# The Singer's Crown

# The Singer's Crown

*Elaine Isaak*

*An Imprint of*
**HarperCollins***Publishers*

FIRST EDITION

*Designed by Lovedog Studio*

Printed on acid-free paper

Library of Congress Cataloging-in-Publication Data

ISBN 0-06-078253-6

05   06   07   08   09   10   9   8   7   6   5   4   3   2   1

To my father,
You know what *you* should do

# Acknowledgments

I WOULD LIKE to thank the following people for their support during the long process of creating this work. Dad for spurring me on by threatening to finish first, Mom for always providing the opportunities for me to make it happen. My grandparents, especially my Grandmother Case, although she cannot be here to see it, she expressed her deep faith in me. My husband, Ed, who remains my hero, even when that seems unwise. My sister, Michelle, with whom I found common ground in the worlds of fantasy.

Jeanne Cavelos, Odyssey workshop leader, and the Odyssey class of 1997, especially Keith and Troy, for thrashing me into a better writer. Early readers Peter, Kathy, Lorraine and Chase, for their excitement—and Peter's wife, Melissa, for the day her car broke down at my house, and she told me to go back upstairs and write. The science fiction readers group at the Toadstool Bookstore, for sharing insights into what readers love, and what they hate. The members of the WWF, the Wilton Writers Foundetion: Mike, Jim, Deb and Linda—my cheering squad through the anxious days.

My agent, Rachel Vater, editor Diana Gill, and the folks over at Eos: together we are laying the foundations of a fantastic future. David Hartwell, for the single word, "yet," which helped me maintain my own faith. And finally, the legion of teachers who make any of this possible, especially Mrs. Krackhardt, Mrs. Tribe, Mr. Fox, and, yes, Mr. Tulloch.

# The Singer's Crown

# Prologue

Year 1215 since the Second Walking
The Queen's Garden, Lochdale,
Kingdom of Lochalyn

"DO YOU see the garden gate there?" the queen whispered, kneeling. Her hand trembled as she pointed across the courtyard to a doorway barely visible in the predawn gray. A gravel path dipped between plots of ragged flowers to come to the iron gate. Beyond it, a shadowy figure waited.

Prince Rhys bobbed his head against her chest, but did not raise his eyes.

She grabbed her son's elbow and spun him to face the yard. "Do you see it?"

"Ouch! Yes!" the child blurted. "You're pinching."

"Jerome's waiting to play with you there. I'll bet you can crawl right under that gate!" She forced a smile. "Why don't you show me how fast you can run there?"

"I'm sleepy. Where's Alyn?" the child asked, turning back to his mother.

"Alyn's not coming," she snapped, wiping her eyes with the back of a pale hand.

"Why?"

"Alyn can't come. He can't play with you anymore." Her voice cracked.

"Because of this?" The prince touched the queen's crown, perched on her tousled hair.

"Yes. Now will you run?"

"Where's Duncan?"

"Your brothers can't come, I told you!" The queen rose, her face hidden behind her hands, red-clad shoulders shaking.

Rhys grabbed the dangling tippet of her sleeve. "Can I go back in the box? I'm sleepy."

"Why won't you run?" the queen exploded, shaking him from her sleeve to gather up her skirts with both hands. "Run!" she screamed again.

Rhys stumbled back a few steps, his lower lip quivering. His mother's hair blew around her face; the crown's points caught the first rays of sunlight, shining like spearheads.

"Run!" She pursued him a few steps, floundering in the heavy skirts, as he scurried to a bench not a horse length distant.

Rhys shook his head, and tears glistened in his eyes. "Mama," he said, half in a wail.

Duke Thorgir strode into the yard, backed by a dozen armed men clad in blood-spattered mail. "Caitrin, don't frighten your son." The duke passed his helmet to a soldier and knelt with a smile on his round face. "Don't be afraid, Rhys. I have a surprise for you!"

"Uncle!" Oblivious to his mother's moan, The prince sprang into the arms of her enemy.

"Since your father left, your mother has decided to let me have the castle," the duke said with a feral grin, "Haven't you, Caitrin?"

The queen could only lower her head and sob.

"Where has your mother been keeping you? Why, I've not seen you for nearly a week!"

"I got to sleep in a huge box under Mama's bed." He looked from his uncle to his weeping mother. "Why is Mama sad?"

"Oh, she's not sad. She is crying because she's happy to see me home safe." Thorgir's smile faded a bit as he looked back to the queen. "Can't you smile for your son's favorite uncle?"

"And what of my other sons? Would you have me smile for them also? Would you treat your favorite nephew as the others were treated?" She raised her eyes to his.

"What have you told him of that?"

"Only that they could not come to play. Not ever again."

"Well, that's all right." He turned his face to the child in his arms, who tugged a little on the man's beard with a quavering smile. "I'll find you some other boys to play with."

"Do not lie to us. You can no more allow him to live than you could his brothers. I will hear no more lies from you."

"Before long, that will be true, Caitrin, but I do not intend that you watch your youngest do the final dance." His eyes narrowed, as if he stared again at the strangled princes, their faces slack, as they were dumped into a grave—denied even a proper funeral. "But on the other hand, I cannot have him breeding whelps to one day move against me."

The prince frowned. "What's a whelp?"

"I could not do away with my favorite nephew, but neither can he father an ambitious lad such as I. Let me think . . ." The Duke began to pace, sighing in mock consternation. Rhys pulled back a little to look at his mother. The breeze stirred a scent of lavender and thyme, and the odor of blood.

"You cannot mean that!" the queen gasped, taking a step toward him. "You shall not make a eunuch of my son!"

The duke laughed aloud, snapping his fingers as if it had just occurred to him. "Your son could join the Virgins of the Goddess. You like the Goddess, don't you, Rhys?" The boy nodded. "And you like to sing very much."

"Oh, yes!" The child's shining eyes matched his uncle's enthusiasm.

"Good, then you shall have both for the rest of your life." He gestured with his head, and one of the guards stepped forward. "This man is my friend, and he's going to take you to temple while I talk to your mother. He and the surgeon will make you ready for your new life."

Rhys frowned at the new man. "Can I sing whenever I want?"

"Anytime at all, Rhys." His uncle kissed him softly as he placed the child into his guard's arms. "Good-bye, nephew. Say good-bye to your son, Caitrin."

"Why didn't you run?" were the only words the queen could say.

Looking back over the guard's shoulder, Rhys saw the duke step up to his mother.

"I'd hoped you and I could come to terms, Caitrin," Thorgir murmured.

The queen turned away sharply, but he slid an arm around her, and his other hand held a glint of steel. With a ladylike moan, she slipped from his grasp and fell to the ground in a rippling pool of mourning velvet. The crown at last escaped her hair, and rolled on the path to fall gently atop the duke's blood-smeared boot.

The soldier clutched the child close as he ducked through the door. Of the boy's last moment as Prince Rhys, only two things would remain clear in his mind: his mother's last words, and the shine of gold against leather and blood as the sun rose full in the sky.

# Chapter 1

Year 1223

A ship on the Southern Sea

"WE'VE NEVER been so far away, Jordan," the singer said as he peered into the wind over the ship's rail. "Do you suppose we'll ever go home again?"

Jordan shrugged. "I don't know what the point would be since the monastery was destroyed." He pulled the monk's hood back from his clean-shaven head to look at the boy, small for a twelve-year-old and still sporting the long, blond curls of his childhood. The orphan looked out to sea, toward the land that was growing before them. "We left four years ago, Kat; that's as long as you lived there. I'm surprised you remember much of it, after our travels."

Kattanan duRhys turned toward his tutor. "Four years is much longer than I've spent anyplace else. By my count, we've had eight masters since we left the mountains."

"I reckon nine, if you leave in the fortnight we were with that spice merchant. Before the week is out, we shall probably have yet another. It's all your fault, Kat," Jordan teased. "Were you a singer of only fair talent, I'd be a happy scribe in some great library rather than keeping you to your lessons in palace after palace."

"It's really your fault for bringing me inside the gate eight years ago." Kattanan gave the usual response, poking the tall man's ribs.

Jordan narrowed his blue eyes and thought a long moment. He was supposed to reply that the boy need not have followed him in, another easy exchange of blame, but instead tried something different. "It's your fault for being left behind there."

The boy stiffened, crossing his arms with a jerk. "It is my fault. It's always been my fault." He did not see the foreign shore, but a garden where his uncle stooped for a fallen crown.

Jordan pushed back his hood all the way, revealing his sharp, handsome features. He touched his pupil's arm lightly. "It's a game, Kat, a joke. I would not wish my life any different. Few teachers ever have a student of such accomplishment."

"Few students have a teacher so difficult," Kattanan replied, lifting his golden head.

Jordan thought he might have seen a tear on the boy's cheek, but made no comment on that. "We're almost there, best to return to the cabin and pick up our things. We can rehearse that new tune you picked up from the boatmen."

The singer frowned. "Do you think that would be appropriate?"

"Let me start and see what you think." Jordan stood calm a moment, then began. The song, which had been a raucous ballad, was smoothed by his low voice into a rising breeze of sound. But Kattanan's voice was the sweetness upon the tune, blending in as he caught on to the changes Jordan had made, as high and clear as ever it had been. Jordan fell back into harmony, as Kattanan's melody surged ahead and swirled around them. Heads raised among the sailors. Jordan sighed, smiling, and shut his eyes. The boy might not ever be a man before the Goddess, but his voice would conquer where strength could not. When Kattanan reached his full potential, no lord with ears would give him up for any price.

As they moved across the gently swaying deck toward the cabin they shared, Jordan imagined the singer as he had first seen him: a trembling child, bound to the monastery gate, bearing a note with his name: Kattanan duRhys—child of Rhys, with no mention of the mother's name. Looking at the adolescent's stooped shoulders and joyless eyes, Jordan realized that, while his singing had become ever more brilliant, he was still a trembling child, bound first to one master, then another. Not long after the orphan had been left in his care, Jordan himself had taken vows that bound him to the Goddess. He fingered the medallion that dangled around his neck, a comfort in the strange and faithless land they would soon be entering.

The wealthy wizard who had brought them beamed when they stepped ashore. He was a stocky man, and affected the dark robes with golden embroidery that his patrons expected of a man who lived by magic. Small, dark-skinned men greeted them, bearing long, feathered spears.

"Smile, lads!" the wizard exhorted them. "This place may be your home if the emir enjoys your music." He slapped Jordan on the back and winked. Turning to Kattanan, he remarked, "I hear his ladies are guarded by men such as yourself, maybe you can make some friends." He laughed loudly, even as the singer flinched. The wizard glowered, and commented in Jordan's ear, "You'd best make sure he is still in fine voice this evening, or both of you shall hear of it. I'll not have my bargain ruined by choirboys."

Jordan stiffened. "Kattanan duRhys has the finest voice yet heard on our side of the ocean. He may seem to you a child, but his song is not a toy, and neither is he."

"I thought you monks were supposed to be respectful and obedient."

"I'm not just his tutor, but also his friend; you may own him and therefore me, but my conscience is guided by a greater hand than yours. Someday that hand shall teach you about respect." Jordan stared at the wizard a long moment, then preceded him into the carriage.

Kattanan flashed him a brief but radiant smile, and whispered, "Let it be soon."

"At least the singer entertained my daughters," said the merchant as he heaved himself into a seat, "but I will not be sorry to see you go."

The rest of the ride passed in silence, with the wizard smiling widely at the curious natives who frequently barred their path. Jordan gazed over Kattanan's head toward the buildings that lined the street, plastered in a myriad of pinks and yellows, and marveled at the variety of sounds assailing them from all sides. It was to this cacophony that Kattanan was attuned, his absolute stillness betraying the intensity of his listening. The years of singing had tuned his ears as well as his voice; Kattanan could describe many people just by hearing them move or speak. Livestock crowded their way, horses, oxen, and camels scraping out a rhythm for the city. Above that, the cries of dogs and monkeys burst into the air, loudly accompanied by foreign laughter and the occasional child's wailing. More subtle songs took time to filter through, those of ladies leaning from the high windows, their faces veiled and voices sliding along strange vowels, those of the peddlers plying their trade, and the beggars' hopeful cries fading away as the carriage passed. The singer's hands were locked together in his lap, lips slightly apart, breathing it in.

After such a journey, the brightly colored palace that at last rose before them was no match. They were led between a phalanx of barely clad guards and into a suite of tapestried rooms to refresh themselves before meeting the emir. A host of slaves greeted them there, taking bags from their bearers and offering scented waters and silken robes. When they would have undressed the men for their bath, Jordan chased them out of the room with a scowl, towering and bizarre in his thick, brown garb. The wizard gladly accepted this surfeit of servants into his adjoining chamber, leering at the monk over his shoulder as he pulled the door shut.

Kattanan stared at the ceiling. "If the throne room is like this, I doubt the Lady Herself would sound good." Rich hangings swaddled the room even to the rafters. "If I'm no good tonight, we'll be stuck with this wizard. Or worse, he might turn us into bugs and crush us." He shuddered. "I wish you hadn't said some of the things you have to him."

"I will not have him treat you as a common slave, or lower.

Besides, he can do nothing to us unless we make a direct request of him. Remember all those lessons on wizards?"

"You told me you didn't know much, and what you did know was doubtful. Besides, it doesn't matter what we ask. What if I made a mistake, and he is already working his magic?"

"I would have noticed if either of us made a slip. Anyhow, you have never disappointed an audience, so we shall be free of the wizard's company as quickly as we were of the merchant's."

"And of the countess's before that," Kattanan commented, dipping a washcloth in the scented water, "and the young abbot's before that. It seems everyone can't wait to be rid of me."

Jordan shook his head as he walked to the singer's side. "All had gains they wished for themselves, Kat, and they were willing to give up any treasure to attain them. It is because you are so gifted that we have moved so often."

"Gifted and given away." Kattanan scrubbed at his travel-stained hands, then asked suddenly, "You wouldn't give me away, Jordan, would you?"

"No, Kattanan, I would not and shall not."

"Not even for a new trade route, as did the merchant?"

"Not for the world."

"Not to gain a lady's heart, like that knight?" He had ceased all pretense of washing, and his hands trembled as if his very life depended on the answer.

Jordan touched the medallion he wore. "What should I do with one if I had it? I have promised myself to the Lady Above."

Kattanan's voice fell to a whisper. "What if She told you to?"

Jordan knelt to look up at the singer. "Her first tenet is never to kill, and to take me from you would surely kill me. I've been with you eight years, where do you think I would go?"

His eyes were shut, shoulders quivering. "I dreamed last night that we sang a duet as we walked through the mountains, but then my voice was lost. I looked everywhere for it, and couldn't find it. When I went back to where I left you, you were gone, too."

"Just a dream, Kat. I am here, and your voice is found," the monk murmured. "Probably the wizard's presence is making you

nervous. Tonight, we'll laugh at him after another perfect song."
But even as he said the words, he felt uneasy and glanced over
his shoulder.

"What did he want me for? He doesn't even like music."

"He was planning for tonight, for some great favor he can
have from this emir."

"What if this wasn't just a dream?" Kattanan pulled away one
hand to wipe at his eyes.

"It would take much more than a dream to separate us." Jordan gestured toward the heavens. "She brought us together for
something greater than this. If it is Her purpose to take you
away, I am sure She will not keep us apart for long. It never hurts
to pray, though." Jordan frowned. "I don't suppose there is a
proper temple around here."

"We passed a missionary house on the way. I heard the prayers
sung in Strelledor."

"That's good to know if we are to stay here any length of
time. I should like to hear prayer in the tongue of the Lady. And
I suppose you could lead me there blindfolded." He had risen
and found a washcloth of his own.

Kattanan shook his head. "Many of the things we passed toward the end were tents and market stalls. I don't know if they
are permanent, and if they were moved, we could end up anywhere. They had a bell tower, though, which might strike the
hours for prayer."

"A bell tower? I'd have noticed that."

"I think it was probably just a bell hung in the upper window
of one of the tall houses. It didn't sound quite the same."

"Very impressive," Jordan remarked. "If you ever tire of singing,
I'm sure we could earn our keep with your amazing ears."

The sun was slanting low through the peaked windows when
the servants came for the pair, bearing a gift of new clothing.
Jordan refused the offering, making emphatic gestures to the servants, who shook their heads and jabbered ever louder. None of
them was even so tall as his shoulder, but there were enough of
them that they seemed to Kattanan as a group of sparrows attacking a hawk. They wore scant garments of long strips of cloth

wrapped around their bodies, concealing little. At least the tunic they gave him was patterned after the northern style, but with sleeves that nearly brushed the ground. The cloth mingled red— the color of mourning—with flaming orange. "Do you think it's right to wear the red?" he asked aloud.

Jordan looked up to take in his companion's new garb. "I should think so, since it is mixed with other colors. You look like a southern prince. That would make me look like a maypole."

Kattanan smiled at this. "Perhaps you could put on the sash, at least."

"The robe I wear is a sign of my devotion to Finistrel. I would not cast aside any part of it so lightly. But how do I explain that to these?" His gesture swept over the heads of the servants, but many of them sprang back, making a sign upon their foreheads.

"I think they are warding off evil. They think you are cursing them to dress as you do."

"Your observation is not half-wrong, Singer," the wizard said, entering through the connecting door. "I am glad to see you, at least, have taken the offered gifts. The emir is easily offended by those who do not." He glowered at Jordan.

"I would ask you to explain why I do not, but no doubt words describing faith and devotion would fall as stones from your lips."

"I would give much to have you ask me just one question. Not that I would have any power against your . . . faith." There was a dangerous light in the wizard's eyes.

"Jordan," Kattanan said, "this is not the best way to prepare for a performance."

"No, indeed." The monk stepped through the jabbering servants to stand by his pupil. "I'm sure our master would not want you to go unprepared before the emir."

Without taking his cold glare from Jordan, the wizard advised, "He likes songs in Strelledor; maybe he finds your religion a curiosity. He also enjoys songs of conquest, I have been told. I have no stomach for either, but suppose I shall suffer through." He emphasized "suffer," in a way that made Kattanan stop breathing for a moment, until the wizard left the room, herding the servants before him.

Even then, Kattanan felt shaky, and his friend's glib good humor failed to comfort him. "You are taunting him, Jordan. He may wait in the city just to find a way to spite you."

Jordan shook his head. "He's too impatient for that, but you have a performance at sundown, and you can't go on in this state."

Kattanan paced, arms crossed. "How can I be calm with that wizard lurking around?"

"Stand still, and look at me, please." Jordan had straightened to his full height, every inch the stern teacher. "He cannot harm me, and he will most certainly not harm you." Every word was solid as stone. "Stop thinking of the wizard and concentrate on the sound. Listen," he said.

Kattanan shut his eyes, and willed himself to be still. Listen. The command had become like a game to him. How far could he hear, and how much recognize? His own heartbeat was the beginning, steady, and slowing with his breathing. Jordan's calm breath came next. Wind whispered in at the window, straight behind Jordan, across from the door. Soft murmuring came under both doors, women's voices—slaves, most likely, making up a bed in the next room. In the hall, voices passed, ladies clad in long, filmy garments that swished around their legs. They wore no jewelry, nor shoes. Outside, through the noise of the city, he heard the bells of the missionary house they had passed. Evening Prayer had begun. Kattanan opened his eyes at this comforting sound. Jordan was smiling faintly at him.

"I heard Her bells, Jordan."

"Even here, She does not forget us. I'm glad this emir enjoys the music of our Lady. We may be alone in the midst of infidels, but at least you can sing in Her words." So saying, he began to hum softly, and intoned the first line of Evening Prayer in his rich tenor. "Oh, Lady of the highest stars, Sweet Finistrel set the spheres to singing."

Kattanan joined in as Jordan let his voice fade back and fall silent. Though Strelledor had been spoken only by priestesses and monks for many centuries, it sprang from Kattanan's lips as if he were born to it. Footsteps halted outside the door, but the servant waited outside. His eyes locked on Jordan's, Kattanan slipped immediately into the seaman's song they had learned on their voyage. It had the roll and fervor of some deep emotion, stirring even in its mystery.

The new servant who entered was not so small as the locals, though he wore similar garments. He bowed briefly, and greeted them in their own tongue. "It were well if you sang this tonight," he offered, "for it tells the story of a hero long renowned by the emir himself."

"Would you tell us what it means?" Kattanan inquired.

"I came only to offer you supper, but it is good to speak with folk of nearer my own country. I, too, crossed the sea many years ago, and feared I would lose the language." The man's hair was steely gray, and he spoke with a strange accent, stumbling over words he had not spoken in a long time. He limped past them into the room. "Let us lay out your meal." A pair of dark men followed him in, laden with trays, which they placed on a low table by the far corner.

"We have only two stools," Jordan pointed out. "Perhaps one can be brought in."

The servant shook his head. "I am well used to the floor." He winced with some old discomfort as he made to seat himself there, but Jordan caught his elbow.

"You should not stoop for us, father. Take my chair."

"I cannot. I am but a slave here, and you the visitor."

"I am a slave to the Lady, who bids us give whatever aid we may, no matter how small it seems. If you do not take my chair, it shall go empty."

"May you serve your Lady long," the old man said, and accepted the seat.

When they were comfortable Jordan began to eat from the fruits and breads laid before them. In deference to his throat, Kattanan accepted only a cup of minted water, gesturing for the old man to begin his tale. As he spoke, the man broke off now and again to quote the foreign words so his listeners could follow the story through the song.

"This happened on the eve of the Lady's Second Walking, after She first slept, but before the great wars awakened Her again. She has another name here, and another language, but I feel certain She is the Lady. There was a race of tall and angry men who lived upon an island but had already grown too numerous for it. Some of the men made a great boat in which to find a new land. After a great storm, when they had sailed many days, they saw a bright green place before them, a place of deep forest and bright rivers flowing to the sea, but a wind blew from it so mightily they could not approach it. They argued about what should be done: some thought they should go on and find an easier shore, but many were weary of their wandering. At last, one of them leapt from the ship and swam to shore, where he lay down upon warm sand in such peace that one by one, they all leapt after him. The steersman struggled to master the wheel and keep the boat close to make the swim easier for his fellows. They wind grew stronger at every moment. The steersman fought with great strength and called for help to make fast the wheel, but they were afraid and did not heed him. Soon they had all gone, and he had but to loose the wheel and leap. Even as he did so, the wind blew most cruelly, and the wheel was wrested from his grasp. He was cast flat, and could not rise until the isle was far behind. So, at times of trouble, it is said the lone sailor can be seen, still struggling against the wind to find that little paradise."

Kattanan frowned. "A curious story. Why should it be one of the emir's favorite songs?"

At this, the old man smiled faintly. "The emir likes to say he is that sailor, holding the ship to the wind so that all others may reach the shore."

"Has he sacrificed so much for his people?"

"For every thing he gives up, he receives back tenfold. The emir is a shrewd man."

"I can't say I look forward to meeting him," Jordan put in.

"Do you know what arrangement is made between the emir and the wizard?"

The servant leaned forward, glancing to be sure no others were near enough to listen. "It involves a very ancient text of the black arts. He has said he may grant this wizard one day with the book in exchange for yourself. I had thought he would not let even the Liren-sha lay eyes upon it."

"The what?" Kattanan asked. Jordan shot him a fierce glance.

"The Liren-sha, the man born who is death to magic."

"I wish he were here; we could show that wizard."

"A legend," Jordan snapped, "no more."

The servant peered at him, with a warning finger wagging. "None has been here in my time, but the Liren-sha is no legend. Somewhere he is born, and lives, and may die never to know his power. Every man born with no magic hopes to meet this man who makes all equal."

Kattanan spoke softly. "This book must be a great thing. Am I worth so much to him?"

The servant looked away from Jordan and nodded to the singer. "There is a lady he would have among his wives. I hear you are to be part of the bride-price."

"And so we travel on." The boy sighed. "How long until the audience?"

At that moment, there was another knock on the door. The wizard strode in without waiting for their answer. "I trust you have enjoyed your meal, but it is time to go. The emir is in a fine mood after our discussion. You will not let me down."

Before Jordan could say something nasty, Kattanan replied, "No, sir, I'll be at my best."

"I am so glad to hear it. Follow." He swept out again in a swirl of colorful fabric. They moved quickly through the dark halls until they stood before a great door cut with vines and flowers. A servant announced them, and Jordan gripped Kattanan's shoulder briefly, smiling down at him. The open door revealed an octagonal chamber with a coffered ceiling lit by the ruddy light of sunset. A few veiled women lounged on cushions to one side, and guards armed with curved blades were placed all around. The emir himself reclined on a heap of furs and pillow under the room's peak. He was bedecked with flashing gems and gold, even in the black hair that trailed down his back. He waved them forward with a casual motion. The other hand rummaged through a bowl of something golden and crunchy, tossing bits between the emir's fleshy lips. As they approached, Kattanan saw that the emir's snack consisted of ants crisped in honey. The singer blanched, doubly glad he had eaten nothing.

"Where is the voice?" the emir purred. His eyes seemed incapable of opening all the way.

The servants vanished to the corners of the room, and the wizard gave a half bow as he presented Kattanan. Jordan, too, stepped aside, leaving the boy exposed to the peculiar regard of the emir. Kattanan bowed low, not knowing what else to do. When the emir still said nothing, he glanced to Jordan. The monk made a surreptitious circle with his hand, raising it to his lips to kiss it in the sign of the Goddess's blessing. Kattanan turned back to the emir, and began the Evening Prayer. He shut his eyes and let the song take him to the ceiling with outstretched arms to bring the Goddess in. The chant ended on a triumphant high; the singer dropped his arms at the same time. He heard the emir's tiny sigh, and knew that the audience was with him. He sang the Morning Prayer then, too, and part of a musical play they had heard in some far-off court.

When he performed "The Song of the Lonely Steersman," Kattanan's voice conjured the strife of the men's home, and the thunder of the storms at sea. Up from an infinite depth he raised the island on a gleaming pinnacle of sound, and when the steersman rose and saw the island dwindling behind him, the magic of the island fled his voice. The emir made no sign between songs, but his lips curled into a smile, and he caught the wizard's eye with an air of approval. Jordan allowed himself to relax. The singer's blond hair glowed in the fading light, in bright contrast with the dark figures around them. When the emir rose, Kattanan fell silent.

"I will take him." The emir motioned to a pair of slaves, who

stepped up to Kattanan. "They will show you your chamber."
He turned back to the wizard.

Jordan started to follow but found himself held back by a
stocky guard with a sharp blade as Kattanan was hurried out. He
turned to the emir. "Am I not to stay with my student?"

The emir ignored him as he addressed the wizard. "My most
trusted men have readied your reward if you will go with them."
A small group of guards stood aside from a dark door. Jordan
moved into the emir's line of sight and repeated his question,
with more than a little concern. The emir laughed soundlessly as
the guards moved forward. Before the monk could respond, they
snapped a chain about his wrists and propelled him toward the
smaller door. "How dare you? I am a servant of the Goddess—
and Kattanan needs me!"

"I will not have men around me of such great stature and
such little humility."

The wizard grinned widely and bowed to the emir.

When Jordan struggled, the little men cast him off-balance,
and dragged him bodily through the door. The wizard followed,
shutting the door behind him. "May the Goddess wreak her justice on both of you!" The monk howled, still forced to his knees.

"Oh, the Goddess—that paltry wench." The wizard looked
around in the dark hall, turning his back to the guards even as
one of them readied his sword. "You would have come to this
without my help. I'm just sorry I cannot stay to witness your
fate, or that of your little student. You never told him about
yourself, and now you've lost the chance. I wonder what you
have been teaching him." The wizard laughed again, and made
an obscene gesture as he turned to go. Jordan tore free from the
guards and sprang at his back, swinging the chain around the
wizard's neck. The man clawed at him, mouthing hoarse words
of power in a vain attempt to defend himself. He was already
off-balance, and fell to the floor with Jordan on top. The chain
tore at Jordan's own wrists even as it bit into the wizard's throat.
The guards stood back and whispered even as the wizard ceased
to struggle and slumped against the floor.

Jordan straightened over the body, panting with the exertion. He untwined the chain from his enemy's throat and stared limply at the mingling blood and the wizard's bulging eyes. One hand leapt to his mouth as he choked back a cry, his own eyes wide. "Oh, Great Lady, what have I done?" Dark hands roughly pulled him away, accompanied by incongruous laughter when they looked upon the wizard's body. His face as pale as his victim's, Jordan no longer fought them as they hauled him along to what fate he neither knew, nor cared.

KATTANAN WAS rushed out the great door, along a different hall. The flush of pride, for a song well made, and well-accepted, still filled him so it was not until they finally stopped before a door that it occurred to him to look for Jordan, the only link he had to his home. The corridor was empty save himself and the servants. "Where is Jordan?" They blinked and mumbled to each other, still gesturing for him to enter the door. "Where is my friend?" Kattanan thrust his arms in the air to indicate the monk's height, and held his hair off his face, as if bald. "Where?"

One of the servants nodded rapidly. "He go . . ." The man stumbled over a foreign word. "How say?" He made as if to surround himself with a long garment, and drew himself up.

"The wizard?" The man grinned, and Kattanan floundered. "He went with the wizard?"

"Yes, wizard. Is go in now?" He offered the open door.

Kattanan looked back down the hall. "When is he coming here?"

"Is not here. Is go with wizard." He added a flurry of his own speech and some inexplicable gestures at which the others nodded firmly.

When the singer took a few steps into the room, the servants bobbed their heads from the hall, then hurried off. There was only one low bed in the room, and one chair at the table. A scented basin and towel had been laid out there. Seeing this, Kattanan turned sharply away. He clamped his hands together to stop them shaking, and shut his eyes.

His ears, though, told him all he needed of the night and the room, dark, empty, and silent in the worst possible way. The awful space was filled by his heartbeat alone.

# Chapter 2

### Year 1229
### The Great Hall,
### palace of the Kingdom of Bernholt

ON THIS NIGHT, the seventeenth birthday of Princess Melisande, nobles crowded the Great Hall of Bernholt. The royal dais, where Melisande waited with her brother, seemed an island of calm above the sea of richly dressed lords and ladies. Dressed in russet velvets, Kattanan stood nervously with his most recent master, one Baron Eadmund of Umberlundt. The party celebrated not only Melisande's birthday, but also the night on which the princess's suitors declared themselves publicly at last. Most—including the baron—had been sending gifts and poetry all year, expressing admiration of the princess in the highest terms. Kattanan was to be Baron Eadmund's final offering in hopes of winning her hand. The baron ran his hands through his hair and glanced often toward the singer, his smiles alternating between doubt and encouragement.

For himself, Kattanan focused on the princess. How would she receive him, and his master by extension? As they slowly moved forward in the line of visitors, he watched the shine of her auburn hair as she flung back her head to laugh. Often, she leaned close to her brother to whisper in his ear and drummed her fingers upon the arms of her throne. Although her gown was rich with ribbons and stitchwork and her posture conveyed all the grace one expected of a princess, Kattanan heard a soft thumping sound, and realized she was kicking her feet against the legs of the throne. At last, only one couple remained before them in line, and Kattanan picked out the princess's quiet voice from the surrounding din.

"Can we not cut short the introductions and go straight to the dancing, Wolfram?" the princess murmured to her brother. She inclined a royal head toward the next of the guests to be received, an elderly couple in old-fashioned silks.

"Lord Harold and Lady Ethelinda," the herald intoned from his post by the thrones.

"How delightful," Wolfram exclaimed. "Lady Ethelinda has come to serve you until Faedre's return. You recall the lady from last year's solstice, I am sure, Sister." He raised a slim eyebrow.

"I do hope your peacocks have recovered. My hounds had never seen such birds before."

The lady straightened stiffly. "The cocks, Your Highness, died."

The princess raised a quick hand to her lips so that Kattanan nearly missed her giggle. "How frightful for you!" She motioned for the herald to approach. "Instruct the gamekeeper that he shall find no less than a dozen peacocks for the lady."

"Your Highness is most kind. I shall look forward to my service." Lady Ethelinda bowed slightly and walked away.

The prince and princess sat on modest thrones, on a small dais below their father's empty royal seat. Rumor had it that the king's long affliction had a magical origin, which might explain the intensity of the guards who confronted every guest on their way in. Given the king's support of the man who now wore his ancestors' crown, Kattanan had trouble feeling the proper concern.

Princess Melisande turned delicately aside to stifle a yawn but was brought back by her brother clearing his throat. "I think this next has not come to seek my royal favors, Sandy," Wolfram whispered, as the baron bowed formally from some distance away.

"Fear not, I shall hear him and smile most graciously upon him," Melisande replied, putting on an air of haughtiness, her nose pushed comically in the air.

"Before laughing him down?"

She shot him a sharp look. "This choice is mine." Immediately, their royal facades descended again. Straining to hear the exchange, Kattanan frowned.

"His Excellency, Eadmund, Baron of Umberlundt," the herald announced.

His Excellency bowed deeply, and flung himself on one knee before Melisande's chair. "Even to my trifling realm, Your Highness, we have heard tell of your great beauty."

"Then you have come so far only to be disappointed by the truth of it," she said.

He looked up at her with narrowed eyes, a scar stippling one cheek. "Your Highness's modesty joins with her fairness in a way most becoming."

"I thank you. Forgive my ill humor, but we must wait so long for the dance, and I cannot even hear the minstrels. If I am short with you, it is only my impatience for music."

The baron flicked graying hair from his sharp eyes. "In that spirit, I should like to offer a gift from my court to yours, although even such a treasure should pale next to you." The baron stood and bowed with a sweeping gesture of his cloak. He stepped off to the side, leaving Kattanan standing before the royal dais. He kept his eyes down as he made obeisance.

"He is both more than a page, and less," the baron explained, uncomfortable as ever with the nature of his singer. "Show her your skill, boy."

At this, Kattanan did raise his head, and from his lips sprang the voice that was his only prize. Though touched with sorrow, the voice was high as a child's, and clear. As his teacher had predicted, Kattanan had come into his own, growing stronger and fuller with every year.

"Oh," the princess gasped, "he's one of the Virgins." Then she fell silent and shut her eyes, her hands pressed together, lips parted, as he sang an ancient song of blessing.

Kattanan watched the princess, observing the way she leaned forward, breathed softly, her lashes flickering upon her cheeks. Never before had he been heard with such intensity. Smoothly, he finished the blessing and began a new song, a ballad of forbidden love between a queen and a hunter. During the queen's lament, he used his sweetest tones to convey the depth of her love, and Melisande's lips curved slowly into a smile. When the hunter rode away from her, Kattanan's voice spoke of a heartbreak he knew well himself. He slipped into his lower range, mourning the queen's loss. Now, Melisande's lips trembled as if she stood there herself. At last, the hunter let fly the hawk upon his fist; high, clear notes drew in the wind and the bird flying. When the hawk returned to the song, Kattanan raised his own hand as if he saw it there, and saw the gift it carried—a silver comb from the queen's own hair.

Wolfram opened his mouth several times before the words came out. "This is truly the most stunning of gifts ever brought before our court."

The baron had eyes only for Melisande. "No treasure is so great that it might equal that of your love. Think on me, your Highness, when you seek a home for that prize."

Melisande murmured, "A Virgin of the Goddess—perhaps the last—" Then she broke off. "Thank you for your generosity. You can be sure you will be in my thoughts, Baron Eadmund."

"He is called Kattanan duRhys. May his music bring you great joy." The baron's cape dragged on the ground as he bowed out of their presence.

Melisande held out a hand to Kattanan. "You shall stay beside me."

"I thank you, most gracious Princess." His voice emerged again as high and clear as his song, from a body that would never be a man's. For a moment, he remembered that his mother had been a queen, that, if events had taken a different turn, he himself might have sought this princess's hand. Kattanan straightened and thrust the thought aside. He took the offered hand gently, and lightly brushed it with his lips, then settled on the dais by her side.

The next guest was a suitor also, one Earl Orie of Gamel's Grove. Younger than the baron—a good deal more handsome, Kattanan noted—the earl did not kneel, but bowed as if he would sweep the floor with his dark hair. "I am not such a great gift-giver, Your Highness, as my worthy competitor. Still, I would offer a token of my affection." From a pouch at his hip, the earl pulled a necklace that sparkled with gold. "May I approach, Your Highness?"

"You may." Melisande straightened her skirts and raised her chin as he came to stand before her. He held out to her the necklace, a golden chain of interwoven flowers, with a jeweled bee as its pendant. She gasped, and met his sparkling black eyes. "I have never seen its like."

"Each bloom was once a wildflower, transformed by wizard's touch into this marvel, as I would have you transform my life, Your Highness." The words tripped smoothly from his lips, as if practiced before a polished plate. Kattanan smiled a little, still aglow from his performance.

"I thank you for the present." Melisande slipped it over her hair, but a link caught at her combs. The singer jumped up and, with careful fingers, untangled it. Once the task was complete, his eyes widened in horror, and he fell to both knees.

"Forgive me, Highness, for having touched your person unbidden." As a child in foreign courts, he had been allowed a certain ignorance. As he grew older, those who felt themselves offended had replied with violence, a sharp blow or a beating intended to teach him the local customs. In his eagerness to please his new mistress the lesson had slipped his mind.

The earl's hand leapt to his hip, where a sword would have hung were this not a royal court. "If this boy has offended, Highness, it shall be my pleasure to punish him for it."

"Be not so quick to anger," the princess responded. "He can

bring me neither shame nor injury. Indeed, he has delivered me from a fight with my own hair. Take your seat in safety, Kattanan. Again, I thank you, good Earl." He bowed out of her presence with a fierce look at Kattanan, who shrank back to his place, his glow forgotten in the trembling of his hands.

By the end of the long procession, no less than twelve men had asked for the princess's favor. Each was received with due courtesy, at least as he came close. Between introductions, though, Melisande rolled her eyes at her brother and sent tiny sighs in his direction. Her fingers tapped even more upon the throne—in the rhythm of his song, Kattanan was pleased to note. At last, the prince rose and clapped his hands together. "Minstrels, my sister requires a dance." He took the princess by the hand, and led her down the few steps to begin the first dance. Kattanan sipped at a goblet of wine, his eyes tracing the path of the princess, his ears listening to her voice.

"Wolfie, I shall never be able to chose among these," Melisande was saying.

"Father and I have already eliminated many men who came first to us."

"It's not the marriage that I mind so much, but these suitors just want to be closer to you, to gain favor for when you are king. They don't ask for my sake."

"Did you not hear all their compliments? And what of the gifts you've had from them? When Esther came of age, she received only five offers, one of whom was our own cousin."

"Esther has the nose of a boar; no man would want to get his heirs from her."

"They just don't know you yet," Wolfram said. "Give them time, and they'll see you as more than your title. You may even begin to see them, as well."

"None of them seems a bad sort, and no doubt I could make a life with any one of them. That just makes the decision more trying. Sometimes, I wish it were done already."

"How about the baron? You must admit that his gift pleased you."

"The voice is divine," she agreed, glancing toward Kattanan, who swiftly looked away.

"The baron knew your love of music—he considers more than your crown."

"That's true." Melisande made a slow curtsy. "Perhaps I shall find him for this next."

Wolfram returned the honor and turned to seek a new partner. The baron intercepted him quickly, with a tug at his sleeve. "Is your sister favorable?"

"My friend, your gift was truly inspired. Catch her and dance with her."

The baron made a move to follow this advice, but Melisande had already been swept away by the son of a senior minister. Eadmund rubbed a hand over his beard, standing first on one foot, then the other. After a moment, he glanced over to the thrones, where Kattanan sat alone on his stool. Approaching the singer, he said, "There's no law against your dancing, boy."

Balls and courtships always made Kattanan uncomfortable, always watching from a distance the moments between men and women. "The dance is not my trade. I was made, or unmade, to sing, and that alone."

"I'm no longer your master, but if I should be again, I'll find one to dance with you."

"I thank you, Excellency, but the Lady assigns to each of us a purpose, and I know my own well enough. The dance is nigh to finished," he pointed out.

The baron hurried off to find Melisande. "If Your Highness would care to dance?"

"Certainly, Excellency." She smiled brilliantly at the older man—much older, he suddenly seemed, with lines like frost around his eyes.

"I fear I was not well tutored, but your grace will perhaps mask my own lack of it."

"Any man can dance, given the right tune."

"You are the tune I would dance to, Your Highness."

The princess laughed, more at his earnestness than at the

compliment. "I shall endeavor to be neither sharp, nor flat. But come, it is beginning."

The baron proved not terribly clumsy and ever generous in his praise. He had been practicing at both in the halls of his keep, trying dance steps, and murmuring to an unseen partner. At the final bow, they stood not far from the thrones. "My singer does not care to dance?"

"No, Highness, he has said his purpose is to sing."

"Why, he must be light of foot. I think I shall ask him." With that, she turned from the baron, and Kattanan glanced away, hoping to seem uninterested.

"Come dance with me," Melisande demanded, holding out her hand.

"I do not know the dances, Your Highness, and I've no wish to embarrass you before your guests," Kattanan protested, to no avail.

"Join me quick, before one of my suitors shows up!" She smiled, beckoning him onward. He accepted the hand delicately into his own, his fingers even more pale than hers. "It begins this way, with a bow, then three small steps . . ." She bent her head to the task of tutoring his feet, but the second time he trod upon her skirt in his nervousness, she stumbled into another dancer and abandoned the task. "For now, I'll accept your ignorance. Fetch me some wine."

"Yes, Highness." He took his leave with relief, his heart pounding in his throat.

"Wolfie," the princess said as she retired to her seat, "this is the first time I have left a dance unfinished. A singer he is, and such he shall remain." She took the offered goblet.

Her brother sighed with her. "It is a shame Father couldn't be here to listen. He'd have told you to marry the man on the spot."

"It is true that the baron is less false than the others." She toyed with the necklace. "He is also one of your favorites, so I would not seem so distant from Father."

"Can I take it he is one of your favorites also?" the prince asked lightly.

"He is near twice my age, but gentle also, unlike that minister's son. That one leers at me and makes it quite clear what he is looking for. What did he give me?"

"A length of fine cloth, as I recall."

Melisande shook her head. "You know how I hate sewing."

"The baron does care for you, Your Highness," Kattanan offered. " 'Tis not my place to speak, but he has often returned to the keep with talk of your goodness."

"Do speak. I should like to know all about him."

"He is a strong man, since he was given the seat at his father's death when he was no older than you. He has had to be a statesman, but prefers an honest battle to quiet counsel. His lady would often chatelaine the keep, as he still rides the borderlands to hold off the Woodfolk." Seeing her hesitation at the mention of Woodfolk, Kattanan went on, "Not that they have attacked since last autumn, and even then, they were soundly defeated. Now, it seems—" He broke off as Earl Orie came before them.

"Your Highness will dance?" He held out an imperative hand.

"Yes, certainly." Melisande looked for someplace to put her goblet and left it in the singer's hands. Kattanan frowned after them. The earl's mention of wizards had made him uneasy. The baron, at least, he knew to be a good man; Earl Orie had the look of thief.

The earl brought her to the floor with long strides, his large hand enshrouding hers. "It is not fit the hostess should not dance at her own ball."

"I appreciate your concern."

"Forgive me for overhearing some of your talk, but has the baron so overshadowed the rest of us that there is no need for me to make my suit?"

"No, assuredly not. I shall be delighted to hear your suit."

"My house is not so large a one as his, nor so old." He emphasized the last word. "But its strength is unmatched. For myself, my interests lie in dancing"—he offered a grin—"and in the realm of magic, hence the necklace."

"Are you, then, a wizard?" Her eyes narrowed.

He shook his head. "I know they are out of favor, what with

the king's illness; however, I have hired a wizard who is willing to tutor me in such arts, but the magic is not strong in my blood, so it takes much time and patience. Fortunately, I have both."

"Have you time for a wife?"

"A man would be a fool not to make time for such as you."

When they finished the dance, Wolfram had gone off and was being fawned over by a cluster of young ladies. "They must know his betrothed is on the way," Melisande remarked to her singer. "That would not be such a bad fate. He doesn't need to decide, but only learn to live with the one who has been chosen for him. Such is the luck of the heir."

A servant dashed up to her throne and knelt quickly. "Would you come to your father, Your Highness? His fever rises, and he is asking for you."

"I am on the way; fetch my brother." Melisande gathered her skirts. "With me, Singer." The pair bounded up the stairs toward the king's chambers, where they were beckoned inside. The princess knelt by her father's bed, while Kattanan hung back.

"It's wizardry," the old man mumbled to his doctor. "This pain is of no earthly means."

"A fever, my liege," the healer said, "brought on by that hunting in the rain."

"Argue not with me! Am I not still king?" He raised his voice to a quavering shout.

"Of course, Father. You shall be king for a good while yet," Melisande said.

He sank back into his pillows, coughing. "Ah, Melisande, I so long to see you wed." He felt for one of her hands and held it to his chest. "Are these suitors to your liking?"

"Some, Father. I don't know how to choose."

"What have they given you? What have they told you to sway your heart?"

"Sire, you should be still," the healer urged. "I've not taken off all the leeches yet."

"Begone, knave! I wanted my daughter here with me, and I mean,"—he gasped another breath—"I mean to talk with her."

"This necklace, Father, was from an earl."

"Orie, was it? He seems a rascal at times, but a good man to have on your side."

Melisande waved Kattanan forward. "This is from the baron of Umberlundt."

"He looks young to be a baron," the king said, squinting up at him.

"No, this is the baron's present to me. He is a singer. Would you sing for the king?"

"A country lay, Your Majesty," Kattanan said, took a moment to collect himself. From this stillness, the song began. In this dark room, his few listeners were rapt as he summoned the song into being. The king moaned softly from his bed. His eyes were red, but not until the voice had died back to a whisper was he sure the king was weeping. Kattanan's pulse quickened. Another mistake, and he might well find out more about foreign dungeons than he ever wanted to know. "I'm sorry, Your Majesty. Please, I did not mean for it to hurt you."

The king caught his wrist in a startlingly strong grip as the singer would have slipped back to his corner. "You have touched my heart, do not apologize for that. Where is this baron?"

The door burst open, and Wolfram ran in. "Father, I came as soon as I could." He dropped to his knees by the old man's bed. "Is it much worse?"

The king did not look at him. "Don't interrupt. Where's the baron?" he prompted.

"I suppose he dances below," Melisande answered

"Tell one of the guards to bring him here, healer."

The man bowed and left the room.

"Melisande, I feel myself leaving, and that boy sent to call me to the stars. Call the healer back in, and the chamberlain, if he is about."

Wolfram did so, as the baron arrived, breathing rapidly.

"Closer, I have not the voice I once had." The gathering obeyed, huddled around the king's bed like so many pilgrims around a campfire. "Seeing as my older daughters saw fit to leave the kingdom, and the younger will shortly do so, I name my son, Wolfram, to serve you as your king, until my recovery, or lack of it." With pale and trembling hands, he lifted the crown from his own head. The chamberlain took it reverently and placed it on Wolfram. The king shook his head vaguely toward the princess. "Do not protest, for I know better than you where my soul is. Melisande, have you any curse for this baron?"

"No, Father, I have none."

"And I trust he has no curse for my daughter?"

"How could I, Your Majesty?" said the baron.

"Then take her hand, and keep her for me." The ailing man wrapped his hand around theirs. "Your worry is lifted, Melisande. Find a priestess and finish the deed."

"Thank you, Your Majesty. I shall hold her always in honor and love." Baron Eadmund lifted the king's hand to his forehead. He glanced to Kattanan, acknowledging the performance with a grin, and Kattanan bowed his head slightly, some of the flush returning to his face.

"I charge you both . . . beware of magic." The old man's voice quavered, and he scowled. "The wizard kills me," he mumbled. "The wizard . . . of Nine Stars. Wizard, I defy you. I will be king a while longer," the king was whispering.

"Please, Father, what wizard? How do I find this man?"

"No. Do not look for wizards. Daughter, do not ask for wizards." The old man patted her hand and lifted his fingers to her cheek. His smile was faint, and his hand sank down again to his breast, his eyes shut.

"He is not strong. You should leave him to rest," the healer admonished.

The baron drew Melisande to her feet, and both paid homage to the king. Wolfram, the crown heavy over his clouded eyes, still waited at his father's side. "I will not leave him, but I will not wake him either. You two go to your own affairs."

They left the room in silence, closely followed by Kattanan, who shut the door behind. "Do you care to dance this night, Princess?" the baron inquired.

Melisande shook her head. "No more, I think, but someone must be with our guests. Come, you shall tell me of this keep where I am to live."

"At your desire, Princess."

"I had not expected that this should be my bridal ball."

"Nor had I. To be sure, I much doubted that I should ever take your hand. The others seemed all so young, so handsome and jovial. I am just an old warrior."

" 'Twas your dancing that won me over. That, and the song." She glanced back to Kattanan with a smile. "It's so fast, I don't know what to feel yet."

They had arrived at the ballroom again, still overflowing with colorful gowns and laughter. Once she set foot on the rushes that covered the floor, all eyes turned to Melisande, and three of the hovering suitors shared whispers. Baron Eadmund held her hand low so as not to crimp the fine silk of her sleeves, but the meaning was clear. Across the hall, Earl Orie stared hard, then whirled abruptly and pushed through the crowd to the outside doors. Melisande ordered a servant to bring wine, and a chair for the baron to sit by her throne.

"What made you seek my hand? Now that you are to have it, it can do no harm to tell."

The baron shifted awkwardly. "I have visited here before, on business, and seen you often, though no doubt I escaped your notice."

"Many of my brother's friends have."

"One afternoon, I saw you in the courtyard with your hounds. The big one knocked you over, and licked your face with such enthusiasm, that I knew you must be kindhearted to put up with him. Such a generous lady would surely be patient with an old baron."

"I will be, only if you are as patient with me."

"I am the luckiest man alive, and not wont to ruin my luck once I have found it. My keep is made more for battle than for festivals, but a lady's hand may temper even that. Now that I shall have someone to come home to, I will ride patrols only when the situation demands."

The baron kept talking, but Kattanan noticed that the princess's eyes were no longer upon him. A slight breeze rippled through as the great doors were opened, and a man entered. The princess straightened instantly, her face turned into the wind, and Kattanan listened, too. From outside came a soft scratch of claws upon the stones of the courtyard. He recalled having seen a pack of hounds there on their way into the hall. Melisande smiled at the sound, then frowned a little. Earl Orie nodded to her across the distance, and seemed to be smiling.

"Melisande, are you well? Forgive me, here I sit speaking of brighter days, with your father so ill. You must think me utterly thoughtless. Let me take you to your chambers."

She looked at him then, momentarily confused. "Yes. I think that—yes."

"Is there a lady who may stay with you? I would not wish to leave you alone."

"My singer will do—my ladies are all dancing, and I'd hate to bother them for this. It's simply the excitement, on top of my father's illness."

"As you wish, Highness." The baron led her around the dancers toward the courtyard.

They walked around the cloister to the heavy door that opened on the princess's chambers, a series of rooms swathed in tapestries and velvet curtains. The first was occupied by an excitable mass of dogs who wriggled their pleasure at having their mistress home again. The hounds huddled close against her and shoved inquiring noses against the baron's finery. She brushed a hand along their backs and muzzles as the baron brought her to her sitting room. Here he released her to sit on a leather-backed chair as he laid a fire. "Would you like me to stay?"

"No, you must make my apologies and let my brother know. I'm sure I'll be fine."

"I can bring the healer."

Melisande managed a small laugh. "I need a few moments peace, Eadmund, that's all."

He kissed her hand, then bowed as he left her with her singer and her dogs.

The room was silent a long moment. Kattanan poked at the growing fire, then took a stool opposite the princess. They watched each other in the flickering light. "What happened to me?" The princess finally asked. "I felt so strange for a moment, as if I were hearing things."

She looked so young, suddenly, and vulnerable. "Perhaps you have asked for wizards."

"I have no fondness or need for them. Especially if one of them made my father ill. Until recently, I rarely even wondered about them. They seem to me to be a nuisance, and quite powerless, for they can do nothing against an enemy who has not asked anything of them. What an absurd notion. Why does anyone bother?"

"Do not think them powerless, Highness. They can send visions by night, or influence things of lesser will. Has Your Highness had any congress with a wizard?"

"No, of course not," she answered firmly, then stopped. Her eyes caught his again, and one hand fingered her necklace. "The earl is no wizard. Besides, what would he want of me?"

"I cannot answer except to say that Your Highness's love would be quite a prize."

"But I am now betrothed. Whatever anyone may try, I am already bound to the baron." A few of the dogs began scratching at the door and whining loudly. "Let them out, would you?"

Kattanan did as she asked. "It is raining, Highness, but they went anyhow."

"The silly beasts don't know what is best for them," she said, with an indulgent smile. She had removed the combs that held up her hair. "Would you brush my hair?" Kattanan found an ivory-backed brush on her table and began his gentle task. "What is it like for you?"

"What, brushing your hair?"

Melisande played with the lacing at her wrists. "I mean, well, being as you are."

"A eunuch, Your Highness?" His voice leapt in the firelight above her head. "What can I answer? If not for that, my voice would be ordinary. I would be as any slave, unremarkable."

"You certainly are remarkable. I read about the Virgins of the Lady when I studied music, but I thought there were none left."

"I was raised at the monastery where a few of the tutors were older Virgins. Their voices were fading, but they remembered how they had learned."

"Can you sing as you brush?"

In answer, he began a song, in an unfamiliar language, sung her ears alone. After the first strange moment she relaxed. His hands upon her hair became an intimate rhythm, and the song tingled along her scalp as the brush stroked her skull. Melisande shut her eyes and lay back into his touch as the long melody went on. Her breathing slowed, her hands slid along the velvet into her lap. When at last the song was done, the princess slept soundly. Kattanan laid the brush down, and stoked the fire. He watched red and golden light dance across the princess's features. Why had that song come to mind, "The Song of the Lonely Steersman?" With one hand, he wiped the tears from his cheeks, and turned away.

THE SCREAMING and snarling woke them both. Jumping up from the floor, Kattanan shared a wild look with Melisande before she ran toward the door. He caught her in the entry chamber. "Princess, no! Listen. That is no friendly beast. You must not open the door."

"Someone screamed, and my dogs are out there." She struggled against his grip.

"The baron would not forgive me if any harm came to you."

The screaming ceased abruptly, replaced by a more horrible snuffling and ripping. Then voices rose with fear, too many to be distinguished. The princess stopped fighting and pulled closer to him. "What is happening?"

"Can I say any more than you?"

"I must open the door." Gasping whines cut through her insistence, and something heavy fell against the door. They stared as dark liquid began to seep underneath and into the rushes. Melisande trembled, then sank against Kattanan, and none too soon, for the door burst open, and a guard stared at him, sword drawn and bloody. "Is the princess injured?"

Beyond the guard, the singer could see what was left of

Melisande's dogs littering the courtyard, surrounding a sodden body. As another guard dragged a hound from the man's throat, the singer turned abruptly away. "Help me take the princess to her bed." The guard dropped his sword and gathered Melisande's skirts in his bloody hands.

Between the two of them, they got the princess to her thick bed and pulled a few blankets over her. The guard waited while Kattanan lit a taper at her bedside, then motioned the singer out with him. "You're the castrate the baron gave her?"

He crossed his arms tight. "He asked me to wait with her as she was not feeling well."

"Come on to the hall."

Kattanan shook his head firmly. "She still should not be alone."

"I'll fetch one of her ladies." The man stuck his fingers in his mouth and whistled loudly. A few heads came up, and one of the servants approached. "Stay with Her Highness." The woman moved past to the bedchamber. "Happy?" Kattanan nodded. The man had smeared blood across his own mouth. "You don't look well yerself. Come on."

They picked their way across the courtyard, passing very near the dead man, though someone had covered him with a cloak. Kattanan balked a moment, his eyes drawn by the palm gaping up at him from beneath. For an instant, he saw it tenderly enfolding the princess's to lead her into the hall. He shook himself and stepped around a hound's bedraggled tail. They reached the doors, where other guards were herding the shocked guests back inside. Through this crowd, Wolfram struggled, his father's crown awkward upon his head. "Where's Eadmund? What happened?" He walked out to raise an edge of the cloak, then bowed his head. "Oh my friend, this should have been your finest day."

"The hounds, Highness," the captain of the guard pointed out. "They had him down already. It was all we could do to kill the curs. They paid us no mind. Funny thing." He frowned, then realized what he had said. "I don't mean funny, Highness, but strange that they did not attack us, as if they were so intent upon the baron that they couldn't be bothered."

"No one saw it?" Heads shook. Wolfram searched the crowd. "Where's my sister?"

"Within, Highness," Kattanan said with a shaky bow. "It was I who let the dogs out, at her request. How could I know?" Tears had sprung to his eyes again.

"No one could have, you only did as she asked." Wolfram gently touched his shoulder.

"She wanted to open the door, when we heard them outside, but I didn't let her. They sounded wild, Your Highness. When blood came under the door, she fainted."

"It's well you kept her in. I do not look forward to telling her this."

"I will tell her, carefully, Highness. If you think that is best."

"Yes, you were his gift, perhaps you should be the one, although I do not envy you the task. Let me know when she awakens. She may have need of family, then."

Kattanan bowed to Wolfram and started across the bloody stones, but hesitated at the center. There, he stared at the covered corpse of his former master. He flung back his head and sang the death chant. Under the roof peaks, the settling doves burst into the air at the sound and vanished into the night. The rain had begun in earnest, washing the blood of man and dogs into the gutters, glazing Kattanan's hair and shoulders as he stood alone. Those who still hovered near the doors bowed their heads, some murmuring the words. He sang it through but once, his hands pressed together as if in prayer, then turned back to Melisande's door before the echoes had even died away. Many of the gathering made the circle-sign of the Goddess as a bolt of lightning smote the sky and struck down the last of the terrible song.

# Chapter 3

MELISANDE AWOKE long after dawn. She could hear the rain still falling and the soft breathing of her dogs, but as she opened her eyes, she discovered her mistake. Only a young man lay sprawled upon the sheepskin by her bed, his clothes bedraggled and stained: her new singer. Melisande pushed back the blankets and pulled on a heavy robe over her chemise, then set her pale feet on the warm rugs. She crept around the sleeping Kattanan, and quietly pushed open the door to the next room. Melisande looked forward to letting the hounds burst in with their usual enthusiasm, and stood well out of the way as she opened the door, but nothing came. The princess craned her neck to see into the next room and found it empty. Pulling her robe around her, she crossed that room as well, to open the outside door. A gust of wind and rain blew her back a few steps and brought the maid running.

"Highness, you mustn't!" said Kattanan

"Where are my hounds? They've not been let out of the courtyard, I trust."

"Come away, Highness, and shut the door."

The princess set one hand on her hip, frowning, but his bleak expression made her pause. She closed the door, and leaned back against it. "What is it?"

"Princess, I would rather you sat down before I begin," the singer said. "Please."

"All right, I'll humor you." Melisande thrust her chin up and strode past to flop into her favorite chair. "What is it? Where are my dogs?"

Kattanan knelt before her. "They are dead, Highness."

She jumped up. "Dead? That was their blood, wasn't it—last night?"

"That is not the complete tale, Highness." He took a deep breath and let it out slowly. "They attacked the baron, and killed him." This said, he released her, and looked toward the fire.

"But, the screams, the barking, the blood—that was him. That poor man." She finished on a breath, which quickly became a sob. "But I don't understand—they would never hurt anyone!" Tears seeped between the fingers covering her face.

Kattanan jerked upright. "The baron is dead! Your betrothed has been killed, and you weep for hounds!"

Melisande looked up at him through her tears. "I am sorry for him, but I didn't know him, not as I knew those dogs. I raised them from puppies. He was a man I met only a day ago. How can that compare?"

"Because he loved you!"

"Loved me? He gave me presents, he flattered me, he wanted me to bear his children, but that's hardly the same as love. I liked him well enough; he was at least more civil than the rest, but love? Don't fool yourself, eunuch."

Kattanan caught himself on a chair and sank into it.

A maidservant appeared with the drowsy prince in tow. "Good sister, how do you fare?" he asked her, with a curious glance at the singer.

"As well as can be expected, I suppose." She sat back down.

"I am so sorry," Wolfram said, coming forward to embrace her. "To lose your husband, before the wedding is even made proper, is a hard thing to bear, but there are still others who care for you." The prince smoothed her hair as he spoke over her head. "Wait as long as you need before we invite the suitors back again. There is no hurry."

Melisande pulled away from her brother. "I would like it to be done as soon as possible, and put all of this behind me."

Wolfram stared at her tear-streaked face. "Of course. Whatever you say, Sandy."

"Don't patronize me, Wolfram. It's important for me to be wed. I don't mean to be callous, but with Father ill, and now this—"

"Hush, I meant nothing by it. I am simply tired and stunned by Eadmund's death."

Melisande put out a hand to him. "You were very close. I should be apologizing to you. We've both had an awful night."

"What happened—" He broke off and looked to the fire. "I can't explain it. Aside from a dislike of peacocks, those dogs wouldn't hurt anyone."

"Perhaps they thought he meant me harm, coming across the court so late at night."

Wolfram watched her through shadowed eyes. "He was no more a danger to you than I. If I had been there, I'd have slaughtered them myself."

"I raised them from pups, and I tell you they would not attack without provocation. Maybe there was a wolf got in, and the hounds were defending, not attacking."

"I am not saying this was your fault. Maybe it was the moon, maybe the weather."

"Maybe the wizard," Kattanan murmured, but a knock came at the door.

"Good morrow, boy, is the princess yet abed?" Earl Orie inquired.

"She keeps counsel with her brother, Your Excellency."

"Bid him enter, Singer," the prince called out. "If you are up to visitors, that is, Melisande."

Melisande shook back her hair and thrust up her chin. "I am."

The singer moved forward as if to announce the visitor, but Earl Orie strode past him before he had the chance. He executed a low bow to the prince, then turned his attention to the princess. Only one of his hands was visible, holding shut his cloak over some unseen burden.

"I hope you will forgive my intrusion, Your Highness, but I

must return to my estate and did not wish to do so without taking my leave."

Wolfram cleared his throat. "I shall leave you, Sister. You might join me for supper. Good day." He inclined his head toward his sister and left the room.

"Do not think me discourteous, Highness, but I'm glad the prince has left us, for I bear a gift he'd not approve of, no doubt." The earl flung back his cloak and held out to her his gift. The tiny puppy shook its ears as it awakened and let out a small bark. "I myself raise hounds, and I know the pain of losing just one. For all of yours to be lost, and in such a brutal manner, must have been quite a shock for you. This one is of a special breed that shall never grow so large that you cannot hide him. After last night, your brother will not want to think of dogs."

Melisande gathered the pup in both hands and pulled it close. She grinned as it licked her chin and cheeks. "Oh, my lord, he is wonderful! Thank you for your kindness."

"I hope you might give me leave to return, and renew my suit."

"I will entertain your suit, good Earl. Do return, and promptly."

"You are the most gracious of ladies, Highness." He bowed again and let himself out.

"Oh, Highness," the maidservant began, "your brother will be so angry."

"And let him be, though I trust he shall not hear of it from you." She cuddled the pup.

"As you wish, Highness. What gown shall I lay out for your supper?"

"The black: it makes me look pale, and Wolfram will be sorry for acting so abominably."

"Very well, Highness." She turned and went about the business of the morning.

Melisande slid down onto her knees and released the warm bundle to wag around the pool of her gown. "What shall I name you, little one?" The puppy stumbled over itself in its eagerness to slurp her hands, and the princess laughed lightly. "I wonder if anyone thought to keep Thor's collar," she mused, then frowned. "No, I shall have to commission another."

"Highness?"

Melisande looked up into the face of the singer, his eyes red and lips pale. "What?"

"I should like to return to the quarters I shared with the baron, Highness. At least for a change of clothes."

She wrinkled her nose as she inspected the blood and rain-stained tunic. "Yes, do. Bring your things here. I should like to have you sing in the evenings." She gathered the puppy into her arms and stood. "There is a chamber off by the fireplace for you. It is small, but you may use my sitting room when I am not entertaining."

"Thank you, your Highness. I shall return promptly." Kattanan bowed and left the room, which was promptly shut behind him. The stained area around the outside door made him shudder as he passed into the courtyard. The diligent rain swept away all trace of the night's disturbance. Kattanan kept to the cloister rather than cross the place where his master had died. The sun outlined the crooked tiles of the roof, but the yard remained close with shadows and puddles. Kattanan made for the archway that would take him swiftly to the guests' quarters.

In the baron's chambers, a half dozen servants with tear-streaked faces clustered in the solar.

"Hello, Kat," one of the young pages whispered.

"How fare you, Thomas?" The singer knelt before the boy.

Thomas looked at him with wide brown eyes. "You weren't here. Sir didn't like that."

At the title, Kattanan's throat felt dry, and he ached from a dozen secret bruises. "He knew the baron's plans, even that I might not be back."

"Are you leaving?"

"Yes, Tom. I belong to someone else now."

"Take me with you."

"I can't," Kattanan said, as gently as he could. "I'm sorry. Now that the baron is gone, though, your parents could take you. They could send you somewhere else."

"I can't tell them," the boy replied, his voice elevating. "Sir said never tell."

"Are they here? In the castle, I mean."

A nod.

"I will tell them something else. Another reason to send you away." He touched the boy's cheek with a delicate finger, then pulled Thomas into a fierce embrace.

Someone nudged his arm, and he looked up to the dark-featured head maid. "Sir will be calling soon."

Thomas trotted into the other room without another word.

"Sulin, can't you watch him?"

She did not change her tight-lipped glower. "You are leaving." He nodded once as he rose to his feet. She shrugged. "Once the funeral is over, I am a free woman. I do not intend to stay on here. Until then, I will mind the chambers, and the others will do my bidding, and his."

"Thomas is a child, and noble-born—"

"In the service of the baron or his heir. Has Sir done anything improper in your sight?"

"Not to Thomas, but the boy knows to fear him. I don't know what he may have seen."

"So perhaps he never will. As to what the child may have seen"—she looked him hard in the eye—"he will learn soon enough the ways and places of men, and of those who must bow to them. Thomas will be a man one day, a man who can keep these places separate."

Kattanan flinched, but held his ground. For himself, it didn't matter—another blow, another ache, but for Thomas—"Doesn't it disturb you to know what he is being taught?"

Sulin shook off the hand that grasped her arm. "He is not old enough to understand what you are. He thinks you're his friend, and that disturbs me. Take your things and leave us be."

"I'm sorry," he offered, as she turned from him. All eyes were studiously on their work, polishing things that already shone. The closed door to the left-hand chamber loomed before him, and he pulled it open with a strength he did not feel.

"So you've come," The baron's squire observed. Montgomery

stood in formal attire, having a red sash bound around his arm by a maid whose hands shook. He was of average height, somewhat stocky, but with an intensity of expression not unlike a cat hunting mice.

"The princess desires that I stay in her hall. I came to fetch my things."

"Sir." Montgomery intoned with a warning glance.

"Forgive me, sir, I am not altogether well."

"Nor are any of us, after last night's doings." He sniffed, and eyed the armband. "Still, the baron would not want us forgetting our manners, would he?"

"No, sir." The singer stared at the squire's feet, at his tall boots with rests for the spurs he had not yet earned.

Following the path of Kattanan's eyes, Montgomery's smirk twisted into a snarl. He snaked out a hand to catch the singer's chin. "But perhaps you need another lesson."

Kattanan's eyes were clamped shut, already tensing in anticipation of the blow that did not come, this time. The squire released him, wiping his palm against his leg. "Thomas! My cloak!" The page fetched it and stumbled after the squire as he strode off down the hall.

Kattanan shivered and sighed. How could the baron have taken this brute into his house? A servant girl clutching a chamber pot focused a withering glare on him. One of her eyes was patched by angry red and rimmed with a painful darkness.

"You didn't come back," she hissed. "You might have warned us."

"I'm sorry. I could not leave the princess."

"You're just relieved it wasn't your precious Thomas he hit."

"We all knew what was coming—that I'd be leaving."

"Oh, I knew? So now I'm to blame? I'll remember that when you are gone for good." She, too, turned away.

Kattanan walked across to grab one handle of his trunk and drag it into a curtained alcove. He found a dark tunic and the hose to match and laid them out on the little bench before peeling off his ruined garb. The skin beneath was as pale as a lady's, except for the darkened patches of fading bruises, bruises the baron had never known were there. It was easy to assume that the singer's sleepless nights and frequent illness were brought on by some lingering trouble he had picked up in his travels. The baron had a singer in fine voice and a squire who could keep the staff in line, and had gone to his death in the happy ignorance of a good man raised more to trust than to question. Kattanan's hands shook. He thanked the Lady not to spend another night in this household—only to feel the instant stab of guilt, knowing that Sir would only choose a new victim and that the chambermaid was right.

He pulled the dark brocade over his golden head and straightened its pleats. He wore his tunics rather longer than the fashion, and tied his sashes loosely so as not to interfere with his breathing. Studying the effect in the mirror, he might almost pass for a nobleman's son, soon to be landed in his own right. So long as he did not open his mouth, the illusion held its power. He dimly recalled a time when men called him "prince." If he were, he could take on Thomas as his own page, maybe even challenge Montgomery to a duel and avenge them all for every beating. His daydream broke against his own reflection: a delicate boy of eighteen, his face framed by the curls that were the envy of many a lady, the face of one abandoned time and again. And if the tunic were slipped away, they would all see the truth, the horrible absence that made him everything he was. He pulled on his hose with small, quick gestures, and did not look that at the mirror again.

Hauling the leather trunk behind him, Kattanan crossed back into the sitting room. Most of the servants had gone, and those that remained did not bid him farewell. He left the baron's place behind him, bearing his own trunk into yet another new life. A mental count brought the tally to fourteen new places in the six years since Jordan had broken his vow and left him. He could no longer count the number of songs he had learned, the number of languages he knew just enough to get by. The thought made him weary beyond his years. Where would he land when this princess cast him aside? But the uproar in the princess's rooms swept away his melancholy.

"You're hurting! I won't have you near me!" The princess shouted, brandishing a hairbrush as she chased a maid out the door. She stopped short when she saw Kattanan staring at her—anger brought out the green of her eyes. He quickly recalled himself, and bowed. "Oh, good," said Melisande. "Maybe you can do a decent job with my hair."

One of the maids rolled her eyes with a good-natured shrug. "If he can serve you as you like, let him try, Highness." As she passed Kattanan, she whispered, "Good luck!"

The singer hauled his trunk to the little room beside the chimney and emerged again. "Would you like me to try, Your Highness?"

"Please." She pushed the brush into his hand and dropped into her seat. "They have me wrapped in this gown, and then want to tie my hair in knots."

He paused in his brushing, trying to read the reason for the mood. "In some places, Highness, maids can be killed for having angered their ladies."

"Oh, I shouldn't go that far." She smiled slightly. "Is that true?"

"I stayed there only a little while," Kattanan responded, "else I should probably have struck a wrong note as well, Your Highness."

"I don't believe it of you. Have you traveled many places then?"

"I have lived in twenty-three, and performed in many more." He paused to work out a tangle.

"Where were you born, then? I don't hear an accent when you speak."

"Not far from here. Over the mountains to the east."

"Lochalyn? Then you must know about the revolution! My father helped to put the proper king on the throne, about fourteen years ago, I guess. Did you know that the queen had taken a lover?" She spoke with delight at the scandal of it all. "She had three sons by this other man while the king was away, then denied it when he had died. She was so ashamed in the end that she went mad and killed them all."

Chilled, Kattanan fumbled the brush.

"I guess you didn't know that." She watched with bright, gentle eyes. "You must have been quite young when you left there."

"Eight, I think, when we left the monastery." He was looking at his hands, and had not resumed brushing.

"We?" she prompted.

"I had," Kattanan's voice trembled, and he started over. "I had a tutor who traveled with me, but he left."

"Why did he do that? I should think he would stay with you just to visit all those places, even if you didn't need him any longer."

"I don't know, Highness." His voice bit so that she glanced at him again.

Her brow furrowed, then she blinked and turned away. "I'm sorry."

"Forgive me," he mumbled. "It must be the lack of sleep."

Melisande tipped back her head, gazing up at him. "Perhaps if you sang?"

He faltered at first, for the song grew steadier—"Morning Prayer to the Goddess." She joined her voice to his after a moment, an unexpected delight for one used to singing alone. She lacked his years of training, but made up for it in spirit. The prayer felt almost like a love song, and Kattanan ended rather abruptly.

"Thank you," said Melisande softly. "I missed prayer this morning. There's a priestess who usually comes, but she always looks so stern and asks me if I have been living a holy life. You've had some dealings with the clergy. Are they all so stuffy?"

"No, not all." He avoided her gaze, trying to master the sudden hitch in his breath.

"Oh." She swallowed, then asked, "Can you do my hair in plaits at the side?"

In silence, Kattanan separated her hair, and braided it with deft fingers. "All done, Highness." He picked up the looking glass and held it before her. She touched his hand lightly, her fingers steadying his. Their faces reflected side by side, and their eyes met.

"It's beautiful," she said, smiling. Outside a bell struck. Melisande's eyes flew wide as she jumped up. "Afternoon bells! Wolfram is waiting supper for me. Where are my maids?" She looked around.

"You sent them off, Highness," Kattanan pointed out.

"Well, I can't go with no escort at all. Attend me."

"But, Highness . . ." Kattanan began to protest, but she had already gathered her skirts and gone for the door.

# Chapter 4

THE BLACK gown did make Melisande look pale indeed, and the braids hanging against her shoulders gave her the air of a wayward child, one certainly not of marrying age. Kattanan hurried to keep up with her as she trotted down familiar halls and arrived breathless outside an oaken door. A liveried servant bowed her in immediately, giving Kattanan a strange look as he trailed after. Within was a large table dominated by a great empty chair at one end. Though he wore his father's crown, Wolfram was not willing to sit at his place. A dozen other courtiers rose to bow to Melisande at her abrupt entrance. Some were wearing scarlet garb, the rest had bound bands of mourning around their arms. Crown Prince Wolfram shone in his red satin, his auburn hair just brushing the shoulder. His face was tired, and his glance at her attendant dubious, but still he took her hand to lead her to her place. When he sat, the others did likewise. Diagonally across from the princess, Montgomery gave Kattanan a hard stare. A stool sat behind each noble's chair for his or her attendant, and Kattanan's stool provided him a clear view of the squire, who sneered at him when the others weren't looking.

"Now that my sister has arrived, we may begin," Wolfram announced. The servers moved forward laden with trays that smelled of exotic spices. As the nobles began their meal, several of the attending ladies brought out needlework to stitch at while whispering to one another. Many glances were cast his way, by both servants and nobility.

After a time, Kattanan relaxed. The duty, it seemed, was simply to sit unless called for by one's master. The courtiers fawned over the princess, offering their condolences. She smiled faintly and paid many compliments to the dead baron.

"You are so gracious to my lord," Sir put in. "Were I highborn, I should press his suit as my own." The smile seemed nearly genuine, and he became, for a moment, the loyal man the baron had always seen.

"Thank you, good squire," Melisande murmured.

"It would gladden my heart to have you call me Montgomery," he said earnestly.

"Very well, Montgomery. I can well see why Eadmund took you to his service."

Sir contrived a sad expression. "I have tried to serve him well, Your Highness, but I fear my service, even to his realm, is at an end. His brother, the new baron, has many good men already. And the keep would hold too many memories for me."

On behalf of all the baron's servants, especially Thomas, Kattanan's heart soared, but his hopes were quickly crushed as the princess responded, "I am sure my brother would be glad to have you join our household, Montgomery. We are ever in need of brave and true men."

Sir smiled widely, looking not at the princess, but at Kattanan. "If you would put in a word for me, Princess, no doubt he would be favorable."

The singer shrank back against the wall, tucking his hands against his sides.

"Kattanan." Melisande narrowed her eyes at him. "Are you quite well? Good. Would you take a message to my brother regarding this good squire?"

He nodded numbly. "What would you have me say, Highness?"

"Tell him his friend the baron would have wished the best for all of us, and especially his loyal man, so I think we should bring him into our service."

Kattanan nodded again, and walked behind the chairs to approach the prince. Wolfram listened, looking down the table to his sister and Sir, who gravely acknowledged his glance.

"The baron has spoken of this Montgomery," the prince whispered, doubt playing across his features as he looked into Kattanan's face. "You knew them both, what do you think? Would he have the man brought to our household, or prefer him to remain there?"

Kattanan was taken off guard. From the way Sir was eyeing the princess, he had some other plan than service. "The baron trusted this squire above all others, it is true, Your Highness. While I am sure he would wish you the finest of men, I think he would wanted a firm hand to govern his household." His heart raced within his chest.

The prince pursed his lips, searching Kattanan's face. "You don't speak all your mind, but say well what you do. I would talk more with you, but not here. Tell my sister that I will think on it and ask that she send you to me after the meal, when she has retired to the garden."

"As you wish, Highness." He bowed slightly as he backed away and returned to his place. Sir's gaze followed him the whole way, beating at him like the sun on the desert.

When the princess had relayed his message, a shadow passed over the squire's face. "I appreciate your intervention, Princess, more than you know. Even more fervently do I desire to serve such an honorable House as yours."

Melisande giggled. "Well, it is all in my brother's hands, now, but I wouldn't mind your reassignment if you always give out such compliments."

The conversation now turned to other things, but Kattanan frequently felt Sir's blazing scrutiny. At last the meal was done, and Melisande gave him leave to go to the prince, after Sir had gently kissed her hand in farewell. Kattanan wanted to cry out in warning but only bowed and stayed behind. He took several wrong turns before he found the prince's chambers at last.

The prince greeted him from a deep window bay that looked out on the garden and dismissed his squire with a negligent wave. "Join me, Singer."

Kattanan bowed to him and approached hesitantly. "I am not sure it is fitting, Highness. I am somewhat less than a servant and unused to conversing with princes."

Wolfram laughed. "Yet you must have spoken with as many as I, in all your travels. Eadmund told me somewhat of your history, what he knew, which was not much. He had a good deal of confidence in you."

Kattanan had no answer to this unexpected turn.

"Please, sit." The prince waved him to the window seat opposite himself. "There is much I would ask you, but we should deal with the business at hand. Eadmund spoke to me of Squire Montgomery as a man who tended his keep well while he was away. I once asked him why he did not bring this man with him on patrol, and he told me of the interrogation of a Woodman they had captured. The squire grew angry at the man and beat him. Eadmund was loath to speak of it, but I gather that the man died. He spoke in terms of his squire's eagerness for truth, yet Montgomery never accompanied him again."

"I had not thought he knew even so much," Kattanan gasped. "Highness, I do not mean to speak so carelessly. I should not be here." He stood up again as if he meant to go.

"Peace." Wolfram looked on him with troubled eyes. "I did not bring you here to test your loyalty. When you spoke to me at supper, you were trembling, and I do not think it was nervousness at speaking to me. At least, I try not to be fearsome, and Montgomery never took his eyes from you. If you speak plainly to me, I will not raise a hand against you, nor allow another to do so." Kattanan wavered uncertainly. "No matter what you claim, you are not just a singer, but also the sort of person who sees and hears many things. I would have you trust me with such things." The prince watched him silently now, leaning forward in his seat.

"Your Highness, I know not how to reply. I fear you misplace your attention in me." Kattanan stared at his shoes a little longer, then sat down quickly. "Squire Montgomery is a cruel man, Your Highness. I don't know his intention today, but in all else he is bent on his own power." The words left him breathless, waiting for the prince to take offense.

The prince quietly regarded his lowered head and put out a hand to him. The touch brought the singer's head up with a jolt. "Do not fear me," Wolfram said. "I have watched my father thinking of how I should be different in his place. My father has been a good king, and strong, but he was not always kind, when that might have gained him more than strength."

Kattanan gazed at him in wonder. He was power's toy, freely passed from one prince to the next for some advantage; kindness was not a word he associated with such men. The fear died away as he heard sincerity in the prince's voice and saw the hand ready to comfort him.

Wolfram smiled a little. "I will not take this man into my household and have any live in fear of him, and thus of me as his lord." He leaned back into the wall. "I can't say I look forward to ruling anyone. You have no idea how hard it is for a prince to make friends. Sooner or later, he finds their parents all have cases before court, or have daughters of the same age."

Kattanan gave a sharp laugh. "Forgive me, Highness, I had thought princes lead lives of luxury, given all they could ask."

"Princesses, maybe. There's my sister for an instance. What do you think of her?"

"It is not my place to speak of that, Highness."

The prince made calming motions with his hands. "I shall tell you, then. When the court is watching, she is the image of propriety and grace; but let them look away, and she is still a little girl: demanding, moody, selfish, inconsiderate. I hope marriage will bring her a little more wisdom. We have two elder sisters, both well married, though neither was so full of youth as Melisande. There was a time I was her most trusted friend, now she seems to think me a royal pest, meddling in her affairs." He contemplated the singer. "Already she places trust in you."

"If you mean bringing me to supper to attend her, it was all quite by accident, Your Highness. She had chased her maids away."

"It is not that, but that she gave you a room adjoining her own; and the priestess came there this morning and did not enter, for she heard the prayers already being sung."

Kattanan blushed, and did not meet the prince's suddenly stern gaze.

"I am still unsure about these suitors. Eadmund was a man I had faith in, these others"—he spread his hands wide—"may be as loyal as their titles, or they may want to increase their attachment to me. I do not believe Melisande will be guided by me in this." Something in his face let the singer know that he had not spoken his true concern, and would not, but a hint of urgency appeared as he continued, "You are in a place to know her mind, and she may speak freely before you as she would not before me."

"You want me to spy on her, Your Highness."

"I'm not asking you to tell me her deepest secrets, nor do I mistrust her, but there are things I may need to know of which she will not speak. Do not answer today, but think on it," the prince urged him, then repeated softly, "Do not fear me."

Kattanan rose, and Wolfram gave him leave to go, but he turned partway to the door, "Your Highness, might I ask a boon of you?" His voice, so drained felt very small now.

"What would you have of me?"

"There is a page in the baron's household named Thomas. If you could bring him to your service, Your Highness; he is young yet, but loyal. I know I have no claim on your goodwill—"

"You have a claim equal to any other, more so because you have my sister's trust."

Kattanan bowed again, and left, but his heart was troubled. Though he had but come into the princess's service, he already shared the castle's concern for her, and the prince asked him to betray that. The singer found himself returned to the Great Hall, empty of dancers and musicians, before the thrones. The largest throne drew his eyes upward in a shaft of sunlight colored by stained glass. Though it had been kept dusted, there was no depression on the cushion, nor wineglass set out for its occupant. The absence dominated the room. As he stood staring, he heard the trot of small feet into the space, in a familiar stride, then Thomas hurried toward him.

"Kat!" The boy's livery was disheveled, and he was quite out of breath.

"Slow down, Tom. I had not hoped to see you, but am I glad anyway."

"I came from the chapel for you." The boy looked behind him as if expecting pursuit. "They are preparing the baron, and Sir isn't there. I thought you might want to come."

Kattanan stroked his hair. "I will come to see him off. Go back before you are missed, and I'll follow as if I hadn't seen you. Thank you!" As Thomas trotted back the way he had come Kattanan set out for the princess's chambers. As he hoped, he found several maids there and pulled one of them aside. "May I borrow your badge?" He pointed to the embroidered ribbon she wore that marked her as the princess's staff. "I need to run an errand."

"Don't forget to give it back." She untied the ribbon from her belt and passed it over.

"Thank you. You shall have it for Evening Prayer. Which way to the chapel?" He followed the direction she pointed at a run, until he was within sight of the doors, where he paused to catch his breath before entering. The royal chapel had the traditional peaked roof, with an opening above the altar to allow in both sunlight and rain. The room was round, with pews rippling out from the altar, and smaller niches at the cardinal directions. In the easternmost of these, the Cave of Death, the baron's corpse had been laid, covered with a red cloth and his sword. Several of his servants worked there, twining ritual cords about bundles of sanctified branches for the cremation at dusk. Kattanan made the sign of the Goddess as he entered and crossed quietly to the Cave. A carved band running along the wall told the times of Her Walking in elegant Strelledor. No one looked up until he picked up a cord and bundle and knelt on the floor beside the others. Then Sulin gave him a sharp glance, not especially glaring at the princess's badge he wore. He mouthed the appropri-

ate prayer as he tied the cord and placed the bundle aside before picking up another. Thomas was at the far end of the
bunch, learning the prayer from a maid. Sulin finished her bundles and left for the funeral ground. Several others soon followed, each bearing seven bundles. Thomas went along with
them, casting a regretful glance at Kattanan, who found himself
alone with the body.

He had just picked up his sixth cord when he heard footsteps
approaching and jumped up as Sir pounded into the chapel and
stopped short. "What are you doing here? I would have you
gone from my sight!"

Kattanan stepped back, holding the branches before him as a
shield. "I came in Mourning, Sir. No harm was meant."

"You are not fit to tie branches for the baron, you piping
swallow." He crossed in four long strides. Kattanan slipped aside
and was backed into the corner, the badge of the princess revealed against his hip. "So you would try to hide behind her."
Sir wrapped a strong hand around the singer's arm and hauled
him up.

"Goddess protect me in this Your house!" Kattanan whispered, and Sir squeezed harder but did not strike him, glancing
around as if he had just realized where he was.

He growled, still hesitating, then flung the singer to the floor.
"Finish your branches and get out." The squire flung himself
into a pew, his stony back to Kattanan.

His final prayers were rushed, and his fingers numb as he tied
the last bundles. Hurriedly, the singer gathered up his bundles,
then paused, hearing another approaching. He glanced to the
door, then thought the better of it, and scrambled under the slab
table behind the red funerary cloth, taking the branches with
him. His every breath was thunder in his ears, his heartbeat an
earthquake as he crouched there. These new footsteps were still
heavy, but not with anger as the squire's had been, and the newcomer barred the door behind him.

"So you are here at last, to watch the ruin of your plans! I
should never have listened to you!" Sir sprang up and approached him, but was stilled by some gesture.

"Are we alone?" the new voice said, chillingly familiar.

"The canary was here, but he's gone, and in a hurry. He's ruined everything."

"Calm down, Montgomery. I have no idea what you're on
about." The voice was both deep and commanding, used to
complete obedience. Earl Orie. There was a creaking sound as
he sat down. "I was to be gone already, and shall have some explaining if I am found here."

"I made the request, as you advised." Sir's voice was still
edged with fury, and he paced as he spoke. "It was over supper,
and she sent the singer to bear her message. The prince returned
that he'd think about it. I gave her every compliment; she is a
pretty girl—"

"That is none of your concern," Orie cut in, with low
menace.

"He sent a servant to tell me no! That it was better I stay on
at Umberlundt in this troubled time. So what of all your fine
plans?"

"My only plan remains to win the heart of the princess, and
I am well on that road, whatever becomes of your ambitions. I
might have already succeeded if not for you."

"It's not my fault the baron kept him out the night before. I
never had a chance to try anything, or believe me I would have
done. Anyway, that doesn't matter now." His pacing steps suddenly turned and came straight for the table. The well-polished
boots filled Kattanan's vision. "A dead man won't turn that lady's
head, or any other." He slapped his palms against the table. "But
now I'm stuck out in nowhere for Goddess-knows how long! I
ache to be rid of that place."

"Before you will get anywhere, you must learn patience. I
haven't gotten this far by making rash moves."

"That's fine for you, you are only a day's ride from here. This
is the first time I've been to the castle in over a year." He turned
swiftly from the table, and hissed, "I would be in residence here,
you said. Why did I listen to you?"

The other groaned, and rose. "Truth be told, I am sick of this
ranting." He strode across to the door and stopped there. "And

you will pay dearly if I hear you making suit to the princess. She is for me. You will gain your precious knighthood in due time."

"Count on it! In spite of your patience." Sir made the word sound like a curse.

"Be silent, fool, and listen well. Without me, you would still be cleaning stables." The dangerous undertone came surging forward. "Don't ruin both our chances with your stupidity." He lifted the bar and was gone. Were it not for the sinister tone, Kattanan could have cheered for Orie so thoroughly condemning Sir's intentions. The squire kicked at a fixed pew and stomped off down the hall, not even bothering to close the chapel door.

It was several minutes before Kattanan could trust himself to move, and longer still before he mastered his heart. No one was coming that he could hear, so he crawled back out from the table and kissed the hem of the red cloth that had concealed him. He stood with the bundles of branches hugged to his breast and gazed on the baron's shrouded form. Making the sign of the Goddess, the singer bowed and left the room, carefully shutting the door. The way to the funeral ground was easy enough, and he added his branches to the pyre. Out in the sunlight, Kattanan began to shake the worry that had descended upon him in the chapel. He crossed the field, then passed under an arch into the garden.

The change was marvelous and instantaneous. A wide lane stretched before him, lined with trees that were just turning green. From this, many smaller ways wandered off, and he could hear sounds of laughter and flowing water. Down the center of the path, water streamed along a channel and down steps set in for that purpose, occasionally vanishing underground to reappear later bubbling into a fountain. The high sunlight touched benches and the far-off roofs of garden houses. Near at hand was a small carillon. Turning this way and that, Kattanan made his way to the outside wall and found a small tower with a platform at its summit. He breathed deeply of the wind and got his first good look at the surrounding lands.

The castle was built on a cliff, in such a way that the wall he looked down fell away almost immediately into a deep canyon, the river far below. Two massive stone bridges crossed the chasm

to the city on the lower plain opposite. This, too, had high walls
for defense, curving snakelike over the several hills they encom-
passed. Narrow streets tangled through the dark mass of houses
punctuated by open plazas and bell towers. On the far side, he
could just make out the tent bazaar and ramshackle wooden
buildings, and fields beyond. Anyone bringing an army could be
seen for miles off, and would be hard-pressed to pass both city
and canyon. He turned his back to this dizzying spectacle and
surveyed what he could see of the castle. The red stone of the
palace blazed in the late-afternoon sun, marked by the white
marble of sills and columns. Its facade rose nearly as sheer as the
cliff below, though cut with towers and tiled roofs. Many of its
buildings still towered at this distance, and mountains rose close
behind. Narrow walls topped by stairs ran up their sides in many
places, terminating in towers that commanded a wide view.
Even now, in peacetime, Kattanan could see the glint of helmeted soldiers manning those posts. The forested slope was also
interrupted by patches of tumbled stone, the fortresses of old,
among which grazed the sheep and cattle of the royal kitchens.

"Oh, great lord of the tower!" a sweet voice called.

Kattanan looked down into the garden to see the princess
with several of her ladies. "I am neither so great, nor so lordly,
but I am at your bidding, Your Highness."

The ladies laughed at this, but Melisande called out, "Sing for
me, then!"

"What, from here, Your Highness?"

"Of course!" She settled on a bench and gazed up at him.

He disappeared from view, pacing the tower roof, then returned with this song:

*If the mountains were more fair, my lady, than thee,*
*it were they that I'd be a-courtin'!*
*If the flowers were so kind, my lady, to me,*
*with them, I would be out sportin'.*

His voice drifted to them from above and echoed from the
hills and rooftops round, so that many came to look out at their

windows. It was perhaps a song below royalty, for the verses told of a young man at grief to win his lady's heart, and of her seduction. Still, the princess laughed and clapped, joined by her ladies, and bid him come down when the song was done. So he walked with the ladies for a time, being shown all the delights of the garden and its many buildings and fountains. They also plied him with questions about his travels, and he found himself describing other mansions and gardens. When they came before the door from the royal dining hall, Melisande put a hand to her lips with a startled look.

"My dear ladies, I must return to my chambers. Kattanan shall attend me, but I do expect you to come for me at dinner, so I shall not be late again."

They made deep curtsies, and moved off to their needlework in a rustle of silks and smiles. Melisande, with the singer in tow, set out to her chambers. "I have completely forgotten the pup!" she whispered to him as they went. "Did you have a nice talk with my brother?"

In his joy at escaping Sir, Kattanan had nearly forgotten and gasped involuntarily. "Yes, Highness. He merely had some questions regarding Squire Montgomery."

"And what was the result?"

"He felt the squire would serve best in Umberlundt with the new baron."

"Do my words count so little? This man asked me! He wanted to be in our staff, not out there." Melisande tied her beribboned sleeves into vicious knots. "Why doesn't he listen to me? I think Montgomery would be an excellent guardsman here." Her mouth set into a petulant frown. "When I am married, I shall choose my own guard and have whomever I want."

"Your brother must look out for all the parts of his realm, Highness, not just this castle." He took a deep swallow before he carried on, hating every word, "I am sure he would have taken Montgomery if he did not know that Umberlundt had need of strong men."

The princess stopped and began untying her knots. Her features lightened somewhat. "I had not looked at it that way. Still, he could have explained it himself." When she burst into her own rooms, she found the maid Laura with a broom in the antechamber, sweeping all of the straw into a heap. "What are you doing there? Who told you to do that?"

"Forgive me, Highness. I thought, with the dogs gone—"

"You know better, Laura. I want new straw here, and a smaller bowl."

Kattanan gathered his courage again, and offered, "If the pup is to be a secret, Your Highness, it were best if there were no sign, here at least."

"Where else is he to be kept? He cannot live in my wardrobe forever."

All three thought on this a moment, then the singer said, "None but we shall ever see inside my room, if we are careful, and he may come out when there is someone to watch him."

Melisande grinned, looking more girlish than ever. "Excellent. Have the straw scattered in that room, and find a table for the singer's things or they will all have bites taken out of them."

Kattanan rolled his eyes a little, and Laura nodded in agreement. "All shall be done before Evening Prayer. Speaking of which . . ." The maid held out her hand to Kattanan, who untied the badge from his belt and passed it over. He had not looked at it closely the last time, and saw that it bore the royal arms, with a dog's head as a crest, complete with a lolling pink tongue.

Melisande noted the exchange. "I shall have one made for you. In the meantime, let's visit my pup." They left Laura to clean up the outer room, and shut the inner door behind them before letting the little dog out of its hiding place. It leapt up, tail wagging, and pawed against Melisande's skirt until she sank to the floor to cuddle the friendly beast.

# Chapter 5

KATTANAN SAT down beside her, and the puppy bounded from one to the other, black ears flapping madly. Melisande played with its soft tail. "I'm glad he likes you, as you are to share a room." Her eyes lit up as she said, "I'll call him Prince. We can talk about him anytime we want, and everyone will think we mean Wolfram. Though this prince is much more fun."

Laura came in with a table clutched in her arms. Kattanan jumped up to help her with it. The room was lit by a single small window, looking over another courtyard and off down the canyon. It had only a small bed, and lamp stand, and Kattanan's leather trunk, which had been hauled just inside. "Should be warm anyway," the maid remarked, "but not much to look at." Prince, having wrested away another ribbon, came barreling through the door, with Melisande in hot pursuit. "I don't envy you that one as a bedmate, singer."

"I may yet regret this," he said, as the lamp stand crashed to the floor, "or I may already."

The princess gathered the puppy into her arms and looked hurt. "He's a puppy, you must expect these things." She wandered back out, crooning to the pup.

"Best get ready for dinner, Highness," Laura advised. "You'd be a sight going like that."

The princess returned and scooped the blanket off the bed to pile it in one corner, snuggling Prince into this makeshift nest.

"You stay here and be good while we are gone." They filed out and shut the door in spite of the puppy's whining.

"He must get used to it, if we are to have any peace," Laura said firmly, noticing Melisande's regretful glance. "And you must have your hair done up again, Highness."

The princess sat down, and pulled the remnants of ribbons from her hair. "I suppose it wouldn't do to have Wolfram see the evidence." Kattanan loosed the braids and brushed her hair out in shining waves upon her shoulders. "There won't be a place for you in the Lords Hall, but ask Laura to bring you to the kitchen. You should be learning your way about."

Moments later came a knock at the door, and the soft voices of her ladies come to fetch her. The sun was sinking low already, and there was still the funeral service to come. Kattanan bowed her out the door and went back inside to wait for Laura. He paced the room and popped his head out the door directly opposite. It opened on a private balcony, with a steep staircase leading down to the courtyard below. A few benches and potted trees were scattered about, along with a water trough that was clearly well used. Shutting that door, Kattanan went to the small bookcase and looked over the volumes. They seemed mainly study books, and religious texts with smooth leather covers unmarred by the oils of the hands. A handful of scrolls joined them, likewise untouched, and a dozen miniature paintings, mostly of dogs. She did have a portrait of the family there, with two older girls he took to be her sisters. There was less of the imp in the young Melisande's smile. He still gazed on her when Laura let herself in. "Help me lay the straw." She carried a cloth-wrapped load, which they spread out on the floor. "Don't know what good this does, except to give them something to spread around the sitting room. Better you than me, that's all I can say. Off for a bite, then?"

"I haven't eaten all day; I did not feel much like it, after last night."

"A sorry business all around. That baron seemed a good man."

Kattanan trailed after her, counting passages and turns so he could find his way again. At last they arrived at the kitchen, a huge high room staffed by cooks and maids in light shifts with sleeves much shorter than was proper. They went about their busy work, filling platters, spicing stews, and turning spits. At the back under a tall window, several tables and benches were set, many already full. All the leavings of the platters, or birds unevenly roasted, were brought there to be devoured by eager servants. Laura pushed her way through the kitchen, and sat on the nearest bench where Kattanan joined her. She tore a wing from a pheasant and set to with vigor, tossing the bones to the floor where a rabble of cats awaited. Kattanan tied back his sleeves and set to work likewise. There was no talking, only the greedy tearing of meat and guttural sounds of well-fed diners. Guards and servants finished up and left, to be quickly replaced by more. Most produced cups from their belts to swig the ale provided in great casks. The singer had none, but the scent of the liquid nearly made him retch, so he figured himself better off without. Foods differed mainly in spice or plainness, but the ale of a new place was more distinctive than the language. Even here, where the tongue was the same as his own, the drink was brewed from some weed of the field as far as he could tell. Grubby cats rubbed their heads against him.

Laura slapped his arm and stood. "Can you get back from here?"

"Yes, I think so."

"Good. When you get back, take Prince for a walk down the back steps."

A few of the servants glanced at him, startled by his fine clothing in such a place, but they did not ask any questions, and he, too, left as soon as he was full. The singer threaded his way back along the passages to Melisande's quarters and let himself in. Prince was overjoyed to see him. With an eager pup tugging at one arm, Kattanan pulled open the back door, and followed the tumbling puppy down the steps. The air was cooling, and he saw he had not much time before sunset. Below, the irregularly shaped courtyard was flagged with old stone and overlooked by few windows. Its outside wall was at the cliff's edge with only a few arrow slits looking through. A watchtower formed the narrow end, guarding an iron gate with access to a narrow road winding away along the canyon. The guardsman above hailed him and resumed his watch over the cliff and road.

After a little while, Kattanan pulled a reluctant Prince back upstairs and let him play in the sitting room while he opened his trunk. He had neither tunic nor robe in mourning red for the evening ceremony. Nevertheless, he changed out of the darker one in favor of the closest color he could find, the swirling pattern of the southern silk he had been given so long ago. He rummaged through to find a small dagger, kept very sharp, and took it with him to the balcony.

"Goddess," he said aloud. "I have none of your color but what flows in my veins. Hold this not against the baron." He made the sign of the Goddess, then pricked his finger. With a steady hand, he traced a circle on his forehead and sheathed the dagger.

"Oh there you are!" cried Melisande. "Help me with this lacing."

"I'll get it!" A familiar lady emerged from the other room, giving Kattanan a queer look.

"I have no red, my lady," he explained briefly.

"We could have found you something," the lady snapped. "There is no call for one of Her Highness's party to mark himself like a peasant."

"I do this as one who loved the baron. He is worthy of such honor as I know how to give."

Melisande smirked at the lady. "It seems, Ethelinda, that my singer is not just fair of speech, but humble before the Goddess as well."

"No doubt we could learn much from him," Ethelinda drawled. She tightened the laces of the princess's crimson gown and stepped back for a look. "If it were of a different color, Your Highness, I should think it a gown of courting rather than mourning."

"It was my mother's," Melisande said, turning away.

Ethelinda's face wore a permanent frown that she turned from Kattanan to the princess as if unsure which was more deserving of her disapproval. "Your Highness, we should be going."

Melisande swept out ahead of them into the deepening day.

"We are to meet my brother before the chapel," she said over her shoulder.

"Very good, Princess, but is that any reason to run?" Ethelinda herself moved across the courtyard in an even glide, her skirt just lifted above the ground but not high enough to reveal her feet. Kattanan walked at the end of this strange parade, breathing carefully to steel himself for the funeral. When they reached the chapel, the prince waited, arrayed in red. She took his arm, and they moved together onto the funeral ground; the other groups moved in behind them until all were arranged on the upwind side of the bier that had been built there. An aging priestess was just finishing the seventh circuit around the body, then stood to address them. She was clad in a monastic robe, bloodred in hue, with a circle of red drawn on her forehead. Kattanan thought her glance to him was not unfavorable.

"When the Goddess first walked," she began, in a voice both tremulous and commanding, "She was alone upon the stone, and it grieved Her. Where She stepped, grass grew up to meet Her. Where She sat, rivers sprang up for Her. Where She lay to sleep, mountains came to honor Her. So full of joy was She at this that She swept a hand through the sky and caused a rain of stars to fall upon Her land. Where they fell, men were born. They were of light and goodness while She stayed, but when She walked from them, the men forgot Her name and grew old and angry, and struck out at each other. She walked far, and returned to find them dead. Long She wept and tore Her hair, and from these things were women born. They were a comfort to Her, and taught Her joy again. In blessing of them, She danced the first circle, and they behind Her. Where their feet tread, they danced upon the dust, and new men rose to follow; men not of star alone, but of all the stuff of earth. By fire we take the earth from this man, returning him to the stars."

"By fire," the crowd murmured.

Squire Montgomery, nearest to a relative the baron had in this city, stepped forward with a brand and lit a corner of the red cloth. Soon it was ablaze, echoing the sunset all around. The priestess began the evening chant, and they followed her until the sky fell dark and the stars and flame were all that remained. Kattanan kept his voice low in the gradual darkness, watching the flickering reflected in the princess's dry eyes long after his own welled up with tears again. Wolfram's head was bowed, but he could not hide his grief from the singer's keen ears. At last, the priestess lowered both arms and voice, made the sign of the Goddess, and vanished into the garden. The crowd filed into the castle and dispersed.

Kattanan hovered in the sitting room until the ladies had all left, and he could open his own door, holding the puppy at bay with one hand. He slipped into a sleeping shift. It was then he realized no extra blanket had been brought for him, and Prince was already worrying the one with his little teeth. He sorted a long cloak out of his trunk, wrapped it around himself, and lay down on the narrow bed. Moonlight filled the little room, shining on the puppy as he growled over his bed. Soon Prince abandoned the blanket in favor of Kattanan's cloak, draping himself over the singer's ribs to gnaw on its hood. Kattanan rolled his eyes, then clamped them shut; at least the dog kept him warmer. Once in a while, a warm tongue sought out his face and smothered him with wet affection. As he lay grumbling to himself, there was a knock on the door. The opened door revealed Laura, carrying a soft bundle. "A blanket," she said, handing it over. She left the singer outlined by moonlight, clutching the gift to his chest.

# Chapter 6

THE NEXT morning, Kattanan discovered that his window also faced the rising sun. Prince awoke once Kattanan started moving, slapping him with his tail and dancing around his feet. Kattanan dressed and let the puppy follow him into the sitting room. All was still and dark there; heavy draperies hung over the windows. A pitcher of water from which he filled his basin to wash his face and hands stood by. He rubbed away the stain where the circle had been drawn on his forehead. Prince dashed between the singer and the door, so Kattanan was forced to take the pup out again, barely holding back its headlong flight down the steep stair. A few servants poured basins out the windows and shook out mats. A pinkish light hung over all, dazzling him from the ornate brickwork of the towers. The outer wall cast a long shadow pierced by the glow of arrow slits.

"Hey, hello!" The guard above waved. "Come on up. Not much company this hour."

Kattanan found a little door by the cliff and followed Prince up the stairs until the pup burst into sunlight again. The guard laughed. He seemed half again as tall as Kattanan and his voice was deep with overtones of the mountain folk, which suited his thick, ruddy beard. He leaned his pike against the wall and knelt to tug the puppy's ears. "Not your'n, I'll wager."

"Please tell no one. He was a gift to the princess, and she fears her brother will be angry."

"She needn't fear him, but I'll be close with her secret if ye bring him to visit." Prince grabbed his huge thumb and pulled fiercely. "We kept dogs on the farm. None so little, though."

"His name is Prince."

The guard laughed even more. "I'm called Rolf." He held out a hand to the singer.

"Kattanan duRhys." Rolf's grip swallowed his hand. "Are you up here every morning?"

"Every morning since the captain said I snored." Another laugh. "Suits me fine. The barracks'll be near empty when I get in, and the others miss this grand show." He waved an arm to take in the sunrise over the canyon and hills. When he turned to the castle, Kattanan saw a large company departing on the near bridge, led by the banner of Umberlundt. He let out a long breath and noticed a sidelong glance from Rolf. "Not sorry ye're stayin' behind?"

Kattanan shook his head. "I did not have many friends there."

"Countrified. They're not used to seeing folk of other breedin' out that way and don't much like to, far's I can see." The big man snorted. "I was paraded for a giant there once."

"Paraded?"

"Aye. The robbers who caught me took me for some kind of idiot, on account of my size. They made the mistake o' bringin' me here, among others from my home, who made them take their punishment and more, in the city street, no less. After some of the guard died, the king was brought in and Prince Wolfram with him. His Majesty was for death for all our lot, but I reckon the prince stayed his hand. He spoke to me and looked at me as a man, though he was not much more than a lad. I'd not understood what he said, but he was clearly decidin' my fate, so I offered him my sword on my knees. He looked just at me, took that sword, and wore it at his side. He took me to his service, so here I stay. It was ten years ago, or more." Kattanan said nothing, as Prince leapt between them, yapping. Rolf regarded him silently, dark eyes slightly narrowed. "Ye have somewhat to think on. Will ye not talk instead?"

The singer shook himself. "I should return to chambers, the princess will be rising soon."

"Twas a question, not a threat." Rolf knelt to tussle with the puppy. "Ye know where I'm found, little man. I've just not found an ear of late, and the men've all heard my tales."

Kattanan felt himself relax. "I would like to hear them. Songs, too, if you have any."

"Haven't I?" Rolf laughed again. "Ye know not what ye're asking, Kattanan duRhys, but I'll more than willingly give it. Bring yer friend again tomorrow if ye can."

"I will come." The singer caught himself bowing to this huge man and smiled briefly instead, dragging the pup back down the winding stair and across to their own steps.

The princess, in fact, had not risen, although several maids were fussing over her chambers already. Among them, Laura flashed a smile. Dark hair, going a little gray, hung braided over her shoulder. Catching his regard, she crossed to the singer. "The priestess was asking if she need come today, I figured not. Was I right?"

"I would gladly sing the Prayers. It keeps me in tune, and Her Highness has a fine voice."

Laura laughed lightly. "'Twas the only lesson of hers she paid heed to. You should see her in court, kicking her throne like a child. She makes faces at the prince when she thinks he's not looking. It's a good thing she's not eldest, or the kingdom would be hers to rule someday."

"I thought they had two elder sisters."

"Well, both of them married foreign princes and are queens now, so it falls to Prince Wolfram. I think the king wanted that anyhow. He has not thought much of the ruling queens he has known. Helped to bring one down in fact, not far from here."

Kattanan looked sharply away. "I've heard. Should I get this puppy out of the way?"

Laura was frowning at him. "That would be best. The fewer that know about him, the better."

With the pup in tow, Kattanan went back to his own room. He left Prince there, whining and scratching against the door. The maids worked around him, drawing back drapes and refilling the basins, resisting his attempts to help, so he was left with little to occupy himself. He picked a book off the shelf and settled into a chair in the corner. The book turned out to be a Strelledor text, a testament of Sofiya, one of the early priestesses, and quite a rare volume. Soon the singer was lost to the world in words both ancient and holy.

"How can you read that stuff?" Melisande demanded as she flounced out of her room.

"Are we feeling petulant this morning, Your Highness?" Laura asked, following with a green gown over her arm.

"I can feel however I like; I'm the princess! Today, I do not feel like green." She eyed the gown and flicked it away. "What is my schedule?"

"You are to sit in court in the morning—"

"Ugh!" Melisande shivered. "Tell Wolfie I'm sick."

"You are not sick, and you ought to go to court, Your Highness," Laura advised.

"It is time for prayers, Your Highness," Kattanan pointed out.

"Begin," she said, sitting down regally and offering him a brush.

As before when he sang the prayer, Melisande joined in smoothly, then Laura. The sound drifted slowly down when they finished, but they held still a long moment, the singer, and the princess glowing before him. Kattanan lifted the brush then and brushed out Melisande's soft hair.

Laura started to go back to the wardrobe, but the princess's voice stopped her, "I think green will be fine, Laura. And my suede slippers; I am going to court, after all." She followed her maid to the bedroom to dress. Another servant came in shortly after with a tray of bread and honey butter and a pitcher of fresh milk for the princess's breakfast. The handful of servants left for their other duties, and Kattanan noticed the lady who had slipped in earlier. She waited calmly on the far side of the fireplace.

"Would my lady care to sit?" he asked.

She turned to look at him with a rustle of her long veil, a deep purple with threads of gold. Her skin was dark, but her face was lit by a lovely smile. The lady herself was neither so tall nor fair as the others of Melisande's service, but with rounded hips and full chest accentuated by a neckline a touch too low. When she spoke, her voice hinted of laughter, and a foreign air. "I will sit at court for many hours, no doubt, so I would stand now. You are the singer. I was not there to hear you at the ball, but I did enjoy your prayer. I am Faedre, late of the east."

"It is a pleasure to meet you, my lady." He remained standing, twitching the brush.

"You have been brushing her hair." Lady Faedre took a step toward him, hands gently clasped at her waist. "The hair is very important here, is it not?"

Kattanan asked uneasily, "Do you not know the Goddess?"

"I was raised in the arms of a joined god and goddess, so if you mean do I worship your Finistrel, I must say I do not. What is this taboo about the hair?"

"We are taught that women grew from Her hair and Her tears. It is why monks and priestesses shave their heads, to show that they are not part of the cycle of creation."

"Then should not you also be bald?" Her smile shone as sweet, but there was a twitch of her brow like the flick of a bowstring.

"That has been said before." Kattanan drew away a little.

"But you do not do this. Are you not so enamored of your Goddess as to make that gesture?" She advanced toward him. Her eyes were as dark as a snake's but as warm as a snake's eyes are cold. "I only ask because I wish to understand."

"I am," he hesitated, "I would not be the same."

"Without your hair, you might be a monk, rather than a singer. Your hair determines your worth." She turned back toward the door from which Melisande would emerge.

Kattanan pulled a chair out and sat down, trembling slightly, glad to escape those eyes. When the door opened, he rose but kept his head bowed.

"Faedre! I am so glad you're here. Are you to escort me to court?" Melisande took the lady's hands in hers and led her toward the breakfast tray.

"I am, and you do not want to be late." She took a post by the princess's chair as Melisande set into her bread. Laura trailed out soon after, polishing a coronet.

"Done, Your Highness." Laura held out the coronet, and Faedre accepted it.

Melisande devoured most of her food, quickly wiped her mouth, and stood.

"Shall we be going, Highness?" Faedre asked, placing the coronet on the princess's head.

"Oh, yes. I'm sure Wolfram will have some words for me before court anyhow."

"He always does."

"With me, Kattanan," the princess called over her shoulder as the lady led her away. The singer flicked a glance at Laura, who was cleaning the butter bowl with a finger. She smirked at him and tossed him a slice of leftover bread. He munched on this as he followed after the women. Faedre walked with a gentle sway, her gown clinging at the waist. The veil ended just above in a row of tassels. Occasionally, a tassel would catch upon her hip and quiver there. Beside her, Melisande lifted her skirt a little higher than propriety would wish. Had she not worn the coronet, the princess might be taken for a lady-in-waiting and her companion for a queen.

Wolfram stood to welcome them when they arrived, and lead his sister to her throne. "I am glad you have joined me today, Melisande."

She nodded vague acknowledgment as she sat down. The room, a chamber off the Great Hall, was bedecked with proud banners and a huge portrait of the king, a young, dashing figure one hand on his sword hilt. His eyes were harsh and brilliant, watching every move his son made. Aside from a small honor guard, they were the only ones present.

"I would speak with you before we hear court this morning," Wolfram said, barely glancing at Kattanan. The lady Faedre had dropped to a deep curtsy, head bowed. She rose slowly, looking up at just the moment to catch the prince's gaze; but she quickly turned and took a seat at the princess's side. "I was visited by one of your ladies this morning."

"The Countess DuLamoor? She visited me yesterday," Melisande remarked.

Wolfram sighed. "She does not approve of your new arrangement." He glanced to Kattanan, who had settled on the dais between them.

"It's not for her to approve me. She's been imperious ever since Mother died."

"Our mother asked her to watch over you. She takes that request very seriously."

"Well, I am not a child anymore! She tries to rule me; and I don't appreciate your taking her side." Melisande shook her hair down her back. "Can I not decide who will serve me?"

"I'm not asking you to take back your decision, only to be more courteous about it. You might begin by apologizing to her." Wolfram held his hands low and beseeching.

"I will not. She insulted my singer and told me I was not acting like royalty. She shall apologize to me if she ever wants to be in my presence again."

"Her husband is quite powerful among the other lords, and we need their support. I know she does not treat you as you would like, but—"

"As I would like? As she ought, don't you mean!" She swished out of the chair and whirled on him. "I can't wait until I am married and out of this place! Faedre!" she snapped, then grabbed handfuls of her gown and ran from the room. The lady rose smoothly, not neglecting to curtsy to the prince, and followed, still swaying. Kattanan rose also, but looked at the prince.

"She will want you there," Wolfram said. His head sank to his hands. "Wine, Thomas."

The page came out of the shadows with a jug and goblet. He grinned briefly at Kattanan, then concentrated on the pouring. The singer set out at a trot after the princess. He found them in a wide sunny room well appointed with cushions and window seats not far away.

"—and I am about to be married! By any measure, I am a woman, but he just won't see that!" Melisande was shouting, arms wide and beating at the air.

Faedre sat watching her, nodding sagely. "It is plain to all save the countess. Your brother has had much to think about and may prefer not to be aware of your problems."

"What? What does he have on his mind? There is no war; Father is sick, but has been for a month. Yes, he lost his friend the baron, but the only event is to be my wedding, if I find a groom who lives! Even if I do, he will still think of me as his little sister. If I were firstborn, I should have married a minor lord and stayed here to be queen, then he would see."

"You would be a bold and lovely queen, not weak-stomached and pensive."

"We are complete opposites, he and I." She planted her fists on her hips. "He'll sit at court all day and decide nothing! What's to think about? Farmers' spats and petty theft."

"He is learning to be king."

"Kings go to battle, or to hunt during peacetime. They make examples of people and command them. That's what Father has always done. If he were to be a true king, my brother would have something more important to worry about than how I choose to run my household. I made a request of him yesterday, one request, and he could not grant it."

"Do not blame that on Prince Wolfram alone," Kattanan suddenly said.

Both women stared at him. "What do you mean by that?" Melisande demanded.

"Only that he asked my opinion of the man, and I gave it, Your Highness. The squire and I do not get on well." Kattanan studied her feet. "I did not expect the prince to listen to me."

Melisande gave a little sigh.

Faedre sighed with her mistress. "The marriage is one decision they cannot make for you. Then you may at least rule a separate household." Faedre watched Kattanan through slitted eyes while she spoke. She allowed a slender ankle to escape the hem of her long skirt. She flexed that foot, and slid it a little farther still. "Your brother tried, though, did he not? Speaking of his friend, the baron, and never of the other suitors. I am sorry I was not here for the ball. My husband was at last released from his suffering." She turned delicately aside.

"Oh, no," the princess said, coming to sit beside her lady. "Why did you say nothing?"

"You have had a difficult time while I was gone, and I would not burden you with my own grief. I should have remained at home to watch over our lands, but I did not want to leave you like that." She gazed at her mistress with a faint smile.

"You are so good to me, Faedre. I do not ever want to be without you. The others just don't understand." Melisande held Faedre's hands in both of hers.

"When you marry," said the lady, "I want to go with you to your new estate. Most of the court ladies would not leave here, but I want to serve you wherever you go."

Melisande grinned. "It doesn't matter whom I marry, I will to have you with me. In spite of everything, as least I have your friendship." The women embraced, and the princess beamed over her lady's shoulder. She caught sight of Kattanan, then, though he had turned away from their intimacy. "And you, Singer. I want you to sing the prayers every morning."

"I would be honored, Your Highness."

Faedre regarded the princess. "You were to sit at court today, Melisande."

"I can't. I hate how he treats me as an adult in public, then as a child when we are alone."

"The only way to show him your strength is to deny him the comfort of your absence. You have as much right to advise as he; more, because you are made as the Goddess. Take your rightful throne and hear your people," she urged.

The smile left her face, but Melisande's eyes were shining. "Yes, Faedre. He will not get the better of me, no matter how angry he makes me. Let us return to court."

In the room where Wolfram held court a large crowd had gathered, so their entrance through the side door was not noticed at first. Flanked by Faedre and Kattanan, Melisande glided forward. Heads turned, then the people scrambled to their feet and bowed deeply. "I am glad you have not waited court for me, brother." She nodded graciously to the crowd.

Wolfram, too, had jumped up, and turned to offer her seat. "Good sister, you are a welcome guest this morning." He tossed a quick glance to Faedre and the singer, eyes dark. "These men have come to ask rights to build a dock on our side of the canyon."

"As I was saying, Your Highnesses," said one of the elegant merchants before them, "landing the goods upriver and hauling them overland, even so short a distance, requires all manner of expenses, especially when the loads are intended for the castle. With your good father's permission, I sent several men to investigate the castle side. They are in the process of mapping a series of tunnels up from the river into the castle itself. There is evidence that a dock had been built there before but was not maintained."

"Is it not possible, my lord, that it was washed out by a flood?

Our river frequently runs high, as you must know," the princess interrupted.

The merchant looked at her with raised brows, then at the prince. "That is possible, Your Highness, but we are willing to undertake the risk in order to provide this service to the castle."

"The question is not about the dock." Wolfram settled back into his throne. "If you build and use it, you will have an advantage over any other merchant we might buy from."

Melisande frowned a little. "But this is easier for both of us, brother."

Wolfram set a calming hand upon hers. "You are indeed correct, but it would be as if this fellow were our royal merchant, and we might feel constrained to buy only from him." Before she could protest, he went on, "There is a solution, however. You may build your dock, and we shall buy it. Any merchant who desires may land his goods and use the passages in his dealings with the castle. We shall have the heralds draw up papers and distribute them to all of the guilds. In return for your excellent initiative and the mapping of the tunnels, we will grant you an exclusive contract for the class of goods of your choice for six months."

At this, the merchants' faces brightened. "Your Highness is both wise and generous."

"When you are ready to begin construction, have a copy of the map sent up to me."

"Yes, Your Highness." He bowed first to the prince, then the princess, and left.

During the pause, Melisande leaned over to her brother. "Wouldn't it be more fair to him to let him keep the dock? He could rent it to the others if they wanted to use it."

"Commerce with the castle is not just another trade agreement. Our business influences how the other nobles purchase as well, and even who holds power in the guilds and councils. To give it all to one man would change the market of all the city, and perhaps beyond."

The princess frowned. "But we might get cheaper goods."

"The world is not so simple as that."

"I know that!" she hissed at him, crossing her arms.

He caught her elbow before she could retreat to the far side of the throne. "I know you know, but you may not know how that applies in this instance."

"I did not come here for a lecture, Wolfram." She shook off his grasp.

"The Royal Messenger of Princess Asenith of Lochalyn, for Prince Wolfram."

Kattanan snapped alert, ricocheting his glance from the prince to the messenger, who wore the royal badge that had once been his. He should have expected some contact with his former home. It seemed unlikely that the Usurper's minions would recognize him after so long, but he felt suddenly exposed, waiting in the arms of trust for someone to betray him again.

"Your betrothed sends warmest greetings unto you, Prince Wolfram," the messenger began, "but regrets that she will be unable to come to you before midsummer. The higher roads are still in snow, and there have been many robbers of late. The king even now prepares a rout of the hills, but he would not have his daughter travel in danger. She begs your continued patience and goodwill, and sends regards to your father and sister."

Wolfram's face fell. "Have there been more threats against my betrothed and her father?"

The messenger shifted his weight. "She does not like to speak of it, but there have been. Still it is not known whence come the rumors, but several of the king's most loyal have vanished. We doubt not that they have been kidnapped by this villain who hurls such accusations against the king, but is not willing to face him. When a message is to be sent, three messengers ride, all separately, and in guise of common men so that we shall not be known for royal men. Myself, Your Highness, I changed into my livery not half an hour ago."

"They are our allies, should we not send aid?" Melisande inquired.

"What aid can I send? I cannot alone raise a small army and march out to meet my bride, much as that might comfort her. Several patrols of ours are already assisting in tracking the kidnappers. I should take this up again with Father, in spite of his illness."

"Asenith is to be your wife; surely you can take some action."

"Good sister," he began, but his voice was tight, "I would like very much to discuss this with you, but this man is waiting on our dismissal to take his rest." He again addressed the messenger, "Thank you for your pains in bringing this message and for sharing your news. Would you join me after supper in my chambers?"

"I would be honored, Your Highness." The man bowed deeply and took his leave.

Melisande, arms crossed, glowered just a bit. "There was no need to rebuke me," she grumbled under her breath. Faedre patted her arm with a nod.

She did not speak for the rest of court, though she managed to acknowledge the supplicants and messengers with some grace. Kattanan sat a little behind her throne, still reeling from the news that Wolfram would wed his cousin. He did not remember much of her, except her laughter. Being two years older than he and taller, she took it on herself to torment him while they were growing up at the castle. He had seen her once since then, at a concert at the monastery shortly before he left. She would be tall and beautiful by now, but when he heard the name, he pictured an eleven-year-old princess, seated among friends, who saw him as he stood to solo and laughed until the abbot asked for her silence, ringing high laughter, piercing as the cry of a hawk. But Wolfram might never have met his bride. Kattanan shifted a little so that he could see the prince in the gap between the thrones. His tawny head was cocked to one side, intent on the old woman before him. He nodded as he listened, and sighed at the end of her tale.

"Ancient hag," Faedre's voice hissed. "It does not surprise me that she was caught stealing from a temple. It does surprise me she was brought before royal court, though."

Melisande nodded absently to this comment, smiling stiffly.

"If it pains you to kneel, then please rise," the prince said. "I would not have you caused more discomfort." As the old woman rose, the hood fell back from her head and showed her naked scalp. The gathering murmured at this revelation. "You are a priestess."

"I was, Your Highness," the woman said through crumbling teeth, "but I have no temple, and those of the city would not have me. Goddess forgive me for taking of their bread." She moved to make the sign of the Goddess, but doubled over, coughing.

"Thomas, some water," the prince ordered, but the page looked around. There was no spare cup. "Use mine. This woman is of the Goddess and deserves at least that much."

The boy offered it to her and held it while she drank deeply. "I thank you, Thomas, and you, Your Highness. When you feel most accursed, then shall you find blessing."

"You do readily admit the theft, Priestess, so it cannot go unnoticed. Take this lady to the temple in the garden there to atone for her wrong, and to pray for those who have wronged her. I give her leave to stay there until her every prayer is done."

She shuffled toward him, waving back the guards, and bent to kiss his boot. Wolfram touched her stooped and ragged shoulder. "I am not the king, you need not do obeisance to me."

"You never will be, Highness, but are more deserving than who shall follow." She shuffled backward then, without explaining, despite the sudden rise in the murmurs of the court.

"What a foul creature! And what she said to you." Melisande shuddered. "If you are accursed, it is by such words." Faedre looked quickly to her mistress; she had been watching the back of the old woman as she was led away.

"Let her alone, sister." Wolfram sighed. "She is aged, and may be feeble. If she is not, then at least I have her blessing as well." He wiped a hand over his face, and Kattanan noticed the droop of his shoulders, as if borne down by the crown above. "How many more?"

"Only two who must be seen today, Your Highness," the herald responded.

"Bring them up and let them be quick."

Fortunately, the last two cases were easily resolved. Wolfram asked Melisande and her attendants to join him in his chambers for supper, and she accepted in the most civil tones but did not take his offered arm. They dined simply in the prince's sitting room, with Thomas sitting tall by Kattanan's side.

"I appreciate your presence in court, Melisande, and that you clearly took interest in it today," the prince said, pushing away his plate.

"I'm so glad you noticed." Melisande dissected the chicken leg that lay on her plate.

"Please tell me what's bothering you."

"Many things," the princess said, "but mostly why you won't help Asenith. I've heard her messages in the past and seen her portrait; I would like to meet her, but you won't do anything, even though you know she is in need!"

"Let me tell you what I could not say while her messenger was there." The force of his words made her draw back a touch. "This is the third time she has postponed coming. She may in fact be in danger, but her father has his own armies, his own spies, and knows much more about the situation than I do. If she were ready to come, and he ready to let her, she would be here by now. I know they have received threats. More than one voice has accused her father of usurping a throne that should not have been his, not saving a kingdom from a madwoman who killed her own sons as he has professed—" Kattanan choked and dropped his fork, but quieted himself when their eyes were upon him. Wolfram continued, "They are still only anonymous voices, though, and not enough to hold back a king from his purposes. So she is hiding behind this excuse, or something else is going on." He caught his breath and stared at his sister, who stared back, but with lowered chin and a guilty air. "I will not send aid they do not want, and I will not go to someone who is not ready."

"How could I know all this, Wolfram? Maybe if I had known, I would have held my tongue in court." Realizing the opening she had left him, Melisande plunged ahead. "If you have so many suspicions, why ask to talk to the messenger? He won't tell the truth beyond what he has already said. What is the purpose?"

"If I ask enough questions of him, I may begin to see what he leaves out of the answers."

Melisande said nothing. Wolfram finally looked away from her. "I do want you to be at court, Melisande, but please trust that I know what I am about."

She snorted at this, but then smiled a little. "Only if you will trust that I know what I am about. I will deal with my household and my ladies as I see fit."

"Fine."

There was a tentative knock, and Thomas, who'd been leaning on his arm through the conversation, slid from his chair to investigate. He came back and whispered to the prince.

"The messenger has arrived. I think it were best if I spoke with him alone." Wolfram raised an eyebrow at Melisande, who grumbled, but rose to go.

Faedre stood and made a brief curtsy, flashing her smile at him and making sure his eyes were on her as she turned to follow.

Thomas looked after Kattanan and sighed, offering a small wave with one hand.

"I shall not have need of you until this evening, Thomas. Perhaps you would like the afternoon with your friend?" Wolfram said, stooping to look the boy in the eye.

"Thank you, Your Highness!" He bobbed into a half bow, but the prince caught him before he could go too far and whispered in his ear. The boy nodded and slipped out the door.

"Kat!" he called out, dashing up behind them. "The prince says I can come with you."

"Wonderful!" The singer took his hand. "I want to hear all about your duties."

Faedre slowed a little. "Thomas, is it? You must be a very good boy to work for the prince."

"He says so." Thomas pulled closer to Kattanan, looking up at her. "You're dark."

Faedre laughed lightly. "I am. I come from a country far from here, but my husband brought me to live in his home."

"Where is he?"

"He went to be with the Goddess in the stars."

"Oh," Thomas said, eyes wide. "But you didn't go home."

"No, Thomas. I have too many friends here. Would you like to be my friend?"

He thought a moment, glancing at Kattanan.

"Here, I'll lift you up so you can see better." They were turning into the garden, and Faedre crouched beside the boy, but he hung back. "You know it isn't nice to refuse a lady." He reluctantly released Kattanan's hand and went to her. "That's better. I can see we're going to be good friends." She took him in her arms and moved away from the singer, talking to Thomas in a low voice.

"I did not know she was so good with children," Melisande commented. "Where shall we walk? I have to go feed Prince soon, but we have a little time. Have you seen the garden house?"

"I don't think so, Your Highness."

"This way, then." She gathered up her skirt and headed toward the far corner of the gardens, with Kattanan trailing after, still watching the way Faedre had taken Thomas.

They passed the spire of the little chapel when a quavering voice called out, "Hail, Sire!"

The pair turned, already half-bowing, and exchanged a startled glance, but no one was there except an old woman. It took a moment before Kattanan recognized her as the priestess from that morning's court; she had been bathed and dressed in a clean robe, but the wrinkles of her face and arms seemed lined with a grime that could not come clean. Melisande straightened immediately, lips pinched.

"Hail, King," the woman said, "and to you also, Royal Highness." Her eyes rolled, one the green of algae, the other a muddy brown.

"Are you blind? I am not the heir to the throne, and this is my singer," Melisande scoffed. "Get you back to the chapel and stop speaking nonsense."

"I speak not sense, but truth," she returned, suddenly focusing both eyes on the princess. "One eye sees the present"—she

shut the green eye for a moment—"the other sees what will be."
Now, only the green eye was visible. "You know not truth from
sense, nor then from now, nor beauty from your own face."

She drew back, her face pale. "You may get pity from my
brother, but you'll have none of me."

"No, none of thee, nor would I want ought of thee." She
turned on Kattanan and bowed again. "But of thee, Sire, a boon
indeed."

"I am no king, nor shall be," Kattanan protested, but his hands
trembled, and he could not keep the tremor from his voice.

Melisande's troubled face turned toward him as if to speak,
but the old woman swept a hand through the air. "Were the
Goddess walking, would you turn her away with no ear?"

"No, Granny, if she chose to speak to me."

"And how shall ye know her, if she walked?" Her eye narrowed on him.

"You are close to sacrilege, Priestess," the princess interrupted, stepping between the madwoman and her singer.

"She walks when She wants, and does not always tell Her
people, Royal Highness. Would that your future were not clear,
and I could shut my eyes upon it and so sever you from glory."

Melisande's eyes flew wide. "Enough, you old witch! Get out
of my garden, or I shall have you thrown out as you deserve. If
Wolfram knew you would insult me, he would have cast you in
the dungeon where dark things belong."

The old woman let out a screech of laughter. "Know you only
sense? Even your brother you do not recognize, nor this one in
guise of a servant. Not long now, and you will see all I say. Hail,
King!" So saying, she turned and vanished into the chapel.

Melisande relaxed and smiled at Kattanan. "Remind me not
to walk this way until that hag is out of the palace."

"Nor I, Your Highness. I have no wish to be accosted by a
madwoman." Even as he said it, he shivered, and the sun could
not warm him. *"Hail, King!"* still echoed through his thoughts.

"I wonder what she thought to ask of you." Melisande studied him. "Maybe we should have heard her out. She deserves my
ridicule more than my anger."

"She is still a priestess, and under your brother's protection, Highness."

There was a pattering of feet behind them, and Thomas ran for Kattanan, clinging to his legs. Close behind, Faedre walked. "He just started crying and ran. What was I to do?"

Kattanan knelt with the page and touched his cheek. "Are you okay, Tom?"

"Is she my friend?" Thomas whispered.

"I don't know. What happened?"

"She said the prince is her friend and he would want her to know what he says to me."

"What did you say?"

"I didn't tell her. The prince said never tell without asking him first."

"You did well, Thomas." But he saw that the tale was not all done. "What is it?"

"She said I shouldn't refuse a lady; she asked if the Lady were here, would I say no to Her?" The boy hesitated again, glancing over where Faedre and Melisande had gone. "If the Lady needed to know what he said, wouldn't she already?"

Kattanan smiled. "You're right."

Thomas sniffled, but smiled back a little. "Then I did right?"

"Yes, you did. When the prince tells you something, you should only tell it if he lets you. He would be very proud of you, and so am I."

Thomas grinned at this. "Do I have to be friends with her?"

"No, you don't. But you should still be nice to her because she is a lady."

"Okay—oh! The prince told me to ask you if you thought about it. What does he mean?"

"You tell the prince I haven't decided yet." They came up to walk behind Faedre and Melisande as they went farther into the garden. Thomas was polite to Faedre, but spoke with her little, so intent was he to tell Kattanan everything he had done in the past two days. They passed the afternoon there, until Melisande's etiquette teacher took her off to study, with Faedre following. Kattanan and Thomas wandered the castle's dark passages and grand halls until evening, when they parted to their respective suppers. The next few days fell into a routine of courts and meals, public and private. Each morning, Kattanan and Prince walked to the watchtower to visit Rolf, where they heard the stories of his land. The guardsman did not ask many questions of his new companion, but ended most days with the offer of his own ear, if the singer had some private story to tell. Kattanan was able to spend his afternoons when he was not attending the princess reading from her library. As for Melisande, she sang with Kattanan in the mornings, sometimes joined by Faedre and Laura, and after supper, she argued the allegories with him while they walked the garden, or watched the rain fall from some covered balcony. The prince took many meals with them to defend his decisions, but did not seek another meeting with the singer, and Kattanan was content to leave it that way until the letter came.

They were sitting at court, very much as the first time Kattanan had gone, except that a small chair had been provided for him beside the princess. Melisande frequently used him to whisper her comments to the prince; Faedre had begun in this role, but all the men of the court watched her as she knelt beside the prince and as she walked back to Melisande. There had been no such messages today, and Kattanan hoped the princess had become more frugal with her opinions, but the day was still young. After a rather tedious matter involving disputed cattle, a richly dressed messenger approached and bowed deeply, first to the princess, then to her brother. "My lord Earl Orie of Gamel's Grove bids me bear his greetings to Your Highnesses, and a letter to the beauteous Princess Melisande."

Melisande straightened immediately. "Pray continue, I am eager for news."

He drew out a folded parchment and held it before him. "'Unto Her Highness, the most gracious and fair Princess Melisande, does Earl Orie of Gamel's Grove send most humble greetings. A week has passed since last I looked upon you, and no week was ever so hard on any man. Often I think on your graceful dance and on your kind voice. Please think me not heartless to press my suit so soon after your intended was sent to the stars. Rather, I would hope you see me for the weak flesh that I am, unable to pass a moment without thought of you. If Your Highness would permit me again the joy of your company, I have need to travel to the city three days hence and would come before you. As before, I cannot stay more than a few days, but little would please me more than to spend them with you. Please send word by this man. I await your reply in loving impatience, your servant, Earl Orie." The man passed it to Melisande unfolded, and she took it lightly. Beneath the signature as read, there was a small postscript: "I hope that my parting gift has given you all the affection due you in my absence."

Melisande laughed at this, despite the queer look Wolfram shot her. "Tell the good earl that I would be most willing to share my company with him, and look forward to his arrival with a joyous heart. May the Goddess walk with him until then."

The messenger bowed again and took his leave, finding a place among the nobles who watched all of these proceedings with smiles and nods.

Wolfram, too, smiled, but the expression seemed at war with the darkness of his eyes. "I see you are well pleased by this, sister. It gladdens me that the death of the baron has not caused you to lose faith or interest in marriage."

"Oh, I should hope not, Wolfram. Rather I hope that we shall both be happily wed afore long and fulfilling the gift of the Goddess to bring new life into this world." She looked upon him with a delicate smile and a tiny sigh, unnoticed by most viewers, but the prince turned away from her and spoke little to her through the rest of court. When he did glance at her, she waved the folded letter before her like a fan and gave that same smile.

At last, court was over, and the prince stiffly gave Melisande his arm. The door had just shut behind them, when she said with a grin, "Jealousy does not become you, Wolfie."

"Nor does gloating become you."

"I am merely pleased that one of my suitors broke with propriety to send his love, and his wish for a meeting. It is a shame your Asenith can't be with us."

"Are you still on about that? I thought you understood why I have taken no action."

"I do understand." Melisande patted his arm, still smiling. "I simply begin to wonder if I won't be married before you even meet your betrothed." She dropped his arm then and walked ahead, chin held high. She had not gone far, though, when she looked back. "Where is Faedre? Kattanan, go and find her."

When he opened the door to the audience chamber, Faedre practically walked into him, then breezed by, but not before he saw what had kept her; the messenger from Gamel's Grove just slipping out the opposite door. Kattanan shut the door and caught up with the small party, though he could hear them before he saw them.

"Perhaps it were best if I ate alone today!" the prince was saying.

"You can't even be happy for me because I have a caring suitor. Instead you stand there cautioning me and mooning over this Lochalyn girl, but can't even bestir yourself to help her!"

"Don't you think I want to do something?"

"I don't know anything of the kind! I hope Father gets well soon, because he would do something about this. And about you! Have you even told him about the message?"

"He doesn't need my worries on top of his own, and his concern about the wizard—"

"That's another thing! Who is this wizard? Have you done anything to find out? Someone may be trying to kill our father, and you're not doing anything about it. You should have been with him on that hunting trip. Instead, you were settling some petty wheatfield squabble when your father needed you! If he dies, it will be on your head. I hate you!" She ran down the hall, pushing through the honor guard. "Don't follow me, I want to be alone!"

"Nothing! Sandy, there was nothing I could have done, even if I'd been there."

"That is no excuse to yell at your sister like a common child. All she wants is for you to be happy for her, and I do not understand why you can't do that, Your Highness." Faedre spoke softly and turned to go, leaving the confused guard and their master standing in the hall in silence.

# Chapter 7

KATTANAN WATCHED them go, then glanced toward the prince, who remained as he had been left. "I cannot both find and avoid a wizard, and I cannot leave the castle while I am needed." He spoke softly, as if still trying to explain to Melisande.

"No one expects it, Yer Highness," one of the guards said, with a familiar accent and a slight nod to Kattanan.

"She expects that and more, that I should single-handedly cross the mountains and fetch my bride, cure my father with a glance, then punish the wizard who may have done it!" The prince threw his hands in the air, then realized with whom he was speaking and stopped himself. "You are not regularly in my guard."

"No, Yer Highness. Bertram of Redstock took ill this morning early."

"I trust you know what is expected of a royal guard."

"To be seen and not heard, to defend the royal family at all costs, Yer Highness." The huge man gave a little bow.

"Why am I hearing you now?" the prince inquired.

Rolf pulled himself straight. "I am ever in yer defense, Yer Highness."

Wolfram continued to scowl for a moment, but a smile played about his lips. "You will need to be quite vigilant to defend me from my sister's accusations. Who are you?"

"I am called Rolf of the Prince's Mercy."

Now Wolfram nearly laughed. "Rolf of the what?"

"The Prince's Mercy, Yer Highness. 'Twas ten years past that you spared my life."

The prince's eyes widened. "You did not speak our language, then."

" 'Tis a trifle to learn the tongue of one's chosen lord, Yer Highness."

"But no trifle to use that tongue to the prince without being asked."

At this, the other guards shifted their eyes away, exchanging smug glances.

"No, Yer Highness. And I deserve no further mercy from ye than what ye have granted."

"You have spoken boldly, and I would find out if you act boldly as well. From this day, I want you in my guard, on call at all hours. If I do not sleep, you will have no rest, understood?"

Rolf bowed low, now. "Aye, Yer Highness, have no fear; I am your man."

"Well, Rolf, since my sister has spurned me, I should dine with my lord, if he will have me. To the king's chambers." The guards shuffled back into order, with Rolf just before the prince. At last, the prince turned his attention to Kattanan. "Will you come, Singer?"

The singer bowed and fell in behind the prince. When they reached the king's door, the guards stood aside, and a servant slipped in to announce the prince. He emerged in a moment, and said, "The king is in conference, and bids you wait his leisure." Wolfram turned aside from the door and shared quiet words with the chamberlain.

Rolf stooped a little to Kattanan's ear. "What's this, the king making his heir wait in the hall, not even the antechamber?"

The singer shrugged. "I don't know the protocols of Bernholt. The king did not seem well when last I saw him, perhaps he speaks with his physician."

"I've heard that there's something sour between the king and his son."

Before Kattanan could comment on this, the door opened, and Lady Faedre curtsied to the prince on her way by. "The king is feeling quite his old self today, Your Highness." She did not look back, but his eyes followed the sway of her hips. Most of the guards nodded and smiled after her, but Rolf watched only the prince, with a small frown.

Wolfram lowered his head, drawing his fingers along the points of the heavy crown. The door reopened, and the prince beckoned Kattanan with him as he entered. The door had barely shut out the light behind them when the king's voice flared. "When would you have told me about the message from Lochalyn?"

Wolfram knelt at the bedside. "It held nothing new for either of us. I saw no need—"

"You saw no need." The old man pushed himself up. "I lie here dying, with you for an heir—" He crumpled back onto the pillows, coughing.

"I saw no need to disturb your rest, Sire," Wolfram continued quietly. "Had there been good news, I would have come to you immediately."

"Is that why I heard of the baron's death from a servant before I heard from you?"

Wolfram looked down at his hands resting on the old man's bed. "He was my friend, Sire. May I not mourn in my own fashion?"

"You are to be king! Nothing is in your own fashion, but in that of kingship alone." Spasms wracked his thin form, shaking the prince's head where he had buried it in his hands. The old man struggled to regain himself, and won. "You are as nothing while I yet live, and were my fool doctor to help me up, I would sit at court myself. Then would you know kingship." One hand slapped against the velvet bedclothes.

"I would help you up, Sire, and take you there." Wolfram's voice was small, and distant.

"You can barely support that crown," the king scoffed. "How could you support the man who should wear it?" He coughed into a handkerchief, leaving a speckling of blood upon his lips. "Faedre tells me I am not the only one you neglect," the king continued in a softer tone. "Aside from the princess you have yet to wed, she says you rebuke your own sister at every turn."

"There are many things Melisande does not understand, Your Majesty," the prince began.

"So my daughter lacks the wisdom you so clearly demonstrate?" the king snapped.

"What do you want from me, Father? If you would just tell me, I would do it. Should I go to Lochalyn? What if it is a ruse, and I caught them at it? How then would they save face? Only by war or further deceit. Should I come to you before I have mastered my own grief and add it to yours? Or should I ask you before I make any choice at all? I did once, and you gave me only anger then as well." Wolfram flung himself away from the bed and towered over his father in the gloom.

"At least you are still man enough to return my anger," the king responded with a feral grin. His eyes were the hard blue of a storm at sea, his lips still flecked with blood. "I wanted you beside me on the hunt; you could not do that, so I doubt you would obey me now." He fluttered a hand toward his wasted form. "I have lain here two months, is it? They give me potions for my pain, but the pain is here"—he tapped at his temple— "knowing you will be unready. If only there were a war to hurl you into manhood."

"You worked hard to see that there was none, Sire," his son said. "I would hope to uphold your peace, not your army."

From where Kattanan knelt, he could see an old argument returning. The old king was carved by the fire of the candles, and by his fever; his son stood mostly in shadow, yet both faces held similar expressions.

"I can wield a sword, and I can strike any target with an

arrow, Father, but these are weapons of fear and of death, and I would use any other means before taking a life."

"People of the Goddess will return to her at death, and those who are not will return to the blackness whence they came: to all a fitting end."

"But to no man before his time."

"They are not men, but animals," the king hissed into the flickering light, "those skulking beasts of the mountains. If they had the wit for magic, I would blame them for this bed I lie in. They are bright enough to provide some sport, but no more than a fox or bear."

"Yet they defend their children. They build homes for themselves. Their speech is harsh to our ears, but they sing."

The king's cackle sent tremors the length of his body. "I would hardly use that term. Would you, Singer?"

Kattanan was trapped by those eyes, by the slightly twisted smile. He thought of Rolf, on the little farm in the mountains where the guard's parents raised sheep and traded wool with the Woodfolk. He could not hear the prince breathing, but felt himself pinned by competing stares. Harsh breaths scraped between the king's lips. The song formed almost before he was aware, creeping to his lips in a whisper. The language curved, rough-hewn into the darkness—a chant of high places, bright stars, and the feel of earth beneath one's feet, pounding after some beast of the forest. His whole body shook under the king's storm-eyes, his voice sinking low as a dangerous growl grew in the old man's throat. The king's eyes narrowed, but still he heard. Without warning, a goblet slashed the air, shattering hard against the wall just over Kattanan's shoulder. Herb-tinged wine splashed his face, and shards of glass fell against his feet.

"A song of the Woodfolk, Your Majesty," the singer said, hardly breathing himself. He sank back on his heels, finally able to lower his head. Nothing stopped the trembling this time.

"He was only answering your question, Father. Please treat him kindly."

"It was a rebellious answer, and unsought-for. I would be

within my rights to kill him now." The king's hand still hovered in the air, tracing the wake of the hurled goblet. Slowly, though, he let it fall back. "But he does please my daughter, and so I shall allow his life, as long as he never again enters my presence unbidden. Should he ever again give such an answer, he will die and his body be left to rot in the dirt. Crawl from my sight, Castrate."

Kattanan lowered his hands to the floor, feeling the bite of broken glass, but he heeded it not, making painful progress toward the door. He pushed it open, then shut himself in the narrow antechamber. Voices were low outside both doors. The guards' laughter occasionally rose into his hearing, but there was no more shouting, no crockery thrown. He pulled his hands against his chest and crouched there on the floor, weeping. When the hand touched him, he jerked away against a bench. The hand lay warm and gentle upon his shoulder, though, and waited until the last of the tremors receded.

"Come with me, Kattanan duRhys," the prince whispered, and the singer rose to his feet, though he wavered there a long moment before he trusted himself to walk. Wolfram opened the door and preceded him into the full light. With a flick of the wrist, he gestured the instantly silent guards ahead of them. "I will dine in my quarters. Inform the kitchen that the king requires meat today; venison if we have it." One of the guard bowed and trotted off down the hall, as the others fell in step. Rolf flashed several worried glances behind him, but marched on, asking no questions until they got to the prince's quarters, where he turned smartly with an abbreviated bow.

"With permission, Highness?" he said, but his eyes were on Kattanan.

"You know each other?" the prince asked; his eyebrows rose.

"Aye, Highness."

"Good, then come in and assist me and you may talk all you want."

"Right gladly, Yer Highness." He swiftly shut the door behind the trio.

Waiting within, Thomas jumped up and dropped into his lowest bow. As he straightened, his rosy mouth was bent with dismay.

Forestalling any protest, Wolfram walked to the boy. "I know you want to stay, but I need you to go outside and be sure no one comes until I tell you otherwise. Can you do that?"

The boy nodded quickly and went into the hall.

"Rolf, some water, warm, if possible." Wolfram escorted Kattanan to a chair and knelt before him to look at his bloody palms. The guard returned quickly with a basin and pitcher and the kettle from the fire.

"Ye have the finer touch, Highness, best you do the cleaning."

Wolfram nodded and began picking slivers of glass from Kattanan's palms. He rinsed them as carefully as he could. Still, Kattanan sucked in his breath and winced. Soon enough, the job was done, and his hands wrapped in white cloth. The prince wiped his own hands then, and offered the towel to Rolf as well.

"May I speak now, Highness?"

"Freely, though we may not be so free with our answers," he cautioned the guard.

"By the mount, what happened in there? I heard shouting, then the song, soft as ye were, lad, I heard it." He fixed Kattanan with a stern look.

Kattanan glanced first to the prince. "This is not my tale to tell, Highness. Much of it I do not know."

Wolfram sighed and pulled up a chair for himself. "The king became ill during a hunt, for the Woodfolk of the mountains." Rolf started at this, but held his peace, and the prince went on. "I did not go with him; there was a land dispute to settle, and I . . . I have no heart for such sport. There was a heavy rain in the mountains, and they could not sight their quarry, but a figure crossed their path, and my father hailed it, asking if there were Woodmen about. I gather he was answered by laughter at first, then the figure responded, 'Oh rashest of monarchs, are you asking me?' 'I am demanding it of you!' 'Few men make demands of the Wizard of Nine Stars,' the stranger said, and lightning flashed. My father was unhorsed; the wizard was gone, if such it was. The king returned weak, coughing, and soon became as you have seen him."

"Ye're not to blame, Highness," Rolf said.

"It is not that, precisely, for which they blame me." The prince took a deep breath. "I have been among the Woodmen, to study them. They trust me, and come to me when I am riding, to see if I have brought them cloth or knives. Had I been there, the king's hunt would not have been frustrated. Whenever I see him now, he finds a way to tell me so, hence today, that they are beasts incapable of humanity. He asked whether Kattanan would say that they sing."

"And so ye sang that one, lad." Rolf shook his head. "You learn tunes too quickly, and not so fast when to keep silent. That song, I felt it here." He tapped his chest.

"And I." Wolfram nodded, his eyes soft upon the singer.

Kattanan gave a tiny shrug. "A song, Your Highness, nothing more."

"When you sang it, it was much more. Kattanan duRhys, I am in your debt."

"For my stupidity? You were nearly in debt to an unshriven corpse, Your Highness." The words flew wildly from him. He looked, blinking back more tears.

"No man has yet stood for me against my father," said Wolfram.

Kattanan let out a short, bitter laugh. "That is still true, Highness."

Silence fell between them. Finally, the prince said, "Be that as it may, you have my thanks, and what protection I can give you shall be yours. At least do not deny my gratitude."

# Chapter 8

"YE'RE BOTH looking like a splash of mead would be welcome," Rolf observed. He fetched a small keg from the table and three fine goblets. He poured them each a cup.

Kattanan held his goblet awkwardly and sipped at the contents. Rolf watched the singer's injured hands. "Curse that Faedre! She riled the king."

"I think she riles everyone," Kattanan said.

"All she did was report what Melisande thinks happened between us. My father hears all things about me with disapproval. Why doesn't he just call Melisande his heir and have done?" The prince took a deep draught of his mead.

There was a rap at the door. "Come, Thomas," the prince called, and the page entered.

"Somebody's here, Your Highness, but not the same one."

"Who is it?"

"I don't know. He said a friend."

"You didn't ask him, did you?" Wolfram leaned forward, and sighed in relief when the boy shook his head. "Good. Tell him to wait just a moment. I'll open the door when I'm ready."

Thomas gave a little bow and exited.

"Your guest is a wizard?" Rolf abruptly set down his drink.

"The man I expected is as trustworthy as a wizard can be; he has been looking into my father's ailment. It seems my man could not come and has sent me a stranger. I would not mind having witnesses to our talk, but best if you both remain silent." He rose and walked toward the door. "Especially ask no questions."

The visitor was a heap of a man with a wide, grinning face. His robe was long and full, sleeves dragging along the ground folded back to reveal a rich undertunic. Despite his girth, he swept into a bow and straightened again, still grinning.

"I do not know you," Wolfram observed.

"Oh, need we stand on protocol?" The man's voice was a purr, his gaze meandering around the room. "After all, I am sent by our mutual friend to fulfill his duty in his absence."

"There is a place for protocol, especially in the lives of kings. Tell me how you are called." The last had an edge to it, accented by the prince's raised eyebrow.

"Ritual greeting, even, good prince." The other shook his head. "Very well, I am the Wizard of the Broken Shell."

"An enigmatic name, unlike the Wizard of Long Valley, whom I had expected."

"An inquiry without a question; I can see you have played this game before. My name refers to turtles. But I shall dispense with vagaries and give you the news you seek. My associate of the drab name has succumbed to temptation. May I be seated?"

The prince gestured him to a seat and resumed his own. "And so he sent you in his stead, while he pursues this temptation."

"Oh, no, I volunteered. I had a yen to see the palace and yourself; I have heard so much about you." The grin grew a little more broad.

"If you continue to bait me to questions, you shall not see either for any length of time."

The wizard sighed, leaning back. "Not one question for me, Prince? I would not take undue advantage." He wafted one hand through the air. "If you wish to play with caution, so be it. I suppose I must submit myself to your rules, but won't you at least introduce your friends?"

Wolfram pointed to Rolf with a smirk. "This is my friend of the ready blade, and this is my friend of the quiet stare."

Laughing, the wizard eyed the pair. "Both well named, and

this one quite pretty also." He turned his merry walnut eyes to
Kattanan. "Have you a voice to match your looks?"

"He has a voice to match the king's, and no less. Tell me what
you came for."

"Yes, the Wizard of Nine Stars, was it not? It was foolish to
allow the name to be known without being commanded to it,
but, of all of us, the Nine Stars can afford to be foolish."

"You know him."

"I would not put it in those terms; you see, one special skill
of this wizard is with illusion. He may project himself in any
fashion, male or female, tall, stout, old, or young. He is most
often seen as an old man, bent, with foul teeth, surrounded by
crackling air. I have been told this is what you expect of a wizard." The man settled in to his role with a gleaming eye. "Many
of my brethren would trade their very souls to master only that
talent of all this wizard has. Illusion may be applied to great effect on oneself with no questions asked."

"If his power is so great, it is strange I have not heard much
of this man's works."

"I have myself heard only rumors, and often from those who
heard them from others."

"I fail to see how an illusion could have so afflicted my
father."

"As do I. Is there no way I might examine him?"

"He would never allow it. He does not see strangers these
days."

"Then tell me how he suffers. What are the symptoms?"

"He is in command of his mind, but his body is wracked with
pains and spasms. His breathing is unsteady, and his hands shake
even at the best of times."

"But the condition varies? He does not merely worsen every
day, but is better on some, then worse again?"

"Yes, and with no cause that we can find."

"It does not sound like magic as I know it." The wizard lost
his grin. "Nor is it the style Nine Stars is said to favor. Were there
no mention of such a wizard, I would have said poison or mere

old age. But then, he is not so very old, is he. You are quite sure of his story?"

"It was confirmed by those who rode with him."

"Assuming"—he held this word a long moment—"assuming there is magic involved, I think it doubtful that the wizard would be operating on his own. He was most likely hired to perform the task." The wizard suddenly focused on the prince. "You are the one with the most to gain by the king's illness or death, it would appear."

Kattanan shot a look at the prince, and Rolf twitched his sword halfway from the scabbard. "Give me another reason, wizard, and ye will meet my ready sword."

But Wolfram laughed and shook his head. "It would seem so, I suppose, to anyone who covets power. For myself, I would prefer honor, or love, or any one of a number of things over the fear this crown earns me. To you it is a shining prize, to me, a small prison."

"Perhaps so, but assuredly a comfortable one. I do not mean to offend, only to point out what I see; you are the heir, after all, and you would do well to consider who else would gain from this. Also, any wizard worth the name holds enough power to kill, not just to inflict some lingering sickness. What can be the purpose?" he drawled.

Wolfram looked a little startled by this thought. "I take it you have an idea."

"In fact, Your Highness, I have none." The man spread his hands wide. "Who could possibly want your father sick, but not dead; you in power, but only tenuously? Has there been anything unusual going on?"

"Nothing that seems relevant," Wolfram answered

"My dear Prince, to believe this plot, if such it is, was hatched just since the king's illness is naive and laughable. Whoever it was must have been setting the stage long before."

Kattanan jerked upright, eyes wide, remembering the temple. All eyes were upon him again, and Wolfram spread a questioning palm.

The wizard drew his glance from the one to the other. "Perhaps you and your friends have things to discuss."

"Perhaps we do," the prince agreed, "but they shall wait a few moments, I trust." He did not take his eyes from Kattanan. "This Nine Stars must be a difficult man to find."

"Impossible, unless you are the Liren-sha and can dispel all magic."

"Then there is just one further point, Wizard of the Broken Shell. He of the Long Valley owed me a favor, and so was beholden to help me, but I do not know why you would do so."

"Let me say that the Nine Stars is no friend of mine. If I could hire the Liren-sha to find and kill him, I would do that, for I must admit myself at a loss to dispatch him otherwise."

"You speak of the Wizard's Bane as if he were more than mere legend."

"Legend? Oh, no, Prince, he is as real as you or I, and deadlier than both of us together. Half of us wizards will tell you he is myth, or dead; some will tell you he is spawn of the time before the Goddess; and some will do all they can to search him out." He let this dangle in the air until he was sure no one would ask him why, then tilted his head and explained, "They think they are immortal, or immune. My brother of the Long Valley will not be returning your favor, Highness, for I have heard that he found the Liren-sha and has joined his legend."

Wolfram met the wizard's eyes. "I am sorry."

"Tempt not fate, or you will find it quicker than you think."

"There's nothing further, except to thank you." Wolfram rose and offered his hand.

The wizard took his hand and smiled. "You are gracious and prudent. I would not mind playing this game with you again. If you find this wizard, let me know. I may not stand against him, but I would be pleased to lend you what support I can."

"Again, thank you. Walk with the Goddess."

"And you, Prince," but he was looking at Kattanan when he said it. Then he was gone.

"He is brimful of secrets and dying t' be asked about it. Good riddance to him!" Rolf said, checking the bar on the door.

Wolfram came to kneel again by Kattanan's chair. "You started; why?"

"I did not think of it before, Your Highness, but as a moment between two angry men."

"What happened? Which men?"

"Hush, now, Highness, let him catch a breath," Rolf chided, coming over beside them.

"It was after you denied Squire Montgomery a position here. I went to the temple to bind branches for the baron. Montgomery came in when I was alone and"—he looked away from the softening of the prince's face—"he asked me to leave. Someone else was coming, though, so I hid in the eastern alcove. I did not see the other, and he was not so angry as the squire, except when some comment was made about your sister, then he defended her. Montgomery said all their plans were ruined, the other told him no, that his goal was and always had been to woo the princess, and he was doing well in that. He counseled patience, and spoke vaguely of his plan. I only thought he meant to win the princess's hand, and was a friend of the squire's. Could it be something to do with this, Your Highness?"

"Could it be," groaned the prince. He sat back on his heels. "How can I tell my sister one of her suitors may be plotting against us? How would that not sound like jealousy to her?"

"The voice, Your Highness," Kattanan began, the ache in his palms suddenly more fierce. "I did not see him, but I feel sure it was Earl Orie. He said nothing against you or the king—I had no reason to think more of it."

"There's the dog," said Rolf suddenly. "He must know how angry ye'd be."

"The dogs are dead." Wolfram scrubbed a hand over his face.

"He gave her a new one, the earl did." Kattanan flinched at the pain that crossed the prince's features. "She's asked us all to keep the secret." He looked away.

The prince stood and paced to the window. "Does she think so little of me that I would deny her every pleasure?" He turned back, framed by bold light. "Kattanan, you have had a hard day already, and I know this will not make it easier, but I must have your answer. This earl is coming three days hence to pay court to my sister. We must assign a chaperone for their meetings; if you will tell me what you witness, I would have you there. She will expect me to ask in any case."

The singer looked down at the badge of the princess, the mark of his fealty, freshly stitched by her own hand, then he cast his gaze to the prince. Wolfram stood tall, but off-balance, as if about to run. The shadows of his eyes were ever-present. The king's crown set above his brow, topping a tumble of ash-blond hair, a crown that would be his perhaps sooner than it ought. "If he makes any threat against the royal family, or to betray the princess, I will tell you. More than that, I cannot promise."

Wolfram nodded. "Quite right. Kattanan, you may return to my sister." He swallowed, and his shoulders slumped. "I would appreciate it if she did not hear what happened in my father's chamber."

"I will invent an accident, Your Highness," Kattanan offered, but he thought of other lies, other wounds concealed just so. He made a brief bow and left the room. He looked at his fingers emerging from the bandaged palms; he would make no braids that night.

# Chapter 9

THE DAY of Orie's visit dawned with drizzle, which made for an abbreviated walk with Prince and a dim breakfast. Melisande slept a bit later that morning, and went first to bathe, returning in her richest robe, attended by no less than seven ladies.

"I do wish you could do my hair today, Kat." He frowned a little at this use of his more familiar name, but then she smiled her most brilliant smile, and he returned it. "I want to be perfect when he comes. Isn't he handsome?"

"Wonderful, Highness," Laura said. "As if we hadn't all said so at least a dozen times."

"Relax," Faedre said. "He is only a man, surely not worth all of this worry."

Melisande's eyes lit on Kattanan. "We have not sung Morning Prayer."

"As you wish," he replied, glancing at the ladies arrayed around the princess. Listen, he told himself, looking away from their silks and velvets. He could not yet be sure that Orie's intentions were wrong; he, too, needed to relax. He was a little surprised when Melisande joined in immediately, as if she recognized the moment he found his voice. They sang lower than usual, staggering their breathing so that the song went on. Melisande had eyes only for the singer. "That was the best ever, I think." She rose to her feet. "Come help me prepare for this man." Faedre took her hand, and the gathering of ladies swished into her room.

In their wake, Kattanan found himself trembling. He checked his image in the mirror and wondered if he looked like a spy. He put out a hand to steady himself against the mantel.

"What's the matter?" Laura asked, coming up behind him.

"Nothing."

"You are shaking, Kattanan. The princess is too nervous to notice, but I do."

He smoothed the gloves that concealed his bandages. "If today goes well, the princess will not be the only one moving to a new castle."

Laura shrugged. "I'd've thought you'd be used to it."

"I have always moved away from a master, never with one. I mean, I was a marriage gift several times, but always found myself left behind, or traded off again."

"Oh, Melisande wouldn't do that." Laura put a hand on his shoulder. "She enjoys your company too much. I never thought of what this must be like to you. The rest of us are here because we chose to serve, but you have had no choice."

"That part, I am used to." The remark rang more bitterly than he had expected, and he pressed his forehead against the mantel, working to master his breathing.

Shaking her head, Laura frowned, but a knock sounded on

the outer door before she could respond. Laura backed toward
it, still watching Kattanan as if expecting him to run.

"Prince Wolfram invites his sister to join him at court,"
Thomas said with practiced care.

"Wait here." The maid tapped at her mistress's door, and was
admitted.

The page shifted from one foot to the other. "You okay, Kat?"
The singer did not look at him. "I'm okay, Tom. Just tired."

"The prince sent this for you." Thomas held out a thin figure
carved of bone, its shield inscribed with the prince's device.
Though Kattanan had seen few of their artifacts, it had the un-
mistakable style of the Woodmen. Kattanan slipped it into the
palm of his glove.

The princess's door opened, and she emerged, surrounded by
her ladies. Wearing a gown of deep green, a circlet with a matching stone, and the earl's flower necklace, she smiled warmly.
Thomas's mouth formed a little O, and the princess laughed.
"Faedre says I am a perfect vision, but I think this thing is giving me a headache."

She was indeed a vision, glowing, her eyes and voice and face
so bright with anticipation.

"Be sure to stand straight, dear," an elderly matron put in.

"And smile, but not too much," offered another.

Melisande shuddered. She grabbed her skirts and sprinted
from their midst, catching the singer's arm. "Walk with me and
protect me from them! Every one of them knows just how I
should be, and act and look. You are so lucky you will never have
to go through this!"

"Your Highness, it's not proper," he protested, but she was already moving toward the door with his arm in hers.

"You are the only one of my household who doesn't pick at
me, or poke me. Besides, I'm the princess—anyone who thinks
I am improper may take it up with me, or with my father."

Despite her bold words, her hand looked pale and delicate on
his arm, and the quick glance she shot him was far from confi-
dent. "You are beautiful, Your Highness," he whispered, and saw
the flash of a smile before he lowered his gaze.

"But what if he thinks me a child? Or if I do something wrong?" she whispered back urgently. "I can't be just beautiful."

He thought of the earl's sharp voice in the chapel—but the anger had all been to put Sir in his place, hadn't it? Kattanan put aside his doubts for Melisande's sake. "He has already seen you in your night robe, but he still wanted this meeting, Your Highness, and he gave you something you love."

She squeezed his arm. "You always know how to make me feel better. I hope he is as good at that as you are."

"Either way, Highness, I will still be with you."

She watched the floor for a time, then said, "This afternoon, we will be given time to ourselves, but with a chaperone. Would you stay with me?"

Kattanan stumbled, and caught his balance. "What about one of your ladies?"

"They all have such plans for me, I—it makes me nervous," she finished quickly.

"I will stay, Your Highness." He smiled then, and lifted his head. His heart raced, and Melisande's hand felt like a ray of sun that had pierced the ceiling and sought him out.

Thomas trotted ahead to announce the princess as they approached the court. The crowd smelled of cloves and civet. Wolfram had risen to welcome her, but faltered a little as he saw her escort. Kattanan gave a tiny shrug as he passed her hand to the prince with a bow, then moved to his own place. Melisande leaned in to whisper to her brother, who cast another glance at the singer, this time with a smile and a nod.

"I am sure you all know," Wolfram began, "that my sister has a suitor waiting in the antechamber to call on her." Cheering greeted this, and the herald had to rap his staff on the floor to regain their attention. "We are all eager to welcome him, so the old business shall have to wait. Have Earl Orie sent in."

The doors opened, and the earl stepped into the aisle. He wore a dark tunic and a flowing cape that swirled along the floor behind him. His hair was darker than night, his eyes seemed as stars beneath it, matched by his glowing smile. He did kneel this time, not to center, but on the step before the princess. "I had not thought it possible that Your Highness could become even more beautiful. If it please you, may I kiss your hand?"

The delight of the audience sparkled through again, but Kattanan felt a chill. Looking back, he caught sight of Faedre, well off the dais among the ladies. Whatever charm she had seemed dead, arms held rigid, smile prim and set. Even the guards were not watching her.

"It pleases me, good Earl, though my beauty would not be so much without the necklace you wrought for me." She offered her hand and blushed as her words brought applause from the onlookers. The earl bent his dark head over her hand, taking it gently, and shut his eyes as he placed the softest of kisses just above her wrist—the place of desire. Melisande felt the color rising again to her cheeks. The earl tilted his face then, to look into her eyes as he withdrew.

"You are well come into our court, Orie," Wolfram said, managing a smile. "We would be delighted if you would join us for supper today."

"I would be most honored, Your Highness," the earl replied, only then sweeping his glance from the princess. "After supper, may I walk with your sweet sister in the gardens here, that she might hear my suit?"

"If it pleases her, and I see it does"—he nodded to Melisande—"then, in my father's stead, I grant you the favor you ask, excepting only that you be accompanied by a chaperone."

"I would accept a dozen, if only I may share her company, Your Highness."

"So be it, then. You may take a place among our court until that time."

Orie smiled as he rose. "So long as I may have a clear view of the splendors of your court, Highness." He bowed low again and took a place cleared for him in the nearest row. Several men clapped him on the back as he sat, and a gesture dismissed his escort.

Kattanan could not keep his mind on the affairs of court, but he had no need, for Melisande seemed inclined simply to exchange glances with the earl and give only half an ear to the matters brought before them. Faedre, now that she was in plain view of the man, seemed to disappear even more, fading in among the ladies. Wolfram alone applied himself to the matters at hand but turned his eyes to the silent conversation that passed between his sister and her suitor. At long last, he declared court at a close and led Melisande toward their refectory, closely followed by the ladies, the earl, and the singer.

"Tell us more about your holdings, Orie," Wolfram said over the meal.

"Gamel's Grove borders the capital lands to the east, and covers from there to Tirey-on-the-River," the earl answered. "I was young to take on such a parcel, but the old earl was lost in the same battle where I distinguished myself in His Majesty's eyes, the Lochalyn affair."

"Oh, do tell us!" Melisande said. "Did you get to see the traitor queen?"

Orie laughed. "Indeed, no. I was but sixteen, and a foot soldier in the service of the earl. We were assigned to capture another stronghold, where the queen's relatives had hidden. There was a terrific battle; I was myself first to reach the gate." He gazed off to the distance. "I had a bad moment when the siege ladder fell from beneath me, but held on with all my strength and topped the wall. I fought my way to the winch and drew up the portcullis to let in our men."

"So the battle was won because of your heroism."

He looked at the princess with a puzzled expression. "Unfortunately, there was nobody there. Somehow the royal family had escaped us. So we won the city but lost our quarry."

"Oh." The princess sighed.

"The earl had no family, so I was given his lands. I also command a garrison of soldiers that would be first on the scene if there is any further trouble for our neighbors."

"I'm not aware of any problems, except the snow that prevents my betrothed from coming," Wolfram observed.

The earl cast him a curious glance. "Only that it seems the very relatives who escaped us would like to press their claim to the throne."

"But they have none!" the princess protested.

"Not directly, no, but they are saying that the royal family was murdered by the man who now sits the throne. If this were true, his claim would be solely by way of treason, and the throne would fall to the queen's family. She had a brother, I believe."

"I take it there is no validity to these claims." Wolfram had pushed away his plate and settled back with a mug of ale.

Orie's manner suddenly stiffened. "I do not think so, Highness, but I was only a soldier, and not privy to all the events that brought us to war."

"I ask only because we've not heard much from Lochalyn, so our information is limited."

"I have had similar problems lately, no doubt owing to the condition of the roads."

"No doubt. I have never been there myself, I was too young to join the campaign, but my father attended the new king's coronation, and there betrothed me to Princess Asenith. I think she was about six at the time."

Melisande exchanged a look with Wolfram, who nodded briefly and rose. "It is a fair afternoon for a walk, I am sure. Perhaps you would not mind if I asked your good singer, Kattanan duRhys, to accompany you?" The question was directed at Melisande, who rose also.

"Very good—if I should run out of conversation, we might enjoy a song."

Orie offered his arm to the princess and led her out to the gardens, with Kattanan trailing after. With girlish excitement, Melisande took the earl up to the tower to look out over the land. The weather had cleared, though gray clouds still hung low overhead. After all the appropriate exclamations were made, Orie asked her to sit, and they settled on a stone bench, exactly as if Kattanan were not there. He perched in one of the crenellations of the wall.

"How is the puppy, Your Highness?"

"Oh, he's wonderful. We named him Prince." They shared a laugh over this, and Orie took her hand lightly.

"Have you thought much of your marriage, Princess? Of what you would like it to be?"

"I have not thought as much as I should, I'm sure. I just want to be happy, as I think my mother was. She had only met Father once before their wedding day, and yet she still chose him. He is strong, powerful—a good king." She looked back toward the castle.

"He is that, Your Highness. He has the obedience of thousands of men, myself included. I only wish he had not taken ill. All of the kingdom waits, dreading to hear bad news, praying for good." The earl hesitated. "Would there be a chance that I could see him?"

"If he is able, I know he would want to see you. We can go whenever you like."

"Right now, I am well pleased to sit right here, but I hope to have an audience later. It has been too long. In any event, we were not discussing your father but what you seek in marriage."

"Yes. I do want children, of course, but I must know that my husband cares as much for me as for our future heirs." She spoke quickly, looking up into the earl's face.

"Be not concerned on my behalf. I gained my lands through my own merit, and so am not as concerned with such things as those of older families. I sought your hand for smaller reasons."

"And what were they, Orie?"

"Several of your dogs were of my breeding stock, and I was curious what manner of princess would want such animals. Also, I love to dance. It is not considered proper for a bachelor-earl to host balls, so I must find a wife who would delight in doing so."

"Have you a fitting hall for such affairs? I was given to understand the keep at Gamel's Grove was rather modest."

"I had one built, Your Highness, with tall alabaster windows. The light is magnificent."

She grinned. "I would like to see it."

"Then you shall. I was not certain of my welcome here—"

"How not?" the princess protested, taking his other hand.

"If you are willing, I would ask your father for the privilege of the Goddess Moon."

"Would you?" She turned away for a moment, her eyes meeting Kattanan's with a look of near panic, but she returned with a smile. "I would have to think on it."

"Of course. Perhaps while I am visiting the king? I do not mean to rush you, nor would I presume on your goodwill. If you choose the Goddess Moon, I would like to have you accompany me back to my home."

"Let me take you to his chamber." The princess rose and preceded them down the stairs.

They had not gone far when they heard a strange song to one side. Turning, the trio saw the ancient priestess weaving among the trees, crooning and bobbing. Before Melisande was able to hurry the earl away, she dashed up to fling herself at Kattanan's feet. "Sire! The boon!"

"What's all this?" Orie asked. "Have we been in company with a king?"

"No, Excellency. This lady is mad," Kattanan stammered.

At that, the woman howled.

"Will you leave me alone?" Kattanan begged. "If I do this thing, will you let me be?"

"Aye, Your Majesty, as alone as I am able, never as alone as you think." She thrust a finger toward his face, making the singer step back.

"What is your boon?" His arms were crossed, gloved hands pressed to his sides.

"A dance, Your Majesty. A circle you will dance with me."

"I can't." He shook his head roughly. "I do not dance."

"The last night before you go, that night, you will dance with me, and with them."

"Who?" the earl inquired. "I see no one."

She flicked a glance at him. "Nor I." Returning to Kattanan, she went on, "They will come, you will dance, I will see—"

Earl Orie grasped her shoulder. "What mean you by that? That you see no one?"

"One eye sees the now, the other sees the later. Now, a man of two halves a heart, soon of a whole kingdom. Reaching, reaching, never holding what you have!" She waved her arms before him, then snatched the princess's hand from his. "Here, here is the future!" She flung Melisande away and spat on the ground. "I dance with kings!" the old woman shouted, prancing a little circle around them as Orie gathered a livid Melisande into his arms. Then the priestess was off down the path, still laughing and flailing her hands.

"If she had a hair on her head, I'd tear it out!" Melisande shouted.

"Insults, yes, but nonsense," Orie said. "What does that hag's spit mean in the eyes of the Goddess? It is she who is worthless, Your Highness."

Hearing this, Melisande looked down at herself, and at him, and pulled gently away to smooth her skirts. "Forgive my lapse, my lord. It's just she is so outrageous. She has no blessing for any of us, only curses."

"Not quite true, Highness," Orie pointed out, glancing at Kattanan.

The singer had not moved, but his shoulders quivered, and his eyes were shut. "I hear curses, too, Excellency. Unlike yourselves, I am no dancer, nor would I care to step with her."

"It's true, you wouldn't even dance with me." Melisande watched him closely, the earl standing firm behind her.

"That ball was the first time I have tried in years." He thought a moment. "Perhaps the first time I have ever tried, Your Highness."

She put out a tentative hand. "Oh, if I'd known, I would not have made you. Forgive me?" Her eyes were soft upon him, any anger forgotten.

He made a small bow. "How could I not?"

"Well," Orie broke in, eyes blacker than ever, "shall we be on?" One arm invited the princess, and he stared hard at the singer, as she accepted, then turned away toward the king's chamber.

# Chapter 10

AFTER ORIE entered the king's chamber, Melisande looked at the singer. "Walk with me?"

"Where to, Highness?"

"Oh, anywhere." She folded her arms. "I feared the earl would not be a comfort. That witch spouts nonsense, but there is more to her than that. Why did she ask you to dance?"

"I do not know."

"Forgive my mentioning it—I know how she upsets you." The princess shook herself. "But we ought to be discussing the Goddess Moon. He expects me to decide now."

"Do not let him rush you, Highness, if you are not ready."

"Many ladies my age are already wed, and it would get me out of the castle."

"If I may, Highness, what is the Goddess Moon?"

"It means that, rather than wait a long time for the wedding, I would go to live with the earl as a friend or sister. At the end of one month we would return and say whether we consider ourselves married. My eldest sister had a Goddess Moon with a minor lord and turned him down to marry the prince she has now."

"It seems a reasonable idea," Kattanan remarked.

"What do you think of the earl, though?" she asked, a smile returning to her lips.

"He—" the singer began, but could not look at her. Orie is friends with a brutal man, he wanted to say. And he knows things about wizards. But both points seemed too vague to mention. "The two of you have much in common."

"But I don't like to leave Father, sick as he is. He does not have the strength to see me most days, but I want to be here when he gets well."

"Gamel's Grove is not far away and your brother would send for you if there is a change."

"Yes, yes I suppose so. Wolfram doesn't like Orie. Did you watch him at supper? No interest at all; he acted like he was talking to himself." Melisande frowned, then met Kattanan's eyes. "No questions! Wolfram did not ask Orie any questions." She let out a cry of rage. "Why is he treating him like the enemy? By the Goddess, what's gotten into my brother? He must be mad! Do you suppose Orie noticed?"

"He still asked for the Goddess Moon, Highness," Kattanan pointed out.

"Then I'm going to do it. Wolfram will have to apologize for the way he's treated him." She nodded smugly. "He'll have to be good to my lord, or I'll never set foot in this castle again. Imagine if I didn't come to my brother's own wedding."

"I doubt Wolfram would let that happen, Highness. He does care for you." Kattanan stared at his palm, the slight bulge where the prince's token was concealed, then looked to the princess. "He found out about the puppy."

"What? How?"

"One of the guards reported it. Your brother knows you need that puppy, but I think he was hurt that you did not tell him."

She narrowed her eyes. "How did you find out that he knew?"

"He questioned me, Your Highness. He wanted to know how you were feeling after the baron's death. It was while you were so angry at him, and he could not ask you himself. He said he would not deny you the pleasure of having the dog, even though he did not want to see another." This was near enough the truth, and gave a good reason for his suspicion of the earl, but Kattanan's heart was racing.

Melisande leaned back against the low wall of the outside

gallery they had entered. Sun shone against her hair and fine features, and she sighed heavily. "Maybe I have been too hard on
him. He has been simply awful about the earl being my suitor,
though." She pushed quickly off from the wall. "He shall have to
learn to like him." Melisande stopped with a grin. "And Orie
does make me happy! Oh, Kat, I know we have not had much
time, but it was wonderful. And the way he looks at me. Maybe
it is love. Could it be?"

The singer only shrugged. "Closer than that of many couples
I have seen wed." He heard Melisande describing all of her
suitor's virtues—strength, bravery, kindness, she went on—and
suddenly saw him through the princess's eyes, a man as strong
and heroic as Kattanan himself could never be. The princess before him glowed so brightly he wanted nothing more than to
shut his eyes forever.

"Princess! Your Highness, your father asks for you," the chamberlain said breathlessly.

"Coming." She gathered her skirts and sprang back the way
they had come.

The guards on duty glowered down at him as he stood there,
so he backed off across the hall and looked down the stairwell.
The clouds had burned off, and sunlight streamed in the
clerestory windows two floors above. A pair of maids washed
their way down the stairs scrubbing at stone rails and the worn-
down centers of the ancient steps. Down at the bottom was a
smooth planc of checked marble, with a statue placed to one
side. Kattanan leaned over the rail, and stared; he could almost
feel the breeze of flight upon his face. His hands ached. In just a
couple of steps, he could end the question of his position once
and for all.

"Kattanan! It is done!" Melisande held aloft the earl's hand,
beaming. "We leave the day after tomorrow, and there is so
much to do. Go to Laura and tell her to start the preparations!
No, wait—first go tell Wolfram the news." Her grin took on a
fierce edge.

The singer bowed low and set out. Behind him, he heard their
brief farewell as the earl went to send messages to his own cham-

berlains. Wolfram was not in his chambers, but a servant directed Kattanan to the library. A few lanterns made pools of light around the high desks of the monks employed there. They glanced up as he passed, some copying manuscripts, some delicately rebinding ancient texts. Wolfram he found by his shadow cast on a tall shelf; the prince's hair was bound back out of his face, distinct from the round-skulled shadows of the busy monks.

"Your Highness—"

Wolfram jumped, but he smiled as he straightened on his feet.

"I am sorry, Highness, I do not mean to disturb you."

"Why have you come?"

"Melisande sent me to inform you"—Kattanan took a deep breath—"she has chosen to take the Goddess Moon with Earl Orie. The king has given his blessing."

Wolfram slammed a fist against the table, upsetting a cup of quill pens, not to mention the nearer monks, though they quickly looked away. "Why can't this wait? Must everything happen at once." He sat down heavily and pulled the crown from his head to run his fingers through his hair. "When?"

"Two days."

"What? How can she do this?"

"Well," the singer began, then stopped.

"Tell me, please. It isn't you I'm angry with."

"She is doing it partly to spite you."

Wolfram groaned. "By the Goddess."

"At supper, she noticed that you did not ask Orie any questions. She already thought you disliked him, but she thinks you were unfair in treating him like a wizard."

"What was I to do? I will not leave myself open to magic to assuage some fear of Melisande's, much as I love her."

"He seems to love her, too, Highness. He asked what she wanted of a marriage, and told her of the dance hall he has built. They may make a good match. He said nothing all day to make me think he is conspiring against the king." His voice trailed off a moment as he thought.

"But you do not seem altogether favorable."

"It is a foolish fear, Highness, and I would not give it over to you."

Wolfram faced him and spoke low. "If I am to find the truth, I must know all doubts, even foolish ones."

"The old priestess you allowed to live in the gardens came to us today."

The prince almost laughed. "I have heard she is prophesying madly out there."

"She called Orie 'a man of two halves a heart, soon of a whole kingdom.' She said he was always reaching, but not holding what he had."

"There is something about her that makes me think she is more than just a crazy old woman." Wolfram considered for a moment. "So, you will both be leaving in two days."

"Yes, Your Highness."

"I am sorry. I think there are some stories of yours you have not told to anyone and am curious enough to want them told." He held up a calming hand. "But you will keep your secrets after all. This is likely my last chance to talk with you alone. Even should you part ways with my sister, Kattanan, you have a friend here. Three, if I may speak for Thomas and Rolf. I hope my friendship has not cost you with my sister."

"No, Highness, I do not think she suspects."

Wolfram studied Kattanan's gloved hands, clasped before him. "I know you have to get ready, but I would like to hear you sing again. Would you come to Evening Prayer tomorrow?"

"I will try, Highness." The prince gazed at him a little longer, but Kattanan said, "The princess is expecting me."

"Walk with the Goddess, Kattanan duRhys."

Kattanan bowed deeply. "And you, Highness."

THE NEXT day, Melisande's chambers were in an uproar; they had been hoping for a move, but certainly not so soon. The ladies fussed even more until the princess blew up at them and chased them all out, leaving her with the meeker servants.

"There is a bed and wardrobe in my new chamber, but I'll want those chairs along."

Laura nodded. "You'll want everything before long, Highness. When I left home to come to work here, I was lonely for what little I had had."

"At least I will get to leave some of those ladies behind. Most of them were posted by Father. Oh!" she said, and sat down on a trunk.

"What is it, Your Highness?" Kattanan asked, still holding the books he was packing.

"When I wed him, I won't be a princess anymore."

"Of course you will," Faedre said, emerging from the bedroom. "The blood will never leave you, nor the bearing. You shall be a princess for all of your life. Rather imagine that your husband will be elevated by you."

"My husband," the princess echoed.

Faedre laughed. "Yes, he will be. Don't look so stunned; he might change his mind."

"You really think so?"

"No, Melisande, everyone has seen how he looks at you."

"Oh," she said, with a little smile. "You will come with me, won't you, Fae?"

"I would not miss this for all the world. You will be a grown woman, a lady for all to see. No one shall think you a child ever again."

"No, they won't."

"Do you want all of these books, Highness? This one seems to have a library chain." Kattanan held up a volume with the broken tail of a chain from its binding.

Melisande laughed aloud. "I'd forgotten that. Wolfie and I weren't supposed to be in the library at all, certainly not the locked section, but that book has the silliest pictures in it, so we stole it. He held the chisel to the chain, I struck the blow. It sounded so loud that servants came running. Father was raging, mostly at Wolfram for bringing me there. He did give me a good talking-to, but then let me take the book on the agreement that I would read the whole thing. It must be eight years ago now."

"I'll pack it, Highness." He placed the prize in among the others. "I do not envy the wagon that must bear all of these trunks."

After the feast that evening, Kattanan noticed that the prince had already gone, and slipped away for the chapel. By this time of night, the priestesses had already sung their prayers. The door swung open silently, and he found the place lit only by the moonlight flooding through the opening in the ceiling and a few small candles. Wolfram moved slowly around the outside wall, making the sign of the Goddess to each cardinal point, with a longer pause by the Cave of Death, and longer still by the Cave of Life opposite. Incense drifted in a cinnamon haze through the room. Kattanan began to sing. He started with no words, and brought the prayer up in tiny steps to fill the room with a glorious murmur, reverberating from the pews all around. By the candles lit at the eastern and western caves, Kattanan could see that this was the fifth of the seven circles of blessing. He kept the song steady, and Wolfram paced with it. At last the seven candles were lit, all the prayers whispered, and Kattanan let the song fall back to the silence from which it had come. Wolfram stood at the center, under the starlight, and turned to the singer. "Thank you."

Kattanan met his gaze. "You are most welcome."

"Will you pray with me?"

"For what do we pray, Highness?"

"For Orie to be a good husband, for Melisande to be happy, for my father to get well."

"For yourself?"

Wolfram laughed soundlessly. "Only what I have always asked, to be a wise man. What for you, Singer? How can I include you in my prayer?"

Caught off guard, Kattanan shut his eyes and whispered, "To be loved." He was not sure the prince had heard, nor that he wanted him to, but he came forward to the altar and stood beside Wolfram. They turned their faces to the stars for a long while. At last, Wolfram made the sign of the Goddess, Kattanan likewise. Silently, the prince crossed to the door and left.

Kattanan knew he should sleep, but the stars called to him. He found his way out to the funeral ground, intending to walk on to the garden, but a small fire burned there, and a figure danced around it, casting huge shadows on the wall. The dance was slow, circling, but the rhythm of her feet was strong. At that distance, he saw her first as a girl, playing there, then as a woman, standing tall and proud as he moved closer, but the hand that grasped his was gnarled and mottled with age. And there was no pain, though the grip was strong.

"Dance with me," she hissed, and he danced.

The steps swayed first forward and on, then back, but it took many times round the fire before he took his eyes from the ground. He let his other hand rise, and found that it was taken. There was no fear, only the music, so he looked to his new companion, a tall, fair lady with a sharp crown upon her head. She, too, looked away at the man beside her, his flowing curls crowned the same as hers. Next danced a pair of boys, younger than he, though he knew they had once been older. Their faces were serene, but they almost smiled. Beside them danced an older man, bearded—the baron. And the lady to his left he had seen in a portrait, opposite the king's in the Great Hall. There were more: a group of men and women mingled who danced well, though their eyes were filled with tears; a line of monks, including the abbot who had once taken him in. A young man danced among them, and Kattanan's relief when he saw that it was not Jordan surprised him. The spiraling dances made rank after rank around them, raising no dust, nor chant, but a steady warmth not made by the fire alone. It was then that he looked to the priestess. Her right hand was raised, but held no partner. Eyes shut, she swayed on. After a time her lips began to move, and he heard the words although she made no sound.

> "*Fear no blessing,*
> *take no revenge,*
> *trust a wizard's word,*
> *doubt a woman's change,*
> *sing a hopeless prayer,*

*hear unwanted tales,*
*raise the man cast down,*
*love a foe-man's child,*
*wed no offered hand,*
*learn a new dance,*
*walk with the Goddess,*
*sing with the stars."*

The litany swelled in Kattanan's head, carried him around the fire, and sometime after moonset, followed him to his own little bed, where he dreamed himself a king.

# Chapter 11

"YOU CAN ride, I trust," the earl said, passing off the reins of a tall bay horse without waiting for the answer. Kattanan held the reins gingerly. The earl's men, the princess's entourage, and three large wagons laden with tapestries and trunks cluttered the courtyard. Melisande, Faedre, and Laura would be traveling by coach, along with Prince, who currently dashed from horse to horse yipping. Kattanan passed his horse off to a groom and chased the puppy, managing to catch his dangling leash and haul him from the path of the first wagon as it started to roll. Walking back toward the carriage, he was hailed by a familiar voice.

"Ho, singer! I just got off and wanted t' wish ye well." Rolf planted a huge hand on the puppy and gave it a fierce rubbing. "Sorry t' see ye go."

"I'm sorry to leave you, Rolf. I'll miss those mornings."

"You remember now, if ye need to, my gate's always open for ye." The guard shot a look toward the earl. "Watch yerself, and don't sing dangerous songs."

"Which ones are those?" Kattanan said lightly. "Yes, I'll be careful. You do the same."

"O' course! 'Tis my job, after all." Rolf flashed one of his huge grins. He swept the singer off the ground in a one-armed embrace and set him back again gently.

"And take care of the prince," the singer urged.

"He'll not come to harm while I stand," Rolf promised. "Fetch yer horse, I think they're mounting!" He drew himself out of traffic, and waved as Kattanan weaved back into the crowd.

Melisande leaned out of the carriage to gather the pup into her arms. "Oh, I was so worried about you," she scolded, then looked up. "Ride beside us if you can, we may want some songs. I wish I could be riding. Carriages are so bumpy, and of course, no jumping."

A cry rang out over the crowd, and Kattanan ran to find his horse. Mounted on a fine black charger, the prince rode with them into the city. There, the prince and his escort reined in to watch the caravan roll by. Wolfram was once more master of his emotions, smiling and waving to his sister and her lord. He caught Kattanan's gaze, made the sign of the Goddess, and shut his eyes—the farewell of an honored companion, "I see only your safe return." Some new and burning thing rose up in Kattanan as he returned the salute.

Once free of the city, they turned along the canyon and passed through farmland and small towns, following the river that flowed in the same direction. On the opposite bank, trees marched down the rough ground to cast great roots into the water. A trail there led to Rolf's gate, narrow and often steep. Melisande grew more interested in Kattanan's songs the farther they got from the castle. He and the earl alternated riding at her side, but it was to him she rolled her eyes and whispered the new gossip the ladies were making.

They arrived at the keep of Gamel's Grove not long after sunset. Orie had ridden ahead some distance but had returned, looking mysterious in the dancing light of the torches, or so Melisande said. He gave Kattanan a commanding glance that

sent him back to the wagons for the remainder of the trip. It was
not far from the wooden palisade to the stone tower at its midst.
They had veered away from the mountains enough that the
tower would command a full view of the open lands to one side
and thick forest to the other. All manner of lords and ladies lined
the steps to the keep, giving a great cry when their master came
into view, especially when they saw he had swept Melisande
from the carriage and bore her across his lap, the princess clinging and laughing until she was set down on a rich carpet laid out
on the ground. The earl dismounted beside her and gave her his
hand to climb the steps. Kattanan slipped gratefully from his
mount, rubbing his thighs with a grimace. Despite gripping the
reins for so long, his hands did not ache, and, in fact, seemed to
feel better. He trailed after the crowd into the keep.

As Orie had said, it was not large, but scaffolds were erected
in many areas, and walls razed to expand the place. Purple cloths
and hanging lanterns garlanded the lot. The Great Hall was
rather low, with a thick, beamed ceiling and no gallery. A reddish
stone made up most of the structure, augmented by marble
columns so recent that stone dust still fluttered from them. All
guards snapped crisply to attention, none smiling. Melisande
glowed even more now, when he could see her, nodding to the
residents as they were introduced and gasping at the grand plans
evidenced by the construction. The procession reached a huge
door deeply carved, where the earl halted, and held up his hand.

"Your Highness, my pride and joy." He flung open the door,
and her eyes flew wide.

The hexagonal room was three stories tall, stone cut by thin
alabaster windows at least half that height. Wooden galleries
climbed, the inner walls reached by narrow stairs. At the center,
a platform rose, supported by slender columns, on which a consort played a merry tune. When the ladder was pulled up,
dancers could pass beneath it and still enjoy the quality of the
sound.

"My lord, it is magnificent!" Melisande began. "Kattanan,
come see." She beckoned him up through the crowd. "My good
earl, could we dance?"

He laughed, and said, "I should have expected as much."

"Kattanan can sing from the platform."

The earl nodded, and the couple swirled onto the intricate mosaic floor.

Kattanan crossed to the ladder and climbed up, ignoring his protesting muscles. The musicians gave him a nod, and he placed himself as near to the center as possible, then sang. The sound of dancing fell away, leaving him on an island of perfect music. He lost track of rounds by the time his throat could take it no longer, and he let loose one great finish and turned to search for water. Setting down his instrument at last, a flute player held out a brimming mug.

"Greetings and welcome. We are well met."

"Leave it, Teir," the harper snapped, focusing scornful, pitch-colored eyes on the singer. "I'll take a man among us, not such at that."

A bright gale of laughter rippled from a lady at the far side from the harper. She set down the hammers by her dulcimer and smiled. "Cassius has a love for music, but mainly for his own. It is a source of constant amazement to me that he can even suffer to play with us." She shook back long silver hair and held out a long hand to Kattanan. "I am Strelana." He took her hand lightly and bowed his head over it.

"Kattanan duRhys, my lady, it is a pleasure."

She laughed again. "Oh, I am but a common woman. Be not fooled by my gown—the earl sought the finest musicians of the county, and dressed us in a manner befitting the music."

The singer took a deep draught from Teir's mug and found it to be a sweet wine.

"Made that myself, Singer. Whets my whistle, you might say." He waved the flute at Kattanan. "Methinks I have heard your name somewhere."

Kattanan shrugged. "I have traveled much, and of course the earl has heard me sing."

"Hmmm." Teir looked doubtful, and Strelana shot him a look.

"Are we forgetting all our manners?" She pointed to the fid-

dler, who watched with quiet interest. "That's Fionvar duNormand, the earl's brother, and the harper is Cassius Nyle. On the
drum, his daughter, Caitlin."

Orie poked his head through the trapdoor and smiled.
"Greetings, brother. What else have you for our dance?"

Fionvar's smile was as wide as Orie's. "Welcome home, Orie.
We can play whatever your pleasure, or hers, more like. She's
more beautiful than you said."

"She is more lovely every day. And don't you be getting
ideas," Orie warned, but the smile had not left his voice.

"I have a lady of my own who'd stand for none of that."

"Good for her. Find a new dance, we don't want to keep the
princess waiting."

Fionvar thought a moment, with a glance at Kattanan. "Make
it 'Bernholt Hills.'"

The singer allowed himself a little smile. The dance, and the
song that accompanied it, mixed fast, rollicking verses with a
long, low chorus, a test of any musician's prowess, and more for
a voice.

Strelana struck the first notes on her dulcimer. Caitlin took
up her drum and beat out the complicated rhythm. As one, the
others joined in, and after one verse so did Kattanan, in flawless
Strelledor. Fionvar fixed him with a stare and began to speed up,
leading the others faster on every verse, accentuating the break
between verse and chorus, and Kattanan sprang with him, eyes
closed, not watching the cues, but hearing every movement.
Below, the dancers spun and frolicked, laughing and shouting
when the tempo pulled them ever faster. Fionvar struck an
abrupt note and pulled back his bow, hissing to the others, who
followed his lead. Finding himself suddenly unaccompanied,
Kattanan finished out the chorus and leapt into the verse at the
same remarkable speed the earl's brother had dropped. The
dancers shouted louder as many slipped or stumbled into each
other and clung like survivors of a drunken revel. The last note
climbed away and sighed into the distance. Applause filled the
space, and cheers for the consort, and for the singer.

After a long swallow of wine, when he could trust his voice

again, Kattanan opened his eyes to Fionvar. "Thank you for the challenge, my lord. I shall look forward to our concerts."

The earl's brother gave a slight nod, but his face seemed deadly still.

Strelana suggested, "Perhaps just a tune so our singer can catch his breath; our dancers, too, for that matter."

Fionvar set his fiddle to his chin and picked out a melody. The group caught on and played in minor key. Kattanan sat at the edge of the platform and looked down on the dancers. When the music began, Melisande had pulled back from where she was leaning against the earl. Her face turned upward a moment, with a toss of her hair in the light of the candle-chandeliers. And she smiled. He could not make out her eyes across this distance, but the smile lit his mind and heart. He leaned his head against the slim brass rail and followed her with his eyes.

The ball lasted only a few songs more, then they began to pack up the instruments with the care of new parents.

Teir slipped his arm around Strelana's waist and squeezed her tight to his side for a moment. "A good party, and not least because of you." He raised his mug to Kattanan. "I hope we have many more chances."

"You shall, I'm sure," Melisande said, coming under the shadow with the earl at her elbow. "Marvelous, all of you."

"Allow me to introduce my brother, Fionvar," the earl said.

"The honor is all mine, Your Highness." His lips brushed the back of her hand.

"Are the two of you alone of your family?"

"Oh, no," Fionvar said, "our parents had eight children to help with all the chores."

"Eight? The Goddess smiled on your mother."

Fionvar looked at Orie, slightly shorter than he, and said, "She might have smiled more. Orie here is the only one of us who amounted to anything."

"Having heard you play, I must disagree."

"As yet, it has gotten me nowhere, Your Highness."

"As yet," his brother agreed, but they shared a smile over the princess's head.

"It is a meager skill compared with heroism in battle."

Melisande eyed him. "Did you not fight also?"

"I was the eldest of us, and Father just in his grave. We lost two brothers to the battle, and a sister to the famine that followed. It was I who bound the branches for their funerals and went back to the plow the next morning."

"A difficult life."

Fionvar looked away as his brother said, "Were it not for Fionvar, I should have had no family to return to, no one to share my good fortune. Two siblings are married and live away, but Fionvar and Lyssa, the youngest, live here with me. They are invaluable, and talented. Lyssa carved some of the more beautiful figures in this hall."

Melisande smiled at one of the columns. "I'll look forward to meeting her."

"Right now, she is a journeyman of the Guild at Lochdale, working on a temple and flirting with a younger prince. But we are all tired after our journey, and the dancing. Strelana, perhaps you can show the singer to his quarters."

"Oh," Melisande began with a start. "I was hoping he would be able to stay near me. He sings the Morning Prayer with me."

"We've prepared only one of the nearer rooms, but I am sure an arrangement can be made tomorrow. For tonight, this will do." His good humor had faded.

"It's too late at night for these concerns," Fionvar said, a shade too quickly.

Melisande watched them both, and sighed. "I suppose. Sleep well, Singer." Orie slipped an arm around her and led her off in the wake of his guests.

"Well, this way then, by your leave, my lord," Strelana said, with a little curtsy.

Fionvar nodded distractedly. "They are a handsome couple."

"Aye, they are that," Teir agreed heartily. "And bloody quick dancers as well." They shared a grin. "Give us some practice, and we'll have them on the floor."

"That we will, Teir." He paused to study Kattanan a moment longer, then turned smartly and left by the great door.

"Not a bad man, Kattanan, just not overfriendly. He'll warm to you."

Strelana murmured her assent. "This way, we're in the lower hall."

"Will my trunk have made it so far?"

"No doubt. The earl's men are nothing if not efficient." The trio passed through a smaller door into a hall that ran perpendicular to the main tower. Many arches looked onto a small courtyard. "The rooms are on the outside wall, so we hope there's no invasion. There's also just arrow slits for windows, though, and those are high up." She came to a door that stood open and ushered them in. Kattanan's trunk shared space with a small bed, square table and chair, and a basin stand. The bed was fitted with a straw mattress, down pillow, and linen sheets. Atop those spread a gray wool blanket, embroidered with the device of the princess.

"That bed may be the loveliest thing I've seen all day," the singer said.

"That door across the courtyard opens into the reading room," Strelana said. "Used to be some monks who came to study, now it's usually empty. The earl is not fond of religious books."

"Nor of religion at all, y'might add." Teir made placating gestures when Strelana shot him a glare.

"Why has he such a place, then, if not to enjoy the books?"

"For Fionvar, if you would know," the woman said. "Taught himself to read before his brother was at war, though the Book of the Goddess was all he had to study. It seems there was some bad blood between the brothers, but the earl had found these books someplace, so he had the library built here. It was the first thing he added to the keep."

"The dance hall came next. Lots of additions, improvements. Wonder where the gold came from to do all that . . ." Teir trailed off.

"Such a gossip, this one!" Strelana took Teir's elbow and guided him toward the door. "Garderobe's the last door. I'll come by for you after dawn to show you around."

"Thank you."

"I'll come by," Teir said, with a sly glance, "after that, to give you all the gossip."

Strelana slapped his arm and swished out through the door, with Teir following in mock humiliation. Kattanan shut the door behind them. He unpacked a bit to find his sleeping tunic, and changed, laying aside his trail-stained clothes. Crossing to the washbasin, the singer peeled off the gloves and found that his hands had all but healed. Only a tracery of pale lines showed that they had been cut. When he turned in to the strange bed, weariness overcame him, and his dreams were of music he could never quite remember, and never quite forget.

# Chapter 12

THE MORNING air was cool and the shadows still heavy when Kattanan emerged from his room. The little garden was green, but not yet budding. It held a few simple benches, but no statues or trees. The opposite door stood open a crack, and a light was moving within. He nudged the door open and slipped inside. A few windows faced the garden, and a pair of study carrels stood before him, one decked with old books. Coming closer, he saw that their covers were charred and water-damaged. Some were missing covers altogether, and all were marked by a familiar seal.

"So I have been discovered." Fionvar held the lantern above his head. He did not smile, and there were circles under his eyes.

"Where did these books come from?" Kattanan asked, trying to master his voice.

"I'd've thought you would recognize the seal, even after, what, ten years?"

He looked back at Fionvar and made a brief bow. "Pardon, my lord. I do not mean to speak so; I was merely startled."

"As well you should be. It is not possible, yet here they are, the books of Strel Arwyn's—as many as could be saved, I think." Kattanan continued to stare at him. "Do you know how and why, my lord?"

"Orie told me he bought them at salvage prices on a brief return trip to Lochalyn." His expression remained bland. "Why would anyone bother to unearth them?"

"I wouldn't know, my lord." Kattanan looked away. "I should not be disturbing you." He moved as if to go, but Fionvar caught his arm.

"'Kattanan duRhys, foundling, castrate, age five.' That's in the students roll. The monks recorded concerts with a noted soloist, some attended by the royal family, the new one, that is. A difficult time for Lochalyn. Don't cringe from me."

Despite the admonishment, Kattanan trembled. "What do you want from me?"

"I want to know how so many others died, but you lived. There is no record, or perhaps it was lost. I want to know why Strel Arwyn's burned." His voice was low, insistent, and his eyes never left his captive audience.

"I was sent away to sing in other places. It was not long after we left that the fire—" He fell silent, remembering.

Fionvar let out a little sound of interest, but let go of Kattanan's arm. "These books frighten you, foundling."

"Memories, my lord, nothing more." He straightened his sleeve, still facing the door. "May I go?"

"You may," said Fionvar, "but not far."

With those words at his back, Kattanan escaped into the garden and back to his room, almost running into Strelana.

"I was just coming for you." She set her hands on his shoulders. "Are you well?"

He nodded. "Morning exercise."

Strelana snorted. "Then don't tell me. The last thing I need is more gossip. The earl's even a harder steward than Fionvar." Kattanan flinched at the name, and Strelana turned bright hazel eyes on him. "What's that for? Don't tell me he got to you last night. I'll grant that his greeting was unkind, but you were unexpected."

"I should not have answered his challenge."

"We'd've taken you for a coward, or ignorant of the song. You've got courage."

"Naught but a streak of foolishness. I have not yet learned when to be silent."

"Man has a talent like yours, it'd be a shame to hide it, especially just to gratify some nobleman's pride." They were turning to a more lively part of the keep and servants roamed the halls, many greeting Strelana as she walked ahead. "Tell me of the princess, and of the palace. I have never been so far from home as that."

Kattanan had never been so near—his homeland lay a few days' ride over the mountains, but he kept quiet about that as he described what little he knew about life at the palace.

In the kitchen, Strelana took a loaf of bread, some butter, and cheese, and brought them to a low table. She pointed to a pitcher of water, which Kattanan brought along, and they settled in to break their fast. "Did you get to see the king?"

Kattanan hesitated. "I met him on the first night I was there. He was sick abed, but has some strength beyond his body, I think."

"I have heard that. I have heard he is a great hunter and rules with a strong hand. Indeed, our taxes here would bear that out. Not that I begrudge him that." Her face betrayed her words, though, and she quickly looked down at her food. "How did you come to be there?"

"I was a gift to the princess, from one of her suitors."

"A gift? But you—" His expression stopped her. "Yet she is here with the earl."

"The baron, my master, was killed by the princess's dogs."

"Oh, I am sorry." She squeezed his arm. "I did not mean to bring up such memories."

"The earl gave her a puppy to replace the dogs she lost. I think that is why she has chosen him now. They have at least two loves in common. Do you know where she is staying? She has asked me to sing Morning Prayer."

"Is she very devout, then?" Strelana started to clear their breakfast things.

"She does keep the morning worship."

"I'll show you." They stood and wandered back into the corridor. This keep had none of the twists and turns of the royal castle and only two staircases to the upper floors. From the small, disused chapel, they crossed outside on a high battlement. The narrow passage opened onto a wide court with overhanging eaves that sheltered a widely spaced pair of doors, one of which was marked by the shield of the earl. Strelana took him to the other and knocked. In a moment, the door drew back, and Laura appeared, wiping her hands. "Kattanan! Come in, and your lady-friend, too."

"I can't stay; I'm attending Morning Prayer at the woods chapel."

"Thank you, Strelana," Kattanan said.

She nodded and went back the way she had come.

The princess's quarters were somewhat smaller than her royal chambers, but had a tall, peaked ceiling painted with forest scenes and hunters. Much of her old furniture had been moved in, but darker corners still hid the trunks and shelves left by the previous occupant. Prince yapped around Kattanan's legs until he was picked up for a good petting.

"Faedre just went in to wake her, so it may be a few minutes." Laura held a dust rag in one hand and gestured toward the ceiling. "Is this a fitting place for a princess? She loves it, though, asked about the artist and the scenes; why, they stayed up talking almost until morning, so it's no wonder she's still abed. 'Tis sure she'll be glad to see you this morning. Of course, the earl's right next door. He says, if they marry, he'll make an arch there by the fireplace so they can share their sitting rooms." Laura's eyes twinkled. "He says all the things a maiden wants to hear, and quite well, too." She shook her head. "Look at me, gossiping away."

"I'll introduce you to Teir; he played the flute last night. Strelana makes him out to be quite the gossipmonger."

"I suppose I'm on because Melisande looks so happy here. You must've seen—"

"Oh, Kattanan, you came!" Melisande sprang from her door and gave him a quick embrace before he could bow to her.

"Princess!" Faedre snapped from the doorway behind.

Melisande scowled back to her. "I am tired of propriety. You wouldn't let me summon him last night when I couldn't sleep, and you're always glaring at him anyhow, and I don't see how he is different from any of the rest of my household." She tossed her hair.

"You don't see it because you are not looking. Would you throw your arms around Laura simply because she was away from you for a single night?"

Frowning, the princess replied, "But he's not a servant."

"No, indeed," Faedre went on smoothly. "But what is he? A gift from a rival of the earl's. How do you think he would feel if he saw you act this way?"

"How absurd! Does Orie get jealous when I kiss Prince? If he did, I would think him touched, and so would you. Here I woke up in marvelous temper, and you have ruined it. I expected better from you, Faedre."

"And I from you, Melisande," the lady responded gravely. "You may have won his heart, but you do not yet have his hand. You must be more reserved. Once you have him, you shall again be queen of your household."

Kattanan softly put in, "The lady speaks rightly, Your Highness. Your attention"—he glanced up at her—"it embarrasses me, and the earl as well, I think."

Faedre gave her most catlike smile. "We all have your best interests at heart, Melisande. After the Goddess Moon, then you may again assert yourself as well you should."

Melisande turned to Kattanan, her face puzzled. "You never told me."

"The fault is mine, Highness, for not maintaining the proper distance. I am sorry."

Faedre's glance to him was almost kind. "You knew no better, I am sure."

Melisande hovered between them, then flopped into her favorite chair. "Does that mean he can no longer brush my hair?" The lady's smile faded. "Once in a while, perhaps."

She held out the brush without looking at him, and relaxed into the chair only when he had taken it. The prayer was a brief solo that morning, then Faedre suggested he go while the princess made ready. As he moved toward the door, turning back to bow, Melisande caught his eye a moment, and he thought she might weep. Laura followed him out. "That was a queer scene, if you don't mind my saying. Faedre knows how much the princess likes doing the prayers with you, now she's as much as said you can't do them. What's the harm?"

"The princess should concentrate on earning the love of her lord, and Faedre knows best how she can do that," Kattanan said, all music gone from his voice.

"And you are some kind of distraction to that?" As she asked the question, Laura peered at him, and sighed, "Oh, no. Faedre thinks you are in love with the princess, doesn't she?"

"How could I be? She is a princess, in line for a throne until Wolfram has heirs, and what am I? Not even a man, nor ever shall be." His hands shook, and he squeezed his eyes shut.

"And if you were, would the answer be the same?"

"If I were?" His voice dropped to a murmur. "How could I not?" He sank to the step and buried his face in his hands.

"Then you're right, you can't go on as you have. Best you become a model servant, and soon." Laura straightened as the door behind them opened.

"Laura, we need your assistance," Faedre purred. The maid bobbed a curtsy and passed her into the room. Hand on the door, the lady stood a moment longer. "You pray well, singer. For what are you praying?" Her voice rang in the hall long after she had shut the door.

Kattanan sat a long while, but then began to hear the sounds of other people rising all around him and fled down the stairs. He ran headlong into the earl's brother who steadied him with one strong hand. "Where are you running to? Or should I say from?"

"Sorry, my lord. I'll be more careful."

"To look at you, anyone would think your heart had broken," Fionvar observed.

"A long ride and a difficult night, my lord," the singer said. "Please, may I go?"

Fionvar released him and continued up the stairs.

Kattanan found himself by the doors to the dance hall and slipped inside. The place glowed with pale pink light from the alabaster panels set in the walls. He crossed to the narrow stair and climbed up into the gallery. At the top level stood a narrow bench topped by a purple cushion. Kattanan flung himself down, quivering. Breathing slowly, he managed to hold back the tears, though he dared not move for fear of their return. It seemed an eternity before he could open his eyes, and his shoulders stopped shaking. He thought of the princess's hair flowing over his hands, of the brave front she put on for the court, of her voice when she joined in the prayers, and her laughter when she walked in the gardens. How had he been so blind, not to see what he was doing? How had he even thought himself worthy to serve her, let alone to touch her? The singer rolled over and stared downward through the rail. The empty space beckoned. He stood then, and faced it, felt its eerie music welling around him. What other end could there be for one who could never marry, never pass on life as the Goddess intended?

A voice rose from the floor. "Kattanan, that you up there?" Teir wandered into the middle of the floor and bent his head back. "Don't you want all the gossip, and a tour of the grounds, perhaps?"

Kattanan caught his breath, not knowing if he should be grateful to be found. A moment sooner, and he would not have been seen. A moment later, and he might have jumped. Perhaps he did not know what the Goddess intended after all. "Coming, Teir," he called. Taking a leisurely way down the stairs, he adjusted his tunic. "Good morrow."

"Y'don't seem too sure 'bout that, Singer." The man examined his face.

"I have been thinking too long, that's all."

"What about?"

"The stars," he said. "Do you believe in the Goddess?"

Teir snorted. "What a fool question!"

"I wonder how closely She watches us."

"Some, She watches like a hawk, ready to pounce; some, She watches like a dog, ready to herd; some, She watches like a lady, ready to love."

Kattanan smiled at him. "If you wanted to, you could earn your way as a mystic."

"Goddess's Toes! You're talking foolishness. I have a flute and a farm, two boys and a fine lady for company, what more do I need?"

"You must be the luckiest man alive."

Teir smiled more gently now. "I would guess that I am. That Orie always wants more for himself, and gets it, too, but I wonder if he can ever say he's happy with what he's got." The man waved an arm at the great room around them. "Does put on a fine show, though. Well, let's get out in the light." He led Kattanan down the steps in the chill morning air. "See, the best place for gossip and sedition is out in the open." When they came to a small walled space just outside the keep walls, he stopped and tucked his hands into his belt. "Ye've seen the chapel up high? Did Lana tell you about the lady of the manor though, the good earl's mother?"

"Only that she was with the stars."

Teir stood a little closer, and said, "When her son came back from war a hero, she was proud, but she turned sour a few years later. Ranted at him, tore down scaffolds, crazy stuff. Called him a traitor to his face over dinner, but nobody knew why. She lived up there, where the princess sleeps, and started going to chapel real regular. Then one night, the priestess was away, and the earl's lady-mother climbed the altar and jumped from the star-hole. Landed right here."

Kattanan stepped back from the place, crossing his arms. "Why are you telling me this?"

"It's why he never goes there. Our good earl thinks the Goddess is responsible for his mother's death. He would've torn down the chapel if his brother hadn't stayed his hand. That priestess was the first one to disappear."

The singer peered at him sidelong. "Perhaps he just sent her away."

Teir shrugged. "She was only the first. The late earl's sister went away, and two of the town burghers who didn't like him much, and a couple of monks who studied those old books."

"I am sure there were explanations."

"I said I'd give you gossip, not evidence. They're too careful for that."

"They?"

"I've heard him talk about his friends, unnamed, who want things thus and so. He also has a wizard, at least one, an old man. I met him myself one night, walking home from a ball here. He looked suspicious, so I gave him the ritual greeting."

Kattanan felt a chill beyond the breeze. "What was his answer?"

"Wizard of Nine Stars." Teir finished with a sly grin. "Didn't ask him anything else, I'll tell you. What's wrong, breakfast disagree with you?"

"I need to send a message to the palace, do you know a way?"

"There's regular riders who go, but what's this all about?"

Kattanan hesitated and shook his head. "It's best if I don't tell you what I know."

Teir grumbled, "I gave you some good gossip, and you repay me by keeping secrets."

"Lives may depend on this; I won't have yours be one of them. About that message?"

Teir set his hands on his hips and scowled. "You keep yer fine palace secret, then, and see if I tell you anything else."

"Please, Teir, someday I'll tell you all the gossip I can think of—I'll make things up, even!"

"Come on, then." Teir started tramping back toward the road. Before they reached it, though, a small party intercepted them, led by the princess and the earl, arm in arm. Kattanan's heartbeat jumped.

Melisande smiled briefly at him. "Already out, I see."

"A fine day for walking, Highness."

"It is indeed," the earl agreed. "Teir, have you a flute? The princess might like a duet."

Teir pulled out his ready instrument. "Aye, Your Excellency."

"We are going to the grove, so you can discuss it until we get there."

The pair fell in behind the gathering of ladies and guards, though Kattanan glanced uneasily back to the road, suddenly torn between sending his message and remaining at Melisande's side. Teir started up naming off songs, and they agreed on a Lochalyn ballad. Tall, silvery trees surrounded the open area of the grove, which held several benches roughly built of old stone and a small pool. Startled frogs leapt from the banks, much to Melisande's delight.

The earl showed her to the longest bench and settled beside her. "This is the original grove, you know, where the man who became Strello Gamel built his hermitage hut. Legend has it that these benches were built of the stones of that same holy hut."

"I have read some of his work. He spoke of finding the Goddess in all things, and especially in simple labor, like the building of his hut."

"I did not have much time for study; my brother is the expert."

Fionvar shrugged. "The volume we have here is not well preserved. It mainly refers to his walks abroad. At one point, it describes him walking over the mountain, and finding the Goddess on the other side, combing Her hair and smiling. She gave him a strand of Her hair, and, when he had descended again, it had become a plow, the one thing he had not brought with him. A story of the wishes a simple man would make." He was looking at his brother when he said it.

"She gave him what he most wanted," Orie said. "Legend has it that whoever sleeps in this grove will find what he most desires." Orie looked down at Melisande, and said, "I do not believe it, for I already have what I desire."

She blushed and looked away, toward Kattanan. For a moment, their eyes met, her gaze as open and lovely as the dawn. Kattanan averted his eyes from the unaccustomed brilliance.

Faedre followed the glance with a withering glare.

"Anyhow, you had asked for a song," Fionvar said quickly. "What have you chosen?"

In answer, Teir played the opening notes, and Kattanan began. The audience applauded afterward, but Melisande seemed lost in thought. When she made no response to the music, Orie touched her shoulder, and said, "What ill thought disturbs you this morning?"

"Only the thought of my father. Lying abed under those paintings brought him to mind."

"You may send messages to him; we have a rider here who goes whenever he is needed."

"Thank you, yes, I think that would help," she said, but the distraction did not leave her.

"I had thought to show you the stables, and the mews, but those can wait until after lunch. Besides, I ought to deal with the business of the manor, but I'll be free to spend more time with you later."

"I'll look forward to the rest of the tour." Melisande rose and took her leave of the earl, with Faedre once again swaying her hips. Orie gestured for the guards to escort the ladies.

Teir bowed to them, and took Kattanan's arm to steer him toward another path. "There's some fine ruins off this way," he said, a bit too loudly. As soon as they were beyond the trees, the path dipped behind a rise, and Teir pulled him down, gesturing for silence. "When Fion gets that look, he wants a talk with his brother," he whispered.

Once the ladies had gone, Fionvar said, "That woman should not be here."

"First, how is that your business; second, how can I help it?"

"It is my business because the princess deserves better."

"She will be marrying me, isn't that good enough? No, you'd best not answer that. Did you really pull me back here to talk about her?"

"I plan on going to visit our friends."

At this, Teir nudged Kattanan with smirk.

"Out of the question," Orie replied, "I can't spare you right now. It would look strange for my own brother not to be present. Why don't you let me relay the message?"

Fionvar's voice fell back a little. "It is a matter of religion, only, and I know you don't like to deal with such things."

"Oh? Is that what you know?" The earl's voice chilled the air. "Orie, why must you assume that everyone is against you? You know very well why I like to go there in person, and that kind of message I would not have you hear first."

"Your lady will wait until I can spare you, no doubt. I'm surprised that you're not already sneaking off with your message."

"I am honoring our agreement, brother, by telling you."

"Nonsense. You need my support, or you are nothing. I have said you will not go. Attend me for court, will you; you seem to have an understanding of these peasants that I lack." The earl strode off, with his brother still breathing angrily behind him.

When they were safely off, Teir sat up. "I'm not the only one who talks more openly outside. I wonder if they fear eavesdroppers." He smirked again.

"Those references meant little to me, Teir."

"I've long thought the earl had taken a lady to his bed. Not that I've seen her, he's very discreet, but things like that conversation tip me off. His brother, see, is a straight arrow about these things. None of us have ever seen his lady, but he won't so much as flirt with another. I gather it's a pretty private affair in any case, or he'd be wed himself."

"I need no more intrigue. Take me to the messenger."

"Suits me; I'll just get in a spot of practice while you write."

The pair set out again, back to Kattanan's chamber where he found parchment and ink. He settled at the desk with the door shut, but he could still hear Teir playing his flute out in the courtyard. The message he wrote was brief, and sealed well, addressed to Prince Wolfram. He rejoined the older man, and they set off to the village at a quick pace. Kattanan did not relax until the letter was in the man's hand. Even then, tension cramped his shoulders throughout the day, and on into the evening, making it hard to concentrate on eating or singing for the dancers. After saying his good-nights, Kattanan shut his own door and quietly chanted Evening Prayer, praying for rest. The creak of the opening door startled him out of prayer. Earl Orie cast back the hood of his cloak and fixed Kattanan with a cold stare.

"Don't bother to change, Singer, unless you'd care for a long walk in your nightshirt," the earl said. "And I wouldn't suggest you take that trunk."

"What do you mean, my lord?" The singer knelt under his window, but his heart raced.

"I have seen the way you look at the princess, and I will not have such perversity under my roof. And another thing—" He pulled a familiar parchment from his belt, and cast it onto the fire. "Go and lie to your beloved prince in person. You spy upon her, then dare accuse me of collusion with wizards. How could you betray the princess for that wretch who would be king?"

"Ask as well how you can betray her." Finding himself caught, Kattanan met the earl's gaze. "Faedre, isn't it? She told you about this morning, and who knows what else."

"She didn't need to tell me; I am not blind."

"But you have not said she didn't." Kattanan stood up.

"Your life is forfeit, castrate, for your treason to the princess."

"And for my knowledge of you," the singer added, with starlight behind him now. "Would you kill me here?"

"I would like to tell her the truth in saying you vanished into the night."

"I do not need much baggage, then," Kattanan said, leaning over his trunk. He pulled out a few random tunics, his ceremonial dagger, and a little volume of parables he had copied himself many years before. These went into a bag he slung over his shoulder. The earl stood watching, arms crossed. Kattanan numbly passed under his gaze and out the door. Orie planted a hand on his shoulder, turning him sharply away from the keep and propelling them both out a small door at the near end of the hall. As Kattanan stumbled into the night, Orie said, "Give my regards to the prince, when next you meet."

The forested path should lead him back to the town, and to refuge. As he started to walk, he heard movement behind him— two men following not too close. His pulse quickened, but he stayed his course. He began to chant under his breath, the high prayer of salvation, reserved for funerals, but he did not suppose they would give him one. "Let them not bury me," he beseeched the sky in a whisper.

As the path turned a corner, it came out upon a wide road. A single mounted figure rode nearer, cautiously, while a few darker forms flitted among the trees, blades occasionally catching the light. The shaking took over, and the urge to run became a voice whispering at his ears—his mother's voice. His head jerked up at that, and he did run, straight past the man on horseback, flying down the road, but he could hear footsteps thundering up as the men in the woods broke cover. Something heavy struck his head, rolling him—dazed—to the rough ground. The blow came again, blurring his eyes and buzzing in his ears. Before he could scramble up again, a man was on his back, jerking on his hair.

"Unhand him!" The new voice rang with strength, echoing from a hall of distant memory. "I am the Liren-sha, you have no blade which can harm me, nor power to defeat me. While I yet stand he will not be harmed."

Kattanan's captor laughed. "I don't see that your army is so great as all that."

The rider drew two swords with a smooth movement. "Then show me your own."

But footfalls behind told Kattanan that his captors had reinforcements. The man on top of him pinned his arms and dragged him up from the ground, a blade at his throat. "We're the earl's men, and you're trespassing."

"I am Finistrel's man and the Goddess frowns on you tonight," declared the voice of the Liren-sha. "A hundred men and fourteen wizards I have sent to meet Her."

"Do you believe this manure?" shouted one of the men. "We're facin' a myth here, and it thinks to show us our tail."

"Well," the Liren-sha drawled. "You haven't any teeth, or you'd have shown me those."

At this, the others moved forward, but the man who held Kattanan scooped him over a shoulder and ran.

"Free him or die!" cried the voice of his rescuer.

The Liren-sha galloped after, easily catching up. The animal reared, dumping its rider, and the kidnapper skidded, then fell. Kattanan rolled onto his side, trying to master his breathing, and could not get his eyes to focus. Swords whistled and clashed over his head. A terrible groan told him one man had met his death on the road, and the swords rang on. Scrambling out of the way of the fight, Kattanan fought his own battle with the pain in his skull, then a voice cut through it, ragged with effort, "Kattanan, listen!"

Listen? The singer could hardly breathe, but he tried. The clash of swords and ragged breathing were difficult to sort out, but then he heard another sound. Soft behind him, someone was creeping through the wood, breathing very low, raising his arm in a muffled chink of mail. Kattanan pulled one foot under him, then launched himself at the lurker, hitting him full in the chest. Both smashed hard into the tree behind, and lay still.

When he came to a moment later, a dark figure leaned over him. "Can you ride?" the man whispered, then, "Forget it, you'll ride with me." The Liren-sha gathered Kattanan into strong arms and walked swiftly back to his horse.

"A couple of those men escaped me—I'm sorry there's no time to rest," he muttered.

One of the stranger's arms was across the singer's waist, supporting him as he leaned back. Kattanan's fingers shook, his eyes still felt worthless, and his head ached. His face rubbed against the soft leather his rescuer wore. The slapping of the twin swords hanging against the horse's flanks steadied into a rhythm. Letting out a shaky breath, Kattanan shivered and pressed closer, hearing the beat of a familiar heart. Part of him tried to remember, to link the voice with a face, but in the chaos of his mind, it would not come clear. And part of him did not want to know. The trail sloped up, then evened out around dawn. Kattanan vaguely remembered some great fuss being made over him as he was borne down a long hall, but mostly he recalled, as he was laid in a soft bed, that someone was singing. The song was little more than a murmur, but it was the Morning Prayer, and he fell into a deep and quiet sleep.

# Chapter 13

"WE'VE GOT only that painting to go on and the word of a traitorous guard, but I believe he has my daughter's face, her coloring. I have been told he has his father's eyes," a regal voice was saying when Kattanan stirred toward consciousness again. "I doubt our people will accept a castrated king, but there are ways around that."

Kattanan lay still, trying to keep his breathing slow as if in slumber.

"Whether he is to be king matters not a whit to me, Duchess," the Liren-sha's voice replied. "We have been parted several years, but he is still the nearest thing I have to family."

"I had forgotten. It is difficult for me to imagine that you were ever a monk."

An instant tension shot through the singer's body, as he flashed back to another land, another pain almost forgotten in the press of recent events. A hand rested against his shoulder, and Kattanan rolled sharply away, ignoring the throb of his head.

"Kat, please." Jordan's voice whispered behind him, touched with a new depth but suddenly bereft of its power of the night before.

"Go away. You left me once, surely you can do it again."

"Please hear me out."

"Go away."

"I thought you said he was your friend," the duchess observed.

"He was, and I pray he can be again." Still, he rose from his chair.

"Find something to eat and have something sent up; my grandson may be hungry."

The door was opened, and shut after a pause, before Kattanan opened his eyes. He turned his head a little to look at the old lady who waited at his bedside. Austere wooden pins caught thick, silvered hair atop her head, accenting sharp eyes the blue of deep water. Her unsmiling face had only the faintest of wrinkles. She wore a grey velvet gown, unadorned except by the badge of a duchy that had long since changed hands.

"You do have his eyes, Rhys."

"I do not know that name, my lady."

"You will come to. In the meantime, we will call you 'Your Majesty,' if you prefer."

"No," he protested in a sigh. "I am no king."

"Oh," the duchess said, but her expression grew fierce. "The king who sits in your place taxes his people beyond measure, letting his soldiers take what they will of the wares and the women. He grows fat and lazy, dallying with maids and whores. The royal chapel is a place of drunken revelry, and boars are roasted over the funeral pyres of nobility. This is the false king—the man who poisoned your father, hanged and beheaded your brothers, and had my daughter, your mother, buried in a common grave." Her eyes, at once harsh and dazzling, never left his face.

The singer winced and shut his eyes against the shine of the sun from a fallen crown.

"We have been hiding here, gathering the loyal, finding the truth, and preparing the way for the rise of Lochalyn." He shook his head, but she went on, "All were told that you were dead, along with your family. Four years ago we heard the rumor that you survived. Our men caught the guard who brought you away from the castle, and he was persuaded to tell all. The monastery had been burned, and all killed, or so we thought for a long time. The Liren-sha brought us the final facts by accident—he was threatening a wizard in our employ at the time." She gave an eloquent shrug. "But I gather you are not interested in his story."

"He abandoned me a long time ago, and no, I don't care to hear from or about him."

"He is invaluable to us, and you will accept that. I will not force you to hear him out, but he is staying." When Kattanan made no reply, his grandmother went on, "As for my family, we were besieged. We did have a way out, by waiting on the wall, and riding down on the counterweight if the gate could be raised and lowered again, but that required one of us to stay behind. As we got there, a young soldier climbed over the wall. We told him where some of our wealth had been hidden in exchange for his assistance. Soon after, in the guise of an elderly aunt, I attended his investiture as the earl of Gamel's Grove." She paused. "You look shocked."

"He is a traitor. He may have hired the wizard who afflicted King Gerrod."

"Yes, he did." She did smile at this, a close-lipped expression of satisfaction. "I would have asked for outright death, but the good earl has his own plans."

Kattanan pushed himself up, staring in horror. "I must get a message to the prince." And warn Melisande, though he hadn't an idea of how to reach her past the earl's defenses.

"That family is our enemy. Do not concern yourself with them. You have your own family and crown to defend now." She rose and looked down on him. "I have been told not to tire you. Someone will be up with a meal. Guards are posted outside the doors should you require anything"—she smiled—"Your Majesty."

Kattanan sank back, clenching a fist. He thought of escape, but realized he had no idea where he was. Shortly after she had gone, the door was opened again. A very tall man entered, clad entirely in red leather even to the red band that held back his dark, wavy hair. A trio of thin scars accentuated his sharp features. He bore a tray of food before him, and it took a moment for Kattanan to recognize his old tutor. "I do not want you here."

"You need to eat." Jordan glanced furtively at the singer as he set down the tray beside him. "And I need you to hear me. I overheard part of your conversation, about a message to the prince. The duchess has declared him an enemy of her cause."

"He has to be warned—and even if they raise me as a king, I will lead no war against him."

"I think the overthrow of that reign belongs to Earl Orie."

"That's what she meant," Kattanan breathed, with a sound like defeat. "An old priestess told me that I would be king, but not Wolfram. There must be a way to stop it from happening."

"I have learned the danger of defying fate." Jordan studied the band of scars at his wrist.

"And you, more than anyone, should have learned what it feels like to abandon someone who trusts you," said Kattanan, pleased at Jordan's flinch. "I must at least try."

"If I carry your message to the prince, will you hear my tale?"

Kattanan finally met Jordan's eyes. He thought of the prince making the sign of farewell not so long ago, and nodded once. "If that is the price I must pay. He needs to know that Orie is working with the Wizard of Nine Stars and that the lady Faedre is Orie's lover. If you take the trail on the far side of the river, you'll come to a watchtower with a gate. At dawn, it's guarded by a man called Rolf of the Prince's Mercy. Tell him I sent you."

"Will they believe me?"

Kattanan frowned, then said, "Was my bag brought here?"

Jordan found it on a table and laid it on the bed, watching as the singer fished through it. He came out with a small bone carving. "You can probably convince Rolf to get you an audience with the prince. Show him this." He dropped the little figure into Jordan's hand.

Before the Liren-sha could speak, the door popped open, and the duchess came in. "We have a guest you must greet as a king." The duchess crossed to a wardrobe and found a tunic and cape in the royal colors of gold and green. "Wear these."

Kattanan numbly shook his head. "I can't do this."

"You will." She turned to Jordan. "I need you there; this is the wizard we spoke of."

"The wizard will not appreciate my presence."

"I would not appreciate my grandson, or any of the rest of us, being overcome by magic. We will wait in the hall." She breezed out, followed by Jordan, to allow Kattanan to change in peace. When he opened the door, he found them waiting there, along with a group of guards and a few liveried servants. One of these approached and opened the box he held. The duchess removed something and held it up to catch the light. With a soft cry, Kattanan went pale and stumbled, not even shaking off Jordan's supportive hand.

"We had it stolen from the palace several years ago. The crown your uncle wears is a mere imitation." She made as if to place it on his head, but he retreated toward the room.

"Please don't make me wear that." He imagined blood seeping around it.

Still, she advanced. "This is the crown of your ancestors, and you will wear it."

"No!" Kattanan cried, as Jordan stepped between him and his grandmother.

"Duchess, now is not the time." Their eyes locked, and hers narrowed.

"You do not make decisions here."

"If anyone is to believe that Kat—that Rhys is the rightful king, then neither do you. He has said he will not wear that crown."

She stared up at him a moment longer, then turned smoothly back to the servant. "The king prefers to be bareheaded today, in deference to his injury. Carry this behind him." The servant bowed and shut the box. Gathering her skirts, the duchess looked back at them. "Four guards will go before, then His Majesty, and his bodyguard. If it please Your Majesty," she paused and made sure she had his attention, "I will do the talking during this interview."

"I think that were best," he said. He did not look at Jordan as the pair fell into the procession. Servants flung open great doors as they advanced, spilling sunlight from the brightly lit room beyond. Smaller than the Bernholt audience hall, the room shimmered with polished stone and golden lanterns. The few people within stood to attention and bowed as Kattanan passed. Pairs of

guards parted to allow him to walk to the throne—a replica of
the one that stood in Lochalyn. With a nervous glance, Kattanan
settled on the edge of the throne. Jordan towered beside him,
and the duchess took a smaller seat to the other side.

At her nod, the opposite door opened, and everyone was on
their feet again, this time murmuring in confusion. The figure
revealed there wavered even as they watched. The vestiges of age
and of fine robes faded into the air, leaving a plain woman clad
in homespun. Her hair was cut raggedly at her shoulders, but she
held herself with remarkable poise, striding into the room trailed
by a pair of protesting guards. The woman ignored all of the audience, stepping up before the throne, but to one side. Her eyes
gleamed the pale yellow of old parchment; a wide nose dominated her long face, and her hands hung indecisive by her sides,
but her whole figure was intent, and she gazed up at the Liren-
sha. "You are he."

"You are a wizard." He matched her even, disdainful tone.

"What is the meaning of this?" the duchess demanded, standing firmly before her chair.

"I felt you some distance off," the wizard continued, ignoring
the duchess. "It is a strange sensation to have one's power slowly
eroded. How is it done?"

"First, it strips your casting ability, then degrades your magic
senses, then finally removes whatever magic may linger around
you, leaving you completely exposed." He held her gaze.

She nodded. "That is what it felt like." At last she turned from
him to the duchess. "We have met before, under other circumstances."

"If it was you I met. I saw an old man who wore long, dark
robes. You are not he."

"An illusion. Would you have hired the woman you now see
before you? Ugly and ill formed? If anything, what you have
seen should make you even more sure of my ability. If not . . ."
The woman shrugged and turned back to the door.

"Even a wizard may not turn her back on the king," the
duchess said.

The woman sketched a curtsy. "If I seem ungraceful, it is because I am more used to bowing, Your Majesty. What service do you require?" Her yellow eyes strayed over his form, then flicked back to the duchess, who had again settled in her chair.

"Have you any skill with illusions of sound, or just with those of sight?"

"I have made all manner of illusions. Sound is, perhaps, less difficult than sight, because few people truly believe their ears. What did you have in mind?"

"The king requires a new voice."

"Ah. Trivial. What sort of voice?"

"Something deep and dignified, I would think."

A little smile played about the wizard's lips as she looked back to Kattanan. "He seems a bit young yet for that. I assume you desire a credible tone, Your Majesty?"

"Of course he does."

"Duchess, I understand it is important to you to conceal certain features of your king, but I cannot work in ignorance. Please let him speak."

"I have never thought of it," Kattanan stammered.

"I can see that. I can't work while the Liren-sha is present, and then there is the price."

"You are in our employ already; is not your retainer enough?"

The woman tilted her head. "I had in mind something less tangible. I would like to be considered a member of the court, with a room here, and all the privileges that implies."

The duchess frowned at this. "An unexpected request." She thought a long moment. "I see no reason not to grant it. You understand that the Liren-sha is in attendance here?"

"You do not understand the implications of that. If he enters the king's presence, the king will lose his voice until that man leaves again. At any time when the voice is important, the Liren-sha must be at least as far away as the antechamber is from here."

"I like it not."

"The choice is not mine to make."

Kattanan, who had been sitting at the far edge of the throne, suddenly realized his opportunity. "That is acceptable." Jordan flashed a glance at him, and the duchess glowered, but the singer ignored them both. "If I am to be forced to endure either the presence of this man or the risk of having a spell cast upon me, I choose the spell."

"The king has spoken," the wizard said. "I will not pretend to understand why you turn aside his protection unless you are yourself a wizard."

"No," Kattanan protested, but saw her little smirk and realized the joke.

"Once the Liren-sha is gone, I can begin."

The duchess nodded her dismissal to Jordan, but he bowed to the throne, and said, "As His Majesty has requested, but may I perform a blessing?"

"You are no longer a man of the Goddess," Kattanan said sharply.

"Not as a monk, but as the Liren-sha. My blessing will prevent the wizard from performing any magic beyond what you yourself request."

"This sounds much like magic in itself," the wizard observed.

"It is more like a lingering sense of my presence on the person so blessed."

"Useful," she commented, as he turned back to Kattanan.

Kneeling before the throne, Jordan held out his hands. "Will you suffer my touch?" he asked under his breath.

Kattanan stiffened, but recalled the words of the ancient priestess. "Do it quickly."

Jordan laid his hands upon the young king's head, and said, "By the blood in my heart, defend this man from magic. May the clouds come down to guard you. May the earth rise up to save you. May the light of the Goddess dance upon you. Your voice alone can divide this blessing, but none shall ever dispel it." A strange lightness rose in Kattanan. The touch hovered there like a caress, even when the Liren-sha had let himself out.

The wizard's form wavered and grew into voluminous robes, stitched with gold. Lines wandered about her face, and her hair grew long and grey down her back. The old man she had become smiled at their renewed confusion. "He is gone. I can begin whenever you ask it."

Kattanan forced himself to relax and nodded. "Wizard, will you give me a new voice?"

"Aye, Sire. Imagine the voice you would choose. It should be strong, but not intimidating. Not so deep as to be unbelievable. A voice that you yourself would trust. It may help if you shut your eyes."

He did so, and was only vaguely aware of the chant of the wizard as it rose around him. A voice he would trust. He cast back in memory for such a voice, and found it, in a young man who found him left by a gate, a novice who carried him gently, who stayed with him for so long. The voice was tenor, not too deep, with the echo of a ready laugh. But that voice later betrayed him. He tried to reject it and find another—too late, he felt the voice become his.

The wizard stepped back then. "It is done."

"So, speak," the duchess prompted.

"I do not feel well," he said softly, but he jumped a little when he heard the voice.

"A good voice," the wizard commented, and the duchess nodded to herself.

"The chamberlain will find a room to suit you, wizard. Thank you for your service."

The wizard bowed to both of them and moved aside.

The duchess stood and signaled the guards as well. "My grandson has had a difficult time and will need to recover. I will handle all other business before this court."

Kattanan rose unsteadily and followed the guards back to his room, shutting the door behind him. He flung off the strange clothing and curled up in the blankets, shaking. He shut his eyes against the mourning red of the berries and tried to remember his own voice.

# Chapter 14

A LONG WHILE passed before Kattanan stirred from his bed. Hunger got the best of him, and he bit into a roll as he paced through the room. The bed was twice as large as any he had been in, and all the bedclothes bore the badge of the Royal House of Lochalyn, as did the curtains and chair backs. Two tall windows opened out onto a small patio, with an unkempt garden beyond. The wardrobe held a variety of tunics, robes, cloaks, and hoods, plus a few finer jerkins and hose in various shades. Seeing that his own undertunic was somewhat disheveled, Kattanan put on one of the others. He returned for some fruit and settled by the shelf between the two windows. Aside from the texts, a miniature painting showed his family in exquisite detail. His father was tall and proud, hand on his sword; Alyn, then crown prince, did a fine imitation of his father. With solemn eyes, Duncan stared out of the frame. Queen Caitrin tilted her head to smile at the shining blond of her youngest son's hair. He perched on her lap, grinning, holding his middle brother's hand.

Kattanan replaced the portrait but looked at his younger self a moment. A knock sounded at the door, and the wizard, in the old man's guise, stepped up to the door and looked down at him. In this form, the eyes were dark, near black, and Kattanan could not see his reflection in them. "How fares the new voice, Sire?"

"Strange."

The old man nodded. "It will take some time to get used to it. Have you recovered?"

Kattanan shrugged and found himself some wine. "I feel better, but not good."

"I am both glad and sorry to hear that."

The duchess brushed aside her wizard. "Where's the Liren-sha?"

"He was told not to come near me."

"He hasn't been seen since court, and that was hours ago."

"Should that be important to me?" When he spoke, the new voice sounded strong, firm, not at all like his own.

The wizard shrugged. "I have no sense of him myself, and my power is intact."

"He talked for weeks about how he'd never leave again," said the duchess darkly. "I asked him to be cautious because of the new voice, but this is going somewhat too far."

"I asked him to go," Kattanan said, with a faint smile. "Apparently he went."

"Where?" the duchess asked.

Kattanan studied his meal. "Away."

"A king must learn to face his enemy as he lies. Where did he go, Sire?"

A breathless servant trotted up behind. "He took his horse, Excellency, but not his red saddle, a different one. He had a very long, black cape, the stableboy said."

"So he is riding in disguise," the wizard observed. He raised a shaggy eyebrow at Kattanan. "And you don't know where."

"And he didn't tell me, so he's doing something he shouldn't." The duchess's eyes grew sharp as daggers. "The message! You wanted a message sent to the prince! You asked him to ride to the enemy? And say what?"

"It doesn't concern this place, or you"

The wizard growled something from deep in his beard. "It doesn't matter what he was told to say, if he gets near the king, we are most likely ruined."

"I have always said you should have killed the king outright," the duchess said. "He has a four-hour lead on anyone we could send. Can we get a message to the earl?"

"No," Kattanan said forcefully.

"He is our ally. I am more sure of him than I am of you."

The wizard said, "We don't know what road he's taken, and unless the earl is already riding that way, he would never catch him."

"What is our real danger?"

"Assuming your grandson is telling the truth, and nothing about your affairs is revealed, only that the Liren-sha gets near King Gerrod. I have no way of knowing how weak the king is, or how much the sudden disillusionment would reveal. If the doctors have stopped bleeding him, he could recover very quickly. So far as I know, this has no effect on your plans, but the earl could be ruined. If he thinks the Liren-sha was sent for this purpose, he may betray you."

"What can we do?"

"If he does meet the king, I must be there as soon after as possible to reinstate the spell."

Kattanan stumbled back and sat down hard. "You're the Wizard of Nine Stars. I let you work magic on me."

"We can spare you for a time," the duchess said, "but return quickly, if you can. Presumably, he will simply deliver the message, and come back, so it should be two days at the most." She turned to Kattanan with a hard look. "I will spend them in helping my grandson to define his loyalties and finding a way to convince the earl that this was not our doing. Rhys does not understand our cause well enough to give it his full support. Starting now, Rhys, you are in training to serve as our king. Do not defy me again."

WHILE HIS former student was being introduced to new tutors, Jordan rode hard down a narrow track. The coming of night forced him to slow down, picking out the trail by moonlight and the lights on passing boats. He rested just before dawn as he waited for the first light of the sun. The horse he tethered to a tree by the river just before mounting the climbing trail. He rounded a final bend and emerged from the shadows not far from the tower.

"Halt there! Tell me how ye're called." A deep voice rolled down at him.

"I am a friend of one who was your friend, Rolf of the Prince's Mercy!"

"Ye be no wizard!"

"Gracious, no!" He tugged at his red gloves and smiled a little.

"Then whose friend are ye?"

"Kattanan duRhys."

"By the mount! I'm coming to the gate, but I'll be armed!"

"As well you should be."

Armored feet clumped down inside the tower as he approached the gate. The man who appeared was as tall as Jordan himself but much more broad, especially with the helmet and breastplate. "How are ye his friend, and how come ye here?"

"To the first, it is a difficult story; to the other, I have a message for Prince Wolfram. Kat thought it was important. He told me you were the watchman here."

The big man mumbled to himself in a foreign tongue. "If I let you in, it'd be my head."

"Can you bring the prince here?"

Rolf set down the butt of his spear. "Ye've got no army waitin' round the bend?"

Jordan checked behind him. "If one comes, I'll hold the gate as long as I can."

The guard let out a snort of laughter.

Jordan fumbled in his pouch, pushing back the cloak. Rolf took a step back at the sight of the red garb and matched swords, but relaxed a little when they were not drawn. Jordan tossed the carved figure between the bars. "Kattanan said to show that to the prince."

Rolf caught it, then raised his head to Jordan. "If that army arrives, tell 'em I'll be back in a blink." Rolf hurried off, disappearing through a door on the far side.

Jordan paced a while, stretching his legs, in the shadow of the tower. As the sun rose overhead, he made the sign of the Goddess, and began to sing Morning Prayer until he heard the guard's return behind him. He turned with a brief bow for the newcomer.

"I have heard only Kattanan sing it that way," the prince said, coming up to the bars. "Where's the key, Rolf?"

Jordan allowed himself a smile. "I am glad to hear he still does." The smile faded as he thought of leaving his friend with a wizard. "I am also glad you have decided to trust me."

"The token you sent means I should either trust you, as he apparently did, or kill you, if you got it by some other means." Despite the hurried appearance of his clothing, and his tawny, uncombed hair, the prince looked grave, as did Rolf as the gate was opened.

"Your Highness, harm intended for him would first have to get past me."

"In that case, come in. We'll talk in the tower if that suits you."

"Not as much as talk in the kitchen, Your Highness, but I'll manage."

Wolfram gave him a sidelong glance and a little smile. "That can be arranged. Rolf, to your duty. I do not think this man intends me ill."

"Not unless he's a cannibal, Your Highness." Rolf climbed back into his tower.

"There's a servants' kitchen not far from here." The prince led the way across the courtyard. "Who are you, if I may be so bold?"

"I was a tutor of Kattanan's a long time ago; as to what I am, I think I'd best wait on that until you have heard the message." They walked silently to the kitchen. Only a pair of scullery maids worked there now, as the servants had already eaten, and the nobles were not expected up for quite some time. The men took a tray of food into a small pantry away from prying ears.

Pouring each of them a drink, Wolfram said, "Speak your message, stranger. We are as safe here as anywhere in the castle, I warrant."

"There were two things he wanted you to know. The first I cannot elaborate on, as I don't know the parties involved, but he said that Earl Orie and Lady Faedre are lovers."

"That blackguard is to marry my sister! Bury him; we knew he was hiding something."

"There's more, Your Highness." Jordan set down his cup. "The Wizard of Nine Stars was hired by the earl."

"Goddess's Tears! What is he up to?"

"I can't say, specifically, but, taken to its logical conclusion, I would assume he is after the crown. You say he is marrying your sister. As I understand it, the wizard is responsible for your father's illness. That leaves only one obstacle to the earl, Your Highness, if this is indeed his intention." Jordan met the prince's gaze.

"Thank the Goddess you came while there is still time to do something." Wolfram took a deep swallow, then started. "How did Kattanan find out these things? Is he all right?"

"The earl did send someone after him; I don't know why he was leaving there. We were able to save him, though, and he was not greatly injured. I have not had much chance to talk with him since then. It was very important to him that this message reach you."

"Where is he, then?"

"He is in," Jordan paused, wrestling with the need for trust over secrecy, "I will not say good hands, but at least in the care of people who mean him no harm."

"You don't trust them."

"Their goals and mine coincide about Kattanan's well-being, but not beyond that. Before you ask, I cannot discuss their plans."

"Then what are yours? You said you would tell me who you are," Wolfram prompted.

Jordan nodded. "I said that I was his tutor. We were separated against our will some six years ago. I was a monk at the time. What I am, what I have always been, is the Wizard's Bane. Kattanan did not know until yesterday. I had forsaken my fate to go to the Goddess; now I have forsaken Her." He fell silent, as wonder spread across the prince's face.

"You are anathema to all magic?"

Jordan nodded.

"Then you can cure my father."

"Perhaps. I don't know the nature of the spell, so it's hard to say what would change, especially if he has taken many medicines since then. What with lying abed and being looked after, he may well be more sick without the magic."

"We have tried everything else. I set myself to find the wizard and try to—I don't know what, actually." Wolfram swirled his goblet with a rueful look. "I did not know what else to do. If I had known you were more than a legend, I suppose I would have looked for you. Will you come to my father?"

"If he will see me, then I will do what I can, Your Highness, for the sake of your friendship with Kattanan."

"Well, he won't be accepting visitors at this hour, so we may at least finish our breakfast. How did you become the Liren-sha?"

Jordan snorted. "I did not become, I was born, although my power seems to have grown with me. My father was a wizard, my mother, a priestess. Shadow-shaper— my father—gave up most of his other studies to try to find out all he could about me. He discovered that I affect stronger wizards, and stronger magic, at a greater distance. He had a certain rival he wished to be rid of, so he arranged to meet the man just outside of the distance at which he would himself lose power. You see, he thought the other man was stronger and so would have less power than himself. He turned out to be wrong, and died in the duel. I was responsible for his death." He fell silent, the old ache returning.

"So you went to the Goddess to atone."

"I thought that She had taken me in, freed me. Years later, I killed again, that time in a rage. I was never worthy to wear those robes." He studied his hands. "The wizard I killed had traded Kattanan to an emir for a chance to look at a book of magic. Obviously, I could not be around when he did, so he asked the man to have me killed. He did not know the guards were ordered to kill him as well. Imagine their amusement when I beat them to it. The guard captain started my new vocation, he dared all wizards to come, and other men as well."

"A wizard I had business with hinted at some of that, that one of his brethren had given in to temptation and met his fate."

"They all believe that weaker wizards are the ones who lose their power, and, being as haughty as they are, each new wizard thinks he will be strong enough to overcome me. I have been tempted more than once to reveal what my father learned, just to stop them coming. They don't believe me, though. Some of the men who came were hired by wizards who hadn't the courage to come themselves; the rest sought only their own fame."

"And the red?" Wolfram prompted softly.

"No man should die without someone to mourn him. I mourn them all." Jordan almost laughed as he inspected his garb. "It also has a good effect on the morale of my opponents. So much of what I am is rumor and dramatics that I surprise myself by being flesh and blood."

"You have surprised me, also. Do you have a name beyond your title?"

"I was once called Jordan, your Highness."

"Jordan, will you come with me to meet the king?"

"I will, and thank you for the meal."

They gathered up the remnants of breakfast and left the little room, mounting the stairs to the upper levels. "If you have not met the earl, then I assume you would have no news of my sister either?"

"No, Highness."

"She is at his keep on a Goddess Moon. Ignorance may serve better than knowledge to keep her safe from the earl—at least for now. I wish I knew why Kattanan was leaving there; it might tell me so much."

"He was on foot, with only a small bag, and it was the middle of the night, so I doubt the journey was by choice. The brigands who assaulted him claimed to be the earl's own men. I was riding to the keep—I had heard that he was there but that his position was tenuous at best."

"You and your associates have spies inside the keep?"

"There are those who bring us tidings."

"Your associates are friends of the earl's."

Jordan paused on the landing to look at the prince through piercing eyes. "You have a way of getting more from a man than he means to say, Your Highness."

Wolfram put out his hands, palm up. "I try to listen very carefully. I certainly do not mean to put you on your guard against me."

"I am always on my guard, Highness." The ghost of a grin came upon his lips. "You speak to many wizards, don't you?"

"When I have to. I speak to as many people as I can. You are avoiding the question I have not asked."

"I know, because I can't be sure of the answer. To the best of my knowledge, my associates have nothing to do with your father's illness. They do not have designs on the kingdom of Bernholt." He watched the prince closely, and Wolfram narrowed his eyes.

"Yet they have knowledge of the wizard, and apparently the earl, but have volunteered nothing. You are wise not to trust them." The prince looked him in the eye. "I hope you can trust them with Kattanan."

"I hope so, too."

"That was a less-than-comforting answer."

Jordan joined him on his stair, then kept on. "Then you will understand why I would like to return there as soon as possible."

Wolfram nodded. "This way." They soon stood before the king's door, facing a file of armed guards as they were announced to the king. The steward returned in a moment and bobbed a brief bow.

"His Royal Majesty, Gerrod of Bernholt, requires proof of your claim," the steward said.

The Liren-sha considered, gazing over the little man's head. "Ask if he has some enchanted trinket that he would not mind losing something cursed by magic, perhaps."

The man returned, this time with a small object in his hand: a toy soldier, worn with play, with a tiny crown that glowed in the daylight.

For a moment Wolfram squeezed his eyes shut. "Why that?" He sighed.

"The king said that this is mere sentiment, and worth little with or without the enchantment." He offered it to Jordan, who glanced aside at the prince but took it without comment, then handed it back. The crown and glow had faded away, leaving just an old toy.

"Return this to your king, and tell him the Liren-sha awaits." When the man had gone, Jordan whispered to the prince, "You do not look well, Highness."

"That was all the magic a seven-year-old could afford. I loved that soldier, even more when he was crowned."

"The king will see you," the steward announced, standing aside from the door. Wolfram let his companion go first, both pausing inside to let their eyes adjust to the dim light. They bowed, and Jordan stepped a little forward.

"May I approach Your Majesty's bedside?"

"Unless you can dispel it from there," the king rasped. He peered at Jordan from beneath heavy brows, coughing into a cloth. "Where have you come from?"

"The North Road. I hear your daughter has just gone that way."

The old king smiled, and gave a faint nod. "She is with a suitor, a strong young earl. Goddess willing, they'll marry soon."

Jordan looked up from his study of the king to meet Wolfram's eyes with a small frown. "By your leave, Your Majesty, I will need to touch your head."

"Come to it then. I have been needled and leeched by every physician and healer for miles around, and not one has even eased the pain." He scowled, eyes focusing on the prince, where he waited off to one side.

Jordan knelt and pulled off his gloves, tucking them into his belt. He took a deep breath, and laid his hands on the king's temples. Their breathing synchronized, and Jordan shut his eyes. King Gerrod's eyes flew open wide, and he jerked away. "Light! Give me light!"

Wolfram drew aside the curtains, letting in a stream of light dyed blue and gold by stained glass. The king cackled and clutched at Jordan's arm. He took deep breaths then, and laughed again. Struggling to push himself upright, though, he growled darkly. "What is this? I am still weak as a child!"

"Sire, the magic is gone. What you feel is the result of your treatments; it will pass."

"I should banish those fool physicians."

"No," Jordan replied, "they did all they could for you, but the sickness was not of the body. There was nothing for them to cure, Your Majesty, but the semblance of sickness."

"This wizard is a master of illusions," Wolfram added, moving a little closer, joy and pain warring on his face.

"You know so much about wizards," the king scoffed.

"I have been learning, to try to find a way to help you."

"Learning! I should have known. Steward, some ale, I think. Take away this drugged wine. I have no need of it." Gerrod looked back to Jordan. "Any reward shall be yours, beginning with a feast in your honor as soon as I am well enough to attend."

"I cannot stay, Your Majesty. I have other matters to attend to." Jordan tried to rise, but the king held his arm.

"I have said you will stay." His grin stopped as his eyes burned at the Liren-sha. "I have a mind to grant you knighthood if you do not have it already."

"The offer is most generous, but I must leave." With a supple twist of the arm, he released himself from the king's grasp and moved quickly out of reach. "It is probable that you have not heard the last of the wizard. The prince will know how to reach me, if you have further need of my services." He bowed, and turned, but Gerrod bellowed, "Guards!"

In an instant, three men crowded into the room, effectively barring the door, swords drawn, eyes flashing. "What is your will, Sire?"

"This man has lifted the sickness from me, and I, by right of birth the King of Bernholt, require him to stay. He is far too useful to go so soon. Give him every luxury."

"Your Majesty," Jordan began, gritting his teeth, "I do appreciate your offer, but my business is urgent. I will leave instructions with Prince Wolfram—"

"Am I not king in my own castle? You are my subject."

"Father, please, this man came of his own will to aid you—"

"I will have silence!" the king roared, breathing hard. "And I will have my crown."''

Wolfram fell to one knee and took the crown from his head, offering it with lowered eyes. Gerrod snatched it away and clapped it to his silvering hair.

With a flicker of a glance to the prince, Jordan sighed, "Very well, where am I to stay?"

"The steward will appoint you one of the finest rooms, and my men will stay nearby, should you have need of them." The king's head was raised, his gaze steady and his smile fixed.

Jordan inclined his head, and turned on his heel to follow the guards. Before Wolfram had even emerged from the chamber, Jordan broke from the guards and streaked around a corner toward the stairs. Taken by surprise, the guards stampeded after him, weighed down by armor. Jordan careered down the stairs and slammed into a chambermaid. They fell in a heap, and her face shifted and changed.

"Bury you, Wizard's Bane," muttered the Wizard of Nine Stars.

"Wizard!" shouted a guard, and they were on the move again, hauling both up from the floor. A small cask of ale spurted out its contents across the stairs beside a fallen tray.

"I'd swear that was Hallie a moment ago!" the guard in front exclaimed, pointing at the ragged woman. "She was to bring the king's ale."

"Bury you in stone!" she hissed at Jordan. "If not for you, I could have slipped past."

"What are you doing here?" Jordan demanded.

"Guess!" she snapped, turning away.

"Tell me how you are called," the guard captain ordered, sword at the ready.

She bared her teeth at him, but could not escape the command. "The Wizard of Nine Stars."

"Treason!" the other bawled. "To death with you, wizard."

The wizard snaked out a hand and caught Jordan's sleeve. "If they kill me, all of my spells are undone. All of them, and we don't know what your precious Kat will be doing at the time." Her eyes bored into him, thin lips set in desperation.

A groan of anguish escaped him. Jordan looked at Wolfram, who had joined the group on the landing.

"So this is the one responsible for the king's ailment," the prince said, studying her.

"I cannot allow her death, Highness," Jordan whispered. "If she dies, Kattanan may be in great danger."

"She cursed my father, the king of this land," Wolfram responded, eyes dark.

"Do you think I have forgotten that?" Jordan looked at her and at the ground. "Chain us together." He met the prince's gaze then, and spoke, louder, "Chain us together. As long as I am present, she can make no magic." He turned to the circle of guards. "I am the Liren-sha, Wizard's Bane. You need not kill her now. Would it not be more fitting to prepare a public execution, so that all may see the reward for treason?"

The captain nodded slowly. "So ye'll be staying."

"If this is how it must be, I will." He fastened his fingers around the wizard's wrist. "I suggest we stay right here until your man returns with the shackles."

"Jordan, don't do this," Wolfram hissed urgently. "I don't know what hold she has over you or Kattanan, but she is a traitor, and it is only a matter of time until she is killed."

"I know, and I need every minute, Highness. I cannot let her die, you cannot let her live."

"If it were anyone other than this wizard—" The prince let his hands fall.

"This wizard has every intention of staying alive, thank you," she snapped, leveling her yellow eyes on him. She darted glances to the floor and ceiling and down to where the guard returned, chains dangling from his hand. She pulled urgently against Jordan's grip, but the iron band was clicked shut about her wrist. He let go then and pushed back his sleeve, offering the scarred wrist to the guard. Hesitating, the man glanced at the scars, then up at him.

"Have done with it," the captain commanded, and the soldier complied, stepping back from the pair. "Best disarm him as well, take no chances."

Wolfram looked to the swords at Jordan's waist, at his bound right hand hovering near the hilt, and said nothing.

"Go tell your father, Highness," the Liren-sha murmured. "Let him hear from you that the wizard has been captured."

Sighing, the prince nodded and started to turn, but the wizard lunged forward. She snatched one long sword from the astonished guard and slapped it before the prince's neck. "We are leaving, and the prince is coming along." Her voice trilled with dangerous power; her hand holding the sword twitched it ever so gently under Wolfram's chin as she knotted her off hand in the back of his tunic.

"Don't do this!" Jordan cried.

"You weren't getting us out of this, Bane, so shut up. Down the stairs, Prince."

The guards shifted, swords wavering, but finally moved aside.

Wolfram stumbled on the first step, and a silky drop of blood crept down his neck.

"Back off, wizard," Jordan growled.

"If you weren't dragging me, this would be much easier."

Stumbling, running when they reached a hallway, the wizard urged on the awkward trio.

"There'll be archers at the gates," the prince breathed carefully.

"Back gate, I have a horse," Jordan said.

They slipped to the servants' stair, crashing into a laden page.

"Clear the way, or your prince dies!" She twitched the blade, and Jordan's hand caught it over Wolfram's shoulder as the page scurried off.

"Do not play with this man's life," Jordan muttered.

The wizard glowered. "You're cutting your hand."

His expression froze, the hand did not move.

"How did you plan to get us out of here?"

"Not by taking this man's life in my hands." Still, Jordan released his hold on the sword, letting his hand hover there as they hurried on.

They burst into sunlight, startling doves off the roof.

The wizard yelled, "Open that gate!"

Scrambling down the stairs, the guard emerged, fumbling the keys. The gate squealed, and he leapt aside as they plunged through.

Flinging Wolfram away from her, the wizard rushed forward, but Jordan held them back a moment.

The prince, on his knees, clapped a hand to his throat. "Get out," he gasped.

"Come on!" the wizard snarled. "They'll follow us!"

"There is no map to where we go," Jordan said, locking his eyes to the prince's, then he ran down the path. Despite his long strides, the wizard kept pace fiercely, brought up short by the chain when he paused to look toward the river. "Bury it! Where's my horse?"

"If you weren't so cursed clever," the wizard panted, shaking the chain at him, "I could be there by now, horse or no."

"We'll cross the river." The pair trotted forward again.

"What? Here at least we have the trees."

"They already know the road we're on, and they will be on horseback. No one will expect us to take the main road."

She growled under her breath. "Maybe a friendly blacksmith will think this was a joke and break this iron for us, too. I should have killed you and the prince and been shut of it!"

"Is that what you were sent to do?" He hauled her to a stop. "Is it?"

"Bury you both! My only concern is the king, and you ruined that. You and the prince together aren't worth half a horseshoe to me."

"How much were you paid for the king?"

Straightening, she grinned. "Not a blessed copper; it was a pleasure. I only wish I could have killed him."

Jordan snorted. "You aren't the first to say that. There's a narrows here. Can you swim?" Her smile faded as his grew.

"This is insane." She paused, listening, then stared down at the water. She thrust the sword back into its sheath on his belt. "You can't let me drown, Bane, or Kattanan's secret goes free."

"Don't remind me."

"Can you do this with the chain?"

"There's one way to find out." He whirled her tight against his chest and jumped.

# Chapter 15

"WHAT SHALL I play for you?" Fionvar asked. Orie, intent on Melisande, made no answer. He lowered the violin and watched the couple, seated on a spread blanket not far away. The sun was almost down, and the benches cast long shadows across the glade. Melisande rolled her goblet between her hands, staring off into the woods as Orie laid out the picnic without taking his eyes off her. Fionvar shifted on his seat. "Orie, Your Highness, what would you like to hear?"

"I don't know, anything," the earl said, and Fionvar lifted the instrument and began.

"Where would he go?" Melisande said, sipping absently. "Didn't he say?"

Orie gritted his teeth. "For the last time, no one saw him leave; no one spoke to him, and no one knows where he went. I wish you could just forget him and enjoy the evening."

"Forget him? I loved his voice, and his company, and he had the gentlest hands."

"And he left you, Melisande, you'd best accept that. You still have Prince to keep you company." He forced a smile.

"A puppy can not replace my singer!"

A strain of "Bernholt Hills" came in to the music. Orie jumped up, looking at his brother. He snatched the violin and smashed it against the bench.

Melisande jerked, dropping her goblet, mouth open.

Fionvar turned the bow carefully in his hands and said nothing as his brother stood trembling before him.

"I didn't mean it," Melisande breathed. "I do love Prince, you know that."

His back loomed hard before her, shoulders rising and falling as he steadied his breathing. "It's just that I hate to see you so upset when there is nothing I can do." His eyes dropped to the ruined instrument in his hands. "Perhaps it's best if I took a walk." He stalked out of the grove, the violin still gripped in his hand.

Melisande stared after him a long moment. "I did not expect him to be so angry."

"Nor I," Fionvar echoed, laying aside the bow at last.

"I just don't understand why Kattanan left; can't he see that?"

"Your Highness," Fionvar began, coming to kneel on the blanket, "having the singer here was a constant reminder that you had chosen another man."

Frowning, she stared at him. "But that was before I really knew Orie; and the baron—" She glanced up to the sky.

"Orie knows all of that, but he seeks to win you both heart and hand, Highness. As long as he is reminded of another, he doubts himself in that task."

"Oh." She narrowed her eyes at Fionvar. "You are saying it's better that Kattanan left."

"I am saying that your singer may have seen this trouble before the rest of us and left, not to hurt you, but to help you and my brother. Orie needs to know that he can have your full attention, Highness."

Her face suddenly lightened. "You must be right; Kattanan would never hurt me. Where's Orie? I should tell him I understand, now." She made as if to rise, but Fionvar stayed her.

"He'll be back when he's ready, Your Highness. I've found it best not to disturb him when he's walking something off."

"Will he get this angry every time?" She looked at her wrist, where a marriage bracelet would lie.

"He gets this way very rarely, but it's hard to tell what might set him off."

"How will I ever learn what to do, or what not to? I can't be expected not to care about certain things just because he might get mad."

Fionvar gave her a curious look. "It might be wise to think about that, though. Or rather, to find different ways to tell him how you feel, Highness. Don't discard him for this one moment. Everyone has difficult days."

She sighed. "I suppose so. How do people ever learn to live with each other? Wolfram and I get along sometimes, then sometimes he is an absolute beast!"

"If you care enough about someone, you will find ways around the arguments. My lady and I have had enough of them, but we know there will be joy ahead as well."

"You have a lady? Why have I not met her?"

He looked away with a little smile. "She is of high birth, while I am not, so her family does not approve. There are so many reasons we shouldn't be together, yet we can't stay apart."

"It sounds so mysterious," Melisande said, breaking off a branch of grapes, "very like a minstrel's tale." She settled back and popped one in her mouth.

"It feels like that as well, like a love the Goddess Herself has given. We met right here in the grove that grants your heart's desire. I was waiting for a messenger, playing my violin, of course. She came up without speaking, and when I saw her at last, she was crying. She said she had not heard such music since—well, since she was a child. We stayed that whole night here, telling all of our stories. It turned out she was carrying the message to my brother, and it was not the last time she did so. Some months passed before she told me they had a husband in mind for her already, a man of the highest blood, and a duty she was raised to."

"Certainly we must consider our position, and our family's, but it is still her choice."

"You must know by now that nothing is ever so easy as that, Your Highness. Especially if even I must agree that the match would give her more than I could ever offer. The essence of love, Highness, is to want to give your lady all the world, if she asks it."

"Well said, brother," Orie responded, emerging from shadows

to rejoin them. He took Melisande's hand and gently kissed it. "When would you like the world, Melisande? I'll have it brought here one stone at a time."

Melisande giggled and glanced down as the earl turned to his brother. "And for you, I apologize about the violin. I will have the finest instrument ever made brought to you."

Fionvar shook his head. "You could not buy an instrument like that."

"It didn't seem so special to me," the earl said, frowning.

"That was the one I made," Fionvar replied quietly.

Orie let out a long breath. "I said I was sorry."

Fionvar looked away. "This will give me an excuse to make another."

Melisande smiled encouragingly at them both. "Well, let's eat, anyhow."

"Certainly; we must be well fed when we meet our heart's desire." Orie gave her a steamy glance as he offered her a honeyed pastry. "I just wish we did not have need of a chaperone."

She blushed. "I would not want to face my brother if he knew you said such things."

Fionvar gathered himself some bread and meat and retreated to one of the benches, studiously watching the sky or the trees. Before long, the pair spoke as if he were not there, and, soon after, Melisande yawned broadly. Orie shook out another blanket and slipped a silk pillow under her head with a smile. When the princess had drifted off to sleep, the earl inched away, and came to stand by his brother's bench. "She is even more beautiful in sleep."

Tilting his head to gaze at her through the moonlight, Fionvar sighed. "I know she is of age, but she is still so much a child."

"She will grow up before very long." Orie watched her a little longer, then fixed his brother with a hard stare. "They found their king, but I believe you already knew that."

"I suspected, nothing more." Fionvar met his eyes.

"Next time you suspect something like that, perhaps you should tell me first instead of telling them. I felt like an idiot when my men were killed." He smiled just a little then. "Nine

Stars told me that the duchess was frantic trying to figure out how they would apologize to me. A castrate king." He snorted and shook his head. "You will not tell Melisande."

"My silence is legendary," Fionvar said, unsmiling.

"Go out to the compound tomorrow, I'll make your excuses here."

Fionvar did smile then. "I thought you wanted me here."

"The wizard is going off someplace, and I think it will be valuable to have someone there who will tell me everything. I do wish you would let us make an oath-bond, then we could communicate anytime, across any distance." The earl's eyes sparkled in the darkness.

"Spare me the glories of your magic, Orie, we have had this conversation before."

"When you wed, you'll take a blood oath with your wife; this is not much different." He stared at his brother.

"My lady and I have already shared more than that."

"What more—" Orie bent suddenly to search his brother's gaze. "She yielded to you?"

Fionvar nodded. "We are wed in all but name. She even carries my child."

"Why have you waited so long to tell me?"

"Her family still won't have it." Fionvar rose suddenly and looked to the stars. "You advised, no, you urged me to lie with her, saying they would be forced to give in, but she won't allow me to reveal it for fear of what they'd do to me!"

Orie turned away to look at Melisande, his grin flaring briefly into the night. When he spoke, his voice was schooled to concern. "That's too bad. I thought they'd come around."

"I am sure of nothing but her love, and now, with the king there—" Fionvar clenched his fists but bit his tongue.

Treading softly, Orie came to stand behind his brother. "Don't you wish I *had* killed him?"

"Go keep your princess company," said Fionvar, crossing his arms against the cold.

The earl lay down by the princess, stroking her hair until he dozed off, with a strange little smile on his face.

Late afternoon the next day found Fionvar dismounting in front of a large gate and making certain signs to the gate-keeper. He was admitted without delay and sent to the throne room within the great house. Inside, he could hear the drone of court, so he let himself in quietly, and took a place in the back of the room. Kattanan, clad in rich robes, sat the throne. The crown of state lay on a velvet pillow set between the throne and the duchess's equally tall chair. Fionvar sought among the small gathering, but his lady was not there. Resigned, he settled back against the wall. Kattanan glanced at him, immediately straightening, and Fionvar wished once more that he had not presented such a forbidding air when first they met.

". . . and we can muster some two hundred men from the border provinces on the far side, as well," a captain was saying, gesturing over a map held by two servants.

The duchess nodded, glancing at her grandson. "We are well prepared for the war, Your Majesty, lacking only the king. Very soon now you may reclaim your birthright."

Kattanan, eyes rimmed with darkness, gave what might have been a grave nod of assent or the gesture of a man in despairing surrender. "But does my uncle not know of these preparations? Surely he must have found out by now."

Heads turned to Fionvar as he choked on a swallow of ale, staring at the singer.

Smiling a little more, the duchess replied, "We were to cover this aspect of the plan in conference today, Sire, but, if it is your will, I shall explain now."

"Please do." Kattanan himself and Fionvar both cringed at the new voice, small though the king tried to make it.

"Your uncle has been distracted on several fronts by false information we have allowed him, by the unseasonable weather in the mountains and by his daughter's rather embarrassing condition on the eve of her intended wedding. He is himself plagued by nightmares, some of which are not even of our doing." The duchess allowed herself a chuckle. "There are many small players in this game, Your Majesty. We have been planning for many years, and we are not alone in our quest to restore our House to the throne."

Shouts of approval rippled through the crowd. Kattanan paled and cast her a swift glance, gripping the arms of the throne.

"In any event," she went on, "most of those present are well aware of these plans, so perhaps we should move on to new business, and I shall answer all of your questions in conference. You may go." The captain bowed out of court, taking the map along. "This next is a bit of old business arranged long ago, but left to today to be fulfilled."

Kattanan leaned toward her. "You promised me no surprises."

Unperturbed, the duchess patted his hand. "I know you are tired yet, from your ordeal of a few days past, but this business is not so burdensome as the last." Her eyes locked on his with a fixed smile.

Fionvar carefully set down his mug.

The duchess rose grandly. "Allow me to introduce Lady Brianna yfRhiannon duMarcelle of the House of Rinvien, your cousin, and your betrothed."

Kattanan whirled to her. "My what?"

A maid brought the lady forward to curtsey before the duchess. A pale gown hung loose from her shoulders, swathing her form, and blond hair drooped around her shoulders. She stared blankly, her face a mask with shadowed eyes.

The duchess's face fell, but she quickly regained her composure, turning to Kattanan with a fierce little grin. "The lady Brianna."

Looking from one to the other, Kattanan opened his mouth, but nothing came. Brianna, a couple of years older than he, stared somewhere beyond him.

"A marriage within the House of Rinvien will strengthen the bloodlines of the family and show the people your commitment to the kingdom," the duchess said, each word perfectly formed and offered with an icy gaze.

The singer blanched, knotted his fingers together, and flicked his eyes away. "I can't."

She leaned to his ear, and whispered, "I will not allow your confusion to stand in the way of what is right for this kingdom. You agreed not to defy me in public when it comes to that."

"But I," he began, glancing at Brianna, "I can't do that."

"Your cousin is with child. Marry her, and the succession is assured."

"What of the father?" he whispered back.

"We can discuss that later; the lady is waiting, as is your audience."

He shut his eyes, taking a deep breath. Silks rustled around him, whispers and coughs rose into his silence, and he opened his eyes again. Turning to face the lady, Kattanan made a small bow. "This is . . . unexpected for me, my lady. I'm sorry if my confusion has offended." His glance slipped to the hand that held up her skirts, letting the folds pool around her abdomen. Something peeked from her sleeve, a narrow bracelet of braided hair, pale and slightly shiny, as if waxed. His eyes widened. "I cannot ask you to accept me before we have come to know each other. If you are willing, I would meet with you at some later time."

Brianna shrugged, still not looking at him as if she utterly refused his presence.

"Perhaps you would meet me in the garden after court, my lady? I shall bring a chaperone so you need not fear." So saying, he sat down heavily in his throne. Brianna turned and walked from the room. Once the door was shut, the duchess returned to her chair.

"I am afraid you did not see her at her best, Your Majesty; she has not been well."

"I look forward to a more private reunion with my cousin," he murmured, scanning the room as if in thought. "I think I will ask my lord Fionvar duNormand to serve as chaperone. He doesn't even like me, so he will be an apt guardian of the lady's honor." His eyes flared briefly to life at this, meeting Fionvar's astonished gaze.

She nodded. "I believe that is all the business of today. I shall have supper laid out in your chambers before your rendezvous." She rose, the audience followed suit, bowing the king out of his throne room. "If my lord Fionvar would attend the king?"

Fionvar gave a brief, graceful bow and trailed after the servants toward the king's chamber. A pair of maids arrived from the other direction, bearing food-laden trays, and began to fuss over the table. With a weary sigh, Kattanan loosed the cape from his shoulders and fell into a chair. Setting a goblet at his elbow, the maid curtsied, flashed a smile at Fionvar, and, with her companion, left the pair alone. Fionvar stood by the door, wearing a puzzled frown. The young man opposite shrank back into his chair, sipping from the goblet. "Don't look at me like that," he whispered. "I planned none of this."

The frown deepened. "I know, Your Majesty."

The singer winced. "I'm not a king, please don't address me as one. I'm not even—I don't know what I am."

"To these people you are the king, or will be, once the battles are fought."

"In name only, and not even a name I recognize." He picked at a piece of bread. "My grandmother is the true ruler."

"The duchess knows what she is about; she will do what's best for Lochalyn. I may be willing to put the kingdom in her hands, even if it must be through you."

"And Brianna?" Kattanan looked at him then. "Would you put her in my hands?"

"It is against my conscience to condone your marrying anyone, but the choice is not mine." He crossed his arms.

"I'm not sure it's mine, either. Clearly she has already chosen. The duchess told me she is with child." He watched for some surprise, but Fionvar only gave him a curious look.

"Would you refuse her because of that?"

"I have always wished for children, knowing that I could never have them, and it could ease many doubts if the duchess gave out that the child was mine."

Fionvar snorted. "I don't like building a kingdom on lies, however useful they might be."

"Is that the reason?"

"No lady should have to submit to a marriage of convenience, a marriage that denies her choice and does not even leave her with a proper husband, especially when—" He broke off, and turned back to Kattanan. "I have said too much, Majesty. I am not here to insult you."

"It is hard to see the woman you love offered to another man." Fionvar did start at that. "I think I misunderstand you."

Kattanan took a deep breath, and plunged in. "When the lady was brought in, everyone was surprised by her appearance. She wished that to be my first impression of her." Fionvar's eyes narrowed. "So, she doesn't want to marry me but won't refuse me outright. However, she's wearing a marriage bracelet already— it's under her chemise, so I assume the union is not formal, but I caught a glimpse during court. I believe the band was made from the hair of a violin bow."

"If you saw all this, why ask me to be your chaperone? Perhaps you brought me here to see how long I would suffer your courting my lady?"

"Great Goddess, no! I couldn't deny her in court, so I had to agree to see her. In front of any other witness, she would go on as she was today and only make her family even more upset. I am sure you want to spend more time together." His hands were clasped before him, the strange new voice pleading.

"My loyalty cannot be bought, neither can hers."

"That's not it." He faltered and looked away. "I already have enough enemies here, and outside. I don't want her to hate me, too."

Fionvar looked down at the singer's bowed head. "I don't hate you. All I know of you is that you are willing to live this lie, that you are not who I was led to believe, and that you have been offered the one thing I want more than anything in this world, yet say you will turn it down. I don't understand you, I'm not sure I can trust you, but I do not hate you."

"Thank you for that." Kattanan glanced sidelong up at him. "Are you hungry? I don't feel much like eating."

"I ate on the ride over. Besides"—he nodded toward the window—"the lady is waiting."

Kattanan looked out into the garden, a small patch of hedges and trees between the manor and the forest. On a bench nearly concealed by branches, Brianna sat with a maidservant. She was reading from a small volume, swatting at the maid's hands when she made as if to braid the lady's hair.

"She really isn't like that," Fionvar commented.

"Well, let's go find out." Kattanan straightened his tunic and let Fionvar lead the way out to the garden. As they approached, Brianna shoved the book under the bench and jumped up. She gasped a little, meeting Fionvar's gaze, but quickly folded into an awkward curtsy. The maid rolled her eyes and eagerly left them alone.

"My lady," Kattanan said, bowing his head, "I think my lord Fionvar has some things to say. I will await your leisure." He turned away and crossed to the other side of the little pond. Fionvar took her arm as if to lead her over, then ducked behind a hedge, dropping them both to their knees. He buried his fingers in her hair and kissed her. Brianna pulled back.

"What are you doing? With the king right there!"

"He knows, Brie. He saw the bracelet."

"Oh, no. I thought it strange that he chose you. So we are discovered." She sat back on her heels.

"Discovered, but not revealed." He stroked her cheek and smiled.

"It would better serve his interests to be rid of you. Isn't that why we've been so careful?"

"He said he does not want to make an enemy of you."

She glanced at Kattanan. "One would think I was already against him, from his expression earlier. I've been greeted in many ways—especially in this outfit—but never before with anything so close to terror. Do I look so fearsome as that?"

He laughed. "Almost. If this were our first meeting, I would have refused you myself."

"If this were our first meeting," she murmured in his ear, "we would not be kissing in the bushes discussing my betrothed. Does he really think I could hate him?"

"He thinks I already do, even before he met you."

"You don't, do you?"

Fionvar tilted his head to look at her. "Why the concern?"

"He just seems so sad and lonely."

"You are attracted to him."

"I am drawn to any lost creature in need of comfort," she said, watching the figure of the king. Eyes wide, she turned back to her lover. "Fion! You're jealous! I hardly know him."

"It's just that I can find so many reasons why you should marry him instead of me." He stared down at his tanned, callused hand enfolding hers so pale and smooth.

"Fion, my heart's desire, I love you, and there is no other on earth nor in the stars who could take your place in my life." She kissed his forehead, then his lips.

"Let's run away, right now. I've a horse in the stables, we could—"

"We could leave all our responsibilities and a cause we have both struggled for that is on the verge of fulfillment. I promise you we will find a way to be together. If this king is to be trusted, he may even help us." Brianna stood and shook out her garments. "We shouldn't leave the king waiting."

"Very well, then," Fionvar grumbled, "but not too much comforting."

Kattanan looked up at their approach, then stood. "My lady."

"My lord King," she returned, with a small curtsy, "I fear I have presented myself in a way less than honest. I hope you can forgive me."

"Only if you don't serve me mud pies, my lady."

Brianna shouted with laughter. "You remember!" Fionvar glowered until she squeezed his hand, and explained, "Rhys was my favorite cousin; we used to play together in the palace gardens. I am the older by three years, though, and I admit I abused my position. Perhaps two months before the Usurper, I made mud pies, and convinced him they were good to eat. If I'd known—" She fell silent as Kattanan looked away. "I'm sorry, Your Majesty."

"Please don't call me that," he said with unusual force. "I feel many things, but majestic has never been one of them."

"Well, what, then?"

"'Kattanan.' It's what I'm used to."

"As you wish." Her brow furrowed, and Fionvar again sought her hand. "Shall we walk, or would you rather sit?"

"Oh, no, I have had enough of sitting."

"You did seem . . . uncomfortable." The three headed for a trail into the woods.

"It isn't right. I don't know what to do up there."

"I'm sure it will feel right, someday. Strello Gamel wrote that we each know all we need to, but that the knowledge lies silent until most needed."

"A little training never hurt, though," Fionvar commented. "It's hard for people to put their faith in a leader whose knowledge still lies silent."

"Fion, there's no need for that," Brianna said.

"He's right, my lady. I have no business here, and we are not the only ones who think so." Kattanan sighed.

"Unless you assert yourself as king, you never will. We defer to the duchess because she clearly intends action on behalf her people." Fionvar moved a bit ahead and looked back over his shoulder, meeting Kattanan's gaze until the singer looked away.

"I had no idea you idolized my grandmother," Brianna snapped, stopping in the path.

"At least she takes action when she sees that something needs doing. I respect that." His dark eyes still searched Kattanan. "She is an old woman, though, and I fear what will happen when she dies."

Brianna scowled, taking another step toward him. "Why are you bringing this up now? Kattanan has already had a difficult day, the last thing he needs is you badgering him."

Fionvar leaned over to her, whispering, "All he has to do is tell me to stop. That is the least of his powers as a king." She continued to glare. "Trust me, please."

"Leave it!" Brianna hissed. "There is a time and a place, and now is neither." She turned back to Kattanan with a smile. "My lord is infamous for speaking his mind, with utter disregard for the feelings of others." When he did not respond, she brushed his arm and pointed. "This manor was the refuge of an ancient order of warrior-priestesses—the Sisters of the Sword. There's an old temple this way. Fionvar's sister and some others have revived the order."

Falling in step, Kattanan nodded vaguely. Fionvar brought up the rear, examining the young man intently. Brianna chattered on, and finally brought them to the overgrown ruin. At this, Kattanan took an interest, brushing aside the vines to touch the inscriptions. "Can we go in? Is it safe?"

"Well, I suppose so. The door is over here." The mound rose not much taller than Fionvar, but its foundation looked to be somewhere farther below. Small trees sprouted from the roof, their roots gripping the ancient stone. Squirrels, crying out indignantly, scattered to the treetops. A tangle of leaves encroached on the door from all sides. Brianna grabbed hold and started clearing the path, but Fionvar laid a hand on hers. "I'll do it."

"I am perfectly capable—"

"You are more than capable, but I'm still in my old riding garb."

"As if my dress were so much to look at." She moved back and watched as he pulled the vines away, revealing a low arch. He squinted, then shrugged, and stooped through. A loud crash followed, and the pair outside stuck their heads in to see Fionvar seated on a floor some four feet lower than the outside ground.

"Are you hurt?"

"Only my pride, love." He picked himself up and looked back at the edge he had tumbled over. "Don't worry, it's not as bad as it sounded." He lifted Brianna down beside him and offered a hand to Kattanan, who refused it to scramble in on his own. Kattanan picked his way to the wall and ran his fingers over it. Standing on the altar, Fionvar cleared the roots that cluttered the Strellezza, shedding the afternoon sun on the crumbling inscriptions. While Kattanan frowned over them, Brianna pulled Fionvar into an alcove, whispering, "Where is your head today? He may be an orphaned singer to you, but he is both my king, and my cousin."

"And a pawn to whoever asks it. I try to reserve judgment until I know someone, but I can't respect him as anything but a singer."

"You were as eager as the rest of us to find the rightful king, in spite of the fact I am to marry him; now that we've found him, you can't even be civil."

"Yes, I wanted to find the king, but I didn't expect him to be like this."

"You knew what was done to him, just what did you expect? I thought you were different, that you helped people rather than just throwing them aside when they got hurt. What happened to patience and compassion?"

"Patience? If the duchess has her way, we go to war in less than a month. I know these soldiers; right now they believe in their cause. How long will that last when they see that their king does not believe? That he is scared to wear his own crown? They might be better off with Thorgir; he's a tyrant, but at least he cares!"

"Never say that! Never again! He is a murderer and a blasphemer who should be hanged from the highest tree, then buried in the deepest hole!" Brianna tore away and stumbled into the temple, but he caught her hand and fell to his knees, eyes shining.

"I'm sorry, Brianna." Fionvar stared up at her. "Please don't turn from me. Goddess' Tears, Brie, I am sorry."

"You've been spending too much time with your brother." She shut her eyes, chin tilted toward the ceiling as tears ran down her cheeks.

"I know. There is so much I can't say to him, that when I am with you I want to speak all the words in the world."

She nodded, sniffling.

"I wish I had not said that. I didn't mean to hurt you, and I know that you are right." He fell silent at last, and she squeezed his hand, then jerked away. She ran the few steps to where Kattanan lay still on the ground.

"Holy Mother!" Fionvar touched the singer's wrist, and let out the breath he had been holding. "Just a faint, I think. He hasn't been eating."

"It had better be; they would never forgive you if something happened."

"I wouldn't forgive myself; he may never be a great king, but then again, he may yet rise to the challenge." Fionvar glanced toward the wall Kattanan had been reading and frowned. "Can't make out much of it. 'Now comes the bless-ed—' something I don't recognize—'he who sings with the stars.' "

"Forget it, Fion. Let's get the king back inside." She touched his pale forehead, and Fionvar watched her sidelong.

"Before you feel it necessary to revive him," he muttered. He gathered Kattanan in his arms and rose.

"I hope you don't think I can be wooed away from you by a mere fainting spell. It would require at least a severe concussion."

# Chapter 16

"Get up, they're gone," the wizard urged, still looking anxiously toward the road. She tugged the chain. "I'm the one who nearly drowned, not you."

Jordan groaned. "I had to swim for both of us and haul you up the bank."

She glared down at him, saying finally, "Well, we could do with a fire, or at least a walk. Lying around in the underbrush won't get us any warmer."

Jordan dragged his eyes open and sighed. "True." He regarded the arm's length of chain that tethered them together. "We should look up that friendly blacksmith."

"It was a joke," she said flatly.

"No, a possibility. We have made it this far, Finistrel will provide a way for us."

"You can't possibly believe She cares what happens to a killer like your."

"I have no illusions about my own salvation, but I may yet have a part to play in that of others." He bent to pull up a bouquet of wildflowers. "Camouflage," he said, "take my hand." He flipped the chain over her head, his arm across her back so that their joined hands rested at her hip.

The wizard, nestled against him, muttered, "I suppose this will keep us warmer."

He thrust the flowers into her off hand. "If any one asks, we're betrothed."

"Nice wedding bracelets."

They ducked under the branches to emerge on the road. Jordan kissed her forehead as a wagon drew near, feeling the stiffness that shot through the wizard's body.

"Nice night for it," the driver called.

"Aye," Jordan returned. "The king's guards passed us more than once, though. Do you know anything of that?"

"Someone tried to assassinate the king and escaped. Not to worry, the town's been searched so whoever it was must be long gone."

"Thank the Lady," the wizard said dryly.

"Indeed." The driver bobbed reined on his horse and soon left them behind.

As they approached the town, they crossed a little bridge, and Jordan glanced at the stream below. "This'll likely lead us to the smithy."

"You don't really propose to ask for his assistance."

"I might. Are you always so contentious?"

"I'm a wizard chained to the Liren-sha; should I dance for joy?"

"All I expect is cooperation so that both of us can get out of this intact. If you'd prefer, I can chop off my hand right now and have done with it."

She cocked her head to look up at him. "You didn't suggest my hand."

"I can fight equally poorly with either hand, and I can't guarantee the survival of the patient, in which case you are the one who must live."

"Is King Rhys so important to you?" When he did not answer, she mused, "Or perhaps that you think this self-sacrifice will redeem you in Finistrel's favor."

He snorted. "Nothing I do can outweigh what I have already done."

"How many men have you killed?" she asked, the tone solemn.

"Of ordinary men, I lost count at one hundred. Of wizards, fourteen."

"Would they not have killed you if they'd gotten the chance? I would have."

"It's not really my life they sought, but that of the Liren-sha. How can I hold it against them that they seek to destroy what makes them powerless?"

"That's absurd! Your purpose's to kill wizards, and part of ours to be sure your power does not spread. And you claim to have no grudge against wizards?"

"How can I hold against any man what birth has made him? You were formed with the ability to perform magic, I with the ability to nullify it. I do not spend my time looking for wizards to kill simply because I can do so. Responsible wizards don't look for people to ask them questions simply to take advantage of them."

"So every wizard you've met is irresponsible, and that's why you killed them?"

"Did I say that I killed every wizard I met, or even that all of them would kill me?"

The wizard looked to the path ahead. "What about me? If I hadn't cast the king's voice, would you have killed me?"

"What crime have you committed that would require your death at my hands?"

"I caused King Gerrod's illness; you yourself said I deserved a public execution."

Jordan stopped suddenly. "I wasn't passing judgment on you,

I was giving them a reason not to kill you right then. I know next to nothing about King Gerrod except that he hates his son and intended to force me to stay there against my will. You made a choice to antagonize a king, knowing that the punishment for your choice is death by their law. I may not approve of your choice or their law, but I have no control over either."

"My choice. Yet if my choice had been to kill the prince rather than release him, I doubt you would have stood by quietly."

"If it is in my power to prevent a wrongful death, I will do so."

"Bold words from one who has caused so many."

"Yes," he murmured. "Finistrel forgive me."

"That could be it ahead." She pulled him into motion again as they came up to a house with a broad, three-sided structure off to one side. It harbored a great hearth, with the coals still glowing. Hammers, tongs, and bars of iron decked one wall. The wizard uncoiled herself from Jordan's arm, dropping the flowers. She plucked a chisel from the shelf and was reaching for a hammer when Jordan flung both of them sideways, landing heavily on top. An arrow glanced off the iron and fell to the dirt.

"This would all be so much easier if you'd stay still, my good wizard." A round face, painted by the fire's glow, peered under a table at them.

"Anything for you, Broken Shell," she hissed, scrambling to her knees, but keeping the table between them. "You were always the first to hunt down our own."

"It's been too long. No one can insult me the way you do. Where is it?"

"I burned it."

The other laughed lightly. "A treasure of our kind, and you burned it. Hardly likely, but I'll get it from you the other way." He raised the bow again.

Jordan lunged against the table, shoving Broken Shell off-balance. The shot flew wild, and the bow likewise. Grabbing Nine Stars by the hand, Jordan dashed around the table and drew his sword. "What is this about?"

"Great wrongs that I mean to right, if you will just give me a clear shot." The other man heaved himself up, smirking.

"You will not kill her."

"The Wizard's Bane, protecting a wizard? Legend of legends! I won't leave you chained to the body. Indeed, I'd be delighted to release you before she breathes her last." He slipped a long knife from his boot, but did not raise it.

"Why? What is her crime?" Jordan asked.

"Lying, stealing, seduction under false pretenses—what crime is not hers?"

"Murder, for one," she said, "torture, rape, to name a few of yours."

"In service to the pursuit of knowledge, a virtuous pursuit, if fraught with hardship."

"They were children! We were children."

"You make me out to be a monster," he chided. Facing Jordan, he added, "Sometimes the search for truth is not a bloodless one; no one regrets it more than I."

"There you are wrong!" spat the Wizard of Nine Stars.

"If I had not done what I did, you might have no name, or not one so intriguing. Haven't you wondered, Liren-sha, how she got her name? I admit they died under my care, but she took the nine stars, then she took my property, and I want it back."

"You weren't bright enough to use it when you had it, or my friends would not have died. Give me the sword, I'll kill him myself." Her yellow eyes flamed as she turned to Jordan. "There were ten of us, wards of the Church. He petitioned the king, claiming noble intent, to take us into his home, and we went."

"Oh, you liked it, you liked me," the large man insisted with a smile. "Life on my estate was better than any orphan could wish. And the cause was noble. You see, I had come into possession of a certain religious text and was eager to discover the truth of it."

"Religious? The *A-strel Nym* is a vile heresy!"

"And you read every word," the other snarled.

"You killed nine children trying to make the blood magic work without knowing what would even happen if it did—and you failed! You didn't understand what that power is about. If I

had not absorbed their power, it would have driven me insane!"
Her hand clenched the chisel.

"If I'd only known you were gifted, I'd have done you first."
He caught Jordan's cold gaze, and said, "The power has so many
possibilities: to heal using one's own blood, or to pass on knowledge. Surely you can see the value in that. But there must be a
wound to heal, and I'd done so well on the cuts and scrapes." He
frowned a little.

"You killed these children to find out if you had the power
to heal them"—Jordan raised an eyebrow—"and now, for some
unholy reason, you are holding a grudge against this woman."

"She took the power, don't you see?" Broken Shell swayed a
little, his tone near pleading. "I didn't realize until the last that
she was taking the power, drawing it from them, so she is really
the reason I couldn't heal them."

"I was eight years old, I didn't even know what I was; but I
learned fast."

"Thanks to the book you stole from me!" The knife flashed
forward, swept aside by the longer blade, but not before it had
drunk blood. Jordan's sword hacked the air, answered by a cry,
then by shouts of alarm as two men bearing lanterns rounded
the corner of the house.

"Hold that chisel!" Jordan cried, stooping to pull his companion over his shoulder before plunging into the night. Crashing through brush, Jordan slithered on the muddy bank into the
stream, regained his balance, and ran on, sword still in hand. After
following the water some distance, he staggered to his knees and
splashed under the low bridge. The wizard wriggled from his
shoulder to collapse, breathless, against the stone beside him.
They lay half in water, not daring a sound, as their pursuers
pounded across the bridge, then trudged back again moments
later, grumbling as they receded.

Jordan slid the sword home to its scabbard. "Where are you
hurt?"

"My leg, just a cut though, and I'm sure this water will do it
a world of good." She inched forward. "Sorry," she mumbled.
"You did what you could."

Jordan stared numbly at his hand and did not answer.

"What? What's wrong?" She tucked the chisel through her rope belt, and studied his palm. The thin slash across his hand seeped blood around his trembling fingers. The wizard tore a strip of cloth from her already ragged shift and held it out to him. "Sorry, Bane; I would not really have killed the prince."

The chain clinked as he wrapped his wound. Jordan glanced to their bound wrists. "Perhaps you'd better do the honors."

Her hands searched under the water and came up with a stone. As she held the chisel against the chain, Jordan did his best to steady it. A few strikes with the stone—painfully loud under the arch—and the chain dangled in two, severed a couple of links from his wrist. The wizard set her tools to the bracelet then, and struck through the hinge pin. She wrapped the length of chain about her wrist. "Once I'm far enough from you, I can take care of this on my own; and you're in no condition to hammer."

He nodded. "I'll wait here and let you get ahead."

"You'll be all right, Bane?"

"I've made it this far, and your enemy won't be able to follow as long as I'm in the area. Goddess walk with you."

"And you, Wizard's Bane." She started to move toward the entrance and looked back at him. "I wonder where we would be if you and I were just ordinary people."

"Fare thee well, my lady," he said, then added, in the most ordinary tone he could muster, "My name is Jordan."

"I don't think I've ever been called 'my lady,' at least not in my natural form." Their eyes met, and she murmured, " 'Alswytha' used to be my name, a long time ago."

"Take my best wishes to King Rhys, Alswytha"—Jordan gave a little smile—"whether he wants them or not."

"I'll do that." She vanished out into the night.

ROLF WAS nodding as his relief arrived, but sleep was not to be. A panting Thomas trotted up, and bobbed into a little bow. "His Highness begs your attendance."

"Begs?" The huge man chuckled. "Aye, lad, I'm coming." He unfastened his helmet as he walked, slinging his shield over his back, where it beat the rhythm of his steps.

They chatted about the boy's studies until they reached the library. Thomas gripped the handle of the massive door, but Rolf caught it over his head and swung it open easily. When their eyes adjusted to the dim light, they worked their way back to the prince's desk. Several large maps spread haphazardly over the desk and bench, with Wolfram yawning as he bent over one, following a line with his finger.

"Good morrow, Your Highness. I trust you had a productive night."

Wolfram flashed him a brief smile. "I think I solved the Lirensha's riddle."

" 'There is no map' he said, Highness, so why all these maps?"

"Look here," the prince said, pointing to a parchment. "Bernholt, right? And this"—he plucked another from the pile—"is Lochalyn; this river forms the border."

"Aye, Highness, nice and wide." Rolf leaned on the desk to peer at the maps, while Thomas lifted his chin to look on.

Wolfram traced it with his finger to a point near Gamel's Grove where the river bent its course away from the high ground toward the ocean. "If this ran straight, we'd have some extra land in the highlands on the other side."

"But it doesn't, Highness."

"On the Lochalyn map, the same river, but the bend is in the opposite direction."

"None of these maps are entirely accurate, Highness, even the ones where they get wizards to fly overhead."

"The people who made these particular maps were aided by the same wizard." He pointed out the scribes' signs in the corner. "So the same wizard looked at the same river and saw two different things."

Rolf yawned himself, and shrugged. "A line in the wrong direction, Highness. It's been a long night, Highness, if ye could be more plain?"

Wolfram shuffled out the parchment he had been working

on, a very thin, translucent skin. It bore only a single crooked line, with the capitals marked on either side. Again he traced it, but this line split into two and rejoined a short distance down. "This is what happens when these two borders are brought together. The lines are very accurate, to a point, here. Then this split occurs, and they come back together again. An island, Rolf, one that does not exist on any map."

"What makes you believe it exists at all? Surely someone would have noticed before now; meaning no disrespect, Your Highness."

"Why look at all? If I walk the Bernholt side of the river, I see the bend exactly as drawn here, assuming this other branch is concealed, somehow. Someone on the Lochalyn side would see it just as it is drawn on that map."

"What about riverboats?"

"A man on a river doesn't use the maps at all, he just follows the river and gets out once he reaches his destination. I'm not saying something like this would be easy to do, but all it takes are a few itinerant cartographers selling new maps to replace the old."

"A mapmakers' conspiracy, Highness?" Rolf raised his shaggy eyebrows.

"Just so." Wolfram grinned, despite the dark circles under his eyes and the edge of a white bandage emerging from his collar. "Wider than that, I shouldn't wonder. Once my father is well enough to take over at court, I'll go off quietly and investigate."

"Not alone, Highness."

"No, Rolf, of course not. I don't think you would stay behind even if I ordered it."

"Not after the past few days, I wouldn't. They were spotted last night downriver a piece, but men and dogs together couldn't find them, Your Highness. They got tools from a blacksmith and had some sort of scuffle. By now, they're well on their way."

"For Jordan, I'm glad; as to the wizard"—Wolfram sighed—"there are too many questions left unanswered, but chances are they never will be. Will you join me to break the fast? I have an early court today."

"Far be it from me to advise the prince," Rolf began gruffly, "but perhaps Yer Highness could find time for a little sleep before the Goddess Walks again, eh?"

"I wish I could, Rolf." Wolfram rolled up his river tracing, leaving the others for the librarian to reorganize. "Even when I sleep, I feel as if I've lain awake all night."

Before the other could answer, boots tramped outside, and they went to the door to find an escort of soldiers awaiting them. "Your Highness," the prince's squire began with a bow, "I trust you are ready to greet your supplicants."

Wolfram frowned. "I haven't eaten, and I need to change. I'll need some time."

"His Royal Majesty has been reviewing the records from the time of his illness, and he feels rescheduling may be in order, Your Highness."

"Right now?"

The squire stared straight ahead as the guards shifted behind him.

"Very well." Wolfram addressed the honor guard. "Whichever of you has seniority may be dismissed so this man may attend me at court."

They looked at Rolf as if he had turned blue, and the squire's frown deepened. "He's not attired for royal court, Your Highness."

"Neither am I. Will you wait while we prepare ourselves?" He drew himself up and straightened his rumpled tunic.

The squire made a sign, and one of the guards saluted and left, making a place for Rolf at the front of the pairings. He replaced his helm and adjusted his shield, then flicked a glance to the man beside him. "Aelfwin, ye've got the wrong shield," he whispered. "That's the king's guard arms, not the prince's."

The other looked at him sharply. "Mind us and watch yer own manners, Rolf." They looked ahead again as the squire took the lead and called them to order. Wolfram trailed along, smoothing his garments as best he could, trying to ignore Thomas's anxious glances. "Just a schedule change, Tom, not to worry." He tried a shaky smile, then turned his attention to the stairs as they descended to the Great Hall. Here, rather than turn aside for the smaller audience chamber, they proceeded in and split apart to let the prince pass. Only the king's large throne sat the dais, empty, and Wolfram turned back with a weak smile to the assembled people. "Someone has forgotten my chair. Thomas, can you find me something to sit on?"

The boy slipped off to the side and disappeared behind the line of guards. Another lad came up with a stool. "All I could find, Highness," the boy murmured, not looking up.

"This will do for now. Send Thomas back, would you?" He moved the stool to his accustomed position and nodded to the herald to call in the first business. A familiar merchant approached, bowing low, and knelt before the prince. "Greetings! Have you completed the task I asked?"

"I have, Highness." The man unrolled a parchment and offered it up. "This is the map of the tunnels we have found thus far. Some do not lead immediately to the river, as you can see, and these are still being explored, but have little relevance for our purposes. Others come so far as the guest wing." The man backed off a little, still beaming. "I am pleased to be able to deliver the map to Your Highness with my own hands."

Wolfram perused it. "When will the construction be finished?"

"Ah, the best part. We have a small structure already erected, and plans for a larger dock alongside. Several boats are tied there awaiting your pleasure, Your Highness. It would be most gracious if you could attend a ceremony to open the dock, perhaps when the first load of goods is delivered here?"

"An excellent suggestion. I shall confer with my clerks to find a good time." The merchant bowed out of court, accompanied by a few servants of his own. Wolfram looked to the herald, "The next business?"

"Is brought by me," a bold voice announced from behind.

Astonished, the prince sprang to his feet and bowed low. A light crossed his features and a smile twitched the corners of his mouth as he looked up the steps at his father. "Welcome, Sire. I am glad to see you about again."

The king, tall and grave in royal velvets, stared back at his son.

The state crown gleamed on his head, and another gleam was in his eyes. Murmurs and rustling filled the room as all the attendants rose and bowed to their king. Gerrod, leaning on a cane, remarked, "You did not use my throne."

"Of course not, Father. Allow me to formally return to you your court."

"So generous of you," the king boomed. "Despite your efforts, I am able, and I am taking my court along with my crown."

Wolfram's jaw dropped as he froze in his father's glare.

"The very picture of astonishment. Have you studied playacting, then, as well?" He tore his gaze from the prince and regarded the lords and ladies who still hovered awkwardly without taking their seats. "Hear you this: that this man"—he thrust a sharp finger at Wolfram—"has conspired with wizards to cause his king illness; that, when it seemed this plot might be revealed, he allowed his king to be healed to make himself out as a savior despite the fact that the wizard was in attendance to cause relapse; that he further conspired to allow the escape of these accomplices by contriving to be taken hostage; that he dared subsequently accuse an earl loyal to our realm of conspiracy against us; that when he held power, he did all he could to undermine his king's authority and supplant it with his own. There is a name for such a beast as this!" The king raised his arm, and the answer was called out by the guards who held every entry, "A traitor, Sire!" Gerrod whirled back to face down his son.

Still agape, the prince stumbled back the few steps to the floor, shaking his head. "Father, no," he gasped, "this is not true!"

"I do not hear the voice of traitors. From this day forth, I have no son, nor ever have. This creature shall be termed the Traitor!" King Gerrod thundered, raising his arm again. Wolfram flinched away, as noise echoed from the galleries. Archers bearing the king's device appeared on all sides.

"Father!" he cried again, but the king's face was raised to the men above. "A cask of gold to him who lands the first arrow, and two for the shot that kills!" With a whirl of velvet, the king flung himself into his throne, a fierce grin upon his face.

The first arrows, hastily aimed, skittered around Wolfram as he spun on his heel, running for the great doors. He screamed, and his body slammed against the marble floor, pain streaking from his shoulder. A cheer came from the archers. Shrieks and a bellow sounded behind him as another point gashed his thigh.

A metal-clad arm swooped from the air and hauled him up. Arrows pinged from an upraised shield. The arm roughly clutched him to a hard breast, and the flight began again head-long. Pain-hazed eyes could barely make out the floor, and the legs of soldiers arrayed across the entrance, sword tips hovering.

Rolf did not slow down. Bellowing he shifted the shield before them and smashed through the ranks, barreling into the door beyond. It burst open, and the man stumbled into the light, clinging tight to his precious burden.

"Guest quarters," Wolfram mumbled, struggling to get his feet under him. "The right, second—" His thin voice failed, but Rolf flung aside his shield, gathering the prince in both arms, and crashed his shoulder through that door as well, finding another courtyard and a stair.

"Which way?" he howled.

"Down," came the weak reply, and down they went, streaking across landings and careering around corners, the guard's legs pounding. At his shouts, maids leapt aside, servants pressed themselves to the walls until there was no one to warn, and the passages grew dank, echoing their passing to the guards in noisy pursuit. Rolf reached a cavern, open to the river, and looked wildly around. Stumbling across, he knocked a workman from the new dock. He laid the prince in the bottom of the nearest boat, then sprang aboard himself, hacking all the moorings he could reach, and lastly, their own. The first archer reached the dock as the renegades, sped into open water, escorted by the empty boats

Rolf, kneeling over Wolfram's still form, paid no heed to the arrows splashing behind. The shaft that held his eyes was embedded in the prince's left shoulder, just at the base of his neck. Tearing off his gauntlet, he clamped a hand against the flesh, cursing the blood that would not stop. He jerked off his helmet and flung it into the bow of the boat. "Bury you, Gerrod!" Rolf screamed into the wind. "Bury you in stone!"

# Chapter 17

WHEN THE rap at the door grew more insistent, Kattanan pushed aside his tray with a sigh. "Who is it?"

"Just me," called Brianna's voice. "May I come in?"

"Please." He pulled his warm robe a little closer, and sipped at his goblet.

The lady curtsied as she entered along with a maid. "I'm glad you're eating."

He looked down. "I just wasn't feeling well that day."

"Grandmother has said you may come to court today, if you are up to it."

"It will be a relief to be let out of my room, even for that." He rose and went to the wardrobe for some kingly attire.

"We don't want to lose our king so soon after finding him."

"I fainted, that's all." Kattanan spent a long moment inspecting his clothes. "Have you just come to check on me?"

"Not at all. The lord Fionvar will be pleased to see you on your feet."

Kattanan snorted. "I'm not so sure I will be pleased to see him."

Brianna walked up beside him, and murmured, "He is a good man, and he does want you to succeed. He just . . ."

"He just doesn't think I will, and I agree."

She shot him a worried look and moved away. "He rode in

this morning, Your Majesty, with tidings from his brother, I hear. He'll be reporting at court."

Dropping the clothes on his bed, Kattanan nodded. "I don't know why we hold court every day only to hear there is no new business."

Brianna commented, "I suppose it is to maintain the air of a normal kingdom."

"What about any of this shall I consider 'normal'?"

"You'll get used to it; besides, the waiting will be over soon."

"Then we shall leave what I'm supposed to get used to and go into battle. That is not something I look forward to."

"But you have not been anticipating that day for nearly fourteen years." She slipped out the door to let him dress. A moment later, garbed in his royal colors, Kattanan followed. The duchess stood there, as expected, along with his guard. She smiled. "The captain of the guard has sent word that he will be late, but bringing something worth our wait. I am glad that Your Majesty is looking well. Will you wear your crown today?"

"I think not," he replied evenly, falling in behind her.

"Also, we have had no contact with the Bernholt royal court since the wizard returned. I believe they are preventing messages leaving the palace." At Kattanan's start, she gestured for silence as they were bowed into the audience hall. Kattanan settled on the throne, watching the gathering rise from its collective bow and sit.

"Fionvar yfSonya duNormand," a herald intoned, stepping back.

Fionvar bowed and came to kneel not far from the throne. "Your Majesty, I bring greetings from my brother, Earl Orie of Gamel's Grove, and his well wishes to all assembled here. He sends word that his lady seems most favorable, and he expects to be wed erelong." His eyes met Kattanan's as the young man flinched.

The duchess smiled and nodded. "We are pleased by these tidings, and to have you return so soon."

"I believe the earl would like time alone with the lady in question, Your Majesty. He felt I might better serve here, and gave me leave to remain a fortnight or more, if you judge it necessary." His gaze did not leave Kattanan.

"That is well, my lord," the duchess responded. "His Majesty may have need of you." She made a gesture of dismissal. He rose and took a seat near the front.

The herald again came forward, but a commotion outside forestalled any announcement. The large doors flew wide, and the guard captain strode in, grinning and stamping mud from his boots. "Excellency, Your Majesty, the business I have must take precedence."

"What is it?" the duchess asked, her tone imperious.

His grin widened. "My men apprehended a certain prisoner last night and have been occupied with interrogation. While the prisoner has little information of value to us, the man himself is worth much, and his story should amuse you."

"I have rarely heard you so eloquent, Captain," the duchess said sharply, "but why did you not inform us that you were holding this captive, if he is worth so much to us?"

"It was important that we gain what knowledge we could without"—he paused, glancing at Kattanan—"interference. I give you the face of the enemy."

At this, two guards hauled forward a battered figure, his arms bound outstretched to a staff, his feet fumbling against the tile. Just past the last row of onlookers, the soldiers jerked the staff down, sending their prisoner to his knees. "With or without our help, he's not long for this world, though by his own account there is now a price on his head." One of soldiers pulled the captive's head back to reveal his bruised face.

"Get to the point," the duchess said. "You are upsetting the king."

"Please, Your Majesty," said the prisoner, gulping at the air, "my companion—" He cried out as the guard cuffed him and raised a hand to repeat the blow.

"No!" Already tearing the heavy cloak from his shoulders, Kattanan sprinted the few yards that separated them and fell to his knees. "Oh, Great Goddess, no," he whispered, touching his friend's forehead with a gentle hand.

"I bring you Wolfram yfNerice duGerrod, former crown prince of Bernholt," the captain finished, "the son of our enemy, betrothed to the Usurper's daughter."

"Your Majesty, what are you doing?" The duchess rose.

Heedless of the consternation behind him, Kattanan hacked at the prince's bonds with his little dagger. "Breathe, Your Highness, please." He loosed one twisted arm and turned to the other, but the captain caught his wrist.

"This man is a foe to all we hold dear, what we have done—"

"What you have done is torture the kindest man I know! Unhand me."

"I would advise you to obey your king, Captain," a new voice snapped. Fionvar glared down at the older man. "You have no right to hold him against his will."

Kattanan twisted his wrist free and set back to his task with grim features.

Clearing her throat, the duchess placed herself between the two men, their eyes locked on each other. "My lord Fionvar makes an excellent point, Captain. Further, you had no right to keep this from us—from the king."

The captain started. "You can't mean to let him release this man, Excellency!"

She lowered her voice with a threatening glance. "I cannot allow anyone to undermine the king's authority—nor my own—in so flagrant a manner." Turning from him, she raised her voice for all to hear. "While it is commendable that this prisoner has been apprehended, the king clearly finds the manner of his treatment deplorable, as do I. Our guard captain has neglected his duty to the king and is hereby dismissed. Fionvar DuNormand is named to replace him."

"What!" cried Fionvar and the captain together. They shared a stunned glance, then Fionvar whirled to face the guards. "Every man of you who had a part in this is confined to the barracks. The prisoner mentioned a companion, where is he?"

The soldier began, "We were under orders, sir—"

"Explanations later; find the man, bring him here. You are dismissed."

"Help me," Kattanan sobbed, cradling Wolfram's head in his lap. Fionvar was beside him then. "Tell me how, Your Majesty."

"There's an arrow—" He pointed out the broken shaft with trembling hands. "Oh, Finistrel, I don't know," he whispered through the tears.

Laying a hand on the fallen man's chest, Fionvar turned quick eyes to Kattanan. "I'll fetch the surgeons myself, if need be. Let's get him to someplace more private."

Kattanan nodded. "My chamber."

"Out of the question, Sire," the duchess put in from above, but they did not turn.

"Close and large enough to work in," Fionvar said. He climbed to his feet, calling over the king's personal guard. "We are moving this man to His Majesty's chamber; you two, get on the other side. You, fetch the surgeons." The new captain touched his king's shoulder. "We can lift him, will you clear the way, Your Majesty?"

"Yes," Kattanan murmured, letting Fionvar take his place. With bloody hands, he held the door to the corridor and shoved open that of his own bedchamber, leaving the duchess to deal with the rumbling crowd. A pair of surgeons hurried in shortly after, calling for hot water and plenty of rags. Kattanan retreated numbly from the new frenzy; he pressed the back of his hand to his lips, but could not hold back the sobs. Now and then as they cut away the remnants of the prince's tunic, the healers drew back, revealing his battered body. Maids arrived with cloth and basins. Fionvar returned moments later, with Brianna close behind. When she saw the scene, she gave him a horrified look.

"My lady, the king has need of comfort," Fionvar said. "As his intended, you may do better than I." But his eyes spoke all the worry that his voice could not.

She nodded once and crossed to Kattanan. "Your Majesty," she whispered, ready with some words of peace. When he turned his anguished face to her, though, she slipped her arms about him and held him tight. Brianna took him to the little bench by the window, stroking his hair. The sobbing subsided after a time, and Fionvar knelt beside him, offering a basin of water. "If Your Majesty would care to wash his hands."

"Thank you," Kattanan said hoarsely, "for the throne room."

Brianna, too, rinsed her hands. "What has happened?"

"The king asked for help with his friend," said Fionvar. "I was just named captain of the guard because my predecessor failed to inform the king that he had been keeping a prisoner, who turned out to be the prince of Bernholt."

"That's him?" she gasped, looking toward the bed.

Fionvar nodded. "Apparently, the prince was disowned by King Gerrod, shot at by the royal archers, and escaped with one of his guards. He was accused of treason in the matter of the king's illness. They were captured near the river bend last evening."

"He hated Wolfram," Kattanan murmured. "King Gerrod did, I mean."

Fionvar went on, "The other prisoner is a huge man, as tall as the Liren-sha—"

"Oh, no." Kattanan groaned.

"He wasn't harmed," Fionvar quickly assured him. "When they threatened the prince, the other fellow dropped his weapons."

All heads turned as the Wizard of Nine Stars entered, transforming as she moved, walking straight to the surgeons. "I heard there was an arrow still in the wound."

"And likely to remain so," the surgeon retorted, wiping the blood from his fingers. "See for yourself; it has to come out, but I can't do anything with it."

She slipped past him and inspected the broken shaft. "I may be able to help."

"Maybe I should wake him up and see if he'll ask you the question."

Giving the man a black look, the wizard said distinctly, "It cannot stay in, you can't remove it without causing more damage, correct? If you are ready to deal with the wound, I can have the arrow out."

"You can't work on his flesh without his knowledge."

"Have I said anything about his flesh?" The wizard covered the arrow shaft with one palm. "I have been talking about the arrow."

"This man is our patient!" protested the surgeon, grabbing her arm.

"This man is badly wounded, and I can help him. Will you let me try?"

Throwing up his hands, he backed off a few paces.

"If the Liren-sha arrives, don't let him in the building for at least half an hour." Staring down at the back of her hand, the wizard began to chant; strange, indistinct words rose up around her as if in a cloud. Her voice took on a coaxing tone and she shifted her hand to grasp the shaft. The wizard raised her arm, lifting the arrow as if from a pool of water, yet leaving the flesh intact. She rose and backed away, the arrow in her hand. With the other hand, she waved the surgeons back to their patient. Turning, she flung the arrow into the fire with a flick of her wrist. She took a few deep breaths, then turned back to the small company. "Forgive me again, Your Majesty. I entered your chamber unbidden and performed magic here. I hope you can see that it was necessary."

Kattanan frowned at her, glanced toward the prince. "He may yet die, though."

"He may, but not from an arrow working toward the heart. There is something else, Majesty, which I would have said in court. My apprentice reports that a royal messenger came to Gamel's Grove to summon the princess to the capital, as the royal heir."

Shutting his eyes, Kattanan said, "How did you remove the arrow?"

"In essence, I convinced it that it was a weak and hollow thing, and so thin that flesh and bone could pass right through it. I had to burn it before it found out I was lying." She gave him a little smile, a smaller curtsy, and left.

"I don't know that I like working with wizards," Fionvar observed.

Brianna shrugged. "So long as you don't expose yourself, they are just like any other mercenaries, eager to help if the price is good. I've grown accustomed to it; our grandmother has had several wizards in her employ since the Betrayal. Some of them are pleasant enough."

"What about this one?"

Brianna cocked her head. "Well, she appears cold, arrogant, I guess, but I have never seen her do anything to harm another."

"She is an illusionist, she may take another form when she is feeling aggressive," Fionvar observed. "And she is responsible for Gerrod's illness, and Asenith's—condition." The pair shared a smirk.

Kattanan looked at them, confused. "My cousin Asenith? What about her?"

"Boils," Brianna said. "Big, oozing, awful boils. No woman would wish to meet her betrothed like that. It was another way to keep the Usurper occupied." She glanced back toward the bed. "I don't suppose the boils will serve much purpose anymore."

"Where is the prince? What have you done with him?" A huge man, shaking off two guards, barreled into the room, where more guards surrounded him.

"Your Majesty, I'm sorry, we couldn't—"

"I'll give your king a piece of my mind!" The man raised his bound hands.

"Rolf!" Kattanan sprang up.

Fionvar rose, searching a loop of keys. "I'm sorry, Captain," the guard began, but Rolf's joined fists slammed into Fionvar's temple, sending him sprawling across the floor.

"Curse you in the name of the Goddess and the Mount!" Rolf cried, pushing the guard aside, then Kattanan caught his arm.

"Rolf, wait, he's not responsible. Rolf!"

Rolf stared at him, narrowing his eyes. "Ye look like him, but the voice—"

"I know. Part of a very long story. Can somebody find the keys?"

"Don't do that, Your Majesty, he's dangerous," the guard warned, sword drawn.

"Fionvar, staggered to his feet. One hand gave over the key ring, while the other was clamped to his forehead. Fionvar swayed to a chair and worked at catching his breath.

Rolf stared down at Kattanan, furrowing his brow. "'Your Majesty'?" he echoed.

"Part of the same story. Have they hurt you?"

Rolf shook his head. "They took the prince and left me chained to a tree," he snapped, glowering down at Fionvar. "Where is His Highness?"

Kattanan gestured toward the bed. "The surgeons are doing what they can."

"If you are the king here, then, by the Goddess, how could you let them?"

"I didn't know until a little while ago. The former captain didn't tell us. I'm sorry, Rolf. I don't know if he'll live." He tried to control the returning sobs.

Rolf set a huge hand on Kattanan's shoulder. "The fault belongs to them as hurt him, and to King Gerrod, may a mountain cover his grave."

"Can we have some room to do our job?" the surgeon demanded.

Fionvar rose unsteadily to his feet again, and Brianna frowned but went to Kattanan. "Shall we wait in the temple, Your Majesty?"

Rolf, leaning to peer between the busy surgeons, followed Kattanan into the hall.

Still fingering the bruise on his forehead, Fionvar sketched a bow. "If it please Your Majesty, I will go have that discussion with those responsible."

"Yes," said Kattanan. "Will you report to me when you are ready?"

"As you wish, Majesty."

Brianna gazed after him as well as the trio began down the hall. A tall archway opened into a small but well-appointed temple, and they settled onto a padded bench with Kattanan in the middle. They looked toward the sky for several minutes, then

Rolf asked gently, "Is this what you would not tell me, back at my tower?"

"I didn't even know about all of this. Well, I knew I had been a prince," Kattanan began, "but until they brought me here, it didn't occur to me that I was heir to anything. I mean, being the way I am." He studied the floor tiles, then his voice sank to a whisper, and the others drew closer as he told them about the scene in the garden, on his last day as a prince. "After—they took me to a monastery, and I learned to sing. The monks let a rich merchant take me away; Jordan, too. We traveled, traded for favors. Then Jordan left me, and I went alone for a while until I came to Bernholt." He trailed off, and Brianna picked up the tale, describing the plans for the king's return and her own role in that future.

As she finished, a surgeon, bowing and clearing his throat, approached the king. "Your Majesty, please forgive the interruption."

"How is he?"

"We have done what we can, Your Majesty. That arrow was the most serious, although the beating was severe. I really can't say what will happen."

Kattanan nodded, eyes shut against renewed tears.

"I have given him something to help him sleep," the man went on, then added, "I can do the same for your, if you would like, Your Majesty."

"Not right now," he answered faintly. "Can I sit with him?"

"I would not advise more than one visitor at the moment." He shot a look to Rolf, who glowered back. "And he needs as much rest as possible."

"I understand," Kattanan replied, but he was already on his way.

Rolf and Brianna followed him as far as the door, then she looked up at the towering guard. "You must be hungry. I'll take you to the kitchens."

"Fine," he growled, "but I'll bring my lunch back here."

Inside his room, with the curtains drawn and only one candle lit by the bed, Kattanan studied the prince's face. The prince's breathing had steadied, though, and the pain seemed to have fled his features. Kattanan pulled his chair close, flashing back for a moment to the long day he had spent in the same bed, with Jordan leaning over him. At least this man could awaken to the company of a true friend. The thought brought something else to mind, and he crossed for a moment to lean out the door and whisper to the guards. A little while later, there was a soft knock, and the wizard entered.

"What is your will, Your Majesty?"

"Can you take this voice away, just for a while?"

"I can, but the duchess—"

"Bury the duchess," Kattanan hissed forcefully.

She examined him in the dim light. "I will do this for you, Majesty. Be careful that you do not speak too freely, then." Her hands passed through the air before him, and hovered gently at his forehead for a moment, then fell. "I'll come back at dawn, unless you summon me sooner."

"Thank you," he said softly, returning to his place as she left. He settled there, resting one hand on Wolfram's, and began to sing, as quietly as he could. He fell silent when the duchess came herself, demanding entry.

"The captain ordered, on behalf of the king, that no one enter this room without express permission from himself and the king."

"Your captain! I may have acted rashly in giving him command. Remove yourselves!"

Kattanan fetched a scrap of parchment and a quill, scratching out a brief message, and slipped it under the door. She snorted at his words. "We certainly will be discussing this later!" the duchess said to the closed door. "I will find your captain and discuss it with him first, and I do not appreciate having an enemy soldier asleep in our hall."

"No one," Rolf said, "not even yer king, will budge me from here."

"We'll discuss that also! And you men should not assume you can hide behind your orders. I will—Captain," she snapped, with a swirl of skirts as she turned to face a newcomer. "Good of you to join us. I was under the impression that your loyalty was above reproach."

"Your Excellency," Fionvar's tired voice replied, "my loyalty remains with the true crown of Lochalyn."

She demanded, "Explain why that crown's most dedicated servant is barred from interview with the king and from examination of an enemy of that crown."

"I believe that king has just had the most terrible reunion one can imagine with a friend. I presumed, perhaps wrongly, that he would wish some time to . . . regain his composure in private. This room is still the king's quarters, after all." Fionvar's voice gained a calm strength, without losing its usual even tone. "If I have misjudged the king's wishes in this, I trust he will let me know, and I hope he will accept my sincerest apology." He paused for a moment, and, when there was no response from the room, went on. "The other occupant of this room, regardless of his birth or circumstances, is recovering from serious wounds, and his doctors prefer that nobody disturb him until tomorrow. That probably extends to discussions in the hall as well. Perhaps we should continue the explanations elsewhere, Your Excellency?"

"My lord Fionvar," the duchess began coldly, "I have always appreciated your candor and your habit of speaking from your conscience; however, I never expected that you would so abuse my appreciation and generosity in this manner. You may recall that the last captain of the guard lost his position precisely because he failed to report to me in an appropriate fashion."

"It was first necessary to see to my command, Your Excellency— to appease certain resentments that the former captain likewise failed to report. Things like desertions, bad rations, and worse punishments."

The duchess turned from him to one of the guards. "Is this true?" When no response was forthcoming, she said, "I will not hold your words against you."

"And the captain, Your Excellency? Would you hold it against him?" The man's voice was hesitant.

"Then I take it he is telling me the truth."

"Aye, Your Excellency, and more. Forty-three bunks empty and the captain won't have us change quarters. The roof of my barrack leaks as if it weren't there, but he says it's not our job to fix it, then he won't find whose job it is. I've got five mates in the infirmary sick from bad meat the cooks wanted thrown out, but he said we'd get no other. I'd've been gone myself, today, if he were still captain—"The guard broke off.

"And you are so convinced things will be different now."

The other guard, an older man, spoke up. "I just came off roof-repair duty, Excellency."

"I see." She paced up the hall a bit, then back. "I have some other business to attend to, but I will be here immediately after Morning Prayer, and I will be admitted. My lord Captain will do me the favor of meeting me here."

"I am at your service, Excellency."

"I am not yet convinced, but I will think on what you have told me." She strode, not too quickly, back down the hall.

"Great Goddess, Fion!" the first guard exploded. "Now's not the time to be rocking the boat."

"You helped. Besides, the duchess will consider what has been said, and I think she will pay a bit more attention now."

"Either that or she'll have your head."

"Then I'll be careful not to lose it anywhere."

"Don't you think it would've been wise to wait at least until morning?"

"And how would I have ever gotten her away from this door? If His Majesty comes out, tell him I am ready to report at his leisure. Otherwise, I'll be here in the morning."

Kattanan returned to his prayers in peace, adding a word of thanks for his friends.

# Chapter 18

FROM HER post by the ballroom door, Faedre watched Orie and Melisande perform a last design, bowing to each other as the music ended. Melisande, young and lovely, was flushed with the dancing, and her partner bowed over her hand, lingering a long while in the kiss. He straightened again, his eyes alight as he looked upon her. "That will be the last for a while, I fear," he murmured.

Melisande clung to his hands. "I really ought to finish my packing." She gazed up at him as if he were the only man who ever lived. He brushed another kiss upon her cheek and bid her go. Faedre burned, but held her tongue, easing into the shadows at the princess passed by. She stepped out as the earl drew nearer, dipping into her lowest courtesy. "My good lord, might I have a word?"

Orie glanced down at her coolly, not even a hint of a smile at the pleasures her body should suggest. "Not now, my lady. I have too much on my mind." In a few strides he was gone, his steps firm—leaving her behind.

Anger suffused her, that his head could be muddled by a trivial creature like his child bride. In his face, his hands, his every movement, Faedre saw the truth: she herself would never be queen. She knotted two fists in her gown and pounded up the stairs.

"Oh!" Laura cried out, as she and Faedre nearly collided. "Are you well, my lady?"

Faedre stopped short. "This place has rats," she snapped. Glancing down at the tray the maid was carrying, she caught her breath and smiled. "This is for the princess?"

"Yes, my lady. She is quite in a state over the summons, and the packing. This should help her to settle for the night."

"I shall take it to her." Smiling, she took the tray, and watched until the maid had gone to her room. Rather than go to Melisande, Faedre went first into her own chamber and quickly added a few things to the tray, including a splash of dark liquid to the mulled wine she bore. She smoothed her hair and gown and carried the drink in to her mistress.

Melisande, hair braided for sleep, sat curled in a chair in front of the fireplace. Around her were stacked the chests of her belongings, ready for the journey. "Oh, Faedre, I'm so glad you're here." She yawned broadly and smiled.

"I brought you wine, plus a little something to help you sleep." The lady's face glowed red in the firelight, her eyes flickering as she raised the goblet to the princess.

"Thank you." Melisande took a long drink, then frowned into her cup. "It's a little bitter," she said, but she did not set it down.

"Take another sip, you'll get used to it." Faedre lifted a small bundle from the tray and unwrapped it. The icon stood a mere four inches tall, but was studded with jewels framing the faces of the two figures. "Ayel and Jonsha, come to me now," she murmured, kissing each figure before placing the statue on the mantel.

Melisande's unfocused gaze wandered, but she sat perfectly still, the goblet lowered to her lap.

"No doubt you feel better already, little queen. Pity you cannot talk to me. Pity that I cannot give you the dose I'd like." She tilted Melisande's chin to stare down into her face. The other hand lifted a slim dagger from the tray. Smiling again, Faedre reached both hands around Melisande's head, fingering the braid which hung down long and thick. Well-honed steel hacked through the hair in quick strokes. Faedre stepped back, dangling the braid from her hand. "May no child of his ever bring you joy. May you bleed in getting them, bleed in birthing them, bleed in raising them, sorrow in losing them. Ayel and Jonsha hear my words. Finistrel, feel my deeds and weep!" She flung the braid to the fire's heart, where it curled as it burned, reeking of curses and the death of dreams.

The moon had gone from the sky by the time she led her mount by stealthy routes to the riverside. Far from any guard, she mounted and urged the horse across a wide ford not far from the island. Faedre grimaced at the soaked hem of her riding garb, but pressed on into the woods, cursing the branches that slapped at her. It seemed an age before she reached the old road, winding up into the mountains. She had not gone far when her horse whinnied into the night, and was answered. "Hush, foul beast!" she hissed at it, trying to pull the animal back into the wood.

"Who's there?" a voice called as the other rider came into view.

"A mere lady who means no harm. Are you a king's man?"

"Which king, my lady?" the other said, easily halting his mount alongside hers. He looked her up and down, and grinned.

Faedre glanced away demurely, letting her cloak fall a bit open. "I am riding to Lochdale, my lord, in hopes I may seek favor with the court."

"I am going there myself, on important business. You should not be riding alone." He frowned a moment. "I've seen you in King Gerrod's court, though, have I not?"

Her glance grew a bit more wary. "I have been there."

"Why would a lady be leaving the comforts of the castle? Running from someone? A husband, perhaps?" His eyes focused upon the low-cut bodice she had revealed.

She smiled a bit. "You are a very perceptive man."

The other grinned at her. "Allow me to protect you on your journey, my lady."

"You must call me Faedre." She held out a hand to him.

He kissed her hand and held it, still grinning. "Most people call me 'Sir,' but Montgomery is my name."

"We are well met, Montgomery."

"We are indeed."

◌◈◌

KATTANAN AWOKE to a touch on his cheek. He raised his head from the blankets, and looked into Wolfram's eyes. "You sang the whole night," the prince breathed.

"As long as I could," the singer whispered.

"I thought perhaps I was dead, or that I dreamed you."

"I am here, Highness."

"'Highness,'" Wolfram repeated. "Not anymore. You must be a dream, then," he went on, shutting his eyes, then spoke carefully, "You are with my sister, the crown princess. No, someone told me that you left her."

"I did not want to, but I couldn't stay."

"He thought you might be in danger. Are you all right?"

Kattanan gave a curious smile. "I am well."

"Rolf?" Worry creased his face.

"Is in the hall, making sure that you are taken care of."

"The king here looks like you, I think."

Before Kattanan could reply to this, there was a soft knock. "Your Majesty?" the wizard's voice inquired.

"I won't go far," he told his friend as he rose. He let the wizard in, and asked her to replace the new voice. "Tell Rolf that Wolfram is awake, and I'll let him in shortly."

"As you wish, Majesty."

Kattanan shut the door.

"Majesty." Wolfram sighed. "The priestess was right about that, too."

"Yes. Someone is coming to see me soon, so I have to leave you."

"A king's work is never done," Wolfram said. "I'm glad I won't have to do it."

Kattanan pulled on a fresh tunic. "Goddess stay with you. Rest well."

"I am so far in your debt that I must live forever to repay you."

Kattanan set his hand on the door handle, and took a deep breath before opening it. Rolf hovered just outside, eyes alight.

Kattanan briefly returned the grin, then ushered the man in to visit his prince. Leaning against the shut door, the young king looked up at the two guards. "When the duchess arrives, tell her I have gone to find something to eat."

"Yes, Your Majesty."

Kattanan smiled a little. "Have you been here all night?"

Startled, the guard glanced at him. "No, Your Majesty, I just came back on duty."

"Thank you."

The man blinked down at him as Kattanan set off for the kitchen, walking purposefully. It was early yet, and the few maids who were about did not look up when he first entered. Kattanan gazed around him, taking in the details his brief tour had not allowed for. As expected, he spotted a table set by the fire, laid out with the servants' morning mess. When he sat down, though, one of the workers glanced over and let out a little cry. "Your Majesty! Forgive us. Let me fix a meal and bring it—"

He shook his head. "I can't eat in my room today. This is fine."

The woman did not rise from her curtsy. "But this is no fit food, Your Majesty."

"I don't need anything more." He picked up a round of cheese. "Unless you have some Teresan tea," he added, looking over at her.

She pulled herself up, brightening visibly. "Of course, Your Majesty." Her kerchiefed head bobbed eagerly as she went into the pantry, then she crowed in triumph, pulling out a small metal box. "Funny, you and the duchess having the same tastes, Your Majesty. Of course, she doesn't drink all of hers unless—"

"Your Majesty," snapped the duchess from the door, and Kattanan sprang to his feet again. "I had not thought to find you here consorting with servants at this hour."

He bowed, and remained with his eyes to the floor, unaware that all the servants had the same posture. "I was hungry, Excellency."

"Come." She turned and left. Kattanan followed, finding Fionvar waiting in the hall for them. The trio entered the conference room, and Kattanan perched on one of the deep chairs.

"I am in charge of this meeting, is that clear?" the duchess began. At his weak nod, she went on, "Both of you have been defying my will and eroding my position. It cannot and will not go on." She pressed both hands to the table, staring at Kattanan.

"Excellency," Fionvar put in, his voice strangely sharp, "this is no way to speak to the one who will take the throne."

"One thing we all agree on is that my grandson is not ready to rule anything. Until such time as he is, I am the Regent of the True Blood and I will be obeyed."

Their eyes locked, and Fionvar crossed his arms. "You are the heart of this place and of this cause, but you are not alone here, and we cannot afford to let our people see that you have no confidence in the man you have presented as their king."

"I have not opened this for discussion yet, Captain."

His voice overrode her. "If anyone can make this thing succeed, it will be you. We are not always friends, but I will be here as long as you let me stay, doing whatever I can. Right now, however, you need to learn a little patience."

"Patience? I have been working toward this for fourteen years!"

"Look at your grandson. Look at him! He's eighteen years old, and he has been cast away from the only life he's known, kidnapped by someone he never wanted to see again, told he is a king, introduced to his future bride, shown maps of battle-grounds, saved his friends from probable execution, kept an all-night vigil, then been embarrassed in front of the servants so he can be yelled at by a grandmother he barely knows! He should be the one standing here yelling back, when he's had every excuse in the world to want us all buried alive!" Fionvar took a deep breath, glancing at Kattanan. "It's not me you should be listening to, it's him."

She sank into her chair, dark skirts spreading around her. "Fine. I am listening."

Still clutching his mug of tea, Kattanan sat up a little straighter. "I don't know what to say," he whispered.

"He does not know what to say," the duchess repeated.

Fionvar shot her a look and faced Kattanan across the table. "If I have made no sense here, please tell me."

The young man swallowed. "Let Prince Wolfram heal. Please just leave him alone. I'm not used to sitting in court; I don't know what to do; maybe someone can teach me that, too. Don't call me 'Sire'; I wish I could be that, but I can't and I never will be. I can't marry anyone." On this last, his voice fell even lower, and the duchess leaned toward him.

"Aren't the two of you getting on well? What has she done to displease you?"

"It is not her fault," he whispered. "I am no fit husband for any woman."

"But it is necessary—"

"Patience," Fionvar broke in firmly. "Is there anything else you need to say right now?" Kattanan shook his head. "My first comment is that we cannot allow the prince to know too much of our plans. He is important to you, but that fact alone will make our allies suspicious. No one will raise a hand against him, and anyone who tries will deal with me. He will always be guarded, for his sake, and for ours. I will need to speak with him as soon as he is able. As to what to do in court, I gather that you have not seen the business list."

The duchess arched her neck. "He will not be making the decisions in any case."

Fionvar's look was pointed. "There is a list the herald keeps of what issues are to come before court. It doesn't prevent surprises, but you may understand what goes on before it actually happens. Someone can be found to tutor you; if all else fails, I'll do it myself." Fionvar let out a long breath.

"If you are through?" the duchess prompted, rising to her feet. "As his behavior yesterday amply proves, he knows nothing about court or kingship or even royal comportment. But I need him. You, on the other hand—I have no tolerance for anyone who thinks to tell me my business in my own manor. Another of your willful displays, and I will personally cast you out before the entire court! By the Goddess, you will have no part of my kingdom!"

"Duchess! I am not my brother." Fionvar met her eyes. "I do not want your kingdom. I do not want a lordship, or even to be captain of your guard. I want you to listen! Unless you listen to your grandson, you'll have to throw him out with me. Everyone here is ready to serve the True Blood, not just you. There he sits. Maybe you just want him to play the part of king, never to make his own decisions. He can do that, just show him how. Teach him the music, and he will sing your song." The duchess flicked a glance to Kattanan, paralyzed in his chair but for the trembling of his hands. Fionvar went on, "All he need do is present the image of royalty to our allies, and you hold the power. Fine, but what happens when you die?" Her eyes snapped back to him as if he had drawn a knife. "All of us die one day or another. You've raised Brianna to be a fine queen, but your neighbors were willing enough to cast down the last Queen of Lochalyn."

"Why should I listen to such defeatist rubbish?"

"You still don't understand." He lowered his voice now, dark eyes shining. "We are not doomed as long as Kattanan lives, but only if you consent to make him a king in fact, not just in name. Teach him, let him see, let him understand. When we reach Lochdale, let him ride before a victorious army, the true heir returned to his home. Give your people a king worth fourteen years of oppression."

"He is little more than a child and will never be much more than that."

"You are saying that because you have never heard him sing."

Shock sprang to her features, and Kattanan's as well, as he dropped the mug at last. "Sing?" the duchess snapped "What has that to do with anything?"

"I have heard him fill a hall with nothing but himself. I played until I thought I'd bleed, and I could neither outlast nor outshine him."

"That was the past. His voice, his singing—all past," she said flatly.

"That is not the point. Yesterday at court you were horrified to see him rush to aid a prince you have always called your enemy. He confronted you to save a man who was his friend.

You see a child who disobeys you, nothing more. I saw courage, honor, loyalty, compassion, righteous anger—everything I would want from my king."

Slowly, she said, "You did not stand forward yesterday because you mistrust me?"

"No."

"And last night, you ordered the guards to deny my entrance . . . ?"

"Out of respect for my king," Fionvar replied.

Kattanan glanced from one to the other. Summoning every ounce of her authority the duchess sat deadly still, face betraying nothing. Fionvar, taller, no less proud, challenged her across the table, but there was no anger. His eyes begged, his hands hovered, empty, and his breath escaped in small, hopeful bursts. When she turned from him, Kattanan saw the exultant smile that flared briefly across Fionvar's face. She examined her grandson, and he lifted his chin a little higher, stilling his hands at last.

"You have been highly praised by one who does not flatter." The chin lowered, but just a touch.

She crossed her arms and frowned. "I, too, will speak with your Prince Wolfram, when the surgeons allow it. And we will speak of your marriage—but now, I think, may be the wrong time." She tilted her head. "You told me that this man did not like you."

He glanced back to Fionvar. "I had no idea," he replied faintly.

"You seem to be ignorant of many things," she observed, "but youth and inexperience may explain that. And both of those are things we shall overcome. It seems my grandson and I have much to discuss. No doubt you have other duties, Captain."

He did not heed her gesture of dismissal, but turned to Kattanan. "Your Majesty requested a report on the circumstances surrounding the capture of the prince." At the young man's nod, Fionvar continued, "Their boat ran aground on the Bernholt side of the island. They surrendered quickly and were taken to the captain. The guards I spoke with said there was a new man with him, someone they hadn't seen before, and it was he who recognized the prince. He also was responsible for the beating. The stranger claimed to be a friend of my brother's and insisted on being called 'Sir'—Majesty, are you ill?"

What little color had returned to Kattanan's face drained away, leaving him pale and trembling, shaking his head vaguely. "Is he still here?"

"No one seems to know. I have several men looking for him, but with no luck so far. This man is known to you?"

Kattanan shut his eyes and swallowed. He nodded once, but would say nothing of it. With a frown, Fionvar went on, "The former captain refuses to speak to me about his part in this. Perhaps Your Excellency can get something out of him later. The four guards directly involved genuinely believed they were acting with the full authority of this regency; and I don't believe they harbored any particular ill will. The prince himself may provide more of the missing pieces. When they found him, he was carrying a diagram of a tunnel system under the castle, as well as a map showing both sides of the river."

"Did the Liren-sha reveal us?" the duchess demanded.

"No. He returned just a few hours ago, and knew nothing of this until I started asking questions."

"We had best move quickly. Bernholt will be in disarray over the succession; any delay will give them more time to come to their ally's aid."

Fionvar agreed and glanced up at Kattanan. "There was another matter, Majesty, which I had discussed with the duchess some time ago. My sister, Lyssa, is in Lochdale, serving as a journeyman sculptor. I had planned to go fetch her before we march on Lochalyn. Jordan will probably ride with me. I did not anticipate being captain of the guard here. Gwythym duLarce can serve as captain in my stead, if you give me leave to go."

"This Gwythym is a friend of yours?" The duchess arched an eyebrow at him.

"My first lieutenant—the man who spoke to you last night outside the king's chamber."

"I see."

Kattanan gave a tiny smile. "You will return quickly?"

"Yes, Majesty."

"If there is nothing else . . . ?" The duchess gestured toward the door.

Fionvar looked to the young king, who whispered, "You may go."

"Thank you, Your Majesty. I will take formal leave at morning court." He rose, bowed briefly to the duchess as well, and left, shutting the door behind him.

Fionvar slipped into court a bit late, after briefing Gwythym on his duties. His face lit for a moment when he saw that Brianna was in attendance, seated at the very front, her eyes upon the king. A man was reading the rolls of the loyal barons, with estimates of their readiness, and Kattanan was clearly doing his best to look interested, but without much success. At last, the speaker droned to a close, and was dismissed. The herald stood to announced the next business, and Fionvar shifted to be ready when his name was called.

Instead, Brianna stepped forward. "I have business with the king." Dressed in her finest, her attention focused on Kattanan alone, she walked carefully and dropped into a small curtsy. "May I approach?"

Fionvar leaned forward, as intent upon her as she upon the king, and his throat felt dry.

With an uncertain gesture, Kattanan invited her. The duchess watched her granddaughter gravely as she came. Brianna bent as if to kneel immediately in front of the throne, then slipped a hand behind him for the little dagger he always wore. Before he could flinch away, she had cut a lock of his hair, and rose again, her face a blank mask. "I choose you, and I will bear the sons of no other but you. This is what our family has asked of us, and I do it freely, Your Majesty."

"Don't," he whispered, too late. "Don't do this." His eyes glistened, his hands trembled.

"It is done," the duchess said firmly, letting a smile touch her lips. "Let it be proclaimed to all our allies that our king shall have a bride." She raised Brianna's hand before them.

A cheer went up in the chamber, and Fionvar sat rooted to

the spot even as the other courtiers rose to congratulate the king. He remained still as the room was cleared around him. The courtiers trickled out until only a handful of people remained—the three by the throne, Fionvar, still as stone, and the wizard looking on without comment.

The duchess, still gripping Brianna's hand, did not lose her smile as she said, "I wish that you had told me."

The lady looked away. "I have made my choices, Grandmother. Perhaps, at last, I have made the right one."

Fionvar found his voice at last, rising, his hands fisted at his sides. "Why?" he blurted.

His love, his light—another man's betrothed—Brianna rose up from her knees. "Fourteen years, we've dedicated ourselves to this. There was a time we could not be sure it would happen." She darted a glance back toward Fionvar, and as quickly looked away. "In these few days, I have . . . reexamined my part in the kingdom that is to come, and I know where I am needed."

"You would marry without love," Fionvar murmured, no longer caring who heard or who knew. He felt as if he might collapse to the floor, as battered as the prince and as bereft.

Brianna faced him then, a hint of color rising in her cheeks, his band no longer upon her wrist. "Love is a fine thing, my lord, a wonderful thing. But it is not everything." Then her eyes returned to Kattanan's bowed head. "I hope you can see it is for the best," she whispered.

"I can't do this," said the king, and Brianna fled the room, a hand pressed to her mouth.

The duchess replied, "You will find a way to do this, or Brianna will be dishonored before the court. Would you do that to her?" She gazed a long moment at Fionvar, turning when the far door opened.

"I am ready," Jordan said. "Forgive me, Your Majesty, I didn't realize you were still here. Or you," he added, glancing toward the wizard. His eyes lingered on her a moment, brows slightly raised.

When the guise of the old man had fallen away, it revealed her, hair newly trimmed, wearing a simple but well-made blue dress. She smoothed it self-consciously. "Brianna helped me." She looked back at Jordan. "I stayed to wish you both well, and safe journey."

Fionvar's head turned at this, but he said nothing.

Jordan nodded to her. "Thank you, my lady."

The wizard smiled brightly.

Sadness darkened Jordan's features as he looked to Kattanan. "Time is of the essence, I know, so I cannot beg an audience. I will return swiftly, and I hope you will hear me then."

Kattanan nodded briefly and rose to cross the floor toward Fionvar. "My lord," he began, his true voice sounding out of place, "this is not as I would have it."

Fionvar met his gaze with dark eyes. "Your Majesty, my heart's desire has left me, but you are still my king. I will return to serve you as long as I am able." He rose to take his leave and found himself facing the duchess once more.

"I look forward to your sister's return and wish you every success." Her smile looked sharper, as if her fangs could at any moment be revealed. "You may go."

He looked to Kattanan, whose eyes were still lowered, but found nothing to say and turned away toward the door.

"Tell Wolfram I am profoundly sorry for my part in what happened, and that I wish him well." Jordan shared another glance with the silent wizard, then followed Fionvar to the hall.

Here, Jordan paused and laid a hand on Fionvar's arm. "Under any other circumstances, I would be overjoyed to help you bring back Lyssa."

Fionvar shook his head. "The only woman I have ever wished to marry has just accepted another, and he cannot deny her."

"He will find a way."

"You don't know him anymore!" Fionvar said forcefully, starting down the stairs. "He hasn't the strength to resist the duchess, especially not with Brianna now on her side."

"At least he will not be completely alone," Jordan said, picking up the pace.

Fionvar gave him a curious look. "What do you mean by that?"

"The wizard will be watching over him."

This almost brought a smile to Fionvar's lips. "The Liren-sha allows a wizard to look after his friend. Perhaps you should have asked Prince Wolfram to be his bodyguard."

"I would. Don't laugh; you haven't spoken with him. Even as wounded as he is, he would keep Kattanan from harm; even if that meant taking it onto himself. As to the wizard"—Jordan paused at the corner of the stables—"we have reached an understanding."

"Ever the dreamer, Jordan." Fionvar sighed. "I have no heart for dreams today."

"Speaking of which, do you think your sister would be willing to marry me now?"

At this, Fionvar did laugh. "As much as she is willing to marry any man, my friend. She's been flirting with one of the younger princes and looking forward to refusing him."

"A lady of fire."

"Of stone—I've yet to meet the artist who could carve a place in her life."

"I'm told the same was once said of you," Jordan replied softly.

"The fiddler who hates to dance. It seems we are both without hope this time."

The Liren-sha shrugged. "I've learned to live with that. So long as I am without hope, I know I have nothing to lose. It's what makes me so good at my job." He gazed into the sky for a moment, then brought his attention back to the task.

"I do have one small hope," Fionvar offered. "I hope I don't have to lash Lyssa to my saddle in order to bring her home."

Jordan laughed aloud. "Then you'll need my help after all."

"I'm glad of the company. Four days' ride through the mountains can get lonely."

"Ask me about the walk from the castle sometime."

Fionvar gave him a half smile and unbolted the gate. "At least we'll have a joyous greeting at the end of this journey."

# Chapter 19

FOR TWO days, it rained, and the wizard gazed up toward the mountains with a little sigh. Brianna, stitching at a favor not far away, looked up at her. "I have only heard that sound from ladies in love, and it wouldn't be either of those two."

"What?" The wizard resumed the comfortable chair where she had been reading. "I don't understand you." Her yellow eyes held steady.

Brianna bent over the embroidery. "Whenever we are here together, you look out that window and sigh. In other ladies, it is a sign that you are awaiting a loved one."

"You may be, perhaps, not I."

"I am betrothed," she declared, pushing an escaped lock of hair back under her veil. "I have had my childish fancies, but I am happy as it is."

"This love you speak of must be a truly fickle thing."

Brianna put aside her work, gaze lingering on her bare wrist. "It is better thus. Stronger bloodlines, the better to cement our ties with our allies and perhaps to convince those who remain uncertain. This is what I've been raised for—what I have lived for."

"Of course," the wizard replied, "Your Excellency."

Brianna shoved herself out of the chair. "That was uncalled for! I brought this up to see if you needed a friend, not to offer myself for judgment!"

"Wait, please," the other said, also standing, one hand gripped in her dress. "It's just . . . I've learned a great many things, but never how to still my tongue. I need—" She looked down at her too-large hands. "I have not had a friend in so very long that I no longer recognize the acts of friendship. You don't know what it is to live as I do."

The lady hesitated. "I forget, sometimes, that you were not brought up as I."

They faced each other for a long moment, then the wizard began tentatively, "You said I am like a lady in love. I would not know love if the Goddess Herself brought it to me."

"I used to think that's what She did," Brianna replied, her voice tinged with a sadness accentuated by the redness of her eyes.

"Can you . . . ? What I mean to ask is, do you know how I would know, if I were, I mean?" She frowned.

A giggle burst from Brianna's lips as her brow wrinkled. "That didn't make much sense, but I think I understand you." She sat very still for a moment. "I thought the world seemed so much clearer when he was near me. I started to do things I thought would please him. I worried at every step what he would think of me." She sighed, hugging herself. "I was such a fool."

The wizard shrugged. "I have done nothing out of the ordinary."

Brianna gestured with one hand at the dress the wizard wore. "Then I restitched that for nothing? I was certain someone had caught your eye."

Shaking her head, the wizard crossed to the fire.

"You are taking me too seriously for simple curiosity's sake. You can tell me, if you wish," Brianna offered. "I am excellent at keeping secrets."

"As you said it could be neither of those two."

"Fionvar is no friend of wizards, and the Liren-sha, well"— her eyes widened—"the Wizard's Bane?" She nearly laughed again, but held back when the wizard turned to face her, chin held high. "That cannot be!"

"No," the wizard agreed, "it cannot be."

"But, how? When?"

"There is nothing between us. We were chained together when we escaped the castle, and he—I was able to say things I cannot say to any other. It made me feel ordinary, for once."

Brianna came to stand beside her. "You know that he has asked Lyssa yfSonya to marry him?" she asked gently.

"As I said, it is of no consequence to me. I have heard her described as the nearest thing to the Goddess walking. And he is the Wizard's Bane, the one man before whom I can be nothing but this, before whom I am nothing."

"Don't say that."

"It's only truth." She held her hands out to the fire, rubbing as if she could not get warm. When she went on, she spoke as if to herself. "Have you ever felt as if you found what you want above all else, and it is the only thing in the world denied to you?"

Brianna covered her face with her hands, shoulders heaving as if she struggled to breathe.

The wizard saw but made no motion until a knock on the door summoned her from her reverie. She glanced at Brianna and went to answer it.

"The prisoner asked to speak with you," said the guard outside.

"Me? I doubt he asked." She cast another glance at Brianna, then shut the door behind her and followed the guard back to the king's chamber.

Neither Rolf nor Kattanan was in the visitor's chair, so she sat down and watched the former prince's face, obscured by one bandaged eye. "I was told you had asked for me."

"I'm not allowed to read or write, so I must amuse myself somehow." He smiled faintly.

"Where is the king?"

"With the armorer. They are preparing for some great battle that I am not to know about, and it is to happen sooner rather than later."

She returned his brief smile. "I was also told that they have not managed to keep much from you yet, though no one speaks with you openly."

"It's no great feat," he responded, his voice soft as his gaze. "You do not count yourself among them."

"I have no part in this quarrel aside from a few tasks I was hired to perform."

"Like giving my father an illness that does not exist."

"You nearly gained a kingdom from it, and now have lost everything because it is no more. And me, well, what is this king or that one to a wizard?" She casually lifted a glowing crown from her own head and cast it aside where it once again vanished.

"I doubt you are so neutral as you pretend. You took a great risk approaching my father at the outset, and a greater one to come into the castle. No, you have a grudge against Bernholt, somehow." He took a few labored breaths.

"Not against you."

He stroked the cloth binding the cut on his neck, and the faint smile returned. "Only against my neck."

"I used the available means to save my life, and the injury to you was slight. I did not come there with any malice toward you, nor do I have any now." Lounging back in her chair, she watched warily.

"Then I forgive you."

"I had a knife at your throat," the wizard pointed out.

"You needed a hostage. If you had known how little my father valued me, you might not have bothered."

"I don't understand you, Highness."

"My name is Wolfram. I should like to know why your apprentice didn't do it himself."

"Because I wanted to." Her eyes narrowed. "Is that what you wanted to know?"

"Among other things." Wolfram took a sip from a nearby mug.

"He asked me to teach him the skill to carry out the deed; part of my price for the apprenticeship was that I do it myself, a partial repayment for what your father did to me and my friends. Both of them still owe so much. Is that all?"

"I would like to know," he said softly, "what the hounds saw when they killed my friend."

The wizard met his eyes, her face set. "I would tell you if I knew. I did not, and I would not have done that."

"Orie will be king."

"He will do everything in his power to be, yes." She studied the prince quietly.

"You are proud of your apprentice," he whispered, eye shut.

"As proud as you are of your father, perhaps."

"He is a strong king; he has done so much for his people," Wolfram replied, his fingers wrapped tightly in the blanket.

"He has done so much to his people, don't you mean? He has been a tyrant when he could, neglectful of the Lady's Law, and cruel to you among others. It amazes me that you can still think of him as a hero."

A tear sparkled at Wolfram's eye and trickled down his cheek

She watched him a moment longer, frowning. "You may have even more reason than I to hate the man who wears that crown."

"A man cannot hate his own father."

"I wouldn't know; I've never had a father. But for all he's done to you—" She gestured toward his shoulder.

"I was a bad son and a worse prince, and I would have been a pathetic king. He had every right to disown me. Sometimes I wish I had been what he wanted."

"A lying, murdering bully," the wizard supplied, "who uses children to barter for favors and supports the false claims of other murderers. An admirable king indeed. If that is your ideal, I should have left the arrow there to rot!"

He opened his eye. "You are not as neutral as you would have me think."

The wizard started as the door was thrust open behind her, and Rolf tensed instantly. "Stay away from him!"

"I asked her here," Wolfram said, with a curious smile. "I may ask her back again if she is willing."

"I may even come." The wizard rose. "But for now, I will let you rest." She gave a little bow, out of habit, and walked to the door, leaving Rolf to puzzle in her wake. Once there, though, she turned and met Wolfram's gaze. "I can heal you, if you allow

it." She did not wait to listen to Rolf's loud protest as she shut
the door between them.

◯⋘◯

THE RAIN persisted through the fourth night when Fionvar
and the Liren-sha at last faced the walls of Lochdale. Huge doors
leaned on either side of a vast arched doorway, not yet fitted to
their place. At the left, the castle wall gaped open for workmen
to haul carts of stone for the construction.

"If she's still as taken with her work as her last letter implied,
then she'll be here," Fionvar said. Indeed, they heard the ringing
of blows from within; as they approached, hammer strikes echoing into the night.

"I wonder how the neighbors feel about that," Jordan said,
with a brief smirk.

A pair of guards flanked the door, leaning on their pikes,
heads down against the rain. "Good watch there, men!" Fionvar
called out, dismounting as he came up to them.

Both men leapt to attention, protesting. "Halt! Tell me how
you are called."

"Fionvar duNormand, a weary traveler," Fionvar said, smiling
as he fingered his damp hair. "My friend and I are coming to
visit my sister, who is a stonemason working on this temple; we
arrived a bit later than expected."

"Yer sister wouldn't be a red-haired vixen, would she now?"

Both travelers laughed. "That would be her. I see you've met."

The other grinned. "So which brother are you?"

"The eldest, possibly referred to as 'that tyrant who ran the
house after Da's death,' or 'the wretched fiddle-player.' "

"Sounds like her, but her term's not up for a while. Any special reason for the visit?" the second guard inquired.

Fionvar glanced to his companion. "This poor fool wants to
marry her. Somehow he thinks that their having been parted
four months will have softened her resolve."

"Ye're welcome to the effort," the guard replied, "but I don't
envy you the response. Go on in and dry off. Horses, too, there's
room inside for hitching."

They passed under the arch then into the torchlit space that was being slowly molded into a church. Wide ribs soared up to support the great span of the roof, but much of the walls between were still stacked to the sides so that the structure resembled a huge spider crouched over them. Leaving the horses, they wandered farther in, seeking out the source of the hammering. A scaffold rose at the side, surrounding one of the great pillars of stone. High up, they caught sight of a figure, absorbed by the rhythm of her blows against the chisel. A dusting of white powder drifted down upon them. Jordan coughed and shook back his hood to squint up, then rapped on the rods supporting the scaffold.

The blows stopped, and the figure peered back at them. "Halloo! Who's there?"

"Lyssa, light of my heart," Jordan called back, "Come down and marry me!"

Gales of laughter followed, but she rose nonetheless and made her nimble way down, brushing even more stone dust into the air. Her bare feet appeared first, followed by legs clad in loose trews, with a skirt hitched up through her belt. The hammer was tucked in as well. A fitted bodice, grubby with sweat and dust, topped the curious garb, sleeveless to provide for the swing of well-muscled arms. She had bound her hair with a scarf but now released it to flow over her shoulders as she embraced her brother. Jordan, she eyed for a moment, shaking her head, then she embraced him also, a stunning smile lighting her features. "I've come, but not to marry. Is that why you traveled all this way?"

Fionvar took her arm and guided her over to great block, where he sat down wearily. "It's time," he said simply, meeting her bright eyes.

Immediately she lost her smile. "No. I have important work here, Fion."

"You should be able to return and finish later, but you cannot stay here when—"

"I just said, 'No,' didn't I? Is it so hard for you to understand? I will be in no danger." She crossed her arms, regarding him.

"You cannot stay, or you may find yourself an unwilling guest," Jordan pointed out.

"They wouldn't use me as a hostage," she scoffed. "I don't think they are bright enough for that, even if they knew about my involvement. All I need to do is claim ignorance and smile. I have put in enough work here to convince them that I have nothing against the royal family."

"If I cannot be sure of your safety," Fionvar replied, "I will be in no fit condition to serve my king. I have enough on my mind that that might just edge me into madness."

Lyssa scowled at him. "Why? What's happened that I should throw away my vocation to play war with you?"

The sigh returned, and Fionvar rubbed his tired eyes. "I have lost the trust of the duchess by supporting some reckless actions on the part of the king, and Brianna has just declared for another man."

"What?" she repeated, eyes wide.

"Lyssa," her brother said softly, "I know that this is your calling, and this temple is the most important thing you have yet been a part of, but I do not want to risk you. I am asking you to come home."

She nodded slowly, then smirked a little. "I reserve the right to complain about it, though; and I want my armor. I'll be riding with the Sisters of the Sword."

Fionvar opened his mouth, then shut it, and gave a brief nod.

"We must be back as soon as possible, so—"

"Hold!" cried a new voice. Clattering steps approached from the castle's entry. "Watch! Don't let them pass!" the leader called, sprinting ahead with sword drawn.

"The horses!" Jordan cried, grabbing Lyssa's hand as the trio ran for their mounts.

"I am a prince!" the young man returned. "I order you to stand!"

"You are an idiot!" Lyssa laughed as Fionvar swung her up behind him. Jordan's horse danced to the side, snorting as he finally scrambled into the saddle. As he kicked it into a gallop, one of the pikemen slashed out at it. The horse shied, stumbled, and fell, slamming the Liren-sha to the ground. Fionvar reined in and turned back, calling out. Jordan gained his feet quickly, if shakily, flinging aside his cloak to reveal the bloodred garb. The men from the castle hesitated a moment at this.

"I am the Liren-sha!" he cried, then, over his shoulder, "Ride, Fionvar!"

Fionvar, struggling to keep the horse steady while slashing at a guard with the other hand, did not heed him.

Favoring his right leg, Jordan moved back a few paces from the advancing men. The prince stopped, unshouldering a crossbow. "The other one! Get the other," he ordered his men.

The shout of the royal guard made Fionvar's attacker whirl, then he screamed as the terrified horse tore lose from Fionvar's grasp and bolted for the door. The riders plunged out into the night as bells rang behind them.

By the time Fionvar had mastered the beast, there was no turning back.

# Chapter 20

"I THINK YOUR game is slipping, Wizard," Wolfram said as he removed a marker from the board on his bedside table.

"I do not like waiting," she replied, frowning over the next move.

"I wouldn't mind if I knew what we are waiting for." He regarded her steadily.

"Do you never give up?" She nudged one of her pieces a little closer to him.

"Not easily." After more than a week, the bruises on his face were much faded, enough to allow his minute smile.

"Hasn't the king told you anything?" She cocked her head, with a slight frown.

"He has not been allowed near me without a witness since the first time I saw him. Neither has Rolf, for that matter—no one has but you, in fact. Strange."

The wizard shrugged. "Not very."

"I don't suppose there'd be much purpose to assigning you a chaperone."

"The duchess trusts me with the enemy, perhaps because she cannot believe that you would trust me. A more interesting question is, why hasn't she visited you herself?"

"Oh, she did, once. She came in the dead of night, when she thought I was sleeping, and stood at the foot of the bed, staring at me. I was expecting an interrogation, or at least an accusation from her, but there has been none."

"She's had other things on her mind." The wizard looked up quickly, with a little smile. "But I suppose you would know nothing of that."

"Well, let's see. Jordan is involved, or he would have come here himself. So is the guard captain, for the same reason. Brianna, Kattanan's betrothed, is involved, but she is playing the role of not being involved. She is also pregnant."

The wizard's eyes widened. "How did you figure that?"

"She carries herself that way." He frowned a little. "I thought that was obvious. Anyhow, if I were to conjecture, I would assume that the father is one of the two missing men, and they have been sent away together, perhaps to remove the distraction from Brianna. Given that, I would probably further assume the father is Jordan, guarding the captain on his mission. Why are you smiling?"

The wizard shrugged. "You amuse me, Prince Wolfram."

Wolfram eyed her a moment longer. "The guard captain is the father."

She leaned in very close to him. "The captain's name is Fionvar duNormand; he helped the king to save your life. He may be the only man of honor in this place—"

"The earl's brother—he's the man who sent me stones!"

"What are you talking about?"

"Two years ago, my father and his barons were holding a Great Council in the south, so I was serving as regent, while Fionvar served for his brother. It was in the middle of a drought, but I had been charged to collect the king's due from the harvest. Gamel's Grove was in a bad way since the river had been diverted to provide a reservoir for the towns upstream. Fionvar sent a load of stones, along with the record specifying that this was one-fifteenth portion of the local harvest, half again as much as the tax, because they had had such a fine crop. My father would have taken it as insolence, and I suppose it was, but it was also the act of a lord who is watching his people starve."

"What did you do?"

"He sent us a chest of silver," Fionvar replied as he walked through the door, "with a message that it was to pay for stronger oxen since our harvest was the heaviest he had yet seen." He managed a smile. "I am surprised you remember that, Your Highness."

"He's not a prince anymore, and certainly not here," the duchess snapped, sweeping in behind. "We are not paying a social call."

"Should I go?" the wizard asked, gathering the playing pieces.

The duchess glowered at her. "You seem to have become well acquainted."

Wolfram said lightly, "Given the absence of my old friends, I was forced to make new ones. And you are . . . ?"

Still glowering, she snapped, "I am Duchess Elyn of the House of Rinvien, Kingdom of Lochalyn."

"An honor, Excellency." He lowered his head reverently. "Were I well enough to stand, I would do you the obeisance you deserve."

Mouth slightly open, she stared.

Fionvar's smile broadened.

Standing, the wizard turned to him, with sudden concern. "The Liren-sha is not with you!"

"No, he is not." Their eyes locked for a moment, and she sighed.

"Very well. I would hear of it when you are disposed to tell me." She made a brief curtsy and left, closing the door behind her.

"What do you know of our plans, and how did you inform our enemies?" the duchess demanded, looming over the bed.

"I know nothing of your plans, Excellency, except that they involve the reclaiming of a throne too long held by a tyrant."

"Don't think you can gain favor by feigning sympathy."

Fionvar shook his head. "Perhaps we should come back when you—"

The warning look she shot him made him reconsider finishing that statement, and she turned back to the invalid. "Your family was responsible for that tyrant reaching power, Former Prince Wolfram, and now you regret it. Why would I ever believe you?"

"My father was responsible; I was a child, and I have learned much since then."

"What could you learn at your father's feet but how to kick those who deserve much better?"

"I did not study at his feet, Excellency. Until four years ago, when my second sister married, I was heir to nothing." Wolfram's gaze was hard. "I learned in his library and from his servants. I rode in the mountains with the people of the wood and walked the streets alone to hear the city's voices. I learned some of the truth of Thorgir's reign, and have come to see more since I have been here. I have been surrounded by teachers far better than my father. It hurts that he has no regard for me, but it does not surprise me."

"Yet you were surprised by his archers," she pointed out.

The faint ironic smile hovered. "How many men can be accused of treason by two kingdoms within the span of a month?"

"I have accused you of nothing, yet."

"You asked how I communicated with your enemies. How many ways can that question be taken?"

With a rap on the door, a guard ushered in Kattanan, looking pale and flustered. Fionvar bowed immediately. "Your Majesty, I am glad you were able to join us."

The duchess narrowed her eyes at him. "Are you not in the midst of your studies, Majesty?"

"I was told," he began, glancing at Wolfram, "that a discussion was taking place that I might find more informative."

"The wizard," the duchess said.

"The acting guard captain," he corrected softly.

Fionvar smirked, and the guard snapped to attention. "Welcome back, sir. I hereby return your command."

"You seem to have discharged your duties quite well, Gwythym. Thank you."

"At your service, sir! Your Majesty." The man bowed and let himself out.

"Is there no one here whom I may trust?" the duchess snarled.

"If you chose," Wolfram offered, "you could trust everyone here. We are none of us your enemies."

"Someone in Lochdale clearly knows at least part of our intentions. How much remains to be seen. Until the source is discovered"—she stared hard at Wolfram—"or proven, there is no one I suspect more than those in this room."

Fionvar darkened, Kattanan paled, but Wolfram only sighed. "Try kindness, Excellency, or faith before you take suspicion as your companion, or you will shortly have no other."

"You dare to paraphrase the Lady's Word to me? How have you come by such arrogance as to preach to me?"

"How have you come by the pride that places you above the Lady's Word, Excellency?"

"Please," Kattanan said, looking from one to the other.

"I thought you might have learned some manners," the duchess hissed, "but it seems I was mistaken. Perhaps you'd like my guards to resume the lessons?"

Clearing his throat, Fionvar said, "You are not what I expected, Highness."

"Nor I," the duchess added dryly. She turned her back toward the bed to catch Kattanan's arm. "Majesty, it is time you were back to your studies. It seems our schedule may be accelerated. Captain, you will join me for dinner."

"I . . ." Kattanan began, then nodded once and allowed himself to be led away.

Left in the room, Fionvar asked Wolfram, "Are you trying to get yourself killed?"

"Actually," he remarked, "I was trying to ensure that, if someone must die, it would not be Kattanan or you. The other options were limited."

"If you are innocent, why ask for her suspicion? It's absurd, Highness."

"Not if you see it from my place. If she believes I am innocent before she ferrets out another suspect, she will assume one of you is guilty. I am the only one of us three who can afford the luxury of her distrust."

Fionvar snorted. "You or I might be expendable, but her grandson is the rightful king. She would never raise a hand against him."

"If he stands between her and the shaming of Thorgir, would she let him stop her?"

"She would never!" Fionvar repeated.

"Perhaps not. You have known her longer than I. Jordan's been taken, hasn't he? What was her reaction?"

"She—" Fionvar broke off, glancing sidelong at Wolfram.

Before he had a chance to speak the door burst open to admit Lyssa and a protesting guard. "She will do nothing!" the young woman howled, pushing the guard aside with a strong arm.

"Lyssa, get out of here at once!"

"I tried to stop her," the guard offered.

"Lyssa," Fionvar growled, "now is not the time, nor is here the place for this discussion."

"By the Goddess, when are you going to listen to me? You bid me be silent all the way back, and I am sick to death of it!"

"This must be your sister, since I do not believe you are married," Wolfram said, giving a lopsided smile.

"Lyssa yfSonya duNormand, may I present Wolfram duGerrod, former crown prince of Bernholt."

She looked him up and down. "You don't look as good as your portrait."

"Can't anyone in this family learn to keep their mouths shut? You've met, now we are going." Fionvar grasped her elbow, but she pulled away to approach the bed.

"I learned all of my ill tempers from my brothers, despite what they may tell you. But then, they seem to be interested in the last word, rather than the truth, so I guess it's to be expected." She shot a glance back to Fionvar, who collapsed into a chair. Lyssa grinned. "I have just been dragged back here against my will, and all I want is a little consideration of my feelings, but that seems to have been too much to ask from him."

"Lyssa," Fionvar said, rubbing his hand over his eyes, "we have been back only two hours, and we could both use some sleep. Can we continue this in the morning?"

"Every moment we delay, Jordan's peril grows. He wants to marry me, or have you forgotten?"

"What would you have me do? Mount a raid, perhaps? Lay siege to the castle? He knew the danger when he rode with me, and he would not ask us to sacrifice everything to rescue him."

"There must be something we can do!"

"I am open to suggestions."

"Talk to the wizard," Wolfram offered.

Lyssa and Fionvar both stared at the former prince. "She has no reason to care what happens to him," Fionvar said. "She probably prefers it this way."

Wolfram replied, "She may surprise you."

"I suspect you know something more about this."

He shrugged one shoulder. "I am in a position to see things that you have not."

Fionvar frowned. "How is it you can lie in bed for not even a fortnight and claim greater understanding than any of us?"

"Fresh eyes? Or perhaps I simply have nothing better to do."

"Or perhaps you are a spy."

"No, Captain, only a student of humanity. By the way, I have not yet thanked you for the night you allowed Kattanan to stay with me. I am already in your debt."

"You are trying to change the subject," Lyssa cut in.

"Yes, I am"—he sighed—"because your brother is right.

Aside from the wizard, who cannot get close to the castle as long as the Liren-sha is there, none of us can do a thing to help him. I am sorry."

She glared at him, then at her brother. "Then I'll go talk to her myself if you won't!" She stormed out of the room, leaving the door standing wide.

The guards outside leaned around the corner. "Problem, Captain?"

"Only the usual ones, I'm afraid. Give us a few minutes privacy, please."

The man nodded and shut the door, but not until Rolf had a chance to salute from his post across the hall. Fionvar chuckled. "I would trade much for a man as loyal to me as your Rolf is to you. I gather you wanted to talk with me alone? I'm impressed with how you got rid of Lyssa, by the way."

"Well, I do think that the wizard is her best chance to help Jordan, but I also think you and I have some things to discuss."

"For example?"

"Does Earl Orie trust you?"

"As much as he trusts anyone. Why?"

"Do you trust him?"

"He's my brother."

"Ignore that for the time being. He is the consort of her who will be queen in Bernholt. You and I both know he made it so. What makes you think he will stop at one kingdom when he could have two?"

Fionvar almost laughed. "Bernholt has always been his ambition in this. He knows who is to rule in Lochalyn."

"And he approves it?"

"He has been supporting it."

"Not the same thing, but I will let that pass, for now. When he is that close to power, he will become a threat to Lochalyn, to everything you are working to build."

"You are looking out for your family, are you not? Trying to encourage me against mine so that yours stands a better chance?"

"Finistrel knows I would like to see my father and sister

live long and happy lives, but that seems to be out of my hands, or even yours. What I am trying to do is encourage you to apply some of that skepticism to a man who will stop at nothing to get what he wants. If, for any reason, you must leave here, go to Orie and watch him. If he trusts you, you may be the only one in a position to stop him from taking another kingdom."

Fionvar's dark eyes flashed as he considered the wounded man. "I am not sure what to make of you. Or why I should not recommend that you be treated like the traitor you may be."

"You should not because I believe in Kattanan as much as you do. I will do everything in my limited power to see that he regains his kingdom. In order to do that, I need as much freedom as you can afford me. I would love to have you trust me, but I will cast doubt on myself if some is cast on Orie as well."

"Why did you think I would listen to even this much?"

"Because you are a man who is willing to take incredible risks for the sake of what is right." He met the other man's gaze for a long while before Fionvar rose and left without saying another word.

# Chapter 21

AFTER THREE days of the duchess's increased urgency, escape to the North Room was a welcome change, even if it was only to do more reading. Flanked by two guards, Kattanan bent over a volume of legends, rubbing his eyes.

Brianna, watched him with concern. "Perhaps Your Majesty would like to attend temple tonight?"

He looked up, but one of the guards said shortly, "The priestess may attend His Majesty in his room, if he wishes."

"She thinks it best I worship in solitude," Kattanan said, "as befits a king."

"She is taking this a little far, I think." Brianna put down her needle and stood. "Would His Majesty accompany me in the gardens?"

The guard cleared his throat and stared down at her.

"Forgive me, but I have not had much time with my betrothed lately. Naturally, we would wish you to be with us."

The guards moved aside uneasily as Kattanan rose. Brianna put out her hand expectantly, and he hesitated, then slipped it over his arm. She nodded, and the pair set out through the tall door. They walked along the grass, turning at the end of a bower of flowering trees. "Run," Brianna whispered, grasping his hand and gathering her skirts as she sprinted through a gap in the trees. He kept pace with her through series of turns, until she finally dropped his hand to scramble up makeshift steps over a wall. Kattanan followed, crouching beside her in the tumbledown enclosure. She gestured urgently for silence as the guards' shouting receded, then sat back and smiled. "A little place of peace, Majesty."

He settled back against the stone. "They will find us."

"Then you'd best enjoy it while you can." She took his hand more gently this time. "How have you been?"

"I am so tired. I wake and go to lessons, then court, then sword lessons." He looked down at his hand, rubbing together new calluses. "I have not been to temple since I came here."

"Well, the priestess is foul-tempered and a poor singer."

He flinched and slipped his hand away from her.

"There is no reason you cannot still sing," she said.

"That is over," he said sharply.

"Forgive me, I thought it might help."

Kattanan shook his head. "I am to leave that behind me."

"Our grandmother's words? Surely she can see that you must have something beyond studying."

"She herself thinks of nothing but this; why should I?"

"She does what she believes to be for the best. Sometimes, one of us must point out that there are other ways."

"Fionvar tried to do that, before he rode for Lochdale. I think it's worse now."

She looked away. "Fionvar has lost her favor. I believe I still have it, and if you think a word from me would help . . ."

"I—Thank you."

They sat in silence for a moment, and a small bird perched on the wall across from them, cocking its head first one way, then the other. "Am I interrupting, Majesty, my lady?" it inquired, with the wizard's voice.

Brianna frowned a little. "How close are the guards?"

"I sent them in another direction." The bird fluttered down, shifting into the more familiar form. "I am sorry to intrude, but I have had a strange message." She plucked a scrap of paper from her pouch and handed it over.

"Greetings good wizard," the note began. "When I arrived here, you offered me a game I did not expect. I may be interested in taking up that challenge, if the offer stands. I await your leisure to visit and share the rules with me. Yours, Wolfram."

Brianna handed it back. "That is certainly strange, what does he mean?"

"It is meant to get past the guards who have orders to read his messages," the wizard explained. "He regrets that he has not been allowed to write to Your Majesty. I believe he wants me to heal him."

At this, the young man started. "You can do that?"

"I can, but it is not easy, and I would rather not have this talent widely known."

"Then why are you telling us?" Brianna asked.

"Because I also need help. I have a way to go to him past the guards, but I will need"—she paused, looking at Kattanan—"I will need your blessing, Majesty."

"If you can heal him without any other harm to him, please do."

The wizard went on, "The way of healing is not unlike the way of bonding, as might be done for an apprentice, it requires blood to be effective. But he will be uninjured when I am

through. I don't need your permission, Majesty, but your blessing in the original sense."

"But I'm not holy," he pointed out.

"It doesn't matter what you are not. You are the last person
blessed by the Liren-sha, and your own good wishes may help
you share a bit of that blessing with me."

"If it helps Wolfram, I would do anything."

The wizard nodded briefly. "Press one finger here." She indicated the center of her forehead. "Say, 'Blessed be she who does
this work tonight, alone, unbound. Let her be blessed.'"The wizard shut her eyes as he took a deep breath and followed the instructions. A smile crept to her lips, then vanished as he
withdrew his hand, glancing toward Brianna. "Thank you,
Majesty. The other message was from my apprentice, Orie, who
reports that he parted ways with his mistress over two weeks ago
and has reason to believe she went to Lochalyn. He claims not
to have said too much to her, but it seems to have been enough
for her to bargain with your enemies."

A commotion over the wall made her fall silent, then, with a
glance toward the pair, she rose and her form once again shifted.
The little bird fluttered away as the first guard's head appeared
over the wall.

◆

"SIRE," JORDAN gasped. He cried out as the lash snapped
once more. "I can say nothing." His head drooped low against
his bare chest.

Thorgir glowered down on his prisoner, raising the lash
again. "I would have expected the Liren-sha to have a greater
tolerance for pain."

"Few have been near enough to hurt me, Sire." He raised his
gaze to his outstretched right arm, to the scars at his wrist and
the new ones in the making.

"What, as poor a swordsman as you are?"

"Even so." He took as deep a breath as he could. "Perhaps you
could just kill me and have done."

"Why, that would hardly be fitting reward for him who saved

my daughter from the sorry state she was in. Am I not a merciful man?"

"If I got the chance to know you—"

"Do they have Rhys?"

"Who?" Jordan asked, with genuine confusion. He tried to focus his eyes on the toe of one of the silent guards, but winced at the effort.

"I should have buried him when I had the chance."

"But you are a merciful man?"

"Mercy? What I did to him was no mercy!" The lash fell again, but not as sharply, as the king reached a hand to his crown. "It was my last triumph over a doomed woman."

"Your last," Jordan echoed.

"I do not understand," said the king, striking once more, "how you can keep up a conversation while you are being tortured."

"Sheer bloody-mindedness." He mustered a crooked smile.

The heavy door swung back, allowing a shaft of light from the hall to merge with that of the flickering torches. "Your Majesty," a new voice greeted Thorgir, "please forgive my intrusion." He bowed deeply and grinned.

"What is it?"

"I heard that your guest was being a bit . . . reticent. I thought I might offer my services to Your Majesty."

"Please!" He ushered in the newcomer. "Do you require anything special?"

He looked down on the Liren-sha. "A mallet and a stone chisel," Montgomery directed. "Oh, and a chopping block, if you have one."

"I need him alive, for the time being."

"As you wish, Sire. Anything for my king." Torchlight glinted from his spurs.

WOLFRAM LAY awake in his room, eyes turned toward the door through which he could hear the guards' shifting on their watch and the occasional whisper of their conversation. His shoulder ached insistently, tempting him to a bit of the healer's philter that had been left by his bedside. Instead, he whispered a prayer reserved for dark moments and tried to lie still. A soft rattle and creak from the window made him turn sharply, doing his shoulder no good. A pale wash of moonlight showed the latch turning, slipping free. The window opened wide to admit a slender shadow.

"Greetings," the prince murmured.

"And to you, Wolfram." The wizard shut the door behind her and approached him. "The guards will not hear us."

"That is a relief."

"You want me to heal you."

"Yes, I do. I cannot lie abed while so many others march for a noble cause."

The wizard laughed. "Are you as idealistic as you seem?"

"No," he replied. "More so."

"Even if you are well, there is no guarantee they will let you out. Besides, the healing is not a painless thing, Wolfram. Are you sure you want to go through it?"

"I'm sure I have been through worse." He smiled lightly.

"Indeed." She knelt at his bedside and stared into his eyes. "You know that I made your father sick, Wolfram. Why do you trust me to heal you?"

"Trust is the most valuable gift any person can give to another, even when he has no other gifts. Finistrel said that our enemies are only friends whom we have not thought to trust."

The wizard frowned at him. "That makes no sense. Trusting an enemy delivers you into his hands to do with as he will."

"Do you still have reason to believe that I am your enemy, or that you are mine?"

"To question a wizard is to gamble with your life."

"This is no gamble, my friend."

"You do not know me, Highness. I am worthy of no man's trust."

"Then you do not know yourself, my lady. Why are you here?"

"To heal you."

"Why? Am I of any use to you? Have I done you any service? No."

"Because you did not deserve this, and I am partly to blame for it."

"Justice, then, and kindness, a sense of responsibility, perhaps of using your talents to help one in need. I wish more people were as 'unworthy' as you are."

They were silent for a long time, then the wizard said, "I will need to lay hands upon the wound."

"So be it."

She slipped a slender knife from her sleeve, and carefully cut away the bandages.

As she did so, Wolfram inquired, "Can you tell me how the healing works?"

"There is not much to tell, short of teaching you how to do it. I will guide your blood to bring together the muscles and skin. If there were bones damaged, I could do nothing for you."

"Then I am indeed fortunate."

"The act itself is very painful, and there is no way I can lessen that, but the pain will recede once I lift my hand, though you will still be weak." She sat on the edge of the bed and rolled back her sleeves. "Are you ready?"

"I am. Goddess be with us."

"Indeed." She pressed her hand over the wound and made no sound. Wolfram shut his eyes tightly and wept to keep from screaming.

# Chapter 22

THE NEXT morning it was Fionvar and a dozen armed guards who roused Kattanan from his borrowed room. The captain shared nothing, but the intensity of his silence convinced Kattanan that the time had come. He chose his finest garb and, with a wince toward the crown bearer, was escorted to court without breakfast.

"Greetings, Grandson," the duchess said, rising with a curtsy and a broad smile.

Brianna did likewise. She now had a seat beside his throne, which she perched upon uneasily. Kattanan took his place, frowning a little when Fionvar moved to stand behind the throne. "Please, take your comfort," he said, gesturing for the assembled people to seat themselves. After two weeks, the words felt almost natural.

"Your Majesty," the duchess began, again with a curtsy, "I am pleased to inform you that our time of waiting is done." A cheer rose from the court, bringing another smile to her lips. "Our armies are preparing to join us to at last serve the Lady's Justice and cast down the Usurper!" Another cheer. "If Your Majesty has no objection, we ride tomorrow." The smile stayed, but her gaze was heavy upon him.

"I can find no reason to delay," he said hesitantly, "nor would I wish to. Fourteen years is a long time to spend away from home."

The duchess beamed as the assembly shouted once more. The

courtiers, expatriate lords and ladies of the former reign, embraced one another and called out blessings to their young king. When the commotion had died down, the duchess announced, "Those among you who have not yet done so are invited to pledge fealty to King Rhys. As to the rest, make ready to ride home!" She raised her fist high.

Some of the crowd filed out the doors as others formed a line to be received by the king. Kattanan leaned over to Brianna. "Is there someone who can bring me a meal?"

"You've not eaten?"

"I slept late today. She was drilling this moment with me halfway to dawn."

She smiled ruefully. "I'll find someone, or fetch it myself." Brianna slipped out of her chair, almost colliding with Fionvar. The color left her cheeks, and she looked away quickly. "Sorry," she murmured, then ducked her head and hurried off.

Kattanan turned his attention to the growing line. At its head stood two men he did not recognize, both grinning as if they shared a joke. The herald summoned them forward, and both knelt before the king. When they raised their heads, the disguises slipped away, eliciting a gasp.

"Forgive us, Your Majesty, for this deception," Wolfram said.

"Yes, certainly!" A smile broke across Kattanan's face as he looked from wizard to prince and back.

The wizard wore the clothing of a common foot soldier, her hair bound back out of her face. She did not smile, but watched him warily, letting her glance flicker toward the guards who had sprung forward at the surprise. Wolfram's tunic was torn, bloodspattered, but the flesh beneath was traced with only the faintest of scars. His eyes betrayed exhaustion, but the prince held himself like royalty.

"We did not know you were well enough," the duchess sputtered, eyes narrowed. "This cannot be allowed, Majesty, surely you see—"

"I have come to swear fealty," Wolfram said. He drew from his belt an arrow, its feathers battered and shaft stained. "In lieu of a sword, I beg leave to swear upon this. When I stood falsely accused, I was struck by two arrows. This one must stand in for that which flew closer to my heart." He looked up into Kattanan's face. "If you are in need, Your Majesty, let my hand serve you. If you are besieged, let my sword defend you. If you are lost, let my steps guide you. If you are silenced, let my voice pray for you. If you are wounded, let my heart bleed for you. Your mercy delivered me; let me stand by you for the chance to repay my deliverance." He held the arrow out. The duchess started forward, but Kattanan place his hands over Wolfram's.

"I accept your sword and service, and thank the Goddess for them. In return, I grant you free passage in my kingdom, and all such aid and honor as befits the honor you do me." The rote words came suddenly to life.

"Blessed be."

"I already am," Kattanan whispered.

The grip held a moment longer, then Wolfram rose, bowed again, and took a seat in the circle. The guards watched him closely; with no order given, they did not move.

Duchess Elyn, too, was watching, but stepped back to her chair and met Wolfram's eyes. He bowed from the waist and tucked the arrow through his belt.

"I have never sworn fealty to any man. I do not intend to do so now," the wizard announced. "However, until the wrongs done you are made right, I will serve you."

Kattanan looked at her for a long time, and, when he answered, his voice said all that his words could not. "Thank you."

"You are most welcome, Majesty." She rose and left the room.

In the wake of the first, the other oaths seemed dry and meaningless, especially as the morning wore on. Kattanan bore it well, with frequent glances toward Wolfram, who smiled gently and did not leave. The minutes passed slowly, until only the guards and a handful of courtiers remained. The herald stepped out to close court, but was forestalled by a look from the captain. Fionvar extricated himself from his post and came to kneel before the throne.

He slid his sword from its sheath and rested both hands upon it. "Your Majesty, I have not yet made my oath, though I trust you know my fealty."

"Yes, Captain," Kattanan replied. He tentatively set his hands upon the other's, watching him with worried eyes.

"I would ride with you to meet your enemies. I would stay with you to drink your health. I would hold only Finistrel above you, and, if I should go to greet the stars, I would do so in your service."

A commotion at the front of the chamber made both men turn to look. Helmet in hand, Lyssa burst into the room, shaking off a concerned chamberlain. "Forgive my lateness. I was only now informed that Your Majesty sat for oaths." She glared at her brother. Red hair flowed over her armor-clad shoulders, and her eyes flashed. She marched up and dropped to one knee.

Kattanan began to protest, but Fionvar said, "I have finished, Majesty."

"Then I accept your sword and service. Goddess walk with you."

"And with you, Majesty." Fionvar got out of the way.

"I come before you as a Sister of the Sword"—she drew a long blade and clasped it before her—"to pledge my soul, mind and body to whatever service Your Majesty requires of me." She smiled a dazzling smile, which grew a little when he covered her hands with his.

"I accept your sword and service. Goddess walk with you."

"And with you, Your Majesty." Catching sight of Wolfram, Lyssa quickly changed course to sit by him.

The herald looked around carefully before announcing, "The oath-making is done." He rapped his staff against the floor, bowed sharply, and left.

Kattanan sank back into his throne with a sigh.

"Well done, Majesty," the duchess said. "Was that part about going home your own invention?" He nodded weakly. "Well done indeed." She let out a chuckle. "Then it is finally begun." Lyssa's laughter caught her attention, and she frowned. "You should not have accepted his service. He was a traitor to his last king, his own father. Why expect better from him?"

"His oath was freely given, Excellency, and I do not believe he is a traitor to anyone." Kattanan's voice was soft, and he did not look at her.

Wolfram bowed to both of them. "Good day, Excellency. Did I hear my name."

"You are healed. How?" the duchess demanded.

"A gift from the Goddess so that I can better serve my king." He smiled. "She cares for those who serve her wholeheartedly."

"What is there between you and the wizard?"

"Friendship, Excellency. And I needed her aid to come here today. Your guards are polite, but firm about their orders."

"As well they should be." She glowered at him, then at Fionvar. "From now on, you do not leave his side. Prove to me that you are worthy of my trust. Much as I hate to admit it, you are both important here. Come, Brianna, there are still preparations to be made."

The lady rose and curtsied to Kattanan, sharing his worried look. "I am coming, Grandmother." The two exited by the far door.

"Is there something else I am supposed to do?" Kattanan looked to Fionvar.

"There are servants to see to your things, Majesty. And to the cleanup here. We must assume that our enemies are even now finding out about this place."

"Jordan would never reveal us," Lyssa protested.

"Not willingly." The siblings locked eyes for a moment.

"Then this is the last time we will be in this place?" Kattanan asked. Fionvar nodded. "Can we walk the grounds before we go?"

"I don't see why not. We can even leave the entourage behind, if Your Majesty prefers."

"He does." The young man stood, leaving his cup behind.

As Fionvar lead the foursome toward the door, Lyssa glanced at Kattanan. "That voice, that's what Jordan sounded like when he was younger, isn't it?"

Kattanan nodded. "His voice has deepened since last we met."

Lyssa's armor gleamed from the polish she had put to it. Sunlight picked out runes etched around her gorget and down the breastplate—words from the Book of the Goddess. Beside her, Wolfram knelt to touch the earth and took a deep breath. To their curious expressions, he said, "You have no idea how good it feels to be outside again."

"Yes," Kattanan replied, "I do."

"You'll both have had enough of it by the time we reach Lochdale. Much as I want this battle met, I do not look forward to the tents and the long days." Fionvar sighed. "Which way do we go, Majesty?"

"This way, toward the temple."

Fionvar narrowed his eyes. "Are you sure?"

"I will be fine," he replied, without conviction.

"The Temple of the Sisterhood, you mean? Did Brianna take you?" Lyssa asked. "She thought of becoming one of us, you know, before she decided her path led a different way." She looked at her brother, then the king, with questioning eyebrows.

"She seems well pleased with the path she has chosen," Fionvar said, "as would any lady set to marry a king."

"No doubt she shall grow to love him as she does you," Wolfram said, matching Fionvar's disinterested tone.

The other turned to him sharply. "What do you mean by that?"

"You and your sister are speaking as if to conceal something all of us here already know. Unless someone here begins to speak openly, we shall all die of secrets."

"There you are wrong. Every secret you learn brings you one step closer to death. You and I are already on borrowed time, and it will be due with interest. The most I can hope for is that I am allowed my freedom until the battles are over."

"Who would raise a hand against you, Fion? The soldiers here worship you, and the duchess thinks—" Lyssa objected.

"The duchess thinks I am dangerous." Fionvar started walking again.

Lyssa grunted, then eyed Wolfram. "You'll need a sword, at least, if you're to ride with us."

"That may be too much to ask," Fionvar said.

Glancing back at them, Kattanan asked, "He is sworn to my

service, is he not? I would not have him march to battle un-armed."

Fionvar sighed. "I will arrange something, but the duchess will not approve."

"I know," Kattanan said softly. "No man in my service will come to harm without just cause."

"I am not sure you have the power to guarantee that." Fionvar's face was hard, closed. "There is more than one reason she would like to be rid of me."

"If you fear for your life, why did you come back? Great Goddess, everyone who has anything to do with me is brought disaster in return. Look at you." Kattanan gestured to Wolfram as the prince rubbed his newly mended shoulder.

"My disaster is my own, Kattanan," said Wolfram. "If you had never come to Bernholt, I would not have escaped that place alive."

"It was Rolf who saved you."

"He would not have been there if not for you. I would have stood alone, and I would be dead. The Lady has brought us together for a reason, and we will not be parked until it is done. You say you bring us disaster; I say you bring us hope. We have all prayed for peace, for justice, for a way out of our own prisons. In you, we see those things closer than they have ever been. Like it or not, you have been touched by the Lady's hand, Kattanan. Trust me, if you cannot trust yourself. And trust Her."

Lyssa's eyes shone as she listened to him, but Fionvar looked darker than ever. Kattanan stared at his friends.

Wolfram smiled. "Take one step to the Goddess, and She will take a dozen steps to meet you." He rested a hand on the young man's shoulder. "Shall we walk?"

Kattanan nodded. The little group went on, silent, until they reached the disused temple. One by one, they ducked through the opening. Kattanan crossed to the place where he had fainted on his last visit, running his hands over the carved characters.

"This island served as a retreat for the Sisters." Lyssa said. "I found it with Orie a long time ago. I think the privacy was what inspired him to bring the duchess here. After the war, I'd like to come back and tend the temple. Rather than seek the Lady's favor through marriage and motherhood, we dedicate ourselves to fighting, and to other arts of strength. We are supposed to keep ourselves apart from men." She noticed Wolfram's attention, and hurried to add, "Of course, it's not forbidden to us, but we would have to leave the Order, laying aside our arms." She gestured to the niches around the wall. From between the stones, the hilts of swords and hafts of axes stuck out, dark with age.

"The last of the Sisters," Lyssa continued, "stayed to tend the fires here, carving prophecies the Goddess had given her. Here"—she crossed to the wall not far from Kattanan and pointed to a group of words carved somewhat deeper than the others—"this is her last writing. She has burned all her hair in the fire, and seen the face of the future, she says. She blesses those who come after her, and leaves to seek the face." She rested a reverent hand on a stone set into the floor. "She placed her sword here, for whoever might come in need of one." At this, Lyssa looked to Wolfram. "You are in need, are you not?"

"Indeed." He made the sign of the Goddess and knelt beside her. "Have I not said the Lady provides for those who love Her?"

They pried up the stone, revealing a cloth-wrapped bundle. Wolfram carefully removed the wrappings to find a sword, long and plain, but well made, in a leather scabbard. When they held it to the light, they found the letters of the Morning Prayer inked into the leather, and shared a smile. Wolfram looked to the sky. "She who offered this blade, let her be blessed."

"Wolfram." Kattanan's voice trembled.

The other went to him immediately. "What is it?"

"I think I may have misinterpreted this passage. Do you know this word?"

"It refers to one of the Virgins of the Lady, but this suffix implies more reverence than that."

Fionvar leaned over them, reading aloud. "'Now comes the bless-ed eunuch's son, of him who sings with the stars. Let his heart be joyous, let his reign be long, let his voice reach from the mountains to the sea.' That's why you fainted, isn't it?"

"I hadn't eaten in two days, that's all."

"This is why you came back here, for those words," Lyssa said. "You are touched by the Goddess."

# Chapter 23

MONTGOMERY SNEERED down at his victim. "Just tell us what we want to know, and all of this can be over." He gestured with the bloody chisel in his hand.

Jordan stared at his hand, bound flat upon the wooden block. "I cannot do that," he said thickly. "Do what you will."

The torturer set the blunt metal against the next digit of Jordan's middle finger. A sharp blow with the hammer, a sickening crunch, and another bone was broken. Jordan sobbed. All strength for screaming had fled him.

"It's pointless," Thorgir burst out. "You'll have to break every bone in his body."

"I can do that," the other offered.

"I don't doubt it." The king turned away. "Bury it—I'm late" He started for the door, but it was pushed open as he approached, and he stopped with a sigh.

"Good husband, it's time for prayer," said a small woman, clad in rich garb.

"Aye, Evaine," the king growled. "Let us to the temple."

"We will pray here." She moved into the room, oblivious to the stench of blood and the soiled straw beneath her feet. "The Hours of the Lady wait for no man," said the queen gently, "and the people here have even more need than we of soothing prayer."

Montgomery straightened from his bow. "As you say, Your Majesty."

Overhead, the evening bells rang. The queen began to chant the prayer. After a moment's hesitation, Thorgir's rough voice joined hers and Montgomery's.

Jordan swallowed hard. He moistened his lips, and began to sing, hoarsely, softly. As if the sound brought solace, his breath returned, and his voice grew, deep and beautiful. His eyes were shut, tears flowing freely. Montgomery glared, and a low snarl entered Thorgir's voice, though he did not stop chanting. The voices blended, Jordan's weaving round them, now leaping above, now falling back.

Evaine broke off abruptly, dabbing at the corner of one eye. "A shame that such a voice belongs to an enemy. I have heard him sing before, I think."

"He was from that monastery in the mountains, the one that burned," Thorgir supplied, narrowing his gaze at both of them.

"Yes," said the queen. "I recall the nest of traitors there. And they would have had us believe them pious men. It is a good thing I do not rule, for I was quite taken in."

"Indeed you were, dearest. No doubt you will be taken in by this one if you stay much longer." He took her by the elbow, but she resisted, and his hand dropped back.

Evaine took a few steps closer to Jordan, and her round face pinched into a frown. "You are no longer a monk, though, nor have been for some time. In fact, you are a murderer, defiling the Goddess's name by your very use of it."

"No, Majesty," he replied gently, "I have lost Her blessing, but I would never defile Her. If my voice has offended you, then I am sorry to have hurt one so diligent in the keeping of Her ways."

"I am not offended. Even a man outcast may pray for forgiveness."

"This is no place for you, Evaine." Thorgir tugged her toward the door.

"Majesty, if you find such pity in you, pray for me," Jordan called after her. He did not hear her reply as Sir slapped his hand across the broken fingers.

"Be quiet in the presence of the queen!" The man whirled away from him to follow the king, taking the torch with him.

Once again, darkness fell.

❦

KATTANAN QUICKLY decided that riding to battle was not for him. He ached everywhere, and no concoction from the healers seemed to last more than a moment. He groaned as he dismounted, though not too loudly.

Still, Wolfram heard, and offered a rueful smile. "I have not ridden so much in years, Majesty. I should be grateful not to do so again." He, too, swung down from his horse, passing off the reins to a squire. He rubbed absently at his shoulder.

"There's no use complaining." Fionvar joined them on the ground, dark-eyed and unsmiling. "At least our allies have prepared the way." He gestured toward the waiting wagons that bore their dinner. "We'd take weeks if we had to haul supplies with us."

Kattanan glanced at the men unloading the casks and loaves. "Surely they are alerted to our coming by now," he muttered.

"Be not so fearful, Majesty," the duchess said, dismounting gracefully. "The guards here, even those in royal livery, are all provided by the duke of Dalycour, one of your greatest admirers. They've laid a tent for you here, Majesty." She guided him off to one side, whispering, "I am sending Brianna to you tonight, alone. She will stay the night and be seen leaving, understood?"

He nodded. "I have not seen much of her. I trust she fares well?"

Her look told him more than her words as she replied, "She does, Majesty, though somewhat heartsore at being separated from you."

Kattanan frowned, but kept his peace as they reached the tent. Lamps had been lit already, and thick rugs covered the dirt, though they barely concealed the knots of tree roots below. His camp stool and the ever-present crown chest awaited. Following his gaze, the duchess said, "Please try that on this evening and see that it fits."

"I'm not ready."

"You must be wearing it five days hence when we reach Lochdale. Our armies must see a king before them, Rhys. Can you still not understand that?"

He sighed. "I will try it on."

"Very well. Someone shall bring you your dinner." Outside, a strange whistle sounded. The duchess glared in the direction of the sound as she left the tent.

Kattanan slumped into the chair, thankful for a seat that did not move. After a moment's rest, he gripped the heel of one boot and began the nightly struggle. The bird whistled again, and a very excited Wolfram popped into the tent, closely followed by Fionvar, who immediately began to apologize for their entry.

Wolfram took no notice and crossed to help Kattanan off with his boots. "Have you heard that sound, Kattanan? It's a Woodman. That's how they communicate on the hunt. I'm going out to meet him."

"Is that safe?"

"They are men, just as we are, and they can be spoken to," said Wolfram.

"If you break the perimeter, the guards will see you," Fionvar pointed out.

Wolfram turned to him. "Are you not to stay with me, Captain?"

"On midnight walks to meet barbarians?" He let out the exasperated sigh that was becoming so familiar. "I will be there."

"Are ye there? May I enter?" asked a voice from the darkness.

"We're here, Rolf," Kattanan answered with a tired smile as the huge man stuck his head into the tent.

"Yer Majesty, yer Highness," he bobbed his head to the two of them, sharing a brief glower with Fionvar. "Sorry to be intruding. Glorious to be on the road, is it not?" The others stared at him. His grin broadened. "Soft nobility, meaning no disrespect. By the mount, this is beautiful country! Ye're from here, then, Kat? Sorry, Yer Majesty?"

"My name is fine, Rolf, in here. My birthplace is more in the lowlands. The monastery was not far from here, though. We used to go walking in these mountains."

" 'Soft nobility,' " Fionvar echoed, looking at his callused hands. "I am a farmer. I was meant to be a farmer, and I should be farming now."

The other three stared at him, Rolf with an incredulous expression. "You, a farmer? Helping things to grow?" He let out a deep chuckle.

"I tended my father's farm after he died, helped my sisters and brothers to grow. Now even I find it hard to believe."

"Yet ye can believe my prince a traitor and Kattanan but a weak child!"

"Rolf, please," Kattanan began, but Fionvar was already on his feet again.

"You have no idea what I believe! Mayhap if you listened rather than opening your mouth, you'd hear something closer to the truth." Fionvar turned to Kattanan, and bowed briefly. "Your Majesty, I am not well." He turned on his heel and left.

"Struck a sore spot, eh?" Rolf murmured, eyes darting from Wolfram to Kattanan and back. "Sorry I'm not so forgiving as yerselves."

Wolfram did not answer this, but instead asked, "Whom would he go to?"

"What do you mean?" Kattanan asked in return.

"That is a man carrying too many burdens. To whom would he go to lift them?"

"Brianna will not speak to him, now." Kattanan frowned. "Lyssa, perhaps."

Wolfram studied the cuffs of his borrowed shirt, thinking, then he shook his head. "I am going after him, by your leave."

"I don't like yer being alone with him, Highness," Rolf protested. "He's more dangerous now than before. The man's liable t' do anything!"

"He is an honest man, Rolf," Kattanan said. "For reasons of his own, he is on my side, and I'd like him to stay."

"Stay here, guard the king," Wolfram ordered, before ducking out of the tent.

Rolf growled, pulling his sword partway out of the sheath and sliding it back. "Why's he got to be so patient with men like that? Begging yer pardon, Kat."

"It's what he does." The wizard slipped into the tent with a heaping tray of food.

"I wish you wouldn't do that," Kattanan said.

"Sorry," the wizard replied, losing her tiny smile. "I am unused to formal entrances. I brought your dinner, and I'll go." She set down the tray. "Sorry again."

Rolf glared at her, hand again on his sword.

"Perhaps you could eat with me," Kattanan suggested.

She shook her head, stifling a yawn. "My work is not yet done. There are more of us than I thought."

"I don't understand you."

"Nobody does. I am relaying our intentions to other wizards helping your allies. This way, the armies will be ready to strike as one. I still have much to do, and it is a job no one can help with, except my apprentice, I suppose. Hmm."

"You aren't telling Orie our plans!"

"Unless I cut him off as my apprentice, I have no choice. And I will not cut him off. He's too talented. If he gets cut off now, who knows what he might do."

"Talent's got nothing to do with it," Rolf snapped. "He's a murdering swine! Ye cannot mean to let her continue with this. Goddess's Tears, Kattanan, ye are surrounded by snakes. Are ye blind? I came t' protect ye and the prince, but how can I when ye both cast yerselves in the mouth o' darkness?"

The wizard fixed him with a cold stare. "You are an ignorant fool, but I have respected your loyalty—until now. I wish you'd ask me a question just so I could shut you up."

"I'd not give ye the pleasure, Wizard. Were ye a man, by the mount, I'd show ye!" The sword flashed in his hand.

"That can be arranged!"

The transformation raced over her, only to be arrested by

Kattanan's cry. "Get out, both of you!" He was on his feet, hands balled into trembling fists. The wizard vanished instantly. Rolf stood a moment longer, mouth open, then snarled as he stormed out of the tent.

At last alone, Kattanan hovered a moment, then fell back into the chair with a groan, burying his face in his hands.

CRWD

WOLFRAM CAUGHT up with Fionvar at the far end of camp, sidling between the tethered horses. "Captain, wait," he called softly.

"Leave me be."

"No," the pursuer answered firmly. "You've been let be a little too long now."

"What do you know about it? Oh, I forgot, you are a student of humanity." Still, he stopped in the trees just beyond the horses.

"Yes, I am." Wolfram came to stand beside him. "We are all here to fight the same battle, yet you are at war with yourself."

"So should I spill my war stories because you are untouched by such trifling battles? As you say, we are here to fight a common enemy, and I cannot allow my personal 'war' to interfere with that."

"It already has. Ask your sister, ask Gwythym, or the duchess, for that matter. I understand you were once praised for always speaking your mind."

"You are the one who told me that I cannot afford the luxury of distrust anymore. Neither can I afford the luxury of anger, especially not when—" He broke off and scanned the tree limbs above.

"Not when you are angry at the man you have sworn to serve," Wolfram provided. "How would that look, the king's staunchest defender raging against his king."

"No. He is the last person alive I can be angry with."

"But you are."

"Goddess's Tears, she can't help but love him! He's so quiet, handsome, young—he needs her so much. If she heard him sing, she'd forget she ever knew another man. Great Goddess, Orie was right, I should be happy to see him dead!" Fionvar whirled to Wolfram desperately. "I didn't mean that! I would never—"

"I know," said Wolfram. "I love him, too."

"Something happened when he sang. I wasn't just a farmer with a fiddle in his hands. But when I spoke to him in the halls, it was as if that singer had never existed. I hate the way he lets the duchess haul him about like a half-wit. If he were strong enough on his own, he wouldn't need a wife to win over his people. Bury it all, he could be so much more, even without her!" Fionvar threw up his hands. "But he won't. Jordan thought he would prevent the marriage, he claims he can protect me— he has no such power."

Wolfram listened, nodded. "If he had that power, the power he has when he sings, the power to defy the duchess yet still lead a victorious army, he would not need any of us to defend him. He would be free to marry or not, as he wills it, rather than as his grandmother wills."

"Yes, exactly."

"How can we best serve this king who would not be king?"

"I thought I served him well to protect him. Was I wrong?"

Wolfram shook his head. "He needed to know he was not alone. But now, he needs to know himself as we have known him. I don't know how to do that."

"Nor I."

Wolfram laid his hand on the other man's shoulder.

Fionvar met his eyes.

"There is no fault in anger, at your king or at the Goddess or at anyone else. You cannot allow it to rule you, whether that means expressing it in violence or denying that it is there. Anger and fear are part of you, as of all of us, and we need you whole."

He glanced away, folding his arms around him. "Strength knows no fear."

"Fools and martyrs know no fear. Strength is to know fear and choose to face it."

Fionvar stared up at the stars beyond the branches. "I am afraid that we will fail," Fionvar whispered. "I am afraid I have forever lost my lady's love. I am afraid that you are right about my brother. I don't feel strong."

"I am afraid I will always be treated as an enemy because fear will cause my friends not to trust me. I am afraid that I will die alone and no one will help me reach the stars. Small fears, compared to yours."

"I have been ordered," Fionvar said softly, "never to leave your side. You will not die alone."

"If we can all stand by each other, we will not fail."

They stood that way a moment, until a call from the camp turned their solemn expressions into shared grimaces of irritation. "Hey, what're you two conspiring about?" Lyssa pushed her way between the horses and came up to them, grinning. The grin became a frown when she saw them. "You haul me away from my true calling and spend a week avoiding me. I'd get a warmer welcome from the enemy!"

Wolfram slipped his hand from Fionvar's shoulder and gave her a slight smile. "It's good to see you, my lady, however, your brother and I were conspiring . . ."

"I do not appreciate the fact that you are always trying to get rid of me. I'm sure the duchess did not mean for the two of you to be skulking off into the woods in the dark. I am in her personal guard, now." She displayed the badge.

"Shouldn't you be guarding her then?" Fionvar asked.

Her eyes narrowed. "I'm off duty. What is it that you don't want me to know about?" Her eyes flew wide suddenly. "You're going to meet the Woodmen!"

"What?" Both men stared at her, astonished.

"That whistling is how they call to one another. Everybody knows that." Fionvar shrugged, but let her continue, "And here you are in the woods. Can you talk to them?"

Wolfram sighed. "Yes, I can. I have spent some time among them closer to the palace, learning from them. I'd like to know why they are here and if they might help us."

"Would they really?"

"Why don't you come with us and see."

"But she's—" Fionvar started to object.

"She's a trained fighter not unlike you. I last heard them in this direction." Wolfram set out into the woods.

Brother and sister shared a look, his, resigned, hers, smug, and followed. Fionvar hailed the lookouts, identified himself, and they passed away from the encampment. Wolfram led the way into the woods until they came to a clearing bordered by white trees that shimmered in the moonlight. Here, he stopped and let out a whistle similar to those they had been hearing. A figure detached itself from the shadows to approach them. He paused several feet away, with an arrow nocked upon his bow, and spoke in a low, rumbling stream. Wolfram replied in kind and received a grin in response. The Woodman whistled again and walked up to him, lowering his weapon. Both reached out, placing one of their palms on each other's foreheads. The stranger wore a combination of leather and furs, with branches tangled in them. His hair hung in several long braids down his back alongside a quiver well laden. His features were darker and broader than the prince's, but lightened by a quick smile.

Abruptly, Wolfram broke contact and began speaking again, a higher version of the Woodman's deep language. The conversation went on for some minutes, while the other two shifted uncomfortably and peered into the woods around them. At last, this, too, halted, and Wolfram turned back to his companions. "I have met this man before, when he served as an emissary to the tribe upstream. His name is Quinan. He tells me that we have disrupted the hunting here with our presence, but that he had been told to look out for me. I gather that my passage on the river did not go unmarked. In turn, I told him our purpose here, and that we do not mean to stay."

"You told him about the king?" Fionvar's face showed concern and suspicion.

"Yes, I did. Quinan is a powerful man in these parts, and he has no love for the Usurper's soldiers. It seems they follow my father's example in killing his people."

"Did you ask him if they can do anything to help us?" Fionvar asked.

Wolfram resumed the conversation for a little while, then the

Woodman, with a sharp gesture, turned and left. "He thinks they are too few, and does not know what could be done. He will talk to the tribes and return to us some other place if he has any more to say."

"Have we offended him?"

"No. If they have no more to say, or some message to relay elsewhere, that takes precedence over formal farewells. It takes some getting used to." He let out another whistle and was answered. "Nothing more to be done here," said Wolfram, turning back to the camp.

Fionvar fell in stride beside him. "You are a man of many talents."

"My father says I spend too long with books and strange studies, and not enough on the ways of kingship. If that is talent, then I am talented indeed."

At the encampment, Duchess Elyn led Brianna by the arm away from their well-appointed pavilion. "You must listen to everything he says, make sure he's really on our side, not Bernholt's. And remind him to try on the crown."

"Yes," Brianna replied. "I can find my way there, Grandmother."

"Too long spent with peasants, it's ruining your manners." Duchess Elyn held Brianna at arm's length. "Well, at least the child will be half-Rinvien. Let's hope that side prevails."

Brianna held up her skirts with both hands, stumbling over roots and stones, picking her way between the lumps of sleeping soldiers. Though they were a small company, it still seemed to take forever to reach her destination. Two guards stood on duty there, and she smiled as sweetly as she could, leaning in close to them. "I would visit my betrothed," she whispered, winking at the men.

They shared a knowing grin, and one stuck his head in to announce her.

Kattanan lay on his back on the rugs, and she hurried to kneel beside him. "Are you well, my lord?"

He nodded. "I was looking at the stars." He pointed up to the gap at the roof peak where the center pole reached toward the sky. "I have so many people there."

Brianna lay down beside him, and followed his gaze. "I, too."

They lay still for a few minutes before Kattanan asked quietly, "Do you remember my father?"

"Not well," she replied after a pause. "He had a beautiful smile, but he always looked worried about something. I remember wondering what it was. Grandmother always spoke well of him, and I know Caitrin loved him dearly. It was she who played with me and the princes." Something occurred to her, and she smiled. "Once, on Finisnez, he brought me a gift. When he leaned down to give it to me, the crown slipped, and I was frightened that it would fall on me, so I ran away. He followed me, laughing, and told me not to be afraid of it, that it was a good thing and could not hurt me."

"I don't remember him, Brie. I know what he looked like, what he did, but I cannot see his face."

She turned her head toward him. "Grandmother reminded me about the crown."

"Must I?' He sighed; even so, he sat up and looked at the box. "I suppose it is nothing to fear." Kattanan crossed to the chest and peered inside. He reached in a tentative hand, then lifted out the crown his parents had worn. Carrying it carefully, he made his way back and sat down with the thing on his lap.

Brianna sat up to watch him, then asked, "Would you prefer I did not look?"

"I am not sure I would want to do this alone." With another sigh, he placed the crown upon his head. It settled there, gleaming in the lamplight, a perfect fit. When he met Brianna's eyes, he saw himself not so much in the reflection, but in her expression of wide-eyed wonder. "I must look foolish," he said, looking away.

"Kattanan, you are the king, in spite of yourself. The crown only makes it more obvious."

He reached up and ran his hands along the points, the chased surface, and the fur lining that smoothed out his curls. "I never wanted this."

"Nevertheless, it is yours. You will have the throne and the castle."

"And the queen." He looked at her again. "It's not right, none of it."

"Can't you stop saying that? If not you, then who? Who will displace the Usurper and return justice to Lochalyn? Every person of your father's line is dead. My grandmother would like to do it, but she knows her time runs short."

"Why not you?"

"Our House is made stronger by marriage, and the child within me will be your heir, but I do not seek the throne by any means. However, I believe that you and I together can do what needs to be done. I wish you could believe as much."

"Brianna, I don't mean that I don't like you. Lochalyn, and you, both deserve better than me." He thought of Melisande, so close now to a crown of her own.

They stared at each other for a long while, then she slipped her hand behind his head and kissed him.

Kattanan broke away. "What about Fionvar?"

"I have claimed this as your child before witnesses; I will marry you," she said with a curious intensity. She kissed him again, and he did not resist.

# Chapter 24

BELLS RANG overhead, but whether they tolled dawn or dusk, Jordan did not know. Daylight could not touch him. His knees ached from kneeling, his shoulders screamed in protest when he tried to move, and so he sat still. He flickered in and out of consciousness, unable to tell one darkness from the next. The door opened and Evaine entered, bearing a small stool and a bowl. He yearned for the food and loathed himself for the yearning.

"Good morrow, Traitor," she said, without malice.

"Good morrow, my lady Queen," he rasped.

"Forgive my lateness. There was a commotion in the halls." She set down the stool and the bowl, tantalizingly close, and began the chant.

He managed to limp through three verses, but each was progressively fainter. Evaine's lips pinched as she glanced down at him, a vague worry played about her eyes, and she finished the prayer alone. Spoon after spoon she patiently watched him swallow, keeping her eyes always on his face, as if she could not see the mess that had been his right hand bound upon the stump. Several times, she opened her mouth as if to speak.

When she had scraped the last spoonful, she asked, "Would you care for water?"

"Please, Your Majesty."

She rose and brought a dipper from the bucket across the room, gently brought it to his lips. "I have been praying for you."

"I have done nothing worthy of your kindnesses, Your Majesty."

Evaine did not answer this. "More?" At his weak nod, she made the trip again.

The door slammed open, spilling light and men into the dungeon. "Montgomery, take care of him. Evaine! Come!" Thorgir barked. Sir immediately went to the prisoner and set to cutting his bonds.

She rose slowly and turned to him. "Why speak to me so roughly, my lord?"

"Hush, woman, I have no time for this."

Evaine stepped back from him. "I am your wife and queen, Thorgir."

His nostrils flared. "Bury it, Evaine! We are besieged!"

KATTANAN PACED the short length of the pavilion, the crown heavy upon his head "Surely even so dense a fog could not conceal us. They have seen us coming; they must know our number, our purpose, everything."

"Why do you imagine we have spent so much on wizards?" She gestured toward the Wizard of Nine Stars, who slumped in a chair with her eyes closed.

"It should not have been so easy," the wizard murmured.

"From the looks of you and the others, it was anything but easy," Wolfram commented. He swiped the polishing cloth once more along his blade and inspected it carefully. "I pray I do not have to use this," he murmured.

"They have the Liren-sha," the wizard said. Then she pushed herself up with sudden urgency and sprinted from the tent.

"Rude," the duchess observed, "but effective."

Fionvar stared after her, then he also rose. "Permission to go, Your Majesty."

"Well, yes, but—"

Wolfram scrambled up also, and, with a nod to Kattanan, ran outside.

"We will have proper officers soon enough, Your Majesty. Are you ready to receive our allies?"

Kattanan stared after his friends, feeling once again abandoned. "I suppose."

Brianna nodded also and accepted his hand to rise. She had not kissed him since that first night, but they had shared a pavilion, talking until daylight when they could not sleep. The lady shook crumbs from her gown of vivid silk. Kattanan watched her, and the duchess's smile grew a little more.

"Come, then." Duchess Elyn led the way out where they were joined by a dozen guards, including Lyssa and three others of the Sisterhood. "You thought they might know our purpose. Not yet, but they soon will. Look—the banners are being raised."

He followed her hand to where groups of soldiers struggled to heave up long poles. Atop each flew the colors of his father, boldly flashing in the wind. A shallow valley separated them from the walled city and the castle that rose above it. All around to both sides spread the encampments of their allies, lords who had kept faith with the exiles, plus a few of the new king's regime who had tired of his ways. Men teemed about, readying arms and horses. From the forest behind came the sound of axes and hammers, more soldiers at work on battering rams and siege engines.

"Now the Usurper knows who stands against him." Around the crescent of the armies, banners rose into the sky, declaring their allegiance.

Below, Fionvar and Wolfram tramped up toward them, and the duchess frowned. Rolf trailed after them, clearly on the former prince's side. "Your choice of companions does occasionally leave something to be desired, King Rhys."

"But I've hardly seen them the past few days," he protested.

"It ill befits a king to consort with traitors and peasants."

He kept silent, though Brianna nodded vaguely, her grip tightening upon his arm.

Fionvar and Wolfram slipped into the procession behind the king, exchanging a grim look. Rolf waited along the sidelines with the common soldiers and servants who looked after the camp. Many men and women had already gathered in the huge pavilion that served for a throne room, some of the exiled nobles who had come with them, but others who were strangers. The procession filed past, dividing at the thrones to allow Kattanan, Brianna, and Elyn to stand before their places. Only when these three had seated themselves did the company settle onto their benches. Kattanan cast his eye over them, seeing pride and excitement in the eager smiles. A few of the newcomers looked vaguely familiar, faces he might have seen when he was very young. At his side, the duchess had begun her speech of welcome.

". . . to see so many of you among us," she was saying, "and it lightens my heart to know that you have seen our cause and know it to be just." A rumble of approval greeted this. "Still, I know there are some here who have doubted our truth and come here to see the proof of it with their own eyes. Doubting friends, you see before you Rhys yfCaitrin of the House of Rinvien, duAlyn of the House of Strel Maria, rightful heir of his father, True King of Lochalyn and all her lands and peoples!" She brought her arm up, and Kattanan stood, greeted with such a noise of joy that he wanted immediately to sit down again.

Still, he bore their cheering and stood until it had died back again. Into this silence, a voice cried, "Let him speak!" This call was now taken up, both by voices reveling in the presence of their long-awaited king, and by those who remembered the rumor of the youngest prince and whose faces held dark doubt.

The duchess looked at him with a hard expression like a veiled threat.

"The day you have all waited so long for has arrived." He spoke softly, but his voice carried through the sudden hush. "And I—I have come home."

A cheer arose, and the smile returned to the duchess's lips.

"There is a proclamation," Kattanan prompted, and a herald came trotting up with a great scroll dangling many wax seals.

At the duchess's nod, the man unrolled his burden and stood in the little space before the thrones. "Unto the Usurper Thorgir yfEvaine from his Royal Nephew, Rhys yfCaitrin of the House of Rinvien duAlyn of the House of Strel Maria, heir to his father, True King of Lochalyn by the Blessing of the Lady Finistrel, come these mighty words. King Rhys will not long wait outside his own gate, nor shall he suffer a tyrant to rule in his stead while he yet lives. Therefore, the Usurper is given one hour to quit the Keep of Lochdale and surrender himself to the Justice of the Lady. If he should fail in this, no sword will defend him, no hall will shield him, no prayer will save him from righteous wrath. Nor shall his family, nor shall his allies escape the woe that is their payment for their True King's betrayal. Let all see before the gate the might of King Rhys and of those who stand with him. Let them tremble to know the power at his hand, for no traitor shall escape him!"

Cries of "Huzzah!" and "Hail the True King!" echoed out on all sides. Kattanan fidgeted, eyes flickering among the faces. Brianna reached up and took his hand—it was cold and trembling. He glanced down at her. "You are the True King," she said. "Smile."

He managed a smile, but his eyes rebelled, and Brianna was not alone in noticing.

NOT FAR outside the new temple, Montgomery stood near the bustle of guards who rushed to prepare a defense for the gaping wound in the castle wall. In a few more weeks, this wall should have been mended by the stonemasons. Now they struggled to fill as much of the gap as they could. Sir, however, had other work. He turned back to Jordan with a sneer. "That's not even deep enough for a fire pit! You'll have to do better than that." He fingered a long knife.

The Liren-sha bent gasping over the handle of a shovel where he had paused for breath. Though he held his right hand tight against his chest, every movement sent out shocks of pain. His left hand clenched the rough wood. A few days ago, he might have had the strength to lash out with it. Now it was all he could do to keep from falling into the shallow excavation.

"Dig," his keeper ordered, brushing the knife along Jordan's good arm. Jordan lifted the shovel again and thrust it into the ground, adding another scoop to the pile of dirt. His ragged breath began to grate even on his own ears.

A horn blew from the field below, and another. Soon, the valley was alive with calls, answered from the castle. The working soldiers glanced up, then redoubled their efforts.

"They are coming," Jordan gasped.

"Not fast enough for you, as if they'd ever take this place."

"There is a hole behind me," he panted, taking another stab with the shovel, "large enough for ten horsemen abreast."

"They'll never get this far," the other snapped. "Thorgir's not so stupid as to ignore that." He gestured to the men working around them. "They'll lose half their men to archers before one even gets this far!" Still, he glanced down the slope and to the opening in the wall.

"You might still run and escape them."

"Shut up and dig!"

The Liren-sha was silent for a few minutes, trying to concentrate. Deep in his throat, he began to hum a rhythm, keeping time with the shovel in the dirt. Before long, he was rasping out the words of "The Lonely Steersman." It was the last song he and Kattanan had sung together, perhaps the last he would ever sing. Jordan stooped and lifted, bit by bit, digging his grave.

⁂

Siege engines rumbled forward with the charge, horses straining against their harnesses. Their progress was slow but unstoppable though arrows flew down among them. The metal-clad steeds dug in their hooves and strained forward, heedless of the bodies of men who had gone down before them. The sky was pierced by ladders, banners, and catapults borne forward with a great cry.

Above the field, Kattanan and a few companions stood, peering out, wincing when they saw their own men fall. Rolf paced, restless to do more than watch. Wolfram divided his worried glances between his faithful guard and his chosen king, who fretted with the buckles of his armor. Kattanan watched the battle with a curious distraction; he could not bear to see yet dared not look away.

Fionvar, too, was distracted, trying not to notice Brianna's hand on the king's arm, her whispers to him, and excited pointing toward the east where a ladder stood against the wall and had not been felled. The first of the catapults was near enough by then, and a great wagon of stones thundered up to it. The guard captain did not watch that spectacle, but instead focused on a banner nearer to them, a wide blue cloth studded with stars, bearing the sign of an arm and sword upright—the banner of the Sisterhood. "Do not let me lose another to this fight," he murmured, making the sign of the Goddess.

Rolf stopped his pacing. "If he's sent out messages, we'll be caught between the castle and his allies. By the mount!"

"I doubt his allies will muster much force in time to be of any use to him," Fionvar remarked. A stone slammed against the wall, and cheers rose from the field as they readied another. "Even the Lord of Athelmark would take a half day, riding hard, and his garrison is small. By that time, we should have breached the wall at the far side. They doubtless expected us to come by the gate, but once there are two holes in their walls, it'll be no small matter to keep us out." He smiled faintly. "Her Excellency's plan is to have us in by sundown, reinforcements or no."

"We will lose many soldiers," Wolfram observed, looking sidelong at Fionvar.

His smile slipped away. "All of these men and women feel they are fighting for a just cause. They would rather die here for King Rhys than live under Thorgir's rule."

"I can't bear it that they should die for me," Kattanan moaned, shutting his eyes.

"Thorgir is a tyrant," Brianna said. "He should have been cast down years ago by his own people. That's why so many of them have joined us."

"These soldiers are here because they believe their land will be better served by having you as king," Fionvar added.

"But I have given them no reason to believe in me. What if they are wrong?"

"They are not wrong," Wolfram said, in a tone of absolute conviction.

Kattanan's eyes locked with his. The king started to say something, but stopped as voices were heard coming toward them.

Duchess Elyn smiled as she approached them and mounted the low rise. "How fares the fight, Your Majesty?"

Brianna answered, "Well, Grandmother. Our catapults are in place, and flaming arrows cannot take them."

"Excellent!"

Two horses, galloping hard, labored up the slope toward them. The riders slid to the ground, removing their helms. Lyssa's eyes were sharp with excitement. "I nearly lost my mount, Majesty, but we completed a circuit of the city. As expected, they have a great many footmen by the temple wall, but these are finding it hard to be patient since no one has come against them."

"And best yet," Gwythym put in, "the east wall begins to falter." He held out a stone. "This is one of the first pieces to crumble.

The duchess took it, glaring. "I care not for the first. Bring me the last, when the wall has fallen!" She tossed the thing over her shoulder, where it bounced down into the bushes. A great rustling erupted, and they stared.

"Spy!" shouted Rolf, springing for the woods. He crashed in, and the others caught a glimpse of a hooded figure sprinting away.

Fionvar and Wolfram leapt to the chase, following Rolf's lead into the woods.

"Should we—?" Lyssa began.

The duchess shook her head. "The man will not get far in that direction. We have troops massing there to assault the temple door. No, you stay and protect the king."

"Look there!" cried Lyssa, pointing. "Mounted knights, and more besides!"

All turned to squint toward the company, still some way off but riding hard. Footmen straggled out behind them. "Can you see the banner?" the duchess demanded.

Lyssa plucked out a simple scope and peered through it. "A white field, two green serpents intertwined."

"Athelmark," the duchess breathed. "He cannot have come so fast."

"They must have already been riding." Gwythym strained to see them for himself.

"What now?" Lyssa asked, hand nervously stroking the great hammer at her side.

"Great Goddess, Rolf was right." All color had drained from Kattanan's face, and Brianna's hand seemed less for comfort than to keep him from falling.

"We'll turn part of the charge," said Gwythym, "The right flank could meet them."

"Go!" the duchess urged, and he scrambled down the hill, calling to the trumpeters. She gathered her skirts to follow, but stopped abruptly as the Wizard of Nine Stars, dashing up the hill, nearly collided with her.

The wizard brushed past the duchess to face Kattanan. "You must come!"

"He's not going anywhere," the duchess snapped.

"What are you talking about?" Kattanan breathed.

"He needs us now, Majesty. If ever you were his friend, you must come," the wizard repeated, her yellow eyes blazing like the sun off bronze.

"Jordan," he said softly.

"Out of the question," the duchess said. "Especially with Athelmark galloping down upon us."

"He left me," Kattanan told the wizard. "He went off with a wizard and left me! Now you expect me to go into a war looking for him? My grandmother is right."

"Left you? He was dragged away in chains!" the wizard snatched Kattanan's wrist. "Haven't you seen the scars? Holy Mother, have you no idea what he has gone through for you?"

"But the wizard," the king protested, thinking back and finding only his grief.

"Jordan killed him," Lyssa put in, beginning to look as anxious as Nine Stars. "That was the first man he killed."

"Forsaking his vows, losing the favor of the Lady, because he had lost you," Nine Stars put in.

"Great Goddess," Kattanan whispered. "What have I done!"

# Chapter 25

"SHUT UP!" Montgomery shouted again, over the din of battle.

Jordan, up to his waist in the hole, went on singing. At first, the sound of his own voice nearly brought him to tears. Most of its beauty had been destroyed years ago by shouting, screaming, and declaring himself before all enemies. Yet even the first prayer he had sung in the dungeon held some of the former promise. Now, only rhythm and strength were left him. His throat ached at every note, just as his hands pulsed with pain. The darkness he had waited so long for finally lay before him, so close he could nearly touch it.

Montgomery growled low in his throat. He paced, staring at the lines of soldiers waiting nearby. They turned at every cry of battle, shifted uneasily at the pound of stones battering the far wall. "Hold your ground!" the captains called, "Look to the forest!"

Still no sign of the enemy from this vantage.

The prisoner broke down coughing for a moment—a blessed end to the singing!—but recovered quickly. Montgomery bounced the knife from hand to hand. Another archer screamed and fell from the corner tower. He paused to watch the fall. "They are coming," he muttered. He had a horrible sense that the city walls would crumble beneath some massive charge yet he would be the last to know. "Bury it, I told you to shut up!"

The Liren-sha spared him a tiny glance, but no silence.

Montgomery crossed to the edge of the grave. "I'm telling you to be quiet!" His hand shook; sunbeams splintered off the knife blade.

The song went on.

"Enough!" He bent and grabbed a handful of Jordan's dark hair, jerking back his chin. Their eyes locked as he plunged the knife deep into the singer's throat.

Shaking, he staggered back from the grave and ran.

"NO!" THE wizard screamed. She pushed Kattanan away, pressing her hands to her head. "He's dying," she moaned.

"Oh, no." Brianna sighed, eyes brimming.

"We have to go," Lyssa urged.

"You cannot," the duchess said. "I forbid it."

"We can't go," Kattanan echoed.

"Listen, the woods are full of our men waiting for the signal," Lyssa said. "We will not ride alone."

The duchess objected. "We will not charge until the far wall crumbles."

Kattanan touched the wizard's shoulder. "You can heal him."

"Only if we hurry."

He looked from the hard face of his grandmother to the distraught wizard, then to the sky. "Finistrel, what can I do?" he breathed.

"Look!" cried Lyssa. "The wall!" The ground trembled with its collapse.

"Give me a horse," Kattanan demanded.

"Not with Athelmark bearing down on us," the duchess insisted.

"The horse!"

Gwythym, returning breathless from his errand, handed Kattanan the reins and boosted him up with a fierce grin. "Hail the True King!"

The wizard scrambled up behind him. "Ride!"

Leaping to her own mount, Lyssa was only a few strides behind as they pounded down the slope into the woods.

"Rhys!" the duchess called, stumbling a few steps, with Brianna beside her.

Gwythym flashed them a glance. "The king rides to battle!"

"He'll be killed!" Brianna shouted. "He knows nothing of war!"

Gwythym was already plunging down the slope, calling the men to arms.

The horses crashed through the trees, bursting upon the soldiers from one side. Kattanan reined in for a moment. "The wall is fallen!" he cried.

The men—his men—cheered, springing up with swords in hand. Mounted knights hailed him, urging forward the charge. He kicked his horse into motion, ducking away from branches as they passed the last trees. From the forest behind him, knights and soldiers streamed. Thorgir's captains shouted and stiffened to meet their enemy. Soldiers flung great shields up before them.

As the shield wall rose, Kattanan hesitated. Pikes and axes bristled up.

"Jump!" the wizard hissed.

"The horse can't—" he began, but he thought of Jordan, and set his heels to the horse's sides. Great muscles bunched and stretched beneath him. The ground flew under the horse's hooves, perilously close. The cries of the enemy rang about him as the horse gathered himself and launched into the air.

His hind feet clipped a shield, and he stumbled as he struck earth. Astonished men scattered even as their captain bawled his orders. Whinnying, the horse jolted back to speed. Kattanan did not look back to the battle, where his own men cried aloud for their king, pouring in among their bewildered foes.

"There!" The wizard pointed past his ear toward an ominous pit.

The pair slid from their mount, and Lyssa galloped through the breach behind them.

The wizard leapt into the grave as Kattanan stared in horror. She touched Jordan's pale cheek, snarled a curse, and pulled back her sleeve. The king scrambled down beside her. "Does he live?"

"He's lost too much blood." She searched her garments. "Give me a knife!"

His glance flicked to the wicked hilt at Jordan's throat, and he nodded, slipping his little dagger from the top of a boot. "What can I do?"

"Nothing! I don't know." She slashed the blade along her skin from her forearm to her palm. She tossed aside the knife, following it with the other. "Sing!" she said, pressing her bloody hand to the wound.

Lyssa slipped in beside him, catching his worried look. She murmured, "Pray."

IN THE woods, some distance from the battle, a hurrying figure stopped suddenly, panting but alert. Orie tossed back his hood and looked intently toward the castle. He felt a trace of pain along his forearm and gripped it absently with his other hand. A smile grew upon his lips, then harsh laughter. Transfixed, Orie did not turn when Rolf bolted into the clearing and flung him to the ground.

"Ye bastard!" the huge man cried. He locked his hands around Orie's neck. "Spying son of a whore!"

They struggled in the dirt, Orie gasping for breath, clawing at Rolf's hands.

"Let go!" Fionvar cried, pushing his way through the branches. "Find out who he is before you kill him!"

Rolf hauled his captive up, but Fionvar slammed into him, breaking his grip and sending the larger man sprawling with a quick blow. "Great Goddess!" he gasped.

"Thanks, brother!" Orie coughed, rubbing his throat. "Can't stay!" he sprang into the trees again.

"Orie, wait!" Fionvar looked after him, then back at where Rolf lay unmoving against a tree.

Wolfram stumbled in and halted. "What's happened?"

"See to him, I'm going after Orie!"

"Orie? He's here?" But Fionvar had already vanished into the woods again.

Wolfram bent over Rolf, checking his breathing. He glanced over his shoulder, hesitating. With a pat on the guard's chest, he whispered, "You'll be fine. He may need me." Still, he gazed at Rolf a moment longer before pulling himself up to resume the chase.

◑❀◐

THE SUN shone warmly down upon him, but it gave the man no comfort. He walked as he had always done, tripping over the occasional stone. He no longer remembered where he was going, though he vaguely felt that this was not the place. What was familiar about it? Only that he was alone.

"You are not alone," said a voice beside him. "I have not left you."

He knew the voice, though he had never heard it. "It was I who left you, wasn't it?" Memory washed over him, and he turned to look upon her.

"You are not alone," she repeated. Her face was plain, lips thin but kind, and skin unmarked. Yet from the unremarkable face, her eyes held him in their bright and steady gaze. The light within them twinkled, a cool and comfortable glow. When she smiled, her features lit as if from within. "Yes, you know me."

"Once, I thought I did. I thought I could walk with the Lady."

"There was a child," she said, "who every day walked among the trees. He was the son of a peasant woman who had been sent to seek something for their supper, yet on this day he could find neither fruit nor fowl. By nightfall, he lifted his eyes from the ground and saw that he did not know his way. At first, he cried, knowing himself lost. His tears blinded him to the village lights behind him, and he walked on. Often he fell and cursed himself for being lost. After a time he cried no more, and said rather, that it was better so, that his mother was poor, and could ill afford to care for him. In wandering, he came upon a little stream and drank from it. He rose and he followed it, for it held lightness and laughter. It led him to the river, where his mother knelt to do her washing. Her heart leapt within her to see him on the farther bank, but he would not come to her, saying 'Mother, I love you, but I have no food for you. I am unworthy to return to you, for I know you have not enough to share with me.' She wept, and where her tears struck the river, they became as silver fishes, and swam into her basket. 'My child,' she said, 'come home. I will always have enough for you.' He dove in and swam to her while the river laughed for joy."The bright eyes watched him, with sadness and with hope.

"But the child turned his back on her. In the forest, he did not look to the lights, but only to his own tears."

"You have strayed a long time in the forest, Jordan. Will you not come home?"

"I have sinned," he said. "I have killed so many. There are so many more deserving of blessing than I am."

"I will always have enough for you," she replied, lifting his chin with a gentle hand. "Do you think me so poor that I cannot spare my love for those who need it most?" She released him, and there were tears upon her cheeks.

He knew that he was crying, too, yet a joy unlike any he had known filled him as he looked to her. Her eyes blazed, but he did not look away. "Lady, forgive me."

She held out her hand to him. "Walk with me."

As he touched her fingers, a firm grasp took his hand, and he stepped forward.

"HE'S ALIVE!" Lyssa shouted, gripping his hand as if to pull him back from the longest journey.

Kattanan's voice rose, tears flowing down his cheeks. His own fingers were entangled in Jordan's hair, his eyes on Jordan's face as the other took a tiny breath, and let it out as a sigh, almost like a song. The wizard, too, sighed, withdrawing her hand at last. The wound she had made along her arm silently sealed itself, but her face was pale. Her eyes shut, and she slumped against the dirt.

Jordan's eyes opened, and he saw her—the most beautiful woman in the world. Sun shone around her head, sparking from her red hair. "My lady," he whispered.

"I am here," Lyssa said.

He shut his eyes again, and wept, hearing the music as if for the first time. "Oh, my King, my friend. I am so sorry."

Kattanan broke off instantly. "I am the one to be sorry. Can you forgive me?"

In answer, Jordan shook off Lyssa's hand and pushed himself weakly up with his left arm. He gathered Kattanan to his chest, smiling and sobbing at the same time.

"DON'T TELL me that!" Thorgir barked.

The herald flinched at his words. " 'Tis true, m'lord. The wall is breached."

"Bury it!" He stomped across the chamber to snatch up his sword from a table. His wife watched silently beside the shuttered window. Thorgir examined the blade for the hundredth time. "What of Athelmark?"

"He has just engaged on the right flank. His men are bold and worthy, Sire," the herald added quickly.

"Then why do you look so worried, little man? Is this not my castle?"

"Yes indeed, Sire." The man flicked a glance to the door as if planning his escape.

Thorgir caught up the front of his tunic and heaved him off his feet. "Tell me!"

"Gently, husband," Evaine cautioned. She picked up her embroidery hoop and examined the stitches.

"Reports from the temple wall, Sire," the man gasped.

"We are attacked on two fronts, what of it?" Thorgir dropped the herald and shoved his sword into the sheath.

"They say the Pretender-king rode there, that his horse flew over them."

"Ha! They are fools tricked by his pet wizards."

"They say that he wore no helm into battle, and his hair glowed like starlight," the man continued in a rush. "Alyn's sword was by his side."

Thorgir backhanded the herald and pushed him toward the door. "They lied! This is Alyn's sword. I am the rightful king here."

"I heard that King Rhys—"

"There is no King Rhys!" he bellowed. "Get out, and I'll take your head if you keep spreading that horse manure!"

The words echoed inside the chamber, but Evaine kept to her stitching. When the king turned back toward her, she said, "Truth is best spoken with quiet words, my lord."

"Not to idiots. With those people, shouting is all they hear."

"It is now, Daddy," Asenith complained. She shut the door behind her. "Shouting is all any of us hear these days." Her boils had gone at last, leaving her features fair, but sharp. She swept her blond hair back over her shoulder. "It's hard enough to be trapped here without listening to you yelling all day."

"You have no idea." He sank into a deep chair and took a long swallow from a flagon of ale. "Where's your friend?"

"Faedre? I don't know." Her features pinched into a frown. "I was going to ask if you'd seen her."

"I have been on the tower most of the day. I wouldn't have seen her unless she was jumping." His tone suggested that this might be a good idea.

"Why don't you like her?"

"She is a stranger and a heathen!"

"Goddess's Tears! At least she isn't half so obnoxious as your Montgomery."

"Nor is she half so valuable."

"What's he done that's so great?"

"With his aid, I was able to guess at their plans and send for Athelmark and the others. Right now, he is doing away with someone who is causing us a lot of trouble."

At this, Evaine's needle slipped, and she pricked her finger. She started to raise it to her lips, then hastily dabbed it to her forehead.

"Farewell to the Wizard's Bane, the reason our wizards have been virtually powerless. Very soon, we should be able to launch a counterattack."

"Finally!" Asenith brightened a bit, then glanced to her mother and back. "You have heard what the soldiers are saying about the Pretender," she said softly.

"I have," said Thorgir.

"Are you sure it isn't . . . ?"

"Not you, too! Do you think anyone would follow him?"

Evaine frowned as she glanced from one to the other. "The princes are all dead. Their mother killed them."

"Yes, yes, of course," Thorgir said, silencing his daughter with a look.

The queen carefully set down her hoop and looked him full in the face. "I know your face when you lie, Thorgir," she said softly. "There are things you must conceal from me, but what is it that my daughter knows that you will not share with me?"

"Prince Rhys was not killed with his brothers. We had thought that he died in another place, and that his treacherous relatives did not know he lived even so long. He was my favorite nephew, so I naturally investigated the rumors. Clearly they have found someone who resembles him to serve as their Pretender. I have tried to keep this from our troops for fear that their loyalties would become confused. You must understand that."

"I understand," she said. She sat still a long moment, then rose. "I am going to temple to pray."

Thorgir caught her and kissed her forehead as she passed. "You are ever faithful and strong for me. Pray that we do not lose too many to put these traitors in their place."

"I shall pray for us all," Evaine said. As she looked up at her husband, she saw that a spot of the blood was on his lips, and it did not seem so out of place.

❧

"ORIE!" FIONVAR called. He rested his hands on his knees to catch his breath.

"What do you want, Fion?" his brother's voice inquired from not far ahead.

"I should ask you that." Fionvar picked his way through a patch of brambles. "Why are you here?" He emerged into a clearing where a great tree had fallen, leaving a hole into the sky.

Orie perched on the tree trunk, one hand pressed to his side. His smile was interrupted by a wince. "Do I not have an interest in what happens here? I, too, have worked for this day."

"You've worked for yourself, you mean." Fionvar shook his head, then started forward. "You're bleeding!"

"That big oaf broke some of my ribs when he fell on me." Orie looked down at his side as if more curious than hurt. "No matter, now. At least, not for long."

"Let me look at it." He walked to the log, but Orie slid down and stepped away. "I'd rather not lose another sibling to this war, Orie."

"I am so sick of you feeling responsible for the rest of us. We're adults now; we don't need you to see our skinned knees, Fion."

A startled frown crossed Fionvar's tired features. "What has come over you? You need help, mine or somebody else's."

"I'd like you to stay where you are," the earl insisted, adding some faint words under his breath.

Fionvar tried to step forward, but found himself rooted to the spot. "Orie, don't do this. Bury your magic!"

"Not mine, hers." Orie laughed lightly. "Well, all mine, now. All the secrets she tried to keep from her own apprentice." He drew a slim sword. A flick of his blade cut a shallow wound across Fionvar's arm. Before Orie could do more, someone broke from the trees. "Who's there?"

"Your destiny, Orie, if I have anything to say about it." Wolfram stepped from the woods, sword drawn.

"Oh, no, Wolfie," Orie sneered. "Perhaps yours." They met in a clash of steel.

⟨∞⟩

"OH!" THE wizard sat bolt upright, staring through her companions.

"Alswytha!" Jordan twisted to look at her, then frowned. "What's wrong?"

"Great Goddess, he was with me!"

Lyssa blinked a few times. "You aren't making sense." She had an arm around Jordan, supporting his shoulders, her left hand cradling his.

Kattanan's eyes widened. "Orie, you mean. He knows!"

"It's a healing, what harm could it do?" Lyssa asked.

"I can only hope he has no idea," the wizard murmured. "There is so much more. I pray he did not see all." She massaged her forehead. "He seeks to sever the bond."

"You healed me," Jordan said softly.

She looked down at his ruined right hand—the skin had pulled together over hopelessly shattered bones. "What I could. I am sorry."

"Sorry?" he stared at her. "My lady, you healed me when I thought I was dying."

Lyssa glowered a little. "Hadn't we best get off the battlefield?"

Above, and all around them, the battle rang on. Kattanan nodded. "I only wish I knew how."

⟨∞⟩

AGAIN, ORIE fell back, gasping. He coughed, and blood spattered his lips. Still, his sword was fast, and his expression, fierce. "You're a pathetic swordsman, Wolfie."

"I have worked for peace, not war," Wolfram panted, dodging a slash.

Fionvar, horribly still, ground his teeth together. His own blade hung just beneath his hand, the hilt brushing his palm, yet he could not lift it. Blood seeped from his arm and he could not stop it.

"Not your fight, Fion," his brother sang, passing him quickly. As he did, he touched the shallow cut he had made, closing his hand around his brother's blood. A hint of color returned to Orie's cheeks, but Fionvar took in a sharp breath, and the touch left him dizzy.

Wolfram glanced toward him, stumbled, and had to twist under the tree trunk to escape.

With another stroke of Fionvar's blood, Orie sprang up to the tree and leapt down by Wolfram again.

The blades slid together, locked, leaving the combatants staring into one another's eyes. There was a flash at Orie's wrist, a finely wrought silver band.

"You stay away from my sister," Wolfram hissed, pulling back, and lunging again.

"Difficult," Orie remarked, parrying. "I am her husband."

"You killed Eadmund."

"Who? Oh—that petty baron of yours!" He danced away around the trunk, hesitating an instant at Fionvar's side. Every time Orie touched blood, his face flushed, and Fionvar's wound stung.

Wolfram's eyes flared as he caught the gesture. "A good man, and more fit husband than you."

"Ask Melisande about that." Orie laughed, spinning away from him.

Wolfram placed himself before Fionvar, and did not follow Orie's taunting.

"Get away from him," Orie said, smile slipping. He feinted again, lunged a bit wildly.

"I do not like what you are doing."

"Me? Nothing!" Still, his eyes were sharp. He ducked under the tree, forcing Wolfram's gaze and turn. Orie scrambled onto the tree, sidestepping Wolfram's thrust. Suddenly he reached out, Wolfram retreated, but the hand slipped to his brother's shoulder, and the sword wavered over Fionvar's head.

"Holy Mother preserve us," Wolfram whispered, letting his sword point dip.

"Too late," Orie snapped. "At least for one of you. I'll be sure to tell my wife."

Fionvar's eyes met Wolfram's, and they held no fear. He gave the slightest bow, as of a duelist conceding a bout. "Tell her what, Orie?" Wolfram asked quietly.

"Tell her that her brother is a fool." He grinned, releasing Fionvar. "Drop your sword."

The sword slid from Wolfram's grasp to the soft earth, and he stepped forward.

"No, stay there." Orie jumped down from the tree, staggering a bit, with his hand to his ribs. "Oh, you have made this too easy." He walked around the former prince.

Breathing steadily, Wolfram held out his hand. "Welcome to my family, brother," he whispered.

Orie laughed, slashing his blade down the outstretched arm, drawing an arc of blood. "Your father has already done that."

"You will be the son he always wanted. I am glad, now, that I was not."

The smile fell from Orie's lips. He clutched Wolfram's bleeding palm to his side.

Blood streamed down the prince's arm, mingling with Orie's, then drawn into the other man's flesh. Orie moaned and grinned like a man with a whore, the pallor leaving his face. Wolfram's back arched, his head flung back. "Dear Lady!" Wolfram cried, breaking off into a terrible scream.

The sound ripped Fionvar's soul, yet he could not look away.

Orie cursed, pulling Wolfram closer in his cruel embrace, wincing at the way the broken ribs moved beneath his flesh. The blood flowed faster. Orie's eyes froze, glaring down at Wolfram's face, then, he, too, was screaming, a deep, awful cry.

Fionvar let out a strangled sob.

Far off, the men on the field shouted in fear, some fled at the sound, making the sign of the Goddess. Others fought harder, hearing some more terrible fate approaching from the forest.

Thorgir slammed the windows of his chamber, cursing.

Below, in a small temple, Evaine flung herself to the ground and begged the Goddess to forgive her, and every sinner.

Brianna cried out at it, burying her head against the duchess's chest. Elyn, disturbed by both the sound and the gesture, flung an arm around her; her sharp eyes searched for a cause and found none.

It pulled Rolf from his darkness, and he covered his ears and prayed.

Kattanan scrambled out of the grave, and stood weeping. Those who saw him, saw a dead man rise behind him, and a fire in his eyes. "I wish I had never heard his voice, and did not know it!" Kattanan cried aloud.

"I wish that I had known it better," Jordan whispered.

Lyssa came beside him, sword drawn. The scream seemed fearsome to her, yet faint, and it did not make her tremble so long had she filled her ears with hammerblows and swords ringing.

The Wizard of Nine Stars curled her arms about her legs and wept.

At last, the woods fell silent.

# Chapter 26

ORIE LET Wolfram's body fall from him, staring at his side. "It hasn't worked!" The skin and torn muscles had closed, but the ribs still pricked him when he moved. He touched the spot carefully, frowning. "Oh," he said, remembering. He cast an absent word toward his brother.

Fionvar at last fell to his knees. One hand groped feebly at his sword, but he had not the strength to draw it. Wolfram's open eyes watched without blinking. "Great Goddess," Fionvar murmured.

The earl finally looked down at his brother. "I would not have killed you, I hope you know that." He still frowned, shook his head slightly, as if to dislodge a ringing in the ears. "It was for us to settle. Frankly, I had expected more of a challenge."

"He was not a man of the sword," Fionvar whispered, tracing Wolfram's features. Agony had twisted his face; one hand was clenched into a fist. His outstretched arm bore a long, deep wound, flesh as dry as bone.

"No, indeed. Gerrod told me his son was thickheaded about the things of war." Orie rubbed his hands together, transferring his vague glance to them. A shudder ran through his body, and he straightened. "You should come with me, meet the king."

"I already have a king."

"You can't believe he'd have you after all of this!" Orie waved his arm about the clearing. "That was a friend of his; you literally watched him die. And I'm sure the duchess is less than pleased with you now."

"She ever has been." His voice felt dead, small and weak compared to the notes that had gone before.

"I never intended you any harm." He smiled. "You are my brother, after all."

"And blood calls to blood." Fionvar looked up, his face blank. "If you do not want to be seen here, now is the time to leave."

"Still looking out for me, eh?" The smile grew, though his eyes were troubled. "You will come to me, one day." He turned to go, not sparing a glance for his victim.

"One thing," Fionvar said, his voice a little stronger. Orie stopped at the edge of the clearing. "Tell me how you are called."

Orie looked back at the dead man, and chuckled. "I am the Wizard of the Prince's Blood. You are indeed privileged to witness the birth of a new power." He started, then stopped again. "Oh, and brother? I would not share that with too many people if I were you." He vanished into the woods, in the direction of Bernholt.

Fionvar sat a moment longer, then crawled the short distance to Wolfram's still form. He reached out a gentle hand and shut the staring eyes.

"NO, THERE is nothing!" Nine Stars wailed, pulling away from Jordan's softest touch.

"My lady, let me help you, please."

"I told you, you can do nothing." The wizard pressed her hands over her ears. "I need rest, I need silence, I need peace, for love of the Lady!"

"Leave her be," Lyssa said, tugging at Jordan's elbow. "We have other problems."

He shot her a glance not altogether friendly. "My last problem was being dead. Forgive me if my priorities have changed a little."

Lyssa gasped at this. "You said you wanted to marry me, now you can't even be civil. Great Goddess! You're as bad as my brother."

"Which one?"

"Either! We are in a grave in the middle of a war. We have the king. He has no helm, and barely enough skill to chop a potato. How do we get out of here?"

Kattanan peered over the edge, then crouched down again. "Storm the castle."

"What?" said Lyssa and Jordan together.

"We are inside the ring of battle. We either fight our way out, or go the other direction." His dirt-streaked face shone with a curious excitement. "You are the only able fighter among us, Lyssa. How many can you take?"

"Oh, this is ridiculous," Lyssa snapped. "There are hundreds of soldiers, ours and theirs, and they'd kill us as soon as step aside, even if you are the True King."

Kattanan smiled. "My point exactly. So we go the other way. The archers can't shoot without harming their own, and only four guards are at the gate."

"How do you propose to get by them?"

Kattanan hesitated, considering that point.

"Tell them to move aside," Jordan answered, meeting Kattanan's eyes. "You are the True King, I am the Liren-sha."

"Now that is ridiculous," the king replied, smiling a little at his friend.

"No," said Jordan. "They will be more surprised by that than by anything else we could dream up. All you need is to master the tone of voice." He drew himself up as much as possible without revealing himself above ground level and proclaimed, " 'I am the Liren-sha. You will surrender this position and submit yourselves to the justice of the True King.' and you would say, 'Or stand your ground before me, and I will smite you with the glory of the Goddess and you will know me.' " His voice was deep and terrible, his gaze commanding. The other three stared. Jordan shrugged. "Most kings are listened to because they demand it in their voices. You know more about your voice than any man alive, Kattanan."

"About the other voice, perhaps—" He broke off. "Why didn't my voice change?"

The wizard displayed her scarred arm. "My blood courses in the veins of the Wizard's Bane."

"Does that mean he isn't, anymore?"

She shook her head. "The one receiving the blood also receives part of the spirit of the giver. He has a little bit of me, now." She smiled for a fraction of a second. "He is still who he was, but perhaps a little more sympathetic toward me and my magic."

Lyssa, too, was shaking her head. "What about the scream, shouldn't we go that way, no matter the difficulty?"

"And do what?" the wizard asked softly.

"Whatever it was you did for Jordan! Don't you think Wolfram deserves the same effort?"

"Even if I were able right now"—Nine Stars sighed—"he is beyond my aid, or anyone's."

Lyssa's eyes flared. "Don't you feel the least bit responsible? Orie used your magic to do whatever he did, didn't he?"

"Lyssa, don't—" Jordan warned, but she went on, "You went through all this for Jordan, and now you won't even try for Wolfram, even though you are the one to blame!"

"Orie killed him; even without magic, he would have found a way," Kattanan said.

"I don't believe that!"

"Lyssa, shut up!" Jordan shouted. She glared, but kept her peace. "We are all grieving, but we cannot sit here all day. Neither can we go back the way we came unless we can fly."

The wizard covered her face with her hands but had no more strength for tears.

Kattanan laid his hand on her shoulder and said nothing.

"You are seriously proposing that we just walk up and tell them who we are," Lyssa said softly. "Why not just turn ourselves in?"

"What is your better idea?" When she did not answer, Jordan said, "I do not know what else to do without jeopardizing Kattanan in open combat. If I could fly, I would be with Wolfram now, dead or alive."

Lyssa's eyes were soft and sad. "I have never met anyone like him."

"Nor I," the wizard murmured, looking up.

The two women looked at each other for a long time before Lyssa nodded. "I have my hammer and a sword. If we do startle them, we can take the men at the gate."

"Have the horses gone?" asked the wizard.

Jordan nodded.

"I don't think I will be able to rise," she whispered. "I am so weak."

"Then I will carry you; Lyssa must have her sword at the ready."

"The king's guard," muttered Kattanan. "Fionvar will be so pleased."

Jordan smiled. "At your service, Your Majesty."

Lyssa slipped her helm into place and stood. "The tide's turned toward us, we must hurry!" She pulled herself out of the grave and reached down to help the wizard, who crumpled to the ground immediately and sat smiling faintly.

The wizard murmured, "Would that I were not right! I am a burden once again."

Jordan gathered the wizard into his arms. Kattanan drew his father's sword and paused, looking to the forest. "We will come to you, Highness." He made the sign of the Goddess and turned away.

The city wall loomed up not far away, dark with growing shadows. The great gap that would be the temple wall was lit by flickering torches already. Kattanan set the sword to his shoulder. "Lady, watch over us."

"She does," said Jordan, with such conviction that the king looked up at him.

"Well, no use standing about," Lyssa put in. "If the Sisterhood could see me now! Rear guard for a four-person assault on Lochdale."

"The stuff of hero's songs," Jordan observed.

She glanced to him, flashing a smile. "You must sing this tale, someday." Her gaze took in the wizard, clinging with what little strength remained to her, and Jordan's ruined hand draped over the other woman's shoulder. "If any survive to tell of it."

"The Lady walks with us, Lyssa. I do not know what lies beyond that wall, but it will not overcome us."

"My uncle waits in there," Kattanan said, face marked with lines of sadness, "and Wolfram's betrothed." They walked carefully, leaving the battle behind them until the wall filled their vision. Another figure appeared in the lighted space, royalty from the response of the guards on duty. The newcomer first stood, then bolted out, but was captured by the guards.

In a few more paces, the foursome could hear the argument raging. "I cannot be too late!" a woman's voice cried.

"Your Majesty, get back inside," from an imperious guard. "This is a war."

"This is a temple! That is holy ground, despoiled by blood." She gestured wildly.

"If you leave, it will be your blood, Majesty. I cannot allow it"

She slapped at him, struggling against his arms. "The Wizard's Bane," she cried suddenly.

"I told you, Your Majesty, he is dead."

"And yet he walks!" Jordan called out, stepping up to their torchlight. "I am the Liren-sha, and even death cannot hold me!"

The guards' faces went pale. Evaine easily slipped their grasp, and made a deep curtsy. "The Lady spoke and told me so." Her plain face shone even as the guardsman started reaching for her again.

"Your Majesty, there is magic here. Come away and let us fight them!" His voice trembled, and his sword wavered now.

Evaine knelt before Kattanan, placing her hand on the ground at his feet. "Your Majesty, I cannot deny you. I pray for your forgiveness. My hand is yours, to be crushed, or to be commanded."

"After what your husband did, you seek forgiveness?" Lyssa blurted.

"How do you know me?" Kattanan asked quietly, frowning down at his aunt.

"By the sunlight on your hair and by the starlight in your eye, Your Majesty." She did not look at him but gazed steadily at the earth before her.

His sword gleamed over her head, matching the spark of the wedding bracelet on her outstretched wrist.

"When I was in the dark, Your Majesty," Jordan said, "she brought me light and comfort."

Kattanan gazed down upon her, not sure how to feel. Had she been there when his brothers died? Did she wear the circlet his mother had before his father was killed? A soft sound came to him; she was crying at his feet. He stooped and took her hand. "Lady Evaine, rise and walk beside me. You are not too late."

◦◦◦

NIGHT GATHERED early under the trees, and Fionvar looked up at last. The sun rapidly faded, even in the gap overhead, yet no one had come. He heard the suggestion of battle beyond and saw a faint glow in the direction of the city. A strange weakness suffused his limbs, and he knew he could not lift Wolfram to carry him back to camp. Fionvar shivered, huddled against a growing breeze. With a frown toward the sky, he roused himself to gather a bit of firewood. Though cloak and

hood had been left behind, he did have his flint and set about to
lay a fire. It took his shaking fingers several tries to strike a spark,
but he had some warmth at last.

"Companion," a gruff voice broke the silence.

Fionvar sprang up, reaching for his sword. "Announce
yourself!"

A dark man entered the clearing; several others hung back in
the shadows. When he had come closer, Fionvar recognized
Quinan, the Woodman who was Wolfram's friend. "You are the
companion?" the other asked, stumbling over the foreign words.

"You speak our language?"

He nodded. "We studied together. He was better student."
Quinan's eyes traced the dead man's face. "Are you his companion?"

Fionvar lowered his sword. "I'm not sure what you mean."

"When a great man dies, he shall be watched over for one
day and one night. If he is of the gods, no beast will come
near except to mourn him, no rain will touch his face, and
whosoever waits with him, the gods will ever hold as one of
their own."

"He is a man of the Lady," Fionvar said.

"The day has passed, night comes. Do you wait with him?"
the other asked impatiently.

"I will not leave him."

Slinging his bow over his shoulder, the Woodman nodded.
He called out something in his own language and received several whistles in answer. With sadness in his features, Quinan
turned to go.

"Wait," Fionvar said, raising his hand. The trees seemed both
dark and cold, now. "Do you not want to stay?"

Eyes shining with tears, Quinan returned to the fire and
pressed his palm to Fionvar's forehead. "You are his Companion!"

Stepping back, Fionvar shook his head. "Only for a short
time. I barely knew him."

"He knew you." Quinan's eyes narrowed. "The man stands at
his death who would be his last and greatest friend. He spoke of
this."

Fionvar shook his head again "That's not possible. If he spoke of a friend, he must have meant Rolf or the king, not me."

"He knew!" said the other. "As I know, as any true man knows his death comes."

"I do not know."

Startled, Quinan took a step back from him. "You do not feel—?" He pressed a hand over his heart.

"I used to feel that I would die an old man, with my lady at my side." Fionvar turned away and sank to the ground, eyes tracing Wolfram's face.

"Knew you knew!" Quinan crowed, clapping him on the back as he dropped down beside him. "The fire-hair lady?"

Now it was Fionvar's turn for surprise. Quinan plucked a long pipe from his belt and began to stuff it with dark weed. "No," Fionvar said at last. "That is my sister. My lady's heart is no longer mine."

"Sister." The man grunted and nodded. He took a long draw on the pipe, smiled, and offered it to Fionvar. "Give her to me?"

"Great Goddess, you are a heathen! I can't give her away, even if I wanted to."

"I give many furs!"

"Women are nearest to the Goddess. They cannot be bought!"

Quinan's face fell, and he sighed. "Wolf not selling his sister, too."

A dark doubt crept into Fionvar's eyes. "Have you no decency?"

"Decency, yes; wife, no. She follow war chief when he ask her."

"Mine too." They gazed silently for a long moment. Fionvar held out his hand, and Quinan set the pipe in it. Wrinkling his nose at the unfamiliar scent, Fionvar nonetheless set it to his lips and drew deeply. He coughed a little, then looked at the pipe again, this time with wonder.

"Better than it smells!" Quinan took it back and inhaled deeply. He blew soft smoke rings into the firelight.

A bell rang in the distance, calling men to prayer. The stars drew Fionvar's gaze, and he began to chant, quietly, the prayer of Evening as he had not done in many years, being too caught up in other things. He was not now riding on his brother's errands, nor awaiting his lady's pleasure, nor even sawing away at his fiddle, though his hands missed it. Flames cast red highlights on Wolfram's hair, the color of the dead. Fionvar's throat ached, and something pricked at his eyes.

Quinan sat quietly, watching his companion, until the prayer was done. "You will take him to his Goddess."

"Yes, I will." Fionvar brushed his silent tears away. "If the Lady is willing, his killer will shortly follow."

# Chapter 27

"GO TO your tent," the duchess said firmly. "You must rest."

"How can I?" Brianna wrapped her cloak a little tighter. "We are at war, and my lord is wandering in darkness." She stared down into one of the small braziers that heated the royal pavilion. The thrones stood before her, but she could not bring herself to sit. Duchess Elyn leaned back in her own chair, a mug of Teresan tea in her hand.

"That is why you must rest. At all costs, you must carry that child."

The young woman shot a dark look over her shoulder. "To be called his heir."

"We need but a midwife to announce the pregnancy, and we will stand as regents for the child. I wish you could have been wed by now, but it cannot be helped."

"He will not die!" Brianna whirled to her grandmother, her face pale. "I will not hear you planning for his death!"

"I am glad to see that you feel so strongly about that. Nevertheless, plans must be made." Her eyes were as twin sapphires, at once cold and gleaming.

"Can you have no feelings, even for this? He is your grandson, and your king!"

"Of course I have feelings!" The duchess was on her feet, and seemed to tower up in the eerie light. "My heart was torn from me the day my daughter died!" She flung the mug away, heedless of the hot liquid splashing across her chest.

"Forgive me," Brianna stammered, but Elyn was not through.

"I have waited fourteen years to see her murderer brought to justice, and no man nor woman nor unborn babe will stand in my way, for that justice is at hand!"

"Do the rest of us mean so little to you that you would see us die to avenge yourself upon one man?"

"That one man took my home and country; he took my joy and left me empty."

"And Rhys, he was her joy, was he not?" Brianna asked softly. "He is the last of her upon this earth." Her hands caressed the life within her.

The duchess stared at her with unseeing eyes. She jerked when the curtains were thrust aside and anxious guards trotted in.

"Is all well, Excellency? Your Excellency?"

"What news of the king?" she asked, her voice resuming its accustomed weight.

"I have none, Excellency," the man replied hesitantly. "Gwythym is just returned escorting the wounded and prisoners; he may have tidings."

"Fetch him to me." As he turned to go, she called out, "What of Captain Fionvar?"

"No sign, Your Excellency, since the scream. That Bernholt giant returned but he will not speak to us. Should I spare men for the search?"

She shook her head. "Go."

Brianna looked sharply back to the fire. "Rolf of the Prince's Mercy, he is called. He might speak to me."

"You may go." The duchess held her chin high. "I will send you word of my grandson if there is any."

With a brief curtsy, Brianna turned for the curtain-door,

which was held aside for her by blood-spattered hands. Gwythym nodded to the lady and entered. "Your Excellency." He bowed deeply and, approached carefully when she did not turn.

"What news of the king?"

"He broke the enemy's shield wall and rode on, Excellency, and Lyssa yfSonya with him. I lost sight of them in the fighting, but one of the wounded saw them dismount not far from the funeral ground. A prisoner told me that he then raised a dead man, and with those three, went to the castle."

"To the castle? The man must be lying."

"He's not the only one telling this tale. Many of Thorgir's men surrendered to us, offering themselves in the service of the True King." He grinned. "I warrant it was the wizard who raised the dead, but our young king is already making his legends."

They stared at one another for a long moment. "Have you any other news?" she breathed.

"Only that we have broken the resistance by the temple. With the coming of night, their archers can do us little harm. The men are eager to follow their king, but the captains dally over the remnant of the enemy and will not command another charge." His face was bright. "I was on my way here to seek your command."

"Can we make good our attack in darkness?" She crossed her arms. "I was rather expecting an embassy from the Usurper after we breached his wall."

"He is not as great a coward as rumor would make him. No doubt he waits for reinforcements from behind our lines."

"He cannot get them. Athelmark was unexpected, but still the nearest. Even had he sent for others at the same time, they cannot prevent our entering the city and laying siege to the castle proper."

"They might arrive at any time now if they march through the darkness."

"Give the order, then. No—hand me my cloak. I shall give this order myself."

CRVD

JORDAN PEERED into the gloom beyond the narrow opening. "There is an army in the temple!"

Evaine offered him a distraught nod. "I fear the castle has not been made ready for the True King's return. Those men await your assault."

Lyssa laughed sharply.

The guards shared worried glances, unsure if they should obey their queen's command.

"Well"—Kattanan turned to Lyssa—"we are now a five-person assault; perhaps that betters our odds?"

She grimaced, tilting her head to examine the wall. "Is the mason's way still open from the vestibule to the well?"

"I believe it may be," Evaine said.

"A pathway opens, Your Majesty. I hope it is long enough, or yours will be the shortest reign in history," Lyssa said.

"Lead on."

"What about these?" Jordan bobbed his head to the guards.

A horn blast startled the little gathering, and they turned to see horse-and footmen launching toward the castle. Within, a captain cried orders, readying the defense.

Jordan and Kattanan shared a wild look, then Lyssa grabbed the king's arm, hauling him off-balance toward the dark wall of the vestibule. Evaine gathered her skirts and ran after, followed by Jordan, with the silent wizard in his arms. Not a moment too soon, for armored men began to pour out of the temple, and they had barely gained the safety of the passage. The guards struggled to reach them or sound an alarm, but were swept aside and lost in the confusion.

A gap in the wall formed a passageway left open to allow the workers a more direct route to the well in the inner court. Lyssa led them between pillars and mounds of paving stone intended for the floors of the inner chambers, a series of dark cells and partial galleries for the clergy who would serve there. Her companions stumbled after, gasping with relief when they finally won through to the courtyard. Jordan lay the wizard down beside the well. He stroked her brow, smiling when her eyes fluttered open. "How do you fare?"

"Tired," she said. The moonlight increased the pallor of her features.

"What can I do?"

She shook her head weakly, shutting her eyes. The Liren-sha leaned back against the stone also, taking deep breaths.

"Where now?" Kattanan asked.

Looking up from a draught from the well, Lyssa shrugged. "This expedition is not my folly, Majesty. Why not wait here for the victorious army?"

In answer, he gestured toward Jordan. "You said yourself that we were not up to this. And I am not certain we should linger so close to the wall, in case they bring the catapults to bear."

Evaine looked from one to the other in surprise. "Then you came here only to escape the battle?"

"Why did you think we came?" Lyssa snapped. "We have two injured members, one but lately returned to life, and I cannot defend the king in pitched battle. Just what did you think we planned to do?"

"I know what my husband is, now, and myself by extension. I thought you came for us, to capture the usurpers," she murmured.

Jordan laughed. "Of course we shall capture the Usurper!"

"You are mad! Or do you jest with us?" Lyssa narrowed her eyes at him. "Is this when we go to Thorgir and demand his surrender?"

"No," said Kattanan thoughtfully, "he will come to us, anyplace we choose."

"Great Goddess!" Lyssa exploded. "Have you all taken leave of your senses or forgotten where we are?"

Kattanan walked once around the well, frowning, arms crossed. "He will come if you are willing to help." He looked to Evaine.

"You are the True King," was her reply. "The Lady has shown me my wrongs, and I repent of them. Let me redeem myself."

"You have a plan, Your Majesty?" Lyssa asked.

Kattanan nodded. "Evaine will tell her husband that I've been captured when I crossed the lines in a vain attempt to reach my friend. If I do not miss my guess, he wants his people to believe I do not even exist, so he should be eager to come and deal with me himself." His face seemed suddenly to have lost its youth. "Does the queen's garden still open out into the orchard?"

"A small gate, near overgrown, Your Majesty," Evaine said.

"I would like to meet him there." His memory flashed back to dawn, and the scents of blood and lavender.

"And we'd be able to get out through this gate?" Lyssa asked.

"It is the way my mother intended for my own escape."

"There may be archers on the wall above, but they will be expecting enemies from without," Evaine said.

"She can bring him to you, Your Majesty, what then?" Lyssa inquired.

"We find a way to disarm and bind him, and bring him out with us."

"Why not just . . . ?" Lyssa trailed off, glancing toward the queen. She nudged the sword that hung by her side.

Kattanan shook his head. "There are too many he has wronged. He should live to see those things set right."

Evaine nodded. "And I, too."

"Then it's agreed." He knelt by Jordan. "I may need your sword," Kattanan whispered. "Are you well enough?"

Jordan met his gaze. "When the time comes, the Liren-sha will not fail you. Mayhap that alone will disarm him." He flashed his most daring grin, but Kattanan could see the darkness of his eyes and the way his breath still labored.

"We must go, then." From the direction of the temple came the cries and clangor of battle, apparently creeping closer.

With a deep breath, Jordan rose and gathered the wizard to his bare chest once again. She pressed her face into his neck with a little sigh. At the first step, he stumbled, and Lyssa caught him. "I can carry her," she said, looking down at the other woman.

Jordan glanced from one to the other, and nodded. "Thank you." He carefully placed the wizard in Lyssa's arms, and the fighter held her gently against her armor.

"Evaine," Kattanan said, "will you lead us?"

She nodded. "I know a way little used, from the old temple up to the queen's chambers. I found it most welcome."

Lifting her skirts once again, Evaine took the lead. Kattanan followed, with Jordan beside him, while Lyssa followed after. "I wish I did not feel so tired," Jordan murmured. "I hope I can be of some good to you."

"Just so long as you live through this, I don't care if I must do it all myself." Glancing up at his tutor, Kattanan added, "I feel such a coward, running for safety and creeping about in the dark."

"On the contrary, Your Majesty," Evaine put in, "those who saw you at the temple spoke of your horse flying over the defenders and of starlight in your hair."

He let out a harsh laugh. "They will be dreadfully disappointed to meet me, then."

"I think not, Your Majesty."

"Nor I," Jordan said. "You have the opportunity here to personally deliver the Usurper to Duchess Elyn, and I believe you could do it alone. You are the True King, and he knows it. He has claimed you dead for years, and may believe that the attack on the monastery indeed killed you. His men have been telling him grand stories of your coming. Look him in the eye, let him believe you are a ghost and a legend, the hand of the Lady come to take back what he stole from you. And the Lady is with you."

"Wolfram said so once, and look what happened to him," Kattanan pointed out.

Jordan shook his head. "Whatever happened, I do not think he feared it."

"I am not Wolfram, and I am afraid."

"Of course you are. You are not used to being a king, or a ghost, or a legend. I have some experience with the last two. I'll teach you all I know."

"And kingship? Is not a king expected first to be a man? I cannot claim even that without lying."

"Is a man defined by flesh alone? Is that all? I'll wake the wizard and get you some illusory testicles!" Jordan shouted, flinging his hands in the air. "Look at Thorgir! Or King Gerrod—both whole men, both cruel, murdering swine, is that all you aspire to? Great Goddess! If ballocks are all it takes to be a good king, then take mine!" He fumbled with his pants. "Give me a knife, and let's take care of this right here!"

Evaine turned away sharply, but the others stared at Jordan standing suddenly naked in the hall before them. Lyssa blinked in astonishment. Oblivious to her gaze, Jordan locked his eyes to Kattanan's.

The younger man had stopped trembling, the shock slowly leaving his face. Jordan's lean, scarred body glimmered with sweat in the faint light. Kattanan could not look away.

"Is that all?" Jordan repeated intently.

Kattanan shut his mouth and folded his arms across his chest. "No one," he began, softly, then cleared his throat, and began again with sudden strength, "No one speaks to the king that way."

Jordan grinned, though tears were in his eyes. "No, Your Majesty."

Tears glistened in his student's eyes as well. "Put your pants on. We have work to do."

# Chapter 28

AFTER DISMISSING the few servants who lingered in her chambers, Evaine ushered the companions into the garden. Kattanan nodded to her, and she set out upon her mission. Together, he and Jordan crossed to the gate and motioned for Lyssa to follow when they had unlocked it. Groves of fruit trees shielded the gate from the other side. Here, she set down the wizard, and straightened. "Where do you want me, Majesty?"

He considered a moment. "Wait here, ready to come if I need you. Keep an eye out for soldiers. I expect they are patrolling somehow. Oh—and listen for our scouts. They'll be on horseback, just inside the forest."

"How am I supposed to hear that?"

He frowned. "I should be my own lookout."

Jordan gave a glimmer of a smile. "Is there a reason I shouldn't stay here to listen?"

"I'd like you with me."

"But he's not well," Lyssa pointed out. "Surely it makes more sense for me to be with you."

"Maybe so, but I need him."

She snorted and turned to peer into the trees. "I'll be here."

"Thank you, Lyssa." The pair walked back to the middle of the garden, but Kattanan glanced again toward the gate and sighed.

"This place is more to you than an escape route you did not take."

"Yes." They reached the bench, and Kattanan sat down uneasily. "This is where I last met my uncle. He killed my mother here." He studied the new stone of the pathways.

"Kattanan."

He looked to Jordan.

"All those times I teased you about being left at the monastery, how it was your fault," Jordan said gently. "I am so sorry."

"I knew you were trying to tell me that you would never leave me. Lyssa and the wizard told me what happened to you. I am sorry I did not trust you more."

"You have not heard the half of it!" Jordan grinned. "You and I will sit by a fire, drinking Teresan tea, and tell each other every bit of the last four years."

"And I should like to know how a monk becomes the Lirensha as well."

"Actually, it was the other way 'round."

Kattanan looked up suddenly, listening intently. "I hear Evaine's footsteps and his. Go! I want him to see me alone and think for just a moment that he's won."

Jordan rose, but leaned to touch Kattanan's shoulder. "You are not alone," he whispered. They shared a brief smile, then Jordan disappeared into the shadows.

Kattanan took a deep breath, making the sign of the Goddess. "Lady, if you let us live through this, I will learn any dance you ask," he murmured toward the sky. Then he slipped his hands behind him as if bound and waited for his uncle to find him in the garden.

Evaine spoke softly, but Thorgir cut her off as he opened the door. "I said wait here, I would see him alone." He turned through the door, and a feral grin crept to his lips. Bringing a torch, he stepped into the garden and shut the door. Kattanan heard a bar slide behind his uncle. Still he waited.

"So you are supposed to be King Rhys." Thorgir approached slowly.

"I am the king," he replied.

Thorgir stopped, and snickered, "Your voice betrays you, Impostor; his voice would be as high as a child's, or a woman's."

"Do you not know me?"

"Of course, you are an actor hired to portray a castrate, doing a very poor job. You are a good likeness, or is that magic?" He walked again, holding the torch aloft.

"Oh, stay there, Uncle."

"Why?" the other barked, immediately sidestepping, looking sharply about.

"That is where you killed my mother."

"She was crazy, she killed her sons—"

"Stop lying!" Kattanan was on his feet, hands still behind him. "You and I are the only men alive who saw! I was here."

"Guard!" he called. "You in the shadow, your prisoner is getting rowdy!"

"Whose prisoner?" Jordan answered tightly, stepping from the shadows. Two swords, provided by Evaine, hung at his sides. He stood at ease, smiling.

Kattanan lifted his father's sword. "Even your sword is a lie, Uncle."

Thorgir tore his gaze from the Liren-sha. "You are both illusions! You are dead!"

"What, at Strel Arwyn's?" Kattanan stepped toward him now. "Did you kill the abbot yourself, or did servants do that for you as well?"

"No one survived that fire!" The sword wavered back and forth between the two men. "Men of the Goddess returned to the stars."

"For that alone, I should bury you," Jordan said, "as you tried to have me buried."

Thorgir took two steps back. "Evaine!"

"She will not help you." Kattanan advanced a little farther. "She repented of her wrongdoings. How did you think we got here?"

"Through the gate. Evaine!"

"Locked." He plucked her key ring from his belt and tossed it to his uncle.

The keys lay at his feet, glinting in the flickering light. Thorgir glanced down, then back to Kattanan. "My right-hand man saw them cut you! You are a eunuch."

"I am a better man than you, Temple-burner. Drop your sword, and I may yet grant you mercy."

"Nothing is in your power to grant," he snarled, thrusting the torch into a stand by the path to grip his sword with both hands. "I am king here, no matter who you are. I have armies at my command."

"Have you not heard?" A strange compassion grew in Kattanan's voice. "Your wall is breached; my soldiers overrun your temple and your common; your own soldiers flock to the banner of the True King. Uncle, your day is done."

"No!" he cried, launching himself toward Kattanan.

As Kattanan sprang aside from the wild swing his eyes flicked to Jordan, who stood at the ready but made no move, then his attention was on his opponent.

Thorgir had gained some sixty pounds in the years of his kingship. His beard showed more gray than brown. His lips sneered, but his eyes were wide with terror.

Seeing this, Kattanan leapt to the offensive. Even as he lunged, parried, and lunged again a voice rang in his ears. *"Fear no blessing,"* it chanted, *"take no revenge."* He pushed it back, remembering his mother, his brothers, his father's face only dimly.

Thorgir scrambled to put the well between them, and they circled warily. "You are a poor swordsman, Impostor."

"As are you, Usurper."

"My brother was dead; the throne should have been mine!"

"By what law? His wife and three heirs yet lived!"

"Not for long. I should have killed you in this garden the first time."

"Now is your chance, murderer." Kattanan backed away from the well, letting his sword point drop. "Or will you yet hide from me?"

"I am not hiding!" Thorgir moved out from behind the stones, but no nearer.

"You are. I can hear it in your voice. You are afraid of me because I should not live, should not be as you see me. You are afraid because the Liren-sha should not live, yet he is my second. Your wife has betrayed you to me; that, too, I can hear." He stood very still and felt his anger ebbing away. "Speak again, Uncle, tell me more."

"No!" His voice was strange, harsh and yet broken.

Kattanan did not move, for a moment his eyes were shut. "You do not want to kill me," he breathed.

"You must die." Thorgir lurched forward again, and still Kattanan did not move.

Jordan slipped out his left-hand sword, tensing.

"Your voice betrays you, Uncle," Kattanan whispered. "You are afraid because you do not want me to die." Slowly he lowered his sword, watching Thorgir's face.

Blinking fiercely, Thorgir advanced. "Of course I want you dead. I tried to kill you, before, and now." He held his sword in shaking hands and raised it.

Kattanan put out one hand to stay Jordan's sudden movement. "Why, Uncle?" he asked, his voice soft, comforting, forgiving. "Why will you not kill me?"

Their eyes met, and Thorgir's were full of tears. "Why did you come to me? I did everything I could to you! You should have hated me, should have run away, or stayed by her or hit me or something, anything!" The voice rose to a ragged cry, then fell back to a whisper. "Oh, Rhys, why didn't you run?" The sword clattered to the ground. Thorgir sank to his knees and wept.

# Chapter 29

A HINT OF dawn touched the sky, lighting the tips of the banners. Breezes played with the pennants and rattled the siege engines, which awaited daylight. Wearily walking the long way around the city, Kattanan led his companions. Evaine had remained in her chambers, eyes brimming with tears at the sight of her husband bound and gagged. She would await full dawn to surrender the city. It was not until they once again reached the temple ground that they were able to acquire four horses from an awestruck squire. As they passed, the soldiers roused themselves. Those clustered around the temple kept a sleepless watch, waiting for dawn's light to finish the conquest they had begun. When the riders reached camp, with Thorgir bound to a horse that trailed Kattanan's, the king asked his heralds for silence.

"These men fought hard, let them sleep," he told the trumpeter. "They will wake to a different world."

"But, Your Majesty, can we not spread word to those who kept the night?" the man asked.

"Tell them only that war is done. I wish to bring the news to the duchess myself."

The trumpeter bowed very low and trotted off about his business.

A little farther along the path, Kattanan turned in his saddle, looking past his prisoner to Jordan. "The healers' hut is down there." He gestured toward a distant flag. "You'll find me at the royal pavilion, with tea ready."

The Liren-sha nodded gravely, reining his horse awkwardly in the new direction. The wizard slumped against him, rubbing her eyes.

Lyssa watched them go, then hurried to catch up with the king. On both sides, groggy knights and footmen rose at their passing and bowed. Kattanan took no notice until they finally reached the great pavilion. The guards there likewise bowed, and moved as if to announce him, but he stopped them.

"Is my grandmother within?"

"Aye, Your Majesty. Asleep, unless I miss my guess."

Kattanan nodded. Darkness circled his eyes, and great weariness was on him, but he smiled and shook back his hair. Self-consciously, he glanced to his soiled garb and the armor he had taken off, which now burdened his horse and Lyssa's.

"You are quite handsome enough, Majesty," she said, sliding down from her horse. "What of the Usurper?"

Thorgir's eyes above the gag flashed at this still, and he straightened.

"Keep him for me a little longer. I would speak with her alone a moment before I share that piece of news."

"As you wish, Majesty." She turned her attention to prisoner, cutting the bonds at his legs and hauling him down. "Stand, you, and don't imagine you can run from us."

He growled low in his throat, but did as she bid him, stretching his legs as they waited.

Pushing aside the flap, Kattanan ducked into the tent. The braziers still burned, and a few bright candles as well. Her cloak flung about her, Duchess Elyn slumped in the throne, snoring softly. One arm dangled from the chair, just above a small object. As he bent over her, he recognized the miniature portrait from his chamber at the manor. Her face creased with worry even in sleep, though it seemed not so hard as usual, perhaps because the piercing eyes were closed. Suddenly, she jerked and pulled herself erect.

Kattanan stood back a little. "Good morrow. I understand you have the only stock of Teresan tea, and I am in dire need."

Elyn pushed herself up, tugging her clothing into place. "Your Majesty!" She started toward him, then stopped herself, the flash of relief swept away. "I heard that you entered the castle. Not to conference with our enemy, I trust?"

"I did not enter for that reason, but I have had speech with him."

"What? Have you surrendered us?" Her hands clenched into fists.

"Peace, Grandmother." He did not shrink before her, and once again her brows twitched her surprise.

"Tell me."

Kattanan shook his head. "The sun is rising. Come outside with me." He offered her his arm; she glanced at him suspiciously.

"Who are you?"

"I am King Rhys," he said quietly. "I am what you wanted of me."

"I think not. I shall discover your secret."

His shoulders drooped, and he lowered his hands. "Please come out, just for a moment."

She breezed past him and stopped short in the doorway, so that he had to slip around her to win free. "What magic is this?" Thorgir locked his eyes on hers, holding his head high.

At Kattanan's nod, Lyssa stepped up and untied the gag.

"Elyn, it has been too long," Thorgir said. "I would offer to kiss your hand, but my own are occupied."

A smile grew on her lips, and she stepped out to walk around him. "I much admire this garb on you. Who is your tailor?" She glanced to Lyssa, who shook her head and pointed back to Kattanan.

"I did not even see the duel, Excellency," Lyssa said.

The duchess's eyebrows rose. "Can this be true?" She looked from one man to the other, and Thorgir turned away. She laughed aloud and smacked her palms together. "Thorgir, you worm, you are mine!" She stalked around him again, gaze sharp.

From the gathering that built around them, a voice called out, "Your Majesty!" and a lady's face lit with joy.

"Brianna!" The crowd cleared between them as Kattanan dashed toward her. She held out her arms, but he stopped short. "Have you heard from Fionvar?"

Her arms fell. "Why should I?"

Kattanan stared at her, but Rolf, coming up behind her, swept him up in a huge embrace. "Ye live! Thank the Lady!" He set him down gently, adding, "Yer Majesty."

The king smiled briefly. "It's good to see you, Rolf. Can you help me find Fionvar, and Wolfram?"

"If that's yer wish, I'll take ye as far as I got before the bastard jumped me. I had my hands at his throat"—his great fingers clenched—"Orie, I mean, then his brother wrestled me down. I knocked my head," Rolf broke off, touching the wound. He looked away. "I was not there."

Kattanan put a hand out to his friend. "Nor was I. So we must be there soon."

"Ye seem more concerned for the other than for His Highness," Rolf grumbled.

"I am more concerned for him because I do not know if he lives." Anger flared in his voice, and he added, "I regret Wolfram's loss more than anything, but Fionvar has done well by me and deserves better than his rewards so far. Lead me where you can, but I will not hear words against him."

Brianna's face paled, and she swayed on her feet. Kattanan caught her against him, lowering her to the ground. "I thought I had lost everything."

"I am here." His concern showed plainly.

"Do you even care for me?" she murmured.

"I do. And I think that you need sleep and food, apparently even more than I."

The duchess crouched. "Are you well? You have not gotten the rest I ordered."

"No," she replied, "but my king has come home; I think I can rest now. Bring me word, would you?" She let herself be helped to her feet.

"I will," he promised, and wondered where her own concerns lay. A pair of guards came to escort her back to her tent, and he told them, "Be sure the lady has all that she needs, and send a healer for her." Quickly, he turned back to the task at hand. "Lyssa, are you coming?"

"They're my brothers," she snapped.

"Your Majesty is not going off again while the world is yet in darkness," the duchess said. She stood as firmly as ever, but seemed to have shrunk, or simply grown much older.

"Two of my friends are lost in the woods, Excellency." With a glance toward the silent Thorgir, he slipped past her, followed by Lyssa and Rolf, who nodded to the duchess with a fierce grin. "A king, indeed."

She could only watch them go.

"First to the healers, to ask after Jordan."

Lyssa nodded. "Shouldn't we bring more assistance, Majesty?"

Kattanan frowned. "We may not want to share too much of whatever has happened there, especially with wizardry involved."

"I knew it," Rolf said.

"The wizard—Alswytha—may be able to tell us something, if she is awake."

Not only was she awake when they arrived, she was doing her best to confound the healers and Jordan both. "I was not unconscious all night," she snapped, pulling away from a flustered-looking woman. "I was gathering my energies. I have them now, thank you." She was clearly tired, but much of her color had returned, especially in the angry flash of her eyes.

"My lady," Jordan said, with a smile, "you do seem much improved, aside from your disposition."

She glowered at him briefly, but a ghost of a smile traced her lips as well.

Both turned their attention when Kattanan entered. The healers bowed and stepped back. "I am glad the patient is well," Kattanan said, but his expression was grim.

"What is it?" Jordan asked, instantly concerned.

"Fionvar's not back yet, nor have any seen sign of him or Wolfram since they left yesterday afternoon."

"There is a clearing with a large tree," Alswytha began, sliding off the table to the ground, "it's down a slope." She aimed another glare at the healers. "If we find the right direction, I may be able to trace the magic."

Rolf snorted. "I know the way we set out in, anyhow."

"Are you well enough?" Kattanan asked.

"No," the wizard replied lightly, "but I do feel"—she looked hard at Lyssa—"responsible in a certain way. I am coming."

Full light had reached the valley, though it was still dark beneath the trees, and they could hear the bright horns calling the camp into motion. The small party blundered through the woods. Finally, they emerged, blinking, into the clearing Alswytha had described.

"Great Goddess!" Kattanan cried, sprinting toward the two men who lay at to the far side. Even as he did so, one of the bodies stirred and passed a hand over his face.

"Thank the Lady!" Lyssa said, as her brother sat up slowly.

Fionvar's frown quickly was replaced by a grin as he saw Jordan and scrambled to his feet. "Wizard's Bane!" He embraced

Jordan with his good arm, tears gleaming in his eyes. "I thought you were dead."

Startled, Jordan returned the embrace. "I was. The wizard brought me back."

Fionvar pulled away, glancing toward the wizard, who had gone to kneel beside Wolfram. "Can she . . . ?" he asked, a faint, wild hope in his voice.

Alswytha shook her head as she studied the wound on Wolfram's arm. A mask made of bark and leaves covered his face with an almost comical expression of peace. She lifted it, sighed, and replaced it gently. "There is nothing. All ties have been severed. Did any blood spill?"

Fionvar, losing any hint of a smile, came beside her. "No. He seemed to—to take it into him."

"Bury it!" she cursed, one hand resting on the dead man's shoulder.

Kattanan had settled by his friend's head, touching his hair with reverence. "Has a death chant been sung for him?"

Fionvar shook his head.

Swallowing hard, Kattanan rose to his feet. Jordan met his gaze and nodded. He began, very low, and Kattanan's new voice joined him. It did not soar above, the way his former voice had, but had a graceful range and rich sound that made their hearts nearly hush to hear it. There was no other sound in the forest as they sang, even though tears ran on the faces of the listeners. Jordan paused after three verses, the number of royalty, but Kattanan went on, and Jordan followed, until they reached seven, the number of holiness. When they had finished, sun shone down through the gap in the trees and lit their hair and features like pure gold.

Several minutes passed before anyone moved. Lyssa took a few steps toward her brother, surprised by the tears on his face. "I've never seen you like this, Fion. He was close to you," she murmured.

"I did not think anyone could say so much to me in so short a time," he whispered. "And he died for me."

"What do you mean?"

"Orie had the power to use someone else's blood, to heal himself, I think. He had taken some of mine, during the fight. Wolfram stopped when Orie threatened me, then he allowed this to happen." He made a gesture toward Wolfram's body. "He let himself be killed so that I would live."

Rolf growled low, glaring at Fionvar. "Why? What hold did ye have on him?"

"I don't know. Surely I did nothing deserving of that." The anger that once would have flared, now did not, and he looked on the huge man with only sadness.

Kattanan said, "I do not think he would have killed to save his own life, but he would die to save another's." He started to look around the clearing. "Perhaps we can make a stretcher, to carry him back."

"I can carry him myself," Rolf insisted.

"Your Majesty," Fionvar said softly, walking to stand before him, "I'm not going back."

"What?"

"Brianna has left me, and the duchess distrusts me; it's only a matter of time before she tries to dissolve my influence on either one of you."

"I can handle the duchess," Kattanan said, and his tone brooked no disbelief.

"I take it something else has happened, Your Majesty."

"It has indeed," Jordan said. "Kattanan faced his uncle, vanquished him, and brought him back to the duchess as a gift. You may find your king a changed man."

"Then it is done. You've won!" The light returned to Fionvar's face. He almost laughed. "If you've done this, you may indeed handle the duchess." The light died quickly. "She is not the only reason I have to go."

"Why, then?" Lyssa demanded, but Kattanan fingered a lock of his hair that had been cut short.

"I don't want to lose you," Kattanan said. "What will you do?"

"Wolfram told me some time ago that if I ever left you, I should go to Orie."

His audience gasped. "Why? How can you go to him after this?"

"Because I might be the only one in a position to stop him from moving against Lochalyn next."

"He wouldn't do that," Lyssa scoffed. "After all we've done to reinstate the True King?"

"Before yesterday, I didn't think he could kill his own brother. I can put nothing past his ambition, now."

"There is something you should know," said the wizard, finally rising. "Several things. First of all, he is a wizard in his own right, now. He has broken the bond with me and worked his first magic without tapping my power in what he did to Wolfram. Has he chosen a name?"

Fionvar nodded. "He called himself 'The Wizard of the Prince's Blood'."

She winced. "If you are wise, you will not share his Namestory with anyone, especially another wizard. That he killed the prince may become common knowledge, but do not let out how."

"I can't. I don't really know how myself."

"The technique is from the *A-strel Nym,* a book of forbidden magic—" She broke off with a frown. Then she shook off her own worry, and resumed. "Only three wizards that I know of have any part of this knowledge, and I believe I am the only one who knows it completely."

"That means Orie knows it, too," Kattanan observed, but she shook her head.

"The only time he had free access to that part of my learning was when I opened myself to heal the Liren-sha. Before that, the blood-bond we shared denied that information as long as I did not use it. This technique needs to work outside of my defenses, though, which is why I asked for your blessing to heal Wolfram at the manor, hoping that would shield me from Orie. He broke the bond too soon, or just in time, depending on your perspective. He does not know everything, and he is apparently not aware of his ignorance."

"He said that he knew all your secrets," Fionvar recalled.

"He saw how to use the blood to heal, but he did not see the cost. Part of the spirit goes with the blood; neither the wizard nor the patient is ever the same if they have shared blood. In this case, Wolfram was not otherwise injured. When Orie took hold of him, he took everything. He has brought too much into himself."

"So Wolfram's spirit is inside Orie," Lyssa said faintly.

"In a manner of speaking. There is no correlation of thoughts and actions of the person so consumed, but the impression of emotion goes with the blood. Orie will feel as Wolfram might have felt and respond based on that if he cannot make the distinction between those sensations and his own."

"What does that mean for me?" Fionvar asked.

"Orie and Wolfram were nearly complete opposites; there is no way to reconcile their feelings within one man." She looked him in the eye, and said simply, "Your brother will go mad."

"Oh, Melisande," Kattanan breathed. Faces turned toward him. "Her brother is dead, her father is a tyrant, and her husband is destined for madness. How can she survive?" His eyes searched the sky in the direction of Bernholt.

"Orie was right; you do have feelings for her," Fionvar said softly.

Kattanan nodded. "I think I have loved her from the first moment I sang for her. You should have seen her face."

"What of Brianna?" he asked. "I would not have her wed where there is no chance of love." Darkness clouded his features as he looked upon his king.

"How many times must I tell you that I will not marry her?"

"Then you will leave her dishonored and humiliated."

"No," said Kattanan. "I will find a way." The man who had brought Thorgir back in bondage suddenly returned. "If you must leave us, then I will keep her safe for you. When you return, she will still be yours."

"If I return," Fionvar said. "If she will have me." He stooped to pick up his sword, thrusting it through his belt. "I have delayed too long already."

Rolf grunted his agreement but said nothing when faced with the sadness of his companions.

"I will miss you," Kattanan said. "And there will always be a place for you." They gripped hands briefly. "Please look out for Melisande."

"Whatever is said of me in my absence, Your Majesty, I serve only you, even now."

Jordan pulled him into another quick embrace. "I'll miss working beside you, listening to your fiddle on those long nights. Take care." He placed his hands on Fionvar's head. "By the blood of my heart, protect this man from magic," he said.

The wizard gave a little smile. "When next we meet, I hope you can let go of some of your distrust of me."

"Wolfram found something in you I had not seen; he did the same for me. We may have more in common than I thought." At last, he turned to his sister. "I'm sorry I was a tyrant to you for so long. I leave the king in your keeping for a while longer, and there are few I would trust with that task more than you."

"Fion!" she cried. "That was an apology I never hoped to hear." She flung her arms around him for a moment.

He started to walk away, then turned back to Kattanan. "See that his funeral is done with the highest honor. I know that was important to him." He let out a bitter chuckle. "A shame I cannot bring him with me and build the pyre under his father's very nose. It's the least of what that bastard deserves—to see his son held in great esteem."

"You may not be able to do that," Kattanan replied, "but I can, and with an army at my back." His smile was sharp. "Look for us, Fionvar."

"I will. Goddess keep your Majesty.

The king made the sign of the Goddess, kissed his fingers, and shut his eyes as Fionvar vanished into the forest, for whatever lay beyond.

# Chapter 30

THE KING'S second procession walked slow and solemn into the lively camp. Soldiers turned, ready to cheer those who had brought back the Usurper, but the cheers died when they saw the expressions of the small company. Kattanan walked at its head, followed by Rolf, who held the prince tightly to him once again. Lyssa and Jordan walked together, and the wizard trailed after, deep in thought. In the field before the royal pavilion, a pillory had been erected to imprison the Usurper, surrounded by jeering men and women of their allies. Thorgir bore the taunting with only an occasional snarl at the crowd. This activity, too, ceased, and the crowds made way. The duchess emerged from the tent with a handful of lords.

"Where is Captain Fionvar? I don't see him among your number." The duchess could not keep her smile from creeping out.

"He begged leave to undertake a dangerous task, and I have let him." The two stared at each other, and those who had not seen it before now whispered of the resemblance between them. Kattanan went on, "Prince Wolfram of Bernholt has fallen in my service. He will lie in state in the temple at Lochdale and be brought to the funeral ground at his home with all ceremony due his rank and honor."

"You can't be serious," the duchess murmured, moving close to him.

"This nation is not secure as long as Orie rules in Bernholt," he whispered. "Don't pretend otherwise." Kattanan turned away from her, addressing the crowd. "When the time comes, I will ask for mounted guard to accompany me, up to one-third part of the army that rode with me. You may wonder why pay this honor to a man who was declared traitor to his father and to our cause. I say to you that he gave me honor unlooked for, kindness without cause, and faith beyond reason. I hope to find myself worthy of his friendship."

"Have I not earned at least a moment of your consideration?" the duchess asked sharply.

Kattanan turned back to her with a sigh. "Forgive me, Excellency. Perhaps weariness has overcome my manners."

"I can see we have need to speak in a more private place." She ducked back into the tent. Kattanan looked back for Rolf, who stood silent, wearing an unfamiliar solemn expression. "By the house of healing, there is a temple arranged, and priestesses who can prepare Wolfram. Will you bring him there and stay by him?"

"As ye wish."

"If you see my squires, send them here to meet me when I am through."

The big man nodded, bowed his head a moment, and set out for the house of healing, there to lay down his sad burden.

"Jordan?"

"I am here."

"Come with me," Kattanan asked, with a hint of his former insecurity. The pair showed themselves into the tent. Kattanan paused in his to dip fresh mugs of tea for himself and his companion, then they walked up to where his grandmother waited.

"What has come over you?" she demanded, before they'd even taken seats.

"Am I to rule here or no?"

"I brought you here! So now you will refuse my counsel and dispute me before an entire army?"

"I know how much you have done." His features softened, and his voice now held sadness alongside his suspicion. "Is that what gives you the right to treat me as somewhat less than a servant?"

"I have made you a king!"

"You were not alone in that. What I meant was the way you speak to me and deal with me. You expect me simply to obey your commands, and smile while doing it."

"Because you know nothing of being royal, or even being noble. You are a—you have been a court entertainer, not a courtier, never mind understanding the intricacies of ruling over men."

"How do you know what I know? You have never asked me. Since I watched my mother die, I have spent little time outside of castles and palaces. I have witnessed weddings and festivals, judgments and executions; I was smuggled away from a revolution by a royal family who then sold me to gain their freedom. Of all the things that Jordan taught me, the most important was a single word: listen. Perhaps I have not ruled over men, but I have heard the voice of kingship from a hundred different mouths. I did not choose that classroom, but I have learned much."

"How can you be truly a king? You are not even a man, or had you forgotten?" Her tone was acid.

He allowed himself a little smile. "Neither are you."

"That is not the point!"

"Then what is?" he snapped back at her, springing to his feet. "That I cannot be king because I cannot have children? I would not be the first to die without issue. Oh, but you have already solved that problem by forcing me together with Brianna, who is conveniently already with child! It seems as if you are planning for my death."

"I am a cautious woman."

"Yes, you planned for everything—except that I might have my own mind and spirit, and that I am tired of being used and discarded for other people's pleasure!'"

"So now that you have some power of your own, you plan to abuse it yourself rather than allow someone else to do it."

"No. I plan to treat people fairly, to listen to them, and to help them when I can. I plan to live by the Lady's way, with mercy and justice."

"More pretty words. If you plan to listen, then listen to me. What you have done is madness! You intend to turn around and leave your place to escort a dead traitor; absurd! And you have let go a man who will betray you at his earliest convenience."

"Fionvar duNormand swore an oath with me and he will not break it. As for the escort for Prince Wolfram, it is not merely an honor guard. Orie knows better than anyone our strength, and my status here. Will his ambition be satisfied with a single throne when another might be within his grasp?"

She sat back, and when she spoke, the fury had abated. "Orie has been my ally for many years."

"While allying himself with Bernholt at the same time."

"We fostered each other's insurrections." She smiled faintly. "Though his will be less bloody."

"Only if he stops where he is. If I ride with a third of the army as escort, he will not think us an easy target. He will also believe that you trust me to lead the men and that I trust you to hold the city in my absence. If he is truly an ally as you say, he will assume this is something I insisted on to honor my friend. If not—we will be prepared."

The duchess studied him carefully. "I may have underestimated you, Rhys."

Kattanan likewise settled back in his place and took another swallow. Jordan stood proudly at his side.

"This is not all we must speak of," she said, going on as if there had been no tension between them. "You brought back the Usurper. We expect emissaries at any time to offer the enemy's surrender. Before they come, Thorgir's fate must be discussed."

"I had not thought of that." He sipped slowly. "I assume that you have."

"If only there were a way to dishonor him as he has dishonored us. Perhaps we might use his family—"

"Absolutely not." He stared at her wide-eyed. "Have you come all this way for revenge alone?"

"Not alone, but in part, yes," she said harshly. "Do you mean to tell me that was not in your mind also?"

"It was," he admitted, "until I fought Thorgir last night."

"How did you come to win?"

"I was full of hatred for him, wishing I had the skill to kill him, but I did not. Then I listened to him. There was something in his voice . . ." he trailed off, remembering. "I could hear a lie in him, below all of the others. What I heard in his voice was an echo of the time before his betrayal, when I knew that he loved me. It was then I knew that he still did, somewhere, that he did not want to kill me."

"He had you castrated, was that not bad enough, or even worse?"

"I used to think so."

"Used to?" she echoed, incredulous.

"For a long while, I was embittered by that wound, even as Thorgir was embittered by jealousy. I was told that I was less than a man, less than human, and I believed. I no longer choose to believe that."

"So you would not have him punished?" Condescension rang in her voice.

"He has committed greater crimes than that, by far. I would have him stand trial for the murders of my family and for the sacrilege of burning the monastery at Strel Arwyn's, any part of which will cause him to be put to death."

"That is more reasonable."

"But if he pleads guilty to these charges, then I would have his death be swift and his funeral be proper."

"Oh, Great Goddess!" She sprang to her feet. "How can I stomach this after what he did to my kingdom, to my daughter, and to me?"

"Thorgir is an abominable human being," Kattanan said quietly. "But I said that I would rule by justice and by mercy. After all that you have railed against his cruelty, how can you ask me to be the same way?"

Her breathing was angry, her eyes were hot, but she had no retort to this.

A shout from the door flap broke their silence, and Jordan

went to investigate. He returned quickly to tell them, "The emissaries have arrived from Lochdale. They await you outside."

"Grandmother?"

The duchess ran a swift hand across her brow and nodded once. "Show them in."

She sat back in her chair, and Kattanan moved to the throne beside her.

The cloth was held aside, and a small, but well-arrayed party was admitted. Each first had to tear his eyes from the spectacle of Thorgir pilloried and taunted. Lyssa and some of the courtiers came in after, quietly settling on the benches. One of the messengers bowed low, and began, "I bear greetings both sad and joyful from Evaine du Thorgir, regent of the city of Lochalyn in the stead of the True King, unto that king. She bids me say that her prayers this morning were for your mercy toward her people, even toward those who stood by the Usurper and those of his blood who have not shown Your Majesty due honor and courtesy. Her sorrow is in seeing the wrongs done you and your family these years past and ongoing, and knowing that she and hers have had the largest part in them. Her joy is in seeing that the True King is a man of valor and wisdom beyond his years, who has at last come into his own. The city will lay down its arms before you, and the archers have quit the walls in anticipation of your return. Neither man nor woman will stand against you and your captains. Further, she begs a boon of you."

Here, he paused, looking to Kattanan, who replied, "Thus far she has spoken well. What is her boon?"

"She wishes to greet you in humility before the gate, and to wash away your righteous wrath with tears of penitence. If you will it, she would walk before you to proclaim you to your people and beseech them to humble aspect and to reverence."

"Tell my aunt that I would have her greet me and go with me, but tell her further that my wrath is spent with her gracious words, and I would not have her weep for my sake."

Several of the courtiers nodded their satisfaction and smiled on their king.

"She has one thing more to ask." At Kattanan's gesture, he continued, "She asks if her husband is well, and if judgment has yet been passed upon him."

Glancing at Kattanan, the duchess answered, "You may say that he is confined as befits his crimes, and that an assembly of lords will judge him on several charges. If he pleads guilty to the charges, his punishment will be swift, in accordance with the king's justice, and his funeral will be proper, in accordance with the king's mercy."

The man bowed to them both. "Your Majesty, Your Excellency, you have been most generous. When may we throw wide the gates and welcome you home?"

"We shall come before the gates in three hours' time," Kattanan replied.

The man and his two companions bowed low, and were dismissed. Duchess Elyn leaned over as they left, and whispered, "Why so long? We can be ready within one."

"I am famished, and there are a few tasks to be taken care of before I can ride into that city."

"As you wish, Majesty." Both rose, and she smiled to the audience. "My lords, and ladies, Lochalyn is once again brought to its true heir." A cheer rose, and she saw, with no little trepidation, that their eyes were on her grandson and the cheer was for him, not simply for the crown.

He did not smile, but his face was bright, his eyes moist, for he heard a sound not far from love in those joined voices.

After many greetings and congratulations, Kattanan was finally allowed to slip out and away from the crowd. His squires awaited him there and fell in with him, while Jordan went in search of fresh clothing with a promise to attend him before long. "I need a band of mourning," the king told his men, "marked for royalty, if possible."

One of the pair bowed curtly and set out at a trot.

Kattanan turned to the second, asking, "How fares the Lady Brianna?"

He hesitated, then responded, "She is less than well, Your Majesty. She is taking her rest but fitfully, and was anxious for tidings."

Kattanan frowned as they arrived at his pavilion, standing by a trio of birches, separated from the surrounding tents. Two guards on duty there snapped to attention. He leaned a little closer to the squire. "I would rather not see her for a little while." Their eyes met, and the man looked concerned, but nodded. "She should rest if she can; and I would like to do likewise, if I am given peace." This got an understanding smile. "When the Liren-sha comes, admit him, but no other." Glancing to the other two men, he ducked into the tent.

Fruit and bread had been set out for him, but Kattanan could not bring himself to eat. Once inside, his knees grew weak and he sank to the floor, hands trembling. He hugged them to himself, eyes lighting upon the crown placed at his bedside. He looked about again and pushed aside a tapestry to reveal a narrow mirror. The glass showed him a young man, face flushed, eyes dark-circled beneath boyish curls; the gaze was anything but childish. "King Rhys," he whispered.

A call from outside let him know that Jordan had arrived, and the tall man was admitted. He wore common clothes, the only red a band of mourning on his arm. He entered smiling, but quickly lost the smile and knelt beside Kattanan. "What's the matter?"

"Am I a king? All I can see is myself."

"You expected perhaps to sprout a beard and a scepter?" He laid a hand on Kattanan's shoulder. "Last night, and this morning, you have been every inch a king."

"And still I tremble." He displayed his hands.

Jordan's smile returned faintly "Before every performance, your hands always shook like leaves." He took them between his own, the left callused but gentle, the right knobbed and contorted. "I do not know what else to tell you, except that the mirror does not show all there is to you. I expect it will take time before you see a king there yourself, but I assure you that many people already do." He paused a moment, then asked, "Something more is bothering you, is it not?"

Briefly, he told Jordan about the mad priestess in the garden at Bernholt and their spiral dance. "I thought that my mother danced beside me, and my father and brothers beyond him, with the monks of Strel Arwyn's. She chanted something to me, which seemed strange then, but now seems more like prophecy."

"I was a monk, Kattanan, I can understand the things of prophecy," the other said gently. "What did she say?"

"Fear no blessing, take no revenge, trust a wizard's word, doubt a woman's change, sing a hopeless prayer, hear unwanted tales, raise the man cast down, love a foe-man's child, wed no of-fered hand, learn a new dance, walk with the Goddess, sing with the stars."

Jordan nodded slowly. "You were afraid of my blessing."

He nodded. "I did not think of it then, this chant she gave me. Had I heard your tale unwanted things might have gone much better for you."

"You raised Wolfram when his father cast him down."

"And will raise him again to send him to the stars."

Jordan smiled. "In a way, She has spoken to you. Few men, even monks, can say that they were given so direct a message from the Lady." He told what he had seen when he lay dying, how the Lady came to him, and he was forgiven. "You must have thought your prayer was hopeless."

" 'Wed no offered hand' seems clear to me, but it might de-stroy Brianna, not to mention what my grandmother would do. I cannot refuse her without disgracing her, and I would not be untouched either. Now I've promised Fionvar to keep her for him. I don't know what to do."

"Nor do I, but I will do what I can, if you ask me."

Kattanan gave a trembling smile. "For so long, I tried not to think about how much I missed you. I did not think anyone would care for me so much without also betraying me."

"I wish there were some way I could have come to you sooner."

"No, it wasn't you; it was me. I betrayed you when I could not trust your love."

Jordan reached out to touch his cheek. "I did not know I should have taught you trust."

"My mother loved me, but I disobeyed her and never saw her again."

"No wonder you were the most obedient child at Strel Arwyn's. I went there to escape what I am, and I failed utterly. You were sent for similar reasons and likewise failed. We can see full well our course in life, and it scares us, so we run away time and again. When I ran away to Strel Arwyn's, I thought that would be the end of it. I would no longer be the Liren-sha, because no wizards would ever come there. Even when we left there, it took some time before my nature caught up with me. The emir's guards trained me to kill, telling me that this is why I was born, and, like an idiot, I believed them, and I hated myself for it. It wasn't until I was chained to Alswytha, trying to make sure she lived, that I saw anything more. Without their magic, she and Broken Shell were just two people, unable to force each other. She said it was a relief to have an ordinary conversation."

"And now," Kattanan observed. "The Liren-sha is part wizard."

"I don't yet know what that means, except that I can stay by you."

Kattanan smiled. "Then I shall be sure to thank her at every opportunity."

# Chapter 31

WHEN THEY had rested and the time was nigh, Jordan summoned the two squires. They sprang to the task of readying the king, pulling fine garments from the chests. Jordan stood back, watching, with a strange light in his eyes. With each garment of silk and thread of gold, Kattanan held himself a little taller. His leggings were a creamy white, topped with a rich purple tunic worked with golden leaves. The silken undershirt peeped through at his neck and wrists. When the squires stepped back, they shared a smile; then one of them went for the crown. "Are you ready?" Jordan asked gravely.

"The time has come." The crown of his sires was set upon his brow. The squires seemed ready to leave, but Kattanan stopped them, prompting, "I asked for a band of mourning."

"I don't think it proper, Majesty, this is a day for—"

"Too many have died to bring me to this day. They deserve at least that honor."

"As you wish." He produced the strip of red cloth, marked with a crown to honor the royal dead, and bound it about Kattanan's arm. They ushered him into the sun. He stood dazzled for a moment, then a shadow stood before him.

"You have been avoiding me," Brianna said. Darkness circled her eyes, and she held herself very carefully.

"I do not know what to say to you."

"Say anything," she pleaded, taking his arm, "but do not leave me alone."

He met her eyes, reading there the fear and sorrow that filled her voice. "I will not, Brianna." He covered her hand with his own.

She offered a tremulous smile, and he returned it.

One of the squires cleared his throat, gesturing toward the city.

Kattanan nodded. "I want Lyssa and the Wizard of Nine Stars to ride in my procession. And Rolf of the Prince's Mercy, if he'll come."

"Aye, Majesty." The man split off to the side as they walked. Gwythym, now arrayed in a fighting man's finery, joined them with a sketch of a bow, still adjusting his baldric.

Duchess Elyn stood waiting on the hilltop, and did not curtsy. She wore a flowing gown of icy blue, with the chain of her duchy resting on her breast. "We do not wish to be late for this, of all things," she said.

"They've waited fourteen years already, Excellency," Jordan pointed out. "Surely a few more minutes can do no harm."

"We have all waited long enough," she snapped. Turning to

Brianna, she began to smile, though, and her eyes lost some of their chill. "I am glad you are able to join us." She turned to the encircling nobles. "Today King Rhys shall regain his birthright, and we shall ride with him!" The crowd cheered and turned to mount their waiting steeds at her gesture.

Lyssa trotted up on her own horse, grinning fiercely. "I'll enjoy rubbing this in the faces of your horrid cousins—no offense, Your Majesty."

"They are horrid, aren't they?" Brianna said lightly. She mounted a calm gray mare, with her skirts rippling over the horse's tail. Her dress, too, was new, with a short bodice and pleated skirt emphasizing her belly.

The wizard toiled up the hill, drawing all eyes to herself because she alone still wore the grubby garb of the day before. She stared back, yellow eyes flashing, face grim.

"Surely you do not plan to bring a wizard in with us," Elyn muttered to Kattanan, reining her horse close to his.

"My lady, I am glad you could join us," he called, ignoring his grandmother. "Have you a horse?"

"No, Your Majesty," she returned politely, "but I can have one at will." She gestured with one hand, and was suddenly holding the reins of a trim stallion dark as night without stars. The crowd around them murmured, drawing back and shifting uneasily.

"Then perhaps you can have some more appropriate clothing," the duchess suggested sharply, casting a look at the Lirensha. Jordan shrugged, and smiled.

"After all she has done for us, how can you mistreat her?" Kattanan asked, but the wizard bobbed her awkward curtsy.

"I am here at the request of King Rhys. I remind you that you gave me a place at your court, and I intend to be there." The wizard drew a hand over her clothes, and suddenly wore a gown of black, sparkling with silver. She set a foot in the stirrup and pulled herself up. As she did so, her hair grew longer, twining itself into a braid down her back. Her features, too, shifted to become a face of uncommon beauty, though the yellow eyes still shone fiercely. "Is this more to your liking?"

"I like it not," the duchess returned. "Many have places at

court who will not enter the city with us today. As a sign of our good faith, we are riding without our armies to the gate. To bring a wizard in our number would alarm them needlessly, not to mention disturbing our own loyal companions. If you wish to cause more fear and bloodshed, then simply continue as you will, with such wanton displays of power."

Kattanan flipped his leg over the horse and slid down to the ground, shaking off his squire's hand. "It seems we are at an impasse, Excellency. I would bring her among my loyal companions, you would not extend her that courtesy. Until you find it in yourself, I am going back to bed," he snapped, turning toward his tent.

The crowd fell suddenly silent, and the duchess let out a hiss of breath. At last, she spoke. "Wizard, I have misjudged your value. Please ride with us."

Kattanan took off the crown, ran his fingers through his hair, then replaced the gleaming gold and turned around. "Grandmother, we are all tired, we are all missing someone. If you will consider this, and grant me some indulgence"—he met her eyes—"I will try to do the same."

"Very well then. We are expected." She turned her horse, and he mounted and moved beside her. Jordan rode behind him, with Brianna at his side, looking relieved.

Kattanan rode in silence across the plain, with the duchess sitting stony alongside. Banner-bearers and heralds rode before, ranging out to form a semicircle at the city gate. Slowly the gate opened, and a portcullis was raised. A small party came forward from the shadows. The lead riders dismounted to meet them.

Evaine, clad in the dull brown of a penitent, curtsied low before them and did not rise until Kattanan touched her shoulder. Then she looked at each of them in turn with tear-filled eyes. "Your Majesty has at last come home. Would that I had been able to greet you sooner."

"Evaine, you are forgiven. Let us think of the time yet to come."

Duchess Elyn's eyes flashed, but she managed a smile. "Indeed, you cannot be held to blame for your husband's vanity.

Rather you are to be commended for coming now to welcome the True King at his own gate."

"I bring you the castle keys," Evaine went on, "to bear with you that you will never more be denied your place." She offered them, and he took her hand gently.

"Then let us go up together. I was young when I left here, and I may not recall the way. Will you guide me?"

"I will, Your Majesty. Finistrel smile upon you."

At this, a bark of laughter sprang up from one of the waiting figures. A tall, fair woman with sharp features laughed again. "The king is a eunuch!" Asenith crowed, crossing her arms. "Finistrel spit upon him."

Brianna reined forward a few steps to look down on her. "The king is the father of my child, Asenith. It is you who are accursed."

Asenith stammered and shut her mouth, flicking a glance to her horror-stricken mother. She met Kattanan's eyes and raised her chin, but did not speak again.

Returning to his horse as one was brought out for Evaine, Kattanan caught Jordan's eye.

"Welcome home," Jordan whispered.

FIONVAR HAD put a distance between himself and the city, cutting back through the woods and trying not to think about his king's welcome. Wiping his brow, Fionvar scrambled up one of the outcrops, turning to look back over the trees. A cooling wind ruffled his hair. The city looked far away already, the armies more like milling insects than men. Still, a strain of bright horns carried on the breeze and brought a smile to his lips. As he watched, the banners of the king were raised on the towers, flickering in the sun.

"You have small friends, but many," someone grunted behind him.

He whirled, hand to his sword, to find Quinan peering from behind him. "No." He sighed. "One of my friends has just become very great, and I was not there to see."

"New king?"

Fionvar nodded.

The Woodman grinned. "Come." He bounded lightly down the rock, heading farther into the mountains.

"Where?" Fionvar called after, scrambling down to catch him up.

"My tribe. You stay with us."

"I have someplace to go."

"Always going," Quinan said with a frown. "Tonight, you stay. Next day, show a shorter way, yes?"

"You don't know where I'm going."

"Find the man who kill Wolf, yes? Kill him, too, yes?"

"We'll see." He followed his dark companion deep into the forest, and always higher. Hemlock trees ruled the forest here, allowing only patchy sunlight to reach them. Even that began to fade, and still Quinan kept his rapid pace. The Woodman disappeared behind a stone. Fionvar wearily pursued him, and the trail fell abruptly away so that he found himself slipping down a steep, rocky slope.

He caught himself on a tree and regained uneven footing. Gales of laughter greeted him from all around. They had come into a sheltered valley packed with bark huts and small fires. Dark faces peered at him from the village, split with merry grins to reveal grubby, broken teeth. Fionvar slithered down the rest of the way. More laughter chased him, but he did not turn. Quinan flapped a quieting hand at the gathering, bringing Fionvar into a long, low building. The floor had been dug down, forming stairs at the entrance and a ledge all the way around where many men were seated. These did not laugh, but watched him gravely. Three fires along the center provided flickering light and thick smoke. Pipeweed scented the smoke, and Fionvar felt strangely relaxed.

Quinan spoke at great length, not inviting his companion to sit, or even move beyond the steps. He gestured wildly, occasionally pointing to Fionvar, and leaping in the air, or trotting back and forth. Suddenly, he stopped short, then fell to his knees and crumpled to the ground. Fionvar jumped forward to kneel beside him, and saw Quinan's open, smiling eyes. A rhythmic pounding sound began as all of the men stamped their feet. Some had strings of bird beaks about their necks and ankles and shook these vigorously.

"They like you," Quinan said.

"You were telling them about Wolfram's death."

The Woodman nodded, then sat up. "A good death, a good story."

"Why should they like me? All I did was stand there and watch.

Quinan scowled like a frustrated tutor. "Wolf not choose death just for any man."

"But why me?"

"Don't know." He shrugged as if the question were irrelevant. Quinan stood up without dusting himself off. "Later, speak death. Perhaps know then." He turned to the other men, tugging Fionvar over to an empty place on the dirt bench. A drumbeat began, quickly joined by flutes, which moaned and murmured in the queer light. The men settled again, as a few crouched down on the floor with their instruments. Two of them had small stringed instruments, with a round gourd at one end and a neck topped by primitive tuning pegs. Fionvar laughed to see these, listening to the melodies they made by plucking or sliding their fingers upon the strings.

Quinan nudged him, gesturing toward the musicians. "Why laugh? Good music!"

"I have an instrument like that one, but I play it in a different way."

"Show!" Quinan pushed Fionvar toward the players.

"Give me your bow," Fionvar said.

Quinan slipped the little hunting bow from his back. Fionvar sat beside one of the musicians, who handed over his instrument. It was crudely made, but sturdy enough. The bell of the gourd was too large to hold upon his shoulder, so he let it rest on the ground as they had, and set the bow slowly to the strings. It had a low hum—no note that Fionvar could identify, but it would do. He slid the bow gently along the three strings, then he shut his eyes and listened to the flutes. It took a few minutes, but he began to feel them, to anticipate their sound, then to make his own. The flutes, one by one, dropped out until he was playing by himself, but still using their rhythm. Around the circle, the men began to stamp their feet; drums and flutes returned, now joined by deep, strange voices. Fionvar did not open his eyes, carried by the music.

The chant rose and fell around him, and pipe smoke curled in the air.

"Speak," Quinan's voice suddenly urged. "Speak your death, Companion."

"I am an old man," Fionvar began, as if he had always known, "and she is there with me. I think we have been walking, trees I do not know are around me. We lie down in the grass. She is crying though I tell her not to. She touches my hair and my face. I think she is speaking, but I can't hear her. There is another lady, one I have always known. She asks me to walk with her, and I do." He opened his eyes, fiddle falling silent. Fionvar caught Quinan's eyes upon him. "It seemed so clear."

"It was true." Quinan walked to the center of the room, to take hold of a small bundle that hung there. He carefully unwrapped it and squatted beside Fionvar. The object inside, a small book, he opened just as reverently, to a page marked with a feather. With a little sigh, and a nod, he passed it to Fionvar. "Read me."

"I am young," Fionvar began. The script was light, but clear on the pages. "I am in a temple of the forest. My last, best friend is with me—I do not know who he is, but he is angry because he cannot help me. He does not know how much he will be needed when I am gone. My sister's husband will kill me because I will not let him hurt my friend. My killer takes me into himself. He does not know what he has done, and I pity him." Fionvar's voice cracked a little, and a tear fell onto the page. "A lady I know stands beside him. She asks me to walk with her, and I go, but I want to tell my friend that I forgive him."

# Chapter 32

FIONVAR AWOKE on the floor in the longhouse, surrounded and partially covered by other slumbering men, with Wolfram's journal still clutched in one hand. He extricated himself from the snoring heap and picked his way toward the door to stand blinking in the sunlight.

"Ah! Awake, good," Quinan shouted, leaping down from a stone where he had been smoking. He tucked the pipe away, picking up a leather pack. "Come!" He set out for a trail that led from the valley toward the higher peaks.

"How can it be shorter to go into the mountains?" Fionvar looked at the book in his hands, then up where the Woodman hovered at the valley's rim, scowling down at him. "Fine. Short way." Tucking the book into his belt, Fionvar scrambled up behind.

The other nodded once, with a brief grin, and was off again. They climbed for most of the day, often following no path that Fionvar could make out. Quinan did not speak much. The pack contained dried strips of meat and a variety of nuts, to be supplemented by drinking from the plentiful streams. After a particularly arduous ascent over boulders, they found themselves suddenly on a broad track carved into the mountainside. Stone towered above, with scraggly trees clinging stubbornly, and the slope fell steeply off to the side.

"Follow to the cave open like a box," Quinan told him, pointing down the road.

He pushed the pack toward Fionvar.

"You're not coming with me?"

The hand withdrew. "Magic blood walk this way."

"Magic blood? Wizards?"

Quinan nodded quickly.

"I'm not sure I like that. How short is this way?"

"Three suns."

"That's impossible! It would be six days by the main road on horseback! I'll have to walk over the mountains, and still cross the river. Great Goddess, why did I listen to you?"

"Not over." A glint of the familiar grin returned to Quinan's eyes. "Not over mountains, Companion." He took the pipe from his belt and handed it to Fionvar. "Believe."

"Believe," Fionvar snorted, shaking his head. He rose to his feet, taking in the heights to his left, the long drop to his right. "What do I have to lose?"

The Woodman was already making his way down among the boulders.

"Thank you," Fionvar called, then the other was gone, and he stood on his way, alone. Wolfram's book was still tucked into his belt; Quinan had not asked for it back, and Fionvar had not offered it. He slid it out now, warm from being held close to him, and placed it with the pipe into his pack. "Great Lady, walk with me." Fionvar shouldered the pack and set out.

RATTANAN STOOD atop the highest tower of his castle. Even now, he gazed from a place nearer the center than the edge. Wind whipped through his hair. The setting sun flamed on the horizon, and evening bells would ring soon. He pulled his cloak a little tighter, turning to face the city. He had forgotten how cold the nights could be, even far into summer. Music drifted up to him from the Great Hall, and occasional faint cheers reminded him that the celebration went on. He heard a footfall from below and slightly labored breathing.

"Good even, Brianna."

"Good evening, Your Majesty," she returned, with a puzzled tone. "How did you know it was me?"

He faced her with a small smile. "I heard your step and your breath. You found it hard to climb all those stairs, which perhaps means you should be resting."

She glowered. "You have been listening to Grandmother, haven't you."

"Do I ever?" he asked lightly.

"Jordan told me where to find you," she said abruptly. "What are you doing up here? You are missed at the celebration of your own victory."

"I cannot stand to be there, Brie." He sighed.

"But why? Even if you do not dance, still your friends wish to see you celebrate, not to mention your lords. It is important that they see you."

"I suppose it is. I just—it feels too strange."

"What feels strange?" She crossed to stand before him, concerned. "To be among those people? To be king?"

He almost laughed. "That is certainly strange!"

"But that's not what is bothering you." Brianna laid her hands upon his crossed arms. "Tell me, Rhys. I am to be your wife."

He flinched, looking away. "It feels strange not to sing. The audience awaits, entertained by jugglers, tumblers, and minstrels, and I am not there to sing."

"But you don't have to do that anymore! You are not an entertainer now, you are the king! You need never sing again, save in prayer, and that only if you wish to."

"But I am a singer!" He stepped back from her, touching his chest. "I feel it here, every time they play a tune I know. I hear these minstrels who cannot recall the simplest ballad, and I want to jump up and show them how it should be. I was born for song."

"You were born a prince, Rhys. It was the Usurper who made you a singer. If it had not been for him, you'd have been a lord of men and captain of soldiers, not just a voice in a choir. With the wizard's help, none need ever know what you were.

Don't you see? You are free." Her voice dropped to an urgent whisper, and her eyes were bright.

"Free. Of course, how could I have missed that?" Kattanan turned away.

"You aren't listening!" she cried. "Look at you! You rule a kingdom, men and women waiting just to do your bidding, a castle full of pleasures all for you, while I—"

He waited a moment, but she did not speak. "While you what? While you are forced to do the duchess's bidding, bearing a child and lying about its father?"

"No! That is not what I meant to say. I am proud to serve. My child will know you alone as his father, and it will be so! I knew this is what she would want of me, but I also choose it. I want this child, and this castle, and I am proud to be its queen."

"Then you have no thought for him at all," Kattanan said softly.

"I have none. He is gone, as it should be, and he is nothing. It is your child I will bear."

"No, it is not! I can have no children. What happens if the baby dies?"

"What a terrible thing to say!" She stumbled back, stunned as much by the force of the question as by the words.

"Babies die all the time. If this baby dies, how do you plan to get another? Perhaps another fool will love you, so he can father my next child."

"Is that what you think of me?"

"What should I think, Brianna? Fionvar loves you. Perhaps he thought that Grandmother would allow the marriage if you were pregnant. How could he know that what he took for love was just a trap to get an heir for a castrate king?"

"No," she whispered, arms about her belly.

He looked her deep in the eyes. "Then do not tell me you have no feelings for him."

She sank to the floor, weeping.

Kattanan stood a moment longer, wavering, then knelt beside her, slinging his cloak about her shoulders. "I'm sorry," he murmured.

"Let me be," she whispered.

"You can't stay here in the wind—"

"Go away!" she screamed, her hair flying. "Leave me alone!"

Kattanan staggered to his feet and down the spiraling stairs to the door. Quickly, he went inside, catching the first serving maid he saw. "Lady Brianna is on the tower. She should not be alone." The woman bobbed her head and moved for the stairs.

Pausing by a mirror in the hall, Kattanan took in his wind-tossed curls and stormy eyes, and wondered what Melisande would think to see him now, a crown upon his head and a kingdom at his feet. What he told Brianna about his feelings had been true, as far as it went. Somehow, to speak of Melisande, of the foolish love he felt for her, would lay him too bare. Steeling himself for the crowd, Kattanan followed the music back to his party.

A stranger came up beside him and bowed before transforming into the Wizard of Nine Stars. "Welcome back, Majesty."

"Thank you," he said, but continued to scan the crowd. "Where's Jordan?"

"Dancing with his lady, where else?" She gestured toward the dance floor.

Now Kattanan saw them and was surprised he had missed them before. Lyssa's brilliant hair streamed out as she spun through the dance. Jordan wore a smile just as bright. Both had chosen dark silks, and they looked more than a match.

"They are the most beautiful couple; everyone agrees," Alswytha observed.

"You could match her in a moment," Kattanan replied. "Why not dance with him yourself?"

"I do not dance."

"Nor do I."

"Besides, they seem happy enough. Why should I ruin their fun?" She spun on her heel and started off, with no obeisance to the king.

"I wish you would not go off without a guard, Your Majesty." Gwythym came up beside him, arms folded, watching the dance. "You do make it hard on me."

"I'm sorry. I simply couldn't stand to be here another moment."

"I'm glad you came back, anyhow, and so's the duchess, if I don't miss my guess."

Kattanan looked in the direction of the man' s nod to see his grandmother working her way through the crowd toward him. "Great Goddess, not now." He sighed. Fortunately, the dance was over, and Jordan and Lyssa came bounding toward him, grinning. Jordan wore soft leather gloves, which did little to conceal his knobbed right hand.

"Your Majesty, did you have a nice walk?" Lyssa asked, but Jordan frowned, releasing the lady.

"We should talk."

"Please," Kattanan agreed.

"Back to your tower?" Jordan offered.

"No, not there."

"I know a place, Your Majesty," Gwythym put in, "if I'm allowed to lead, that is."

"By all means, and fast!" the king said, as the duchess's bland expression turned sour.

Gwythym led the way up a flight of stairs and down several hallways until they stood before a door that was deeply carved with a pattern of intertwining feathers. "Came upon this place while exploring,"—the man smiled—"and thought you'd like it." He opened the door grandly, ushering them down a short hall into a seven-sided room with a high, sloping roof and windows of stained glass. The three inner walls were lined with half-empty shelves, while the center was dominated by a curved bench with embroidered cushions. Gwythym moved about the room, lighting oil lamps with a torch from the hallway. The beams of the ceiling were carved as well, and gleamed with gilding. "I'm thinking it was a king's study, Your Majesty."

Kattanan nodded, smiling faintly. "It will serve."

"I'll be in the hall should you need me, Majesty." Gwythym made a short bow and left, shutting the door behind him.

"What's the matter, then?" Jordan asked, sprawling onto the bench.

Dropping the crown onto a cushion, Kattanan crossed his

arms and frowned. "I've just done the most hateful thing, Jordan." He told of Brianna's coming to the tower and what he had said to her before leaving her in tears.

When he finished, Jordan was shaking his head quietly. "You know so little of women."

"And you, who were a monk, I should take for an expert?"

Jordan briefly lost his smile. "I am a monk no longer. The last thing she wants is for you to leave her. She wants you to love her, as she believes she loves you."

"You are not making sense! She loves Fionvar, not me. What reason under the stars does she have to love me? She knows what I am."

"More than that, she knows who you are, or thinks she does. She went to your tent every night while you were riding to battle. Why do you think she did that?"

"Because the duchess told her to, to make people believe that we are lovers." His voice grew soft, and he remembered the kiss. "She kissed me, the first night."

"And you did not object," Jordan supplied.

A look of panic filled Kattanan's eyes. "Fionvar is the one who loves her. She should have been kissing him!"

"I had my first kiss in a brothel not far from the emir's palace. The guards had taken me there as a sort of joke on the man of the Goddess. A woman I had never seen before put her arms around me and kissed me. I had been cast out by the Goddess, why should any woman wish to be near me? It wasn't right. And at the same time, that kiss felt wonderful." His blue eyes seemed not so piercing as they had before. "My heart and mind cried out against it, but my body reminded me that a Man of the Goddess is still just a man."

"But I am not," Kattanan breathed. "No woman should love me."

"I thought we had discussed this, in some dark passage." He gave a little smile.

Kattanan shook his head. "Manhood may not be the prime qualification of a good king. But to be a husband, to love a woman, and be loved by her in return?"

"To give her children, perhaps, but to be loved by her? Only the heart of a woman knows what her love requires. And to love her? You said yourself that you loved Melisande from the first time you sang for her."

"And now Brianna wants me to love her."

Jordan nodded. "From what I've seen."

"I might have loved her, if not for Fionvar . . . and Melisande. It would be easier to love her, and to marry her, and better for the kingdom, too."

"Fionvar would blame himself more than you, and would agree that it is better thus. As for Melisande, she might never know the difference." Jordan noted Kattanan's quick glance. "But then again, she might."

"My grandmother would call me a fool for thinking that a princess might care for me and for allowing that to prevent my marriage. How can I place that slim hope against the fact that this marriage would seal the monarchy?"

"That's not a question I can answer, but I will say this, that if the question of Melisande will hold you back from this, or any other chance for love, then you must settle the question. You must stand before her and judge for yourself if she bears you any feeling."

"But she is married."

"I know."

"Her husband despises me, as does her father."

"I know that, too."

"So how would I ever be allowed to see her?"

"You are the king." Jordan gestured toward the crown between them. "Knowing how Orie and King Gerrod feel, I should think she would be the only person there in a position to greet you without giving the greatest possible offense to a visiting monarch."

"Once again, you think I should assault the castle." A slim smile lit Kattanan's face.

Jordan grinned. "You know that's what I would do."

Kattanan contemplated the crown for a moment. "I did not ask for this. Even when I was a prince, all I ever wanted was to sing. Now I am not allowed that. Brianna said that I was free. I have the freedom to do anything but what I love."

"The walls here are thick, Kattanan. The windows are shut, and none but Gwythym stands outside that door." Jordan's voice was as comforting as it had ever been.

Glancing about, Kattanan asked, "But what shall I sing?"

"I think it's time that you chose your own song."

# Chapter 33

AFTER PASSING a cold night huddled in a shallow cave, Fionvar was annoyed to find the sky overcast and rain beginning to fall. He was doubly grateful to Quinan for the pack, for he found it also held a half cape of stitched suede. Now he pulled on the garment and chewed on a handful of nuts. With his eyes to the road just ahead, he found that he had been joined by a set of empty footprints carved into the paving stones. He paused to crouch by the first, rubbing away grime with his fingers. There he felt minuscule letters incised. A little more cleaning revealed the text, in Strelledor, by an anonymous priestess. She had carved the steps to show believers the path that Finistrel had used to cross the mountains, and to bless those who walked the same path. He followed until he saw a tall cave opening, square, flanked by columns that had once been figures but now bore little trace of any human hand beyond the suggestion of hips and breasts.

"Finistrel, forgive me if I profane a sacred place," Fionvar said aloud, then he stepped into the cavern. The round inner chamber had a hole pierced high above, letting in feeble light and driving rain. The prayers carved into the walls could still be made out, framing the three alcoves. The Cave of Death drew his eye, to his left, and he was sorry he had no candle to light there, to speed Wolfram's spirit. Still, he unslung the pack to find flint and steel. A few branches from the stunted trees near the entry provided fuel for a small fire by the altar. A channel carved in the floor allowed the rainwater to flow into a basin by the alcove to his right, the Cave of Life. If Brianna kept the tradition, she would drink of the water in the temple every seven days, to ask blessing for her child. Their child. Fionvar turned his back to the water, crossing to the Cave of Death.

The altar within was long enough to bear a man's body and had been hewn from the living rock. Dim patterns of red paint marked the walls. Waxy stumps of candles stood along a shelf at the height of the lettering, so the temple had regular visitors who prayed for the dead. Fionvar stood there gazing into the darkness for a long while.

Sighing, he turned away at last, taking up the pack. Once more, his fingers traced the circle, and he brought them to his lips. "I am not a devout man," he said awkwardly to the opening in the ceiling, "you know that. Yet Wolfram died in a temple of the forest, and I believe that he is with you. He said once that if a man takes one step toward you, that you take ten steps out to meet him. I cannot walk with you while I have murder in my heart." He paused a moment, and a chill ran through him, as if acknowledging his words. "I know I walk alone upon that path, but if you could see fit . . ." He trailed off again, looking away. "If I could stand just once more with my lady, I will not stray from you again." Fionvar turned on his heel.

He stopped short at the sight of a small woman standing at the entrance. "You are looking for the way," she said.

Taking in her bald head, Fionvar gave a slight bow, and said, "Yes, Priestess, I am."

"The Lady brought you this far, and it is for me to show you the last few steps." She passed by him to the Cave of the Spirit, a deep recess farthest from the light. "The Nezinstrel," she murmured, "Night without Stars."

As Fionvar came up beside her, he knew what Quinan meant when he said not to go over the mountains. At the back of the Cave, a narrow archway led down into the belly of the earth.

Fionvar frowned. "I'll need a torch," he muttered.

She shook her head. "How many can you carry? The damp-ness inside puts them out almost as you light them, if you can get them lit, that is. Besides, you'll have to climb a bit, and it's best to have your hands free."

"Then how can I find my way?"

"The Lady provides." She smiled, ducking under the door and brought him to the side of a pool. Kneeling, she dipped one finger into it. The finger shed an eerie light in the dim cave. "Fill a waterskin with this, and dip your hands into it. As you enter the cave, you'll see the handprints of other travelers." She pressed her finger to the stone, leaving a glowing mark. "Press your hand beside them, and follow the hands."

"Is this magic?" He peered at the stuff.

"Almost. Those with torches cannot see the hands and lose their way." She stood up and looked down at him. "You'll be under-ground for the best part of two days." She smiled a little, and turned away. "Goddess walk with you." She vanished back into the rain.

Fionvar looked again at the strange liquid, then pulled one of the two skins from his pack and emptied the water. He held the skin in the pool with both hands, raising them, glowing, in wonder. The passage she had left him in joined with a larger cave toward the back, across a wide pond from the entrance. Water dripped from the ceiling and babbled from the pond down one side of a wider passage. Just beside the opening, sev-eral handprints were set, some quite dim indeed. Fionvar placed his mark beside them and plunged into the earth, leaving the sky behind him.

"I WISH THE king could ride in a carriage," Kattanan grum-bled, watching the horses mill about the yard below. He leaned his forehead against the leaded glass of the tall window.

"You rode well in battle, Your Majesty, or so I'm told," Gwythym remarked.

"I flew over the heads of the enemy on a steed made more of starlight than of flesh, if you believe all you are told."

The captain grinned. "Oh, a little starlight never hurt anyone, Majesty." He stroked the oiled suede one last time over the hilt of the king's sword and sighed, turning it in his hands. "A thing of beauty indeed."

Kattanan turned from the window. "I'll try not to get any blood on it."

"You do that," Gwythym returned without a trace of humor. He offered the sword hilt first, and Kattanan slid it home into its scabbard. The squires had left them alone in the chamber, off about last-minute preparations. Dawn's light did little to lift the shadows from the dark paneling or heavy tapestries. The two doors stood open, allowing a clear view of the bustle of maids, and the echoes of the soldiers' talk as they readied themselves in the lower hall. "Your tea's gone cold, Majesty," Gwythym pointed out. "Shall I send for a maid?"

"No, I'll only find myself distracted and leave it again."

The captain looked the king up and down and turned to lift the crown from its cushion. "I should be going with you, Majesty."

"I know it." He accepted the crown and set it on his head. "I wish you could, but I need someone here I can trust."

"You can trust me," Brianna said, entering behind them. "Can you not?" She wore a flowing gown of golden velvet, with a circlet upon her head. Her hands gripped each other as she gazed upon him.

"Of course." Kattanan crossed to touch her shoulder. "Of course I trust you, but there are places you cannot go, even on my behalf. And our grandmother—"

"Thorgir is vanquished, you are king, and we are to be married on your return. She has all that she has ever wanted, Rhys. As have I." Brianna took his hand.

"Please don't," he whispered, withdrawing the hand.

"I thought we were agreed," she matched his tone. Gwythym walked self-consciously to stoke the fire. "Now that Fionvar is gone . . ."

"I still hope for his safe return, and I have promised to keep you for him."

"He is devoted to you, Rhys. He would be the first to tell you to marry me. I miss him less and less, and he, too, will move on." She paused, studying him. "There's something else, isn't there? Some other reason you are afraid."

He sighed, and faced the truth. "I, too, have loved another."

"Why did you not speak of this before? Who is she?" Brianna crossed her arms.

"She is of high rank, and"—he sighed—"she is now married."

"Rhys," Brianna said gently, "I know it hurts to let go, but if she is married, then surely there is little hope." She touched his arm. "Do not let a hopeless love come between us."

"I cannot let go until I am sure it is hopeless."

"But her husband! Rhys, you make no sense. Look at me. I admit that I loved another, and I must also admit that it's better this way. I am betrothed to you by holy law—"

"By your own hand. Should I be bound by a lock of hair for the sake of a kingdom, to forswear myself and forsake my own heart?"

Her lips trembled. "Must we always hurt each other? I come to you in grief and parting. Lay aside your anger, cousin, if not for me, today, then for what once had been."

"So much may change again, Brianna, before I return here."

"Then simply tell me you will return, and when you do, we will speak of this. Perhaps then, you will hear me out?"

He took both of her hands in his, eyes searching her face. "I will hear you, if you will let me sing to you just one song of my own choosing. I know you do not want to be reminded, but you must know who I am."

"Do you know, Rhys?" she asked. "Do you know who you are?" She shook her head. "No, forgive me for asking. When you return, I will hear you sing."

They embraced and held each other a long time, then broke apart and offered awkward smiles. "In the meantime, you will take care of yourself," Kattanan said.

"And you, Your Majesty."

Gwythym cleared his throat. "Shall we go down, Majesty, my lady?"

Kattanan offered Brianna his arm, and they led the way down the corridor toward the broad front stairs. They had not gone far, however, when a breathless Jordan dashed up and made a little bow.

"Forgive my tardiness, Majesty." His face was flushed, and he seemed not to be sure whether to smile or frown. "I was detained by a lady." He wore black gloves with his riding garb and two swords at his waist.

Lyssa swept into view behind him, wearing her armor, with her war hammer at her side. Her radiant red hair streamed over her shoulders, and she glowed. The badge of the Sisterhood that had always hung at her side had been replaced by the badge of the king.

"Jordan, is there something we should discuss?" Kattanan narrowed his eyes.

"Time enough for that on the road."

Lyssa bowed, then winked at the king, and fell in with his guards behind. Brianna raised her eyebrows, and the gathering continued down the stairs.

The duchess met them in the narrow hall that led out to the yard. She curtsied and rose without smiling. "Your Majesty looks well and eager to be going."

"This is not a task I am eager for, but since it must be done, I am ready enough." He offered his other arm, and she accepted, laying a cold hand upon him. "While I am there, I intend to call upon the king of Bernholt," he continued lightly, "and see that the facts of this succession and the last are clear in his mind."

"An excellent idea," Brianna put in quickly.

"Still, there is risk involved, Your Majesty, if King Gerrod chooses not to acknowledge you and supports Thorgir's claim," Duchess Elyn said.

"His new son knows the right, and I think the heir, his daughter, will see the truth."

"Yes, but if anything were to go wrong," Elyn purred, "wouldn't you rather be assured of your own successor here? A marriage ceremony need not be lengthy."

Kattanan paused to stare at her. "Lady Brianna deserves the honor of a state ceremony."

"As you wish, Majesty." The duchess paced a little faster, drawing them up to the mouth of the passage where the gate stood open to the crowded square. A hail rose from the assembled knights. The duchess smiled gravely and nodded to them. Kattanan's eyes came to rest upon the wagon draped with red, the heart of the procession and the reason they were gathered. Rolf sat the driver's bench, quietly sobbing. Kattanan slipped his arms from the ladies and went out. The knights bowed their heads to him, and silence radiated out from his path. Footsteps from behind told him that his entourage followed, though with some trepidation.

"Rolf." Kattanan stopped, looking up to the driver. "It's me, Rolf."

Rolf lifted his face from his hands. "I failed him." Tears trembled in his mustache and beard.

"You did all that you could, Rolf." Kattanan pulled himself up onto the wagon, perching on the frame in front of his friend.

"No! I could have been there! I could have—" He cut off his words, lowering his head. "I don't know." He mashed away the tears with one hand.

"I don't know either, Rolf, and we never will. But there is something we can do for him now. You and I will take him home, with all of the majesty and honor he deserves. We will stand before King Gerrod and tell him that his son was no traitor, and we will not leave until he knows that it is true."

"Can we stay long enough to bury the bastard?"

"Maybe not, but I plan to bury the bastard who killed him."

Rolf looked up, brows raised. "Rough language for a king."

Kattanan gave a little smile. "It may get rougher from here on out."

"Ye're not the same lad I met a few months ago, Kat, but I'm proud t' ride w' ye. When we get there, ye won't leave me outside at the gate?"

"I want you with me, especially then."

"Then ye'd best take yer horse."

"Must I?" Kattanan sighed, but Rolf let out a snort of laughter.

"Aye, Yer Majesty, that ye must." Rolf gripped his shoulder briefly.

Kattanan sprang down beside the wagon and turned to the waiting company. "Grandmother, Brianna, I will look forward to returning. In the meantime, may the Lady watch over you both."

"Goddess walk with you, Your Majesty," the duchess returned, stepping aside as his horse was brought up.

Brianna leaned forward to swiftly kiss his cheek.

Kattanan set his foot in the stirrup and pulled himself into the saddle. All around him, the knights were mounting, and his friends found their steeds, coming through the crowd to join him before the wagon. The wizard, wearing no disguise but the garb of a common man, rode up easily, bowing her head briefly to the king. She reined in beside him. "Where would you have me ride, Majesty?"

"Ride with me, if you will, my lady."

"I am not good company, but you honor me." Her words were short, her eyes distant.

Up ahead, a horn sounded, and the leaders clucked their horses into motion. Bells rang from the temple, and the chant of Morning Prayer began. Gwythym patted Kattanan's horse and looked up at him. "Take care, then, Majesty, and watch your back."

Gwythym made the sign of the Goddess. The line before Kattanan began to move, and he turned from the crowd to take his place. He gripped the reins tightly, feeling the familiar aches hint already about their return. Once outside the city, they veered toward the mountains. In a week's time, he would be beyond them, returning to Bernholt to face its king. And more, to face the king's daughter. Which would be the greater trial? He gripped the reins a little tighter, and joined, softly, in the prayer.

# Chapter 34

SCRAGGLY WHISKERS had filled in along Fionvar's jaw by
the time the palace of Bernholt rose into view. As he absently
scratched his cheek, Fionvar reflected that a decent shave would
be in order before he paid a call on his brother. That, and a pair
of boots that hadn't taken the plunge into an underground river.
Along both sides of the road, peddlers set up their wares, and
beggars approached the few travelers. After two days under-
ground and more trudging down this road, Fionvar felt barely
human, and most of the beggars thought him beneath their notice. He was pleased enough to ignore them, until a brown-clad
monk fetched up beside him, matching his pace.

"You look familiar, my lord," the monk began.

"You don't know me, and I'm no lord."

"Those aren't workman's hands," the monk observed.

Fionvar scowled down at his hands, no longer callused. He
wondered how he should ever play the fiddle again—assuming
he had the chance. "What do you want?"

The monk popped in front of him, eyes widening. "The
earl!" he whispered.

Forced to stop or run the man down, Fionvar sighed. He
ought to have expected someone to notice the resemblance.

"Some relative of his? Or perhaps you are the Wizard of Nine
Stars, disguised to travel through Bernholt. But why should she,
why should you, that is, come back here?"

"Why indeed," Fionvar echoed. "When wizardry is banned."

A smile spreading over the monk's face. "Then you do know her."

Fionvar grew wary, a bit too late, it seemed. "I did not say that."

The monk kept up, speaking softly and urgently. "You did not deny that Nine Stars is a woman. Few are privy to that knowledge, outside of certain circles."

"You're not ignorant yourself, stranger."

"Please, call me Brother Turtle. She and I are . . . old friends. There is a price upon her head, and I've been trying to infiltrate the city. She will come here—either as a prisoner, or of her own will, to take her justice from the king." He spoke quickly, hooking his arm through Fionvar's to draw them closer together and off the road. "If I were a better wizard myself, I might find a way past their questions. I would never betray her." He gazed steadily into Fionvar's eyes.

Fionvar took a deep breath. "Nor would I."

"Why are you going to the city?"

"That is my business." He straightened immediately.

"It's something to do with Wolfram, is it? The traitor prince?"

Fionvar flinched—then cursed himself. He must learn to conceal his feelings if he were to infiltrate in his own right.

Brother Turtle's eyebrows pinched together. "I thought him a fine man, and I believe he is innocent of the charges laid upon him."

"What if I do not? You may endanger yourself by revealing these thoughts."

"You carry something of his, and I can feel his trace upon you. But perhaps you are going to sell this thing to King Gerrod as a final betrayal of his son."

Fionvar started walking again, trying to leave the strange monk behind him.

"Oh," said the monk as he hurried up alongside, "the prince is dead, isn't he? But you are not going to seek fame by claiming his death upon your sword. You are a friend of Wolfram's, and of Nine Stars, yet you go to their enemies."

"Yes, if you will leave me be."

"I should like to be there when you arrive." Brother Turtle

kept up as they approached the gate. "I suspect it will be most entertaining. May I accompany you?"

"I can't stop you from following me," Fionvar pointed out, "but those guards may have something else to say about it."

"My peril is my own," said the monk. "And I shall not let it touch upon you, so long as you do nothing to reveal me as other than a simple monk."

Fionvar looked at him and thought of Wolfram with his gift of trust. "Agreed," he said, and the monk grinned in return.

They found the city gate barred, and Fionvar approached the pair of guards, making the sign of the Goddess. Despite the heat of the day, both guards wore coats of mail and peaked helmets that revealed only a narrow sliver of the faces below.

"Tell me how you are called," the taller man barked, lowering his spear to hover in the region of Fionvar's heart. "And state your business here."

"I am Fionvar yfSonya duNormand. I am here to pay a call on my family."

The second guard cleared his throat and prodded his companion, but the first turned to face Brother Turtle. "Tell me how you are called."

Fionvar glanced casually at his scuffed boots, his heart pounding in his ears. The wizard could not avoid this demand, nor could he lie. Why had he been such a fool as to accept the monk's companionship?

"I am the Wizard of Broken Shell, of course!" Brother Turtle drew himself up importantly. "I'd expect you to know that. Aren't you the Wizard of Pointy Stick?"

The guard stiffened, sucking in his breath.

"And this"—the monk slapped Fionvar's shoulder—"is the Wizard of Sloshing Boots!" He crowed with laughter, his belly bouncing as tears twinkled from his eyes.

"This is a poor joke, Brother," Fionvar snapped, as the guard's gaze returned.

"Oh." The monk sighed. "You've no sense of humor."

"I am no wizard," Fionvar growled. "Are you going to give these men a proper answer before you get us both arrested?"

"Many pardons, please." Brother Turtle bowed to the guards. "It's simply been so long since I left the monastery that I forget myself. I am known as Brother Turtle, and I am seeking a certain priestess here."

"Then you are not a wizard."

"Would a wizard come to your front gate, knowing of the penalty hanging over him? I'm sure the nasty creatures are far from here."

"Hey," the second guard spoke up at last, "Normand's your father's name?"

"It is," Fionvar replied.

"You're the prince's brother, eh?"

"I am." Fionvar shifted on his feet, his boot linings squelching slightly. The journey plus the moisture had left its mark in blisters. "Look, if you won't let us in, then take a message to my brother, and we'll sit outside the gate until he comes."

The two helmeted heads swiveled to regard each other, then the men stepped aside, and the taller man struck the bell signaling that the pass door should be opened.

Brother Turtle grinned, tossing off blessings to them both as he walked inside.

"Your companion's a fool, or an idiot," the second guard murmured to Fionvar.

"Or both, but he's agreeable enough company for a walk."

The man bobbed his head. "You won't give a bad report to the prince, will you?"

Fionvar arched his eyebrows at the man, with a little shake of his head. "You were simply doing your job."

"Just so, my lord. Just so. Enjoy your visit!"

Brother Turtle waited a few paces inside and let out a peal of laughter when Fionvar narrowed his gaze upon him. "Just having a joke for the guards, no more."

The other did not respond, and they walked silently out from the shade of the thick wall into a dusty square. Only a few carts and blankets dotted the marketplace at this time of day, but the travelers were quickly accosted by the handful of merchants. Pushing an armload of silk scarves "for yer lady" out of his face,

Fionvar quickened his steps. They wound down the dirt streets, and a few paved with stones where the finer ladies were apt to shop, and found their way to the palace bridge. The guards there immediately seized upon Fionvar's family resemblance, and they crossed the rushing river to the courtyard on the other side.

"Thank you," Brother Turtle murmured. "Best of luck with your business, whatever it may be."

"And with yours," Fionvar returned, then the monk walked on ahead, turning toward the garden with quickening steps.

The outer court gates stood wide, though only a handful of guards and servants moved there. A page greeted Fionvar at the wall of the inner court, letting him into an antechamber before trotting off to tell his brother that he had arrived.

Fionvar flopped onto a cushioned bench, anticipating a long wait, but the door popped open immediately. "Fion! I knew you'd come!" Orie pulled him to his feet with a fierce grip on his arm. "There's so much to do!" The newly titled prince wore a doublet richly embroidered in gold over patterned silk and leggings of a similar flamboyant style. Orie's hair had grown out to lie in waves upon his shoulders, and he wore a thin, curling mustache. His dark eyes looked feverish.

"Have you been sleeping well?" Fionvar asked cautiously.

Orie's exuberance fell away abruptly. "I hope you did not come here to try to be my father again."

"I did not."

"Come with me." He renewed his grasp on Fionvar's arm. "We've just had puppies, and Melisande is with them."

"How is Her Royal Highness?"

"Well. Wonderful!" He leaned in closer. "I think she may be pregnant."

"Congratulations." Fionvar let himself be pulled along the hallway and outside. A door across the courtyard stood ajar, and an excited yipping came from within. Five tall hunting hounds stalked about the court, stepping out of Orie's way and peering after him with soft woofing. Straw covered the floors with nests of blankets and heavy bowls at intervals along the walls. A few dogs snored among the straw. The inner chamber still held a bed and small table for a dog-keeper as well as a low enclosure in the far corner. Melisande knelt there, looking in, with two servants beside her. She wore a plain kerchief over her hair and a gray dress with close sleeves. Ragged edges showed along the hem and straw stuck out all over it. Inside the enclosure, a dark, shaggy hound nosed at her squirming litter.

"Dearest," Orie said, "My brother's come to call."

"Well, let me change and—" She turned and rose, stopping quickly when she saw him there. Her fair face had lost a bit of its roundness, and her eyebrows were plucked to graceful arches. Her mouth pinched as she ran a hand over her garments. "I wish you would not just bring people unannounced, Orie, when I am a complete mess."

"Your Highness is as fair as ever," Fionvar offered, bowing.

"I am glad to see you again, Fionvar. Please, you must call me Melisande."

Orie pushed between them. "How are the puppies?"

Melisande swallowed, losing her smile. She placed her hands carefully together. "I think the runt is dead, but she does not want to give him up." She shrugged slightly. "Your brother has been very concerned over this litter."

"So I see. Perhaps someone could show me to a room, and we may meet again when you have had some time."

"Certainly, my lord," one of the maids put in. "I'll make a place for you."

Fionvar recognized Laura and gave her a nod.

"Aha!" Orie stood again, with a little bundle clutched in his hand. The weary suckling mother whimpered, and started to shake off her remaining puppies.

"Orie, let it be. We should not upset her now." Melisande reached out for the pale dead puppy, but Orie drew it out of reach.

"It doesn't do to get attached to something worthless. Best to give it up now." He prodded the other servant to rise and dropped the puppy into his hands. "Get rid of this." The man bowed quickly and left. "She's too sentimental with them," Orie said. "When it's our own children, she'll understand the need for a firm hand."

Still stroking the dog, Melisande lifted her head. "When it is, we shall discuss it. Laura, would you show our guest to the guest quarters. I believe the Fox Room is ready."

"Yes, Highness. If you'll follow me, my lord?"

"We'll let you rest 'til supper, then, Fion. And I will have some matters to discuss with you afterward."

The Fox Room proved to be named for the deep carving upon its door, a fox captured in twisting leap over a squirrel. The fox's face made Fionvar think of the wildness in his brother's eyes. Laura pushed the door open to reveal a well-appointed chamber with a large bed and chest, and a private entrance into the garderobe. Two windows with inset benches provided ample light and a view into the gardens.

"Make yourself comfortable here, my lord. Do you know how long you'll be staying?" Laura fluffed the pillows, and checked the oil in the lamps.

"A little bit longer than I'm welcome, I think."

She raised her eyebrows. "I did not think you were given to humor, my lord."

"I'm not," he replied. "Has my brother been ill lately?"

"Not as such, my lord." Her tone lowered along with her eyes. "I am sure he's not caught any sickness since he came here."

"But he has changed since then."

"It's not my business to study my betters."

"Perhaps not, but I think Kattanan counted you among his friends. Is that true?"

She snapped her arms across her chest and stared him full in the face. "If there's anything you want, the hall maid is just next door, my lord." She whirled out of the room, leaving the door wide open.

He crossed to the table and chair and kicked off his boots. Fionvar shaved with a basin and mirror, then settled again at the table, poring over a volume of genealogy as the sun sloped past his window. A knock interrupted his reverie when a servant brought him a bundle of clothing. They must have been the least ostentatious of Orie's clothes, but would suit his brother well. The servant also brought word that supper was not far off, so he would wait for Fionvar to get ready, and they set off together into the depths of the palace.

The king's dining hall opened onto the main stairwell in a series of arches. Banners of gold decorated the columns and banisters, and liveried servants greeted him as he entered, escorting him toward the head table. King Gerrod stood at the center, the brilliant blue of his robe commanding the gazes of his courtiers. His crown gleamed, as did his teeth as he laughed over something his companion was saying. Drinking deeply from a great flagon, he motioned the servants closer. Fionvar followed, and bowed.

"Gerrod, my brother, Fionvar, steward of my keep, and the man who saved us from starvation after our father's untimely death." Orie swept his arm toward his brother. It was he to whom the king had been listening so closely.

"Your Majesty does me great honor in allowing me to attend the feast with the highest of the court," Fionvar said, straightening to look again upon the king. The high table stood on a platform so that the king and his companions towered over the rest. The king's white hair framed a face that was all angles, with keen blue eyes.

"Nonsense," Gerrod snorted. "If all your brother says is true, then you readily deserve a place among us. Come up!" He urged Fionvar up the two steps to stand on equal footing, though across the table from them. "I have looked forward to this. Have you come to stay?"

"I may be needed elsewhere, Your Majesty—" Fionvar began.

"Nonsense!" Orie snorted, drawing his eyebrows into a line matching the sternness of the king's own brow. Gerrod roared with laughter, and Orie switched to a little, twisted grin. "You'll not escape our welcome that easily. Find a seat."

"Your brother shall sit by me," Melisande offered as she stepped up to the table from the back stair. Though the cloth still covered her hair, a simple gown of subdued green highlighted

her auburn brows and lightly painted lips as she smiled. Faint
darkness still haunted her eyes, but her tone was light as she held
out a hand for him. "You find me much better prepared now, do
you not?"

Fionvar lightly kissed her hand, dazzled a little by the chased
gold band of her marriage bracelet. "Your Highness has never
looked so lovely."

At this, Orie remarked, "Do not make any designs upon my
wife, Fion, or it'll be my dungeon you're trying to escape from."

A hint of color rising in her cheeks, Melisande slipped her
hand from Fionvar's.

"I would not make such designs, Orie, nor would your wife
entertain them."

"Of course not!" Gerrod put in. "Do take your seats, both of
you. Let us feast!" So saying, the king thrust himself into his own
tall chair and was pushed closer to the table by quick servants.
Orie and Melisande sat to either side, and Fionvar walked awkwardly around the table to sit beside the princess. Pairs of servants emerged bearing great platters of food, which they
paraded before the high table. An enormous boar, decked out
with herbs and staring with eyes made from berries, formed the
centerpiece of this parade. As the servants brought it forward,
Gerrod raised his flagon. "He fought well and died a hero!" A
cheer went up around the room.

Fionvar sampled a pheasant pie, and grinned at the cinnamon
scent of baked apples. He'd done that for his family once, after
trading a good laying hen for the right to pick their neighbor's
apple tree. It had been a feast, indeed, to have spiced fruits after
their meager bread and porridge. Orie had looked up at him
with that lightning grin. *"When I am king,"* he'd said, *"I will have
apples for dinner every night."* Fionvar nearly choked, thumping
down his mug.

Melisande glanced over at him. "Orie told us you introduced
him to this." She gestured with a forkful of apple.

"I had forgotten that until just now, Highness. At the time, I
couldn't even get him to help pick the apples."

"Tell me about when he was a child. Was he very different?"

"He wanted to be good at everything, and he would keep at it until he was. Vaulting, riding, dancing, when he got older. The village girls followed him everywhere."

Melisande's laughter rang. "Oh, the ladies here are just the same. At the marriage ball, we had only two dances together."

"As it should be," Gerrod put in firmly. "Orie has to meet all the members of the court. A prince cannot spend all his time on romance. Not that Orie would have done. He has already made himself invaluable to me. Melisande's choice was clearly for the best." He raised his drink to his new son and took a deep swallow.

Melisande smiled and looked away. "Is there no music tonight?" She turned to Fionvar, placing a hand on his arm. "You've not brought your violin, have you?"

He shook his head. "I took a difficult road to come here, Highness, and that was left behind."

"Then you did not come from Gamel's Grove?" she inquired, poking the last sliver of apple on her plate.

"Not directly."

"And neither could you bring a horse. It must have been difficult indeed." Her gaze rested on him. Something in her tone and the set of her jaw brought her brother instantly to mind, with his way of seeking knowledge without asking.

Fionvar opened his mouth to remark upon it, then recalled himself with a little shake of the head.

A sudden rapping brought their attention back to the floor. Three musicians arrived there, with a striking dark woman, evidently a singer.

"Excellent! My daughter requires song."

The small group bowed and began a sprightly air. The woman's voice flew lightly up and down the scales of the song, though it grated a little at the high end and faded at the low. They concluded to a smattering of applause, which Melisande did not join in as she clutched her goblet in her hands. The woman frowned a little toward the princess, but started a ballad, and her drummer managed to keep up with the slower song. At the end of this, Fionvar gently touched the princess's hand. "They are looking for your approval, Majesty."

"Oh, yes." She put down the glass and applauded loudly. Heartened, the entertainers went on.

Orie suddenly announced, "Gerrod, did I tell you that my brother plays upon the fiddle? He is part of the consort for dancing at my own keep."

"Excellent. You entertain us then; this girl is not to my liking." He fluttered a bejeweled hand toward the singer, who had faltered to a stop.

"I do not have my instrument, Your Majesty."

"Here, fiddler!" Orie cried to the musician. "Loan us your fiddle."

"You flatter me, brother, but I would rather not."

Orie swung away from him, calling out to the dinner guests, "This is my brother, to whom I owe my sanity, if not my life. Would you like to hear him play for you?"

Gerrod roared assent, raising his flagon, and the cheer echoed around the room.

Clapping his brother on the shoulder, Orie leaned across the table to take the fiddle from the glowering musician. Fionvar rose slowly, bowed his head to the princess, and took the instrument down the back stairs. He breathed softly for a moment, hearing the shouts of the crowd, who were well plied with ale. Coming around to the center floor, he set the fiddle on his shoulder and began. He picked out the tune so carefully that some of the audience winced. "In Bernholt hills they'll find me, lying with my lady/ dancing in the starlight, and laughing in the rain." He paused, and a few people grimly clapped.

Orie waved his hands, however. "Hush, that is only the beginning. Fion would not embarrass me by leaving off there. You have not heard the likes of this before. Do play on." The gleam returned to his eyes, and he measured his words by beating his fist slowly on the tall back of Melisande's chair. The princess leaned just a little forward, with one nod of encouragement.

Fionvar started again at a faster pace, his agile fingers dancing upon the strings. Faster he played, and faster, his eyes never leaving his brother's face. There was no other sound while the violin leapt into the lamplight. His fingers sprang from note to note, and he was sure he must miss them, must send the bow slashing off into the audience or catch his fingers among the strings and foul them, but still he played, and in his mind he heard the song and the singer who had claimed it. The brilliant voice anticipated his speed and urged him on. Orie's stony grin told him his brother heard it, too. Orie's hands clenched the back of the chair.

Fionvar played even faster, breathing in quick gasps. The fabric of the shirt tore softly across his shoulder, letting in the touch of a cool breeze, like a hand upon his arm, and he at last fell silent with a final stroke upon the strings. The audience let out their breath around him, then applauded, not needing their royalty to show them how. Their sound thundered upon his ears as he bowed once and again approached the high table. Melisande did not applaud. Her hands were raised to her bright cheeks, and one finger smeared away what might have been a tear.

"He is coming, isn't he," said Orie in a harsh whisper.

"Yes," Fionvar replied. "Yes he is."

# Chapter 35

MELISANDE WORE a gown of brilliant green, with flowing sleeves cut like oak leaves and lined with gold. She turned from her companions to look upon him, and said nothing as he approached. Kattanan saw that he carried a marriage bracelet, a narrow silver band etched with lines like music. He held it out to her. A smile spread across her lips, then she burst into laughter. She patted his head, as she might pat a dog, and walked away. The bracelet wriggled in his hands, now a silver serpent that twitched from his grasp and writhed across the floor toward the throne. He knew he must catch it, and ran after it, but stopped short. Wolfram leaned against the throne with his face in his hands, weeping. Kattanan tried to speak, but the words were a song. The smooth, sibilant tones flowed from his lips, forming verses he did not understand. Bewildered, he clapped a hand over his own mouth, but the song went on, and suddenly he knew the voice.

Kattanan awoke abruptly, but did not move. Faedre's voice whispered ever so softly around him, and the feeble glow of a candle came from behind him. Leather rubbed as she moved, followed by a quiet crunching of dried herbs. A slight scent of evergreen drifted toward him. Cautiously, he slipped his hand beneath his pillow, finding the hilt of his dagger. How had she gotten in? Where were his guards? Faedre crept around the bedding, sheltering something in her hands. As she leaned in, Kattanan sprang up, slapping her hands aside. The incense pot flew across the tent, scattering its scent over his blankets and furs.

Faedre gasped, snatching for a short blade at her side.

"Jordan!" Kattanan caught her arm, pressing her back as he scrambled out of bed. "Guards! Bury it," he cursed as she twisted away.

Now her knife was out, and she tried to sidle away from the corner.

The door flap flew open and three men burst through.

"Oh, Your Majesty," Faedre cried, dropping the weapon as if it burned her. "I thought," she stammered, "I mean, I was sent for, have I come to the wrong place?" She wore dark riding leathers, cut for a man, and her hair was bound back with a simple tie. One hand trailed up her thigh and hip to settle just above the roundness of her breast. Her expression faltered into a sly smile, and she let her eyes wander over the guards. Three stern faces met her gaze, and their swords did not waver.

"Majesty, are you all right?"

"Yes. Whatever she meant to do, she has failed."

"Only to make you feel good, Majesty. Don't you think I could?" She pulled the tie from her hair, letting the rich black tresses swirl down onto her shoulder.

One of the guards cleared his throat.

"This woman is no friend of mine, nor ever shall be." Kattanan took a few steps toward her, chilled by the breeze from a new gap at the back of the tent. He gripped the dagger and met her dark eyes. "Why are you here? Who sent you?"

"I was sent for, Majesty," she purred. "Just to give you a little pleasure."

"What is that incense?" He gestured toward the fallen pot with his free hand.

One of the guards bent over, retrieved it, and brought it to his nose. The man sniffed deeply, then shook his head. "I think it's just—" He swayed, and toppled loudly to the ground. The second guard knelt beside him, while the third advanced to stand by Kattanan.

"Sleeping" was the terse report as the kneeling guard scooped up the pot and as much incense as he could and dumped the lot into a pitcher of water.

"Bind this woman, take her back to Lochdale, and throw her in the dungeon," Kattanan snapped.

"I am a lady, your Majesty, and I have done nothing wrong."

He gestured toward the unconscious guard. "I take that as evidence of your intent."

"To ease your slumber, nothing more." She reached a pleading hand toward him.

"Orie is behind this, is he not?"

Withdrawing the hand, Faedre threw back her head and laughed. "You know nothing of Orie."

He listened to her fading chuckle. "I am going to visit him very soon. Shall I return you to him?"

Her dark features fell suddenly slack. "Of course, take me back to him."

Kattanan took a step closer despite his guards' warning noises. "Perhaps I will," he breathed. "What are you afraid of, Faedre?"

"I am not afraid." She tossed back her hair.

"Have you betrayed him as well? Or perhaps he cooled toward you, now that he and Melisande—" His throat caught on the words, and Faedre flashed a smile at the guard. "It's Melisande, isn't it? You've done something to offend her, or worse."

Her eyes came back to his, and her breathing was quick. "What does it matter what you think I've done?"

"If you have hurt her, I'll—"

"You'll what, Majesty?" she sneered. "You'll ride in like a hero of legend and avenge her wounded pride? She would laugh in your face, eunuch. She knows what you are! Everyone knows."

The guard slammed his sword into its sheath and grabbed her, pulling her away from the king. "The dungeon, your Majesty?"

Faedre struggled, baring her teeth. "Ayel and Jonsha avenge me!" she howled.

"Get her out of here." Kattanan did not turn around as the other man gathered Faedre's kicking legs, and they bundled her off. He stood staring at his feet. Melisande would laugh at him. Of course she would.

"Your Majesty," a gruff voice called out. "We've come to take him—"

Kattanan waved them about their business and heard the scuffling of feet as several men hefted their fallen companion and shuffled out the door.

Breathless, Jordan pushed inside. "Are you hurt? I came as quickly as I could."

"Given that you were not here"—he gestured at Jordan's untouched bedding laid out beside his own—"I suppose you did."

Jordan carefully slid the end of his belt into the buckle and pulled it snug about his waist. "I did not know I was forbidden to leave your side." He hooked his gloved hands over the belt. "Better to ask your guards why they left their post."

"I will ask them, but now I'm asking you. I thought you swore not to leave me."

"I was gone less than an hour, Kattanan, and I am here now."

"Only a few minutes late." Kattanan dropped the dagger by his pillow and poured a draught of wine.

"But you had already disarmed the villain," Jordan pointed out. Kattanan took a long swallow. Jordan added, a bit softer, "I am sorry I wasn't here. It will not happen again. Does that help?"

"You were with Lyssa."

"Yes, I was. I intend to marry her, and I think she will have me."

"Of course she will. Who wouldn't?"

Jordan let out a delighted laugh. "You're not afraid of being alone, you're just jealous."

"What?" Kattanan spun to face him. "I am not! It's just . . ." He shut his mouth into a grim line.

Still grinning, Jordan nodded quickly, running his good hand through his ruffled hair. "I never thought I'd see the day when you'd be jealous of me."

"Fine. So what if I am? Don't I have a right to be?"

"Well, you have a woman who loves you—wait, don't interrupt—and one whom you love. The problem is they are two different people. Part of the reason for this trip is to narrow that number, to see if Melisande might love you as well. Then there's just her husband to deal with."

"And her father." Kattanan swirled the last sip of wine in his goblet. "And then there is Brianna."

"Indeed there is. She has a lot to offer you."

Kattanan shook his head. "She offers only one thing that might sway me to her, Jordan, that someone might call me 'Father.' "

"Well I never . . ." Jordan murmured. "I had no idea you wanted a child."

Now it was Kattanan's turn to chuckle. "How could I, Kattanan duRhys, castrated singer, ever say I wanted a child? What would have been the point?"

"But King Rhys of Lochalyn would want children, would need them, in fact."

"And there is Brianna who believes it is her duty to serve." The two studied each other in the dim light.

"And there she is."

SITTING ON the edge of the royal dais, Fionvar sighed to himself. His third evening at the palace seemed destined to end as the other two, without a private word with Orie. The entire

drunken court had adjourned to the main hall, complete with
the bested musicians of the first evening, to dance the night
away. Fionvar himself, after winning acclaim as a fiddler, sat unnoticed. If his own brother could not see fit to speak to him,
why should the other nobles? As he contemplated this,
Melisande breezed up to perch beside him.

"Perhaps I have at last had enough dancing," she said, flapping
a painted paper fan. "You don't mind if I join you?"

"Certainly not, Your Highness. I had been wanting company."

"Thomas!" Melisande called out. "Do you need a drink,
Fionvar?"

"I'm fine, Your Highness. I've not been wearing my shoes
through as you have."

The page trotted up and gave a little bow. "Yes, Highness?"

"I'll have some water, if you please, Master Thomas. Then
perhaps you'll dance with me?"

The boy ducked his head with a giggle. "He'd not like it."

"Who wouldn't like it?" Melisande stopped smiling.

"Your—your husband, Highness."

She gently lifted his chin so that he looked into her eyes. "My
husband is the prince, and you must call him that."

Thomas took a little sniffle. "Yes, Your Highness. I'll bring
water."

Melisande turned back to Fionvar with a tiny smile. "He's
only seven, and so much has changed here that he doesn't understand."

"Neither do I, Your Highness."

The smile vanished and her eyes narrowed. "The king has recovered, and we are still celebrating that, as well as my marriage.
We are at peace and we are happy. I even have new puppies to
tend. What else is there to concern us?"

Fionvar regarded the princess. The king above them was
deeply involved in a discussion with one of his stewards. Fionvar lowered his voice. "If there were more, Highness, I might be
willing to talk about things otherwise left silent."

Her eyes flared, and she swallowed deeply. Thomas appeared
at her elbow with a jug and two goblets, which he placed on the

dais beside her and gave a little bow, then disappeared back to his place.

Melisande slowly poured herself a drink. "I should have asked for wine."

"Shall I call him back?"

She shook her head quickly. "For now, silence is best."

"As you wish." Fionvar watched the dancers, and they spoke of other things.

Orie finally left his latest partner to weave toward them. He planted a kiss on Melisande's brow. "It's not like you to sit out so long. Are you well? Or is my brother entreating your company?"

"All my fault," Fionvar said. "I asked for news of the princess's sisters abroad, and she was obliging me."

"Obliging, was she."

"Do you need some water?" Melisande held up her goblet to him, but he straightened away from her.

"You are not dancing, either, Fion. Is this some sort of conspiracy?"

Fionvar rose, inches away from his brother. "Nothing of the kind."

"There's no call to act as if you are protecting my wife."

"I'm not." Fionvar held up both hands. "I am protecting you."

"You are what?" Orie laughed aloud. "You are protecting me? From what?"

"From embarrassing yourself and your wife in public," Fionvar murmured.

Orie's fist relaxed, and he took a step back. "Always my big brother!" He clapped Fionvar on the back. "Let's go someplace and get reacquainted, shall we?" He steered them away from the dais, calling over his shoulder, "Farewell, my sweet."

They left by a back door and took a narrow flight of stairs into a servant's corridor. The passages grew quickly darker as they left behind the public rooms and Orie grabbed a torch from the wall to light their way.

"Where are we going? Are your quarters not toward the garden?"

"This is a special place, a place I have never taken anyone, but

I do not think you will betray my secrets." He turned suddenly, holding the torch low to cast his huge shadow upon the wall. "You never have before."

"They do not know you are a—"

"Of course not. You haven't tried to tell anyone, have you?"

"I see no reason to share that if you don't."

Orie frowned. "You have been awfully close to that eunuch, and to the Liren-sha. Perhaps I should not be so free with you."

Fionvar allowed himself a little grin. "You've hardly spoken to me since I got here. I hoped for a warmer welcome after walking under an entire mountain range."

"You never had a sense of humor before, Fion. I'm not sure I like it."

"You need to see it from my point of view. My lady is going to marry a castrated king and take my child with her. I admire him a great deal, but this does alter my plans. I was assigned to guard one man, just one, and he got killed. So I came to you after all." Fionvar tilted his head, and added, "I thought you might have need of me."

"Indeed I do, brother." Orie grabbed his arm again, and they were off. "She cut me off too soon, the wizard did. Now it is up to me to find out the rest."

"To find out what?" Fionvar stumbled as Orie stopped short and motioned him to silence. He quickly pushed open a door that had been nearly lost in shadows. Still silent, Orie pulled Fionvar after him, then shut the door again.

He placed the torch in a brace on the wall, revealing a small room with a very high ceiling, as if it were a tower with no interior floors. A staircase wound about the inside wall, twining up into the darkness past empty galleries. A workbench dominated the floor, swept clean of any clutter. Smaller tables held a few books, bottles, and knives, intermingled with preserved animals. At least, Fionvar thought they were preserved, until the smell hit him. He reeled against the wall, clapping a hand over his mouth.

"It's been too long," Orie muttered. He gathered the putrefying animals into his arms, heedless of his brocade tunic, and toted them beyond a curtained arch.

"What is this place?" choked Fionvar.

Lighting fire to a bundle of twigs, Orie said, "It is my work-room. Once, it was the queen's library. Gerrod, in a fit of senti-mentality, forbade anyone to come here. It is distant from the main quarters and suits my needs well." He walked slowly around the room, wafting the smoking twigs. Making several circles of smoke about Fionvar's head, he noted, "The scent hardly bothers me anymore."

"Perhaps I'd rather not know what you do here." The smoke, which smelled faintly of pine and mushrooms, eased his breathing.

"But I have worked alone long enough. I should find myself an apprentice."

Fionvar retreated a few step. "No. Absolutely not."

"Not you," Orie snorted. "Though you will be useful to me in other respects. You won't even participate directly in my spells."

Ducking Orie's gaze, Fionvar walked a few steps away from the door. Deep red stained the workbench and tables. One of Orie's victims—a tiny, pale puppy—lay entangled in a cloth. He spun back toward the door. "I cannot do this, Orie. I cannot be a part of this."

"Melisande might, if properly motivated," Orie mused.

"No. Great Lady, what have you become?"

"Ah, it's what I will become, with your help and my wife's. You have lost your cause, Fionvar, and begun to care about something beyond your great ideal. I am letting you glimpse a cause so much greater. A mage-king, Fion," Orie murmured, his hands held out. "Think of all those who could benefit from my power, yourself not least of all. Think of the people I could heal with these hands. Our father, Fion, our mother could have been saved. Could still be saved."

Fionvar shook his head slowly. "They're dead, Orie. There is nothing to save."

"You have always been so shortsighted. Think of the Liren-sha, then, how he was returned to life. Or better, think of the prince, your king's precious friend."

"It's too late, Orie, you killed him!"

"But I would not be averse to bringing him back."

"It cannot be done. The wizard said so herself!"

"Even she did not know everything."

"And you do."

"What if I could heal your king, Fionvar? What would you do then?"

A chill flickered the flames and shivered down Fionvar's neck. His dark eyes met Orie's—the younger brother who had more than once been called his twin. He took a deep breath. "What are you asking me to do, brother?"

# Chapter 36

JORDAN WATCHED the first messengers from Bernholt in quick retreat as Kattanan called for water. "On the whole," Jordan commented, "that went well." Kattanan stared, and Jordan's face broke into his ready grin. "King Gerrod does not believe you are Rhys, he did not know of the succession, he has put a bounty on Wolfram's death and banned the prince's name. This trip begins to look exciting."

"Exciting! I just hope I have not made trouble for the messenger." He took a sip of water. "He will accept that I am Rhys, I think, having few other options. And he probably has heard of the succession at least as a rumor from Orie. I wonder why he did not broadcast the news of Wolfram's death since he must have heard that also."

"Not necessarily. Orie may not wish to reveal his involvement, especially since Wolfram and Melisande had been close. We still don't know Melisande's thoughts about her brother."

"True." He drained the goblet and got up. "There's nothing for it but to wait, I suppose. Shall we have lunch?"

Two hours passed in dining and arranging the camp, in particular the king's sumptuous pavilion. The duchess had insisted he should travel as a king, since this was a royal visit to another court, and had sent him off with a great many banners and official seals. So it was at his reception tent that he next met the royal messenger. If the little man had looked strained before, he now fairly crept into Kattanan's presence. Bright redness spotted his cheeks, and his hands trembled. Kattanan glanced down to his own hands, surprised to find them still.

"I gather from your demeanor that the messages you carry are not altogether pleasant ones," Kattanan said, schooling his voice to gentleness.

"Your Majesty may not be pleased to hear them. King Gerrod again sends his greetings to his royal cousin, Rhys of Lochalyn. He finds that he may have been lied to and betrayed by the usurper of your throne. However, he is willing to accept that you are the rightful heir. In this capacity, you will be received by the court as soon as proper arrangements can be made."

"That is well enough, if not an apology."

"Your Majesty and his knights are also offered free access to the city, provided there be no wizards among you." The man's eyes peered up through his brows.

"And to the other matter we spoke of?"

"To that, Gerrod, High and Terrible King of Bernholt by Right of Blood, sends the following response." The man fumbled with a scroll and managed to open it. He cleared his throat, and took a step to the side so that one of the guards could pass him and set down a small chest. "Whereas the bounty on the head of the Traitor was set at five sacks of gold coin should the Traitor's remains be brought before the king, and whereas this deed has been done by the hand of one King Rhys yfCaitrin duAlyn of Lochalyn, His Royal Majesty herewith sends the promised reward"—Kattanan let out a cry of indignation, echoed by his companions—"and further recommends to the aforementioned King Rhys that he should dispose of said remains,'" he cringed as he finished, "as he would the corpse of any foul beast.'" He clutched the scroll with both hands.

Kattanan leapt to his feet, seething, then stopped himself. He took a moment to steady his breathing.

"If you will not tell Gerrod to bury himself," Lyssa burst out, "then I will. I will march up there and—"

Kattanan whirled to face her. "No, you will not. And neither will I. I have taken it upon myself to do this thing, he has chosen to both accept and insult me. So be it."

"Won't you at least face this, deal with this?" She waved a hand toward the messenger, who backed off a few steps.

"Give me a moment to think." Kattanan walked slowly back and forth, then stopped, straining his eyes to look toward the city. "We have free passage in Bernholt City. I will petition the priestess of the principal temple to use her funeral ground and her prayers at the service. If she is afraid of reprisals, then I will bring Wolfram to the temple square and send him to the stars with the help of our own priestess."

The messenger gasped.

"What about that?" Lyssa indicated the chest of gold.

Kattanan stared down at it. "Send it back." He raised an eyebrow to the messenger. "Tell His Majesty that if he wishes to commemorate his son's death with money, he will be better served to build a school."

"Then you do not answer the insult," Jordan observed.

"That was never Wolfram's way, and it will not be mine. Further inform His Majesty that we regret that he will not offer the Royal Temple for the services, but that they shall be held two days from now, at sundown, and that all are welcome to attend the rites and join me in celebrating the life of Prince Wolfram."

"I much doubt, Your Majesty," the man whispered, "that anyone would be allowed."

Kattanan considered this for a moment, then said, "Jordan, take a few of the knights and go into the city, to every cloth merchant you can find and pay for red hoods to be made. These will be brought to every temple in the city and any man or woman who fears to openly attend the funeral may therefore come disguised. King Gerrod may say what he likes about his son; I believe that he is alone in saying it. Oh," Kattanan added to the messenger, "also thank him for his salutation and inform him that we shall await his welcome here. That is all."

Bowing low, the man replied, "Goddess grant you favor, Your Majesty." He turned and left, followed by the guards, who once again took up the chest.

The wizard, disguised as squire, sauntered up and made a casual bow. "There's a death ban on wizards, as well, Your Majesty. I thought you'd like to know."

"There's no need for you to go to the castle, anyhow, and you should be able to pass in the city."

She shook her head. "I did not wish to speak of this before, Your Majesty, but there is a certain book I must find here, before it is found by our enemies. I have reason to believe that it is inside the castle. After the funeral, I may not be able to await Gerrod's leisure in entertaining you."

"You may take care of your own business," Kattanan replied, "but be careful."

"As best I can, Majesty."

"I'll come with you," said Jordan, "if I can, if you think that would help."

She nodded abruptly. "It may. Thank you." A slender smile.

Lyssa glowered. "Shouldn't we be off to town to order those hoods?"

"Coming," he said.

"I shall go to the temple myself," said Kattanan. "It has been too long."

"You should not go anywhere alone, Kattanan," Jordan murmured. "Gerrod does not trust you, and we should be ready for trouble."

"Then Rolf can go with me. He's kept vigil long enough."

"Rolf! The king has no more liking for him than for you, perhaps less."

"Then I'll ask the wizard as well."

Jordan rolled his eyes. "Are you trying to provoke Gerrod or me?"

"Neither. I simply would like some privacy."

"Do what you like. I suppose you will in any case." Jordan crossed his arms, looking down at Kattanan.

Kattanan raised his head to return the look, giving way to a little smirk when he realized he did not have to look up so far as before. "We may yet see eye to eye."

Lyssa, who had gone on a few paces, hovered there, frowning at them and scuffing her feet loudly.

Jordan glanced to her and back to his king. "You will take care of yourself?"

"I will. Don't keep her waiting!"

Grinning, Jordan replied, "One day, I hope to say the same to you." Then he turned and trotted to catch up with Lyssa.

"BUILD A SCHOOL!" King Gerrod thundered. He surged to his feet, pacing the dais. "That King Rhys is indeed an insolent dog and the son of cowards! I will never see him."

Melisande to his right, and Orie to hers, watched the king's tirade. Fionvar, standing behind his brother, watched Melisande for sign of her feelings. She had borne the news of Wolfram's death in stony silence, now her face, already pale with lack of sleep, grew ever more pinched as she clutched the arms of her throne. The two guards stood at attention behind the cowering messenger, with the bold chest between them.

"Well," said Orie at length, "I suppose someone shall have to see him."

"Why?" snapped the king. "He's done nothing worthy of our welcome."

"He is a king, now, and has the power to raise an army against us if he chooses."

"We'd clobber the little runt." Gerrod's blue eyes glinted, and he stopped his pacing to stand firmly at the center. "Perhaps war would not be such a bad thing."

Melisande jerked her hands from her throne to curl them in her lap. "Father, crops have grown but poorly. Our citizens would not like to give up such a feeble harvest to feed an army."

"Our honor has been offended, Melisande. Any loyal man would stand for that cause." He whirled back to the messenger. "What manner of king is this Rhys?"

"As I said, Your Majesty"—the man gulped—"he is quite young, but fierce and proud, too. His knights seem loyal and eager to uphold him."

"How did you find him? Immature, naive? Does he wish to provoke us?"

"I would not say so, Your Majesty. He appeared . . . in command of himself. He and his retainers were angered, but he had no wish to return angry words to Your Majesty." The man ducked his head.

"Father?" Melisande asked softly. When his face turned toward hers, his manner somewhat more subdued, she said, "It may be, if you allow this to escalate into a war, that your righteous anger will be seen as something different, as a wish to suppress what this king says about—about the Traitor. If you respond with your disdain, if you show him that this traitor, and he himself, is unworthy of your anger, your lords will see how strong is your resolve that the truth of what the Traitor has done should be known."

"Unworthy of my anger," the king mused.

Melisande shrank a little into her cushions.

"There may be wisdom in you yet, daughter. Let him burn his rubbish, this king will not hear from me. From now on, you will send him word. You will meet with him and tell him again of the Traitor's deeds. He may be young enough to be tractable."

Orie shifted uncomfortably. He reached out an imperious hand, and Melisande slid hers into it. "Darling," he murmured, "this seems a good plan to avoid war. Find out all you can from this little king, so that we may exploit his weaknesses when the time comes." His eyes searched her face, and she nodded to him.

"It may be ideal, in fact," King Gerrod said, resuming his throne and dismissing the messenger with a flick of his hand. "He may feel he has the advantage over you and reveal too much. Wear something attractive when you meet him, Melisande."

"Yes, Father."

"You may go, then. I'll call for you if I need you." The couple rose to go, but Gerrod stayed Orie. "Let your brother escort the princess, I'd like a word with you."

Fionvar took Melisande's hand upon his arm as Orie's greedy gaze followed. Orie turned back to the king. "What did you wish to speak of, Gerrod?"

"You have said this eunuch king has lusted for my daughter, as repulsive as that is. Do you not fear this meeting will revive those feelings?"

"Oh, I am counting on that, Your Majesty. Rhys will feel that he can trust her, so he will be more free with her. But for her part, Melisande was furious when her singer left her. She will feel betrayed by him because he never tried to contact her and never told her about his past. Believe me, Gerrod, when she finds out who he is, she will do anything we wish to cut him down to size." The two men grinned.

ONCE OUT of earshot, Melisande stopped Fionvar and looked him in the eyes. "There is too much happening here, Fionvar. My father is keeping things from me, things that I must know if I am to act for the best."

"For whose best, Highness?" he asked.

"For the people of this palace and this kingdom. I begin to think—" She broke off, looking back, then urged him on again until they reached a little chamber where she shut the door. "I begin to see that my father does not tell all. As the king, this is his right. It is his duty, even more than mine, to uphold the laws and ways of this kingdom."

Fionvar nodded, not sure where this was going.

"You have said that you would speak of things kept silent," she continued more quietly, standing very near him. "Will you still?"

"If I am at liberty to do so."

At this answer, her eyes roved over his face, so like her husband's. "Can you assure me that you will not reveal what I say to you here?"

"I am at your service, Your Highness."

"It isn't that I don't trust my father, believe me," she said forcefully, "nor that I mistrust Orie, but I have to know." She took a deep breath. "How did my brother die?"

Fionvar considered. Melisande's cheeks held spots of rosy color, and her raised chin, bared a slim and lovely neck. He swallowed, suddenly seeing why his brother guarded her so jealously; her very defiance roused him. "He died as he lived, Highness; with the greatest of honor."

"You know what I meant."

Fionvar perched on the window ledge where the sun might warm him. "My lady," he said, "I hold your brother in very high regard, but that regard is treasonous. If I reveal much more, you might just as easily betray my treason as I could betray your doubts." He shook his head, smiling wryly. "I used to be one who would speak the truth with no qualms at all."

"Yet now you conceal it. You do not trust me."

"How much do you love my brother?"

Taken aback by the change of subject, Melisande crossed her arms and walked to stand face-to-face. "What sort of question is that? Orie is my chosen husband and will be the father of my child. He is your brother; how much do you love him?"

"Enough to see how much he's changed and to ache because of it."

Melisande let her arms slide apart and touched his shoulder. "Then let us say," she whispered, "that I love him at least that much as well."

"Then do not ask me to tell you how Wolfram died."

Her hand dropped, and she narrowed her eyes. "Orie had a part in his death?"

"Yes."

The princess nodded. As she did, one hairpin tumbled to the floor, and the veil over her hair slipped. Quickly, she bent for the pin to replace it, but not before Fionvar saw her hair, or what little remained of it. He sucked in a startled breath, and she again met his gaze, the veil fixed in place. "I loved my brother as well, Fionvar. My father has declared him to be a traitor for reasons of his own. I can't say what happened between them, but I can say this: Wolfram had no wish to be king. I cannot dispute my father in his belief that Wolfram was a traitor, but I also cannot say that it makes sense to me."

"In your position, I would be cautious, too."

"If you will not tell me how he died, can you not at least tell me how he lived? How did he meet you and how did he come to serve with this King Rhys, if that is true?"

"Oh, it is true. I have been long in service to the True King of Lochalyn. Wolfram came because he and Rhys were . . ." he hesitated. "They were old friends."

"How can that be?"

Fionvar shifted his weight on the stone ledge. "I think your husband and father do not wish you to know that now. I can't say that I agree with them, but it might go badly for us both if I told you."

"Very well then. What was his story about his flight from Bernholt?"

Fionvar told her what he knew, from the prince and from Rolf. He described Wolfram brought before the king, and Melisande let out a little moan. She turned from him, but indicated that he should go on. Haltingly, he spoke of his gradual friendship for the exile. When he reached the scene of the great battle, he broke off the narrative. "Here on are things I cannot speak of without endangering both of us."

Melisande held her face in her hands. Her shoulders quivered slightly.

Fionvar's hands reached out to hold and comfort her, but he stopped himself and crossed his arms. That was an intimacy he had no right to offer or to take. He waited until her quivering had stilled, and asked, "Is there anything else I may safely tell you?"

"There is one thing." Her voice had changed now to steel.

"You say you hold Wolfram in high esteem, and that Orie had some part in his death. If those things are so, why have you come here?"

"Wolfram told me to, when we first met. He was concerned for you, and worried about our new king and how King Gerrod would react"—this was most of the truth, anyhow—"so he told me, if I should leave Lochalyn, that I should come to my brother."

"I'm glad you're here, Fionvar," Melisande said. "I know Orie is, too. Since you came he has been . . . he has felt better." She ducked her head.

"I know he is not well, Highness. That's another reason I came."

"He was injured falling down the stairs." She touched her side to indicate the injury. "I think he may have been a little fevered as well. How did you know that?"

"Brother's intuition," Fionvar replied weakly.

She stiffened. "I once believed everyone told me the truth because they loved me. Now I know how many are liars, but some are better at it than others." She shot him a fiery glance. "If you can't be honest with me, at least do me the honor of telling me so."

"You know I can't be open, Highness."

Suddenly her eyes widened. "How can I trust anything you say?"

"My only lies to you have been lies of omission."

"So you have given me just enough of the truth to reveal my emotions? Or is it that you claim to love your brother but still plan his harm? Perhaps he is not himself, but he will get better!"

Fionvar rose, shaking his head. "Please, Highness, what can I tell you? What can I say to help you trust me?"

"Tell me how my brother died."

He shut his eyes. "That would be no help at all." What trust could there be for an avowed friend of traitors who would deal behind his own brother's back? Again, he thought of Wolfram and how quickly the prince had given his trust, even to his enemy's brother. Now that Wolfram was gone, Fionvar learned how much he missed that easy, absolute faith. Instantly, he knew what to do.

Melisande scowled down at him as she turned to go.

Fionvar snatched her elbow; her body went rigid at his touch. "You wish to go to his funeral?" he breathed.

"There is no way I can do that, even were I so inclined. Let me go."

"Please listen, Highness, I know you miss him, even if you cannot say so. Give me seven ribbons, and I will tie bundles for you. Your prayers will be burned with him."

She inched a little closer. "You can't. If my father found out— or Orie!"

"I think I can gain Orie's assistance. Give me seven ribbons, Highness, and your brother will know you have not forgotten him."

"Seven ribbons, Great Goddess." She pulled away. "You could be killed."

"We cannot afford to fear each other when there are so many other dangers."

"I do not wish to hear any more treason from you, sir," Melisande said lightly. She gathered her skirts and plunged down the hall.

Fionvar did not follow her. His heart raced, and it took a long while to control his breathing. Still, a little smile played about his lips. Impulsively, he had become as foolish and trusting as Wolfram had ever been. What better tribute to the fallen?

A hand gripped his shoulder, and he started violently. "What were you speaking of so closely, brother?" Orie hissed. His eyes and hair seemed wild in the sunlight, his grip was iron.

Fionvar let out a long breath. "If you must know, we fought. I expressed some concerns about her ability to handle meeting King Rhys. She got upset."

"Hmm. You did not tell her who he is, did you?"

"No, of course not. I assume you have a good reason for that secret. Do you think the meeting is wise, Orie, knowing how he feels about her?"

"You are so innocent in these matters." Orie laughed, releasing him. "Wise? It's perfect. She hates Kattanan because he left her, and she can't bear having her playthings taken away. When she sees him again, she'll know how deeply she was betrayed. She'll hate him even more. I hate to say it"—he sighed indulgently—"but my lovely wife really is a spoiled child at heart. Chances are she'll send us even more surely toward war than her father would."

"Doesn't that worry you?"

"Oh, I'm exaggerating, brother dear. There will be no war. Your King Rhys really doesn't have the stomach for it, or he would've declared one once we sent him the bounty on Wolfram."

"Speaking of which . . ." Fionvar began.

"What is it?"

"The funeral's to be in two days. Do you suppose anyone will go?"

Orie considered this and shrugged. "Well, a few of the former prince's staff might try, perhaps some townsfolk, since Rhys has gone to all the bother of providing them with disguises. Just a few fools defying their king."

Fionvar looked surprised. "You mean you haven't thought of it? That this funeral, this whole visit, might be simply an excuse to foment rebellion against Gerrod?"

"Of course I've considered that," Orie scoffed, watching his brother closely.

"Now Melisande's talked him out of a hostile response— which is wise, I agree—we might not even see what goes on there. How could His Majesty send anyone to report without seeming to condone it, which would undermine his own decrees, or condemn it, which might enrage the conspirators? Now, don't look at me like that!"

"No, Fion, you bring up an excellent point. Gerrod can't do anything, shan't do anything, but we should keep an eye on things. Or rather, you should. If the enemy recognized you, he would hardly be surprised to find you there."

"Behind the king's back? Are you mad? Gerrod would bury

me!" He backed away, waving his hands. "I came to look out for you, but not like that."

"Of course you'll go. Gerrod likes you, Fion. Everything will be fine" Orie turned smartly and went back inside.

Fionvar looked after his brother, then in the direction Melisande had gone, and thought of the seven ribbons. He smiled grimly. One way and another, Wolfram would not be alone.

# Chapter 37

**THE DAY** of the funeral, at a summons from Orie, Fionvar emerged onto the lower courtyard into a scene that was almost idyllic were it not for the clouds. A mess of barking, whimpering, howling dogs gamboled about the stone yard, tussling with one another, and their master and mistress. Melisande wore the rumpled gray gown he had first seen her in, and Orie wore old hunting clothes. The two played catch over the dogs' heads with a comet ball, its bright tail streaming out behind. The frustrated dogs leapt in the air and galloped in glee when the ball was tossed their way.

"Fion! Good to see you at last!" Orie called.

Melisande turned toward him, her white veil fluttering in the breeze over her ruined hair. "Catch!" she cried, tossing the ball. Fionvar lunged, and grabbed it by its ribbon tail.

"What a miraculous dive! You should've been a retriever," Orie announced.

"Anything for the honor of the family." Fionvar offered the comet back to Melisande, but she refused it.

"It is time you had a remembrance of me, dear brother. And you performed so well!" She turned quickly to Orie. "You see, he can be taught, it simply requires a woman's touch."

"I will keep it with reverence, your Highness," Fionvar grumbled.

Orie kissed her lightly, then pulled her closer for a longer one. Fionvar shifted uneasily, watching the scuffling dogs.

Grinning, Orie nuzzled Melisande's ear. "Why don't you go wait inside for me? I'll pack up the pets."

Released from his embrace, Melisande bit her lip, then smiled, bobbed a little curtsy, and made for the stairs. Orie turned to his brother. "One last game before we go in." He bounded into action, calling over his shoulder, "A race!"

A rippling tide of dogs compelled Fionvar to follow, stumbling, across the court until the canine wave swept up against the far wall. Orie leaned there nonchalantly, one arm braced upon an ornate metal gate set in the base of the tower. "Oh, well done, brother. You might have beaten me, if that brindle brute hadn't gotten in the way."

"Why are you playing with me, Orie?" Fionvar panted.

Orie pushed a little on the gate, which swung silently open. "There's a bridge along a bit, and a path to the city. The gate will be unlocked. I do think we'll have rain, though. Such a pity if Wolfram's fire wouldn't light; or if there were no star for his soul to aspire toward. Go to! And keep your eyes open."

"You can trust me, Orie."

"Of course I can." Orie winked as he shut the gate behind his brother.

Fionvar paced down the road. Now, Melisande would have no chance to give him the ribbons, even if she'd wanted to. Of course, judging from her closeness to Orie the previous day, she'd never intended to. Nervously, he tossed the comet ball from hand to hand, then caught the ball again and held it up before him. The body was a pouch of red wool, somewhat stained, and something crinkled inside it, padding a slender weight. For its tail hung seven long ribbons.

KATTANAN WATCHED the sky with growing concern. Thunder, rain, even overcast could be taken as a sign that his actions had been rash, that Wolfram was indeed a traitor and to give him a funeral with honor was sacrilege against the Lady. He put down another armload of dry twigs with the growing heap at the edge of the funeral ground.

"At least we know it's not magic," Jordan said, coming up behind.

"Great Lady!" Kattanan glowered. "How can a man so tall move so lightly?"

Arching an eyebrow at him, Jordan dropped his own load. "It's not like you to be startled by anyone. I noticed you looking up to the palace."

"Are you sure Orie wouldn't be able to summon rain? He was Alswytha's apprentice, after all, and she can perform her magic."

Jordan said, "He only has a little bit of her blood. There's still too much of his own in his veins. Something should be done about that." He gave a fierce grin.

"If there's bloodletting of his to be done," Rolf put in, joining them from the makeshift altar where he had been cutting ribbons, "ye'd best stand in line behind me."

"I'll arm wrestle you for it," Jordan replied, offering his left hand.

Rolf actually laughed at that, just a short chuckle, but the sound brought a smile to Kattanan's face.

Lyssa, carrying a bundle of her own, murmured, "It strikes me strangely to hear my friends talk of killing my brother as if it were a laughing matter."

"I didn't realize how much this hurt you, Lyssa," Jordan said.

Lyssa shook back her hair and took a step away from him. "No, I'm sure you didn't mean to hurt me. But it does. It does." She whirled away and strode swiftly from the grounds, losing herself among the buildings.

"Bury it," Jordan murmured. "I was a monk too long, and now I don't know the first thing about women. I'd better go after her."

As Kattanan and Rolf finished their bundles, a trickle of people in red hoods were likewise taking sticks from the pile, and ribbons from a few servants who passed among them. Many of those disguised were Kattanan's own knights, trying to comfort the townsfolk who might be afraid to come out. Still, the edges of the cloaks swished to reveal bare feet or delicate slippers, and he knew they were coming. Kattanan carried his bundles to lay them beside the bier where Wolfram's body, draped in red, lay waiting the flame. He knelt again, making the sign of the Goddess, and recalled for a moment the day he had left. Again he saw Wolfram astride a proud horse, shutting his eyes to wish Kattanan a safe return. But the singer had returned as a king, and the prince rode home on a funeral wagon.

Tears sprang to his eyes, and he pressed his hands to them. He rose and turned away, then stopped, stunned.

All around him, red-hooded mourners gathered, some wearing rough hoods of their own making. In defiance of their king's order, they had come, were still coming, furtively at first, then walking boldly when they saw how many others waited there. Jordan, Rolf, and Lyssa stood by, faces raised to the sky in silent prayer. His own priestess walked the sacred circles around the bier, followed by three others, all hooded, and one ragged crone who met his gaze with her mismatched eyes. He took a step toward her, but suddenly felt something pressed into his hand.

A tall man in a red hood and cloak leaned toward him, whispering, "For your eyes, Your Majesty, and for the fire."

"Fionvar," Kattanan murmured. "How's the music at the palace?"

"Awful," the other replied, but with a trace of a smile. "Pray for me, and for her."

"I do."

With the slightest tilt of his head, Fionvar placed two groups of bound bundles at the bier, then faded back into the crowd. Kattanan longed to follow, but suddenly felt as if all the eyes peering out from those hoods were focused on him. There was some truth to this, of course, since the townsfolk had heard stories of the new king. They might have come to mourn Prince Wolfram, but they did not waste the chance to study the king for themselves. Accordingly, he made a little show of reaching into his pouch, then lifting the thing Fionvar had pushed into his hand as if he'd had it all along. The circle of red wool enclosed a small square of parchment, and a single open link of chain. Incised patterns decorated the link, echoing the tooling on fine book bindings: a library chain, meant to protect a precious volume. He smoothed out the parchment to find a simple blessing in Strelledor: *May you rise up in the flames, and look down from the stars. The chain of earth is broken; you are free.* He remembered packing Melisande's things for the Goddess Moon, when he had held up to her a book with a library chain still dangling from it. Wolfram had held the chisel while Melisande struck the blow. Melisande! With a sudden leap of hope, Kattanan brought the chain to his lips and kissed it. Then she did not believe Wolfram to be a traitor. A twinge of guilt touched him through the rush of excitement. Then he let himself smile just a little. Surely, Wolfram would understand. With a regretful sigh, Kattanan bound up the little packet once more and placed it gently on the red cloth. A ray of late sun gilded his hand, and the still form beneath the cloth. High above, the dark clouds still clustered, but a great hole gaped through them, and the setting sun blazed with crimson fire.

HIGH ON a garden tower overlooking the city, King Gerrod scowled at the sky. "Magic," he snorted, "or trickery." When Melisande and Orie said nothing, Gerrod trained a spyglass on the funerary ground. "They're all wearing those accursed hoods. Of course, it could just be a ploy to make us believe that our people are attending. All those hoods could be worn by this upstart's own knights."

"Many of them are," Orie put in. "The guards watching their camp reported that many of the knights put on red hoods before they left there."

"Ha! I knew it wouldn't work." He slapped the spyglass onto the parapet and grinned. "He's putting on a show to impress the townsfolk, but nothing will come of it."

"May I?" Orie put out a hand for the glass and trained it on the gathering. "Three of the priestesses are hooded; it may be time to investigate the temple, Gerrod."

"They always were on his side."

Turning away, Melisande leaned her back against the wall. A wave of nausea overwhelmed her for a moment, and she shut her eyes, one hand pressed to her belly. Slowly, the wave passed, and she refocused on the little temple in the garden, with its slender bell tower.

"Melisande," King Gerrod's stern voice called back her gaze. "If you are not well, you should be abed. No reason to risk your health, or my grandchild's."

She shook her head. "No, Father. I, too, should know what happens." She took two steps to stand between them, leaning on the stone.

"King Rhys is standing for family," Orie reported, his eyes never leaving the scene below. "He's got the torch." Down in the city, a tiny flame licked at the red cloth, then caught. It crept among the sticks, growing steadily toward the still form at the center. Smoke swirled up and raced along a breeze straight toward the watchers.

Gerrod coughed sharply, batting the smoke away with his hand.

Melisande, eyes stinging, turned away, taking deep breaths of the cleaner air behind, but the smoke chased her, eddying about her until her eyes welled with tears.

Suddenly, Orie screamed, and the spyglass fell from his hands to shatter on stone. He clutched his side, slumping to his knees behind the parapet. Melisande crouched by him, while Gerrod, determined not to be afflicted by the smoke, stood erect.

"Orie, what's wrong?" Melisande touched his arm, but he screamed again.

Orie's right hand reached out for her, and she took it, wincing at the strength of his grip. She cradled his shoulders in her lap. "Shhh," she murmured, rocking slowly.

His eyes sprang open, eyebrows pinched together in a look of confusion and sadness. "Melisande?" he whispered.

"I'm here."

"I'm sorry."

"What for?"

"I didn't mean to hurt you, Sandy."

Melisande started. "That's what he used to call me."

He opened his mouth to speak, but a bell pealed out somewhere close by, and Melisande looked up. Gerrod crossed the floor in three furious steps. "No bells! I decreed there would be no bells for that traitor," he roared.

The bell rang out again, clear and strong, from the temple in their own garden. "Guards! Bring the ringer to me, and I shall throw him from this tower!"

The guards crashed back down the stairs.

Weakly, Orie pushed himself up until he sat against the wall. "Are you well?" Melisande asked, not letting go of his hand.

"I'm fine." He struggled to his feet, clutching the stone. "What's happening?"

"Some treacherous bastard has been ringing the bell, but they've caught him," Gerrod crowed, "and I will show him what it means to betray his king."

Brushing the tears from her eyes, Melisande rose, then gasped as the guards reemerged onto the platform. Young Thomas dangled between them, both arms held tight by the armed men.

Gerrod yanked up the boy's chin to stare into his tear-streaked face. "You rang the bloody bell," the king snarled.

"For the dead, Sire," the page blurted, his breath coming in ragged gasps.

"The act of a traitor," Gerrod snapped, looming over the prisoner. He grabbed the boy's arm and jerked him away from the guards. Thomas cried out as he was hauled to the edge and flung upon the top of the broad wall, his head hanging over the stone toward the rushing river.

"Father!" Melisande flung herself forward, clinging to her father's arm. "He's a child, he doesn't know what he's done!"

He shook her off, a low animal snarl building in his throat. "I'm his king; he knows enough to obey." She screamed as he thrust Thomas over the edge, but he had not yet released his iron grip on the boy's arm. Gerrod turned blazing eyes to his daughter.

Melisande knelt on the floor at his feet, her hands raised in supplication. "Father, I am begging you not to do this."

"Am I not the king here? And do I not have the right to administer justice to my subjects?" he demanded, spitting each word like a curse.

"Yes, Father, yes." She forced herself to meet his gaze, hearing the windborne sobs of his prisoner. "But he's just a child; some things he still does not understand. All he knows is the man who was his master is dead, and he wants to honor him."

Gerrod let the growl out again at this, but his eyes remained locked to hers.

"He only knows what he's taught, and we haven't—I haven't taught him enough to understand. I have failed in teaching him, my lord." Breathing heavily, she lowered her head. "By the Goddess, your Majesty, do not punish him for my failure."

A stony silence descended, broken only by Melisande's breathing and the unseen child's soft whimper.

Gerrod yanked his arm back, throwing Thomas to the floor and turning away.

Melisande let her arms fall to support herself, and glanced up. Thomas crouched before her, shaking all over.

"Sire?" one of the guards inquired softly, gesturing toward the boy.

Gerrod did not look back. "Throw him in the dungeon. If my daughter wants to teach him, she can do so there." He pounded down the stairs.

The guards clanked forward, but Melisande rose to her knees and held up her hand to stop them. "We have orders, Your Highness," one mumbled awkwardly.

"Give me one minute before you obey them." She shot him a furious glance, daring his approach. While they hesitated, Melisande inched closer to Thomas and gathered him to her chest, stroking his ruffled hair until the trembling subsided.

The guard cleared his throat, and Melisande pulled back, searching the boy's face. She smiled her most glowing smile for him, but the large arms descended to pull him to his feet. Thomas kept looking back until he was out of sight down the stairs.

Melisande sat back, pushing a short clump of hair back under her skewed veil.

"How touching," Orie murmured.

Tilting her head, Melisande regarded him quietly.

"How long will he last in the dungeon, Melisande?"

"I should have let him die?"

"I'm not saying that." He put up his hands to deny it, his voice suddenly wavering toward uncertainty as he looked at her. "But the consequences. Gerrod may be angry at you for days. I know you don't want that," he said soothingly.

"So, better Thomas than me." She carefully rose to her feet, not bothering to brush the dust from her skirts. "Better Thomas be thrown to the wind so that I can avoid a few days discomfort. I don't know you anymore, Orie. I don't know who you are."

"Do you think Gerrod won't find ways to punish you? To punish both of us?" He folded his arms, shaking his head. "Maybe it's him you don't know anymore."

"No. My father has always had these moments, perhaps not so serious, but he did not have the same concerns back then. I was always his favorite child. I'll get silence for three days, then he'll command me out for a ride, and we'll both act as if nothing has happened. In a week or so, I'll convince him that Thomas has learned his lesson. I understand my father, Orie, but you—" She gave an ironic smile. "You reminded me of him, even in your anger. You would get so angry, then come back apologizing, asking for my forgiveness."

"And it's always so nice to make up, isn't it?" Orie murmured, running a finger along her gown between her breasts.

Melisande shifted subtly back, refusing to be sidetracked. "It was, Orie. But now you brood, or you dismiss me without bothering to get angry. And now this." She raised her arms to indicate the tower platform. "Where were you when I needed you? You keep watching my father, and you aren't paying attention to me anymore."

"Oh, no, Melisande." Creases of worry tracked his forehead. "I love you so much. It's just—your father is so demanding. I need to learn how to live here, with him, how to be a prince. Let me give him some attention now, then I can be a more fitting husband to you. The Lady knows you deserve so much more than I give you."

He wrapped his arms around her, feeling her heat and her breath on his cheek. Looking over her shoulder, Orie lost his smile as the first star gleamed down on the embers of Wolfram's fire.

# Chapter 38

ORIE PACED the length of the paved yard and returned to where Fionvar stood. All around them, servants hurried with benches and brooms, readying the garden for the princess. "I cannot believe he was so arrogant as to insist upon changing the meeting place," Orie grumbled. "I don't like it. And why did she agree? This is her palace, she can choose where or even if she will meet with him."

Spreading his arms, Fionvar took in the fruit trees and fragrant roses. "Melisande likes gardens. If it had been left to her, she might have suggested this herself."

"She doesn't know the first thing about statesmanship. She should have asked me, or Gerrod, at the least, before she agreed to such a change."

Now, Fionvar faced his brother, his humor gone. "I think the king knows precisely why this particular delegation will not enter the throne room."

Orie eyed him quietly. "Are you with me or with my enemy?"

"Why do you consider him an enemy?"

"For Wolfram's sake," he replied, "and for Melisande's. For his own sake, if it comes to that. He can't have forgotten my men would have killed him that night. He seemed more important then." Orie laughed. "Funny, that he seemed more important when he was just a eunuch. I wonder how much he's changed. He was such a pathetic creature before."

Fionvar stared rigidly at a rosebud bobbing in the wind. "If he is of so little consequence to you, why call him your enemy? What are you afraid of?"

Orie snorted. "Nothing he can do, I assure you," he snapped. "He is no match for me." Orie's face shifted briefly into a smooth mask, then he shuddered violently and clutched at Fionvar's arm. His eyes were suddenly wild and dark.

"What's the matter? Orie?" Instinctively, he reached out to steady his brother and thought of what the wizard had told him of madness. "Orie, what's wrong?"

"Nothing," Orie insisted, though his teeth chattered. He clamped his jaw shut and shook off Fionvar's arm and straightened. "Thank you, I am fine."

"That's nonsense, Orie. Great Goddess, everyone can see that you are not well."

Shaking his head, Orie said, "I have been . . . different since the battle. Nine Stars seems loath to speak to me, so I must figure it out for myself. I just need a few more nights' study in my workroom, Fion, and I'll understand what's happened."

Fionvar blanched at the thought of returning to that room, witnessing his brother's bloody experiments. "Perhaps you just need sleep. Lady knows I do."

Orie let out a gale of laughter and clapped Fionvar on the shoulder. "I am close to knowing it all, brother, I feel it. All we need do is—but here comes my wife!" He took a few quick steps away to hail Melisande with a wide grin. "Your father suggested attractive clothing, Melisande, but you are positively radiant!"

Clad in a well-fit gown of russet silks, Melisande approached and took his hands in hers, offering a tiny smile in return. Her grip was strong and damp with sweat.

"Darling, there's no need to be nervous." Orie rubbed her hands gently.

She ducked her head. "I know I must get used to these things, but I feel so anxious, Orie. It's not as if King Rhys is the first I've ever met."

"Maybe so, but we are asking you to defuse a difficult situation." Orie stroked her cheek with thumb. "You stand between Gerrod and this person he despises, yet you must receive this other king with grace and honor. It cannot be easy for you."

Melisande nodded and turned to smile at Fionvar. "At least you will be with me, and all of my ladies, so I shall not feel alone."

"Your Highness is both brave and strong. I have no doubt you will be perfect," Fionvar told her, mustering himself to sincerity. How would she respond to seeing Kattanan again, and under such circumstances? She little knew what a trial she faced.

Orie flicked him a glance. "I will be watching at a distance, as well. If you feel the need to break off the meeting, of course you may. If he offends you, simply stand and raise your goblet, and I will be at your side. You are a vision, my love," Orie told her, "every inch the queen you will be."

She flushed a pretty pink. "I hope to be much more attractive by then."

"A difficult goal, Melisande, considering how beautiful you already are." Orie pulled her close and nuzzled against her neck.

Fionvar contemplated the flowers. A sudden blast of horns brought his head up instantly, and he looked again to his brother. "The delegation has arrived."

Orie nodded once, releasing Melisande, who had lost her color. Orie murmured, "We shall be in that tower, should you need us. Just raise your goblet."

Smoothing her skirts, Melisande stepped back. "I know. I doubt I shall have need, though. I am, after all, a daughter of kings." She raised her head and smiled.

"Remember that," Orie admonished her, "whatever this king seems to be, you are at least as much, and more." He winked at Fionvar as he turned to go.

Sighing, Fionvar watched his brother's retreating figure, then faced the princess, offering his arm. "May I escort you to your throne, Your Highness?"

"Indeed you may." She placed a delicate hand upon his arm and let him lead her to the hastily prepared court. A long purple carpet marked the path from the palace gate, stretching between rows of benches for the courtiers and King Rhys's followers. At the head of the carpet stood Melisande's tall throne, with the gilded device of the heir of Bernholt. Her ladies, in all their finery, assembled behind like an animated bouquet with a backdrop of the shiny green leaves of orange trees. Off to the right, the marble spire of the garden chapel gleamed in the sunlight, a brilliant contrast to the red walls of the palace, especially now that the stain of the funeral smoke marred the stonework. Guardsmen formed a perimeter around the meeting place, sunlight limning their helmets and breastplates where they stood amongst the flower beds. From farther into the gardens, the caged birds' subdued chatter drifted into the day, along with the trickle of the fountains. As Melisande settled in her throne, Fionvar crossed to stand behind her. The sound of marching feet approached from the courtyard, growing louder.

The herald stepped forward, made a brief bow, and announced, "Rhys yfCaitrin of the House of Rinvien, duAlyn of the House of Strel Maria, by grace of Finistrel, King of Lochalyn and all of her territories."

Fionvar straightened up as his king entered the garden.

Twelve knights led the procession, gracefully stepping to the sides, to form an aisle for the delegation. Jordan, clad again in red, and Lyssa, in gleaming chain mail with her war hammer at her side, marched along the carpet, then separated at its head, standing at attention. Two more guards, both huge and fierce, followed behind their king, dropping to one knee when they reached the end of the seating. The king himself walked tall, his red shirt of mourning softened by the cream velvet doublet and trailing cloak embroidered with leaves and crowns. Upon his head, the crown of his parents shone again in the sun, capping his golden curls. He swept into a low bow as he passed between the last benches, then another when he stood just a few feet short of Melisande's throne.

The princess rose to return his courtesy. As the king straightened and stood before her, she froze, lips parted, and all of her grand words of greeting died away.

Kattanan, eyes at first shining, then anxious, searched her face. Her eyebrows arched with a tiny shake of the head, then furrowed down again as she pursed her lips. "Good King Rhys," she began, then faltered. Color flared into her cheeks, and her glance shot toward the tower, then returned.

"Your Royal Highness," Kattanan said, giving her a moment to absorb the sound of his new voice. He continued more softly, "You do me great honor in once again welcoming me before you. The court of Bernholt is blessed by the Lady for a palace so grand, a day so bright, and a princess so fair."

The dark crease had returned to her brow, and Melisande gestured for a goblet with a tiny motion of one hand. "Good King Rhys," she said, her voice strong, near snapping with fire, "I regret that my father and husband could not be here, but I do hope that we may become acquainted so that our two kingdoms will stand as allies for many years to come." She said the practiced words with a rising edge of bitterness.

A page scurried up, bobbed a tiny bow, and offered the bejeweled goblet. Kattanan, hopeful, stared down at the boy but saw it was not Thomas, and let his gaze return to the princess. Melisande, too, let her glance slip to the boy, then back to the man before her. Their eyes met, hers green and flashing, his honey-hazel, warm and sad. Melisande began to raise her goblet, took a sip, then lowered it again slowly.

"That is my hope as well, Your Highness," Kattanan said. He felt his hands tremble ever so slightly and tucked them behind him before continuing carefully. "However, there is a history between your kingdom and mine that must be resolved before we can make such alliance."

At a word from Melisande, another throne—not so grand as her own, but still finely carved and gilded—was brought for the king, and she paused a moment in deference to his crown before likewise seating herself. Kattanan's retainers stood at ease, as he began his story, the story of his parents' betrayal, and his own. The courtiers leaned a little closer, but Kattanan spoke only to the princess, watching her every gesture for a sign from her. All he saw was coldness and anger suppressed behind her royal air.

For a moment, Kattanan's gaze rested upon Fionvar, who stood straight and quiet behind Melisande. His eyes gleamed, and the set of his shoulders revealed his pride, knowing that he had been among those to right the old injustice.

"The friend of my uncle," Kattanan began again, stronger now, "did indeed take me to the temple, but he had compassion for me still—" Here the king's voice wavered a little, and he held his goblet a little tighter. "Rather than bring the surgeons, he brought a wizard who disguised me so that I could hide among the boys of the monastery and be taken for one of the Verge duStrel, the Virgins of the Goddess, who sing for the glory of Finistrel and no other lady. He gave me a new name, and what I knew of my former life became ever more distant. I became a singer in truth." Briefly he told the events leading up to the surrender of the city, and finished by saying, "So my mother and brothers were finally avenged." He took a long swallow of wine and let his goblet be refilled.

Melisande nodded, absorbing what he had said. She suddenly recalled her childish fascination with the traitor-queen, and how her singer had lost his light whenever she spoke of it. "What has become of the Usurper, Your Majesty?" The title felt strange upon her lips.

"He will undergo the trial of lords, Your Highness. When he is found guilty, he will be put to death as mercifully as may be."

"Mercifully?" For a moment, she imagined how it must have been for him, how his life might have been so very different. "After all that you have just told us?"

"My mother was right; his love for me was his undoing. And I had had enough of killing, Your Highness. I have been shown better examples of nobility." He glanced to her left, where her brother's throne would once have stood.

Melisande's cheeks reddened. "So there is business yet undone in your own kingdom. May I ask Your Majesty why you have come all this way when your own ascension is less than secure?"

Kattanan bristled at the change in her. "I would not say that my crown is not secure, Your Highness. But I had ties of friend-ship before I ever was a prince again, and I felt it right to do them honor. I came to speak the truth about your brother, Prince Wolfram."

Instantly, she held up a hand to stop him, her voice cracking even as her gaze turned hard. "Now is not the time."

Meeting her fiery gaze, Kattanan allowed a slight nod.

"I will need to think on all you have said, King Rhys," she said, trying to reconcile her memories with the moment. "If you wish, I shall have a meal laid for you and your retainers here, and you may enjoy the beauty of these gardens."

"I shall indeed enjoy them, Your Highness," he replied. They both rose, Kattanan offering a bow and Melisande a slight curtsy before she made her way down the purple carpet. Her first steps seemed unsteady, but she stood a little straighter as her ladies fol-lowed her out. Fionvar made a little bow to Kattanan, then hur-ried to follow the princess. Slowly, the benches emptied, with many a gaze still turned toward the new king, until the party from Lochalyn were left alone with a few guards and servants to lay tables for the meal.

Kattanan turned to Jordan. "So what do you think?"

"You told your tale well, Kat; it remains to be seen what they will make of it."

"That isn't what I meant," Kattanan murmured. "What about the princess?"

"She is beautiful, proud, and angry, but she has not dismissed us right away, so that is a hopeful sign." Jordan shrugged, then eyed the servants bringing out laden platters. "Which one of us should taste your food?"

Kattanan let out a wounded sigh. "A hopeful sign indeed. If that's how you express your hope, then I tremble to see your warning."

⟨◈⟩

"YOU KNEW!" Melisande shouted the moment the door had closed behind her. "All of you! And yet you saw fit to keep it from me. Why?" She glared first at her husband, then her father, then whirled to stare at Fionvar, and he thought her gaze held him an instant longer. "Great Goddess, I felt like a fool." She flung up her hands.

The three men stood quietly, only Fionvar letting his shoulders droop in mute acknowledgment. It was certainly not his place to answer her.

"Melisande, how could we explain—" Orie began patiently, but Gerrod overrode his calm rebuttal by announcing, "We needed to gauge his reactions, Melisande. How could we watch his honest response if he wasn't to see any of your emotions? As it was, you've not given us much to work with."

"I thought you were giving me some responsibility, yet it seems you are still just using me, not trusting me to make the judgments. Father, I am no longer a child."

Gerrod snorted, crossing his arms. "When you act this way, that is exactly how you appear. A child."

This brought her up short, and though the rage flared in her eyes, and her entire body stiffened, she did not lash out.

"Gerrod," Orie murmured, shaking his head as if to chide the king. "In fact, we wanted you to be angry." Orie placed a soothing hand on Melisande's shoulder. "He approached the meeting presuming on your friendship, now he is off-balance, unsure of how he stands with you. We've got him right where we want him, thanks to you."

"If that was your purpose, I could have served it better had I known what you wanted of me," she replied softly, arms crossed. Melisande turned from her husband and found herself looking at Fionvar. She blinked, her features hard, and he wondered if Kattanan could be any more off-balance than the princess.

Orie, too, glanced at Fionvar and smiled, reassured of his brother's trustworthiness. For himself, Fionvar doubted Melisande would again come close to trusting him. As far as the princess was concerned, the three men were conspiring against her, assuming her role in their plotting was secure. How secure,

Fionvar did not wish to hazard a guess. From where he stood, their decision to keep the secret began to look like a terrible mistake.

"You knew him best, Melisande," Orie said. "How did he seem to you?"

Glancing from her father to her husband, Melisande flopped into a chair. As they settled to either side of her, Fionvar remained standing, a little apart, occasionally looking out the window to the feast being laid in the gardens.

Melisande frowned. "He has the sort of presence he used to have while singing. He projects the air of royalty very well, as if it were a new performance. He always had a way of commanding an audience." She paused to mull this over, and Fionvar allowed a little smile, recalling his speech to the duchess about this very thing. The princess went on. "He lets himself show more feeling, now, as well. He got a little angry with me, and I imagine he's made an excellent impression on the courtiers present."

"I was hoping they would make an impression on him," Gerrod snorted, "remind him of how many armies I can summon at a moment's notice."

Melisande shook her head. "I don't believe that he cares. It seemed as if—"

They waited for her to continue, then Orie prompted, "As if what?"

"As if it didn't matter how many nobles or how many guards we brought there, I was the only one of importance." The furrows of her brow smoothed out a little as she realized this, and Orie shared a look with her father over her head. "Is his story true?"

Gerrod replied slowly, "Thorgir should have been more careful, and his subjects would not have risen against him—certainly not to put a castrate on the throne."

She looked up quickly. "Then he is . . . ? When he told the story, he said that was a disguise, and his voice is certainly different."

"Trickery," Orie said. "What we see now is what he wishes us to see." He shrugged. "Still, we ought to play along with this new lie until we decide how to handle him." Orie leaned forward and took her hands. "There is another reason, though, why he spoke only to you. I hesitate to bring this up." Gerrod nodded sternly for him to go on, and he did, but haltingly. "I do not know if you were aware of this, but several of your servants and ladies have confirmed that they believe he was in love with you."

"With me?" Her eyes flew wide. "But he's a castrate, not even—and I . . ." She trailed off, her face grave. "It's absurd. Impossible." She shook her head.

"Naturally, but still he dared." Orie let that dangle a moment, then continued, "I recall when I first arrived at your ball, and he was so presumptuous as to touch your hair without permission. What would such a creature not dare?"

"I remember how quick you were to leap to my defense," Melisande murmured. "To think that he was so close to me. If I had suspected how he felt, things would have been very different." She lowered her head a little. "You told me to wear something attractive because you wanted him to reveal his feelings for me."

Orie nodded. "And I think he made them very clear. I believe you could have King Rhys polishing your boots if you so desire."

Melisande smiled a little at that.

"He will want a royal apology," Gerrod put in abruptly, "for our part in Thorgir's actions. I would, in his position. If my daughter is correct, he will have no trouble becoming a leader of men. What I hear from Lochdale is that he appeared like a miracle, riding bareheaded into the heart of the battle on a magical steed. He may be a legend already, and it is hard to defeat a legend if we should come to war one day, so—much as I'd like to—I ought not to offend the little king."

"But a eunuch?" Orie inquired. "I find it hard to believe that all of his people have forgotten that rumor."

"On the other hand, if we accept his ascension, and his overtures of friendship, we will be subjected to more talk about the Traitor," Gerrod snarled, his fist clenching.

"Also true, Father," said Melisande, "but we could offer the apology under the condition that he make no more demands about the Traitor."

Fionvar held his tongue, but his right hand clenched briefly, and he kept his eyes on the princess, trying to judge how much of her talk was true.

"Why not have a ball?" Orie suggested.

Gerrod laughed. "What are we celebrating?"

"Hear me out, Your Majesty. We shall announce a ball in his honor, in perhaps two days, if he can wait so long for all of the barons to attend. I mean a huge state affair." He flung his arms wide to indicate the magnitude of the event. "You will apologize formally for assisting Thorgir and take his hand in front of all the nobles we can muster. He will be completely overawed by the festivities."

"I doubt it," Melisande remarked.

Orie lowered his voice to murmur, "If he is seated beside you, my love, I think he will forget he ever cared about anything else."

She squared her shoulders. "Very well then; I shall return to the garden and offer your invitation."

Rising, Gerrod patted her hand. "I understand how distasteful this must be to you, considering his perverse interest in you, but, for the good of the kingdom, you must persevere. I'll see you to your ladies to refresh yourself." The king and his daughter left arm in arm.

Fionvar moved a little closer to Orie. "How've you been, brother?"

Orie replied. "I am quite well."

"I heard what happened on the tower. Do you think that Wolfram's—"

"The Traitor," Orie corrected. "You don't wish Gerrod to get the wrong idea."

Refusing to be sidetracked, Fionvar repeated, "Do you think that the traitor's"—his voice struggled with the word—"blood had anything to do with it?"

"How should I know?" came the harsh response. "The stupid

wizard shielded her knowledge from me. We had an arrangement, and she broke it."

This piqued Fionvar's curiosity, and he asked, "What did she get from this arrangement?"

Orie cast a dark sidelong glance at him, considering. "Something she wanted. Something I no longer need."

Fionvar crossed his arms. "Why don't you trust me, Orie, even that much?"

The sudden laughter caught Fionvar by surprise, making him take a step back. "Oh, Fion. Someday soon, you'll find out. I hope you think it's as funny as I do." He craned his neck, looking toward the window, and crossed to lean out of it. "There goes my beautiful bride."

"I am surprised you are so eager for her to do this, Orie." Fionvar came to stand beside him, watching the progress of Melisande's little procession into the garden.

"She loves me, Fion." A shadow of a frown crossed his features. "She is also a little afraid of me, which serves me well. It encourages her to obey."

Fionvar opened his mouth to reply, then thought better of it. He turned to see Melisande in the distance curtsy to his king, and the king's grave bow in response. Orie was underestimating both of them. His wife was not the child she had been, nor was King Rhys the weakling Orie believed. Orie would be wrong about this; he must be.

# Chapter 39

"YOUR MEN seem to be enjoying the feast," Melisande said after she delivered the king's message, "Are you not eating, Your Majesty?"

His title on her lips sounded so wooden that he wondered if she said it that way on purpose. "I never eat before a performance, Your Highness."

She lowered her chin just a touch. "Is that what this is for you, a performance?"

"Am I not onstage before your court, and before your father?" He gestured toward the palace, continuing, "And you, Your Highness. Am I not onstage before you, this time on my own behalf?" Kattanan said this last at a low pitch, almost a sigh.

Stiffening, she took a step back from him, her tone instantly frosty. "I think not, Your Majesty. You are here on behalf of your kingdom, a diplomatic visit."

A moment passed, then he saw how she had misunderstood him, recalling the first time they had met when she was being courted. Kattanan shook his head, and little sparks danced from the gemstones of his crown. "I meant only that I must somehow convince you of my good intentions. I am to present myself in the best possible way to show you that what I say is true."

At this, she raised her eyebrows and said nothing.

The expression reminded him so much of Wolfram that Kattanan felt a shiver run through him, sobering him. "You are wondering how you can believe anything I say."

Melisande stroked unseen dust from her skirts. She looked away from him, toward the tables where most of his knights were being served. "I came only to deliver my father's message, Your Majesty. I have done so. Perhaps on your next visit, the opportunity—"

"Will you walk with me?" he broke into her stream of regal language, bringing her eyes back to him. "Your Highness, will you walk with me?"

She glanced wildly back toward the palace, then regained her royal facade. "If it is your wish to walk in the garden, I will accompany you, Your Majesty." He offered his arm, but she stepped ahead of him down the path, her pace quickening as it had when he had been her singer, and she had not been heir to a kingdom. Clasping his hands behind him, he caught up with her.

"Where should we walk, Your Majesty?"

"Here," he said, indicating a path, "toward the songbirds."

"How fitting," she replied, not looking at him.

When they stood before the cage, watching the swirling blue-and-gold birds, Kattanan turned to face her. With the birdsong rising about them, no other could hear him say, "Your Highness, you need not try so hard to wound me. When last we met, my will was not my own. Finistrel knows, I never meant to deceive you."

"Yet you did, Your Majesty." She clutched the bars of the cage, staring at the whirlwind of birds. "You deceived all of us, biding your time until you could appear as king and savior of your people. How did you expect me to receive you?"

"What you see today is the lie, Your Highness. What I was then, how I felt—those things were true. I was not born to be a king, and it was never what I wanted."

The tilt of her head revealed her sidelong glance. Just as quickly, she looked away. "What did you want, then? What do you want now?"

Kattanan met that shadowed gaze and did not trust himself to answer.

Even so, she burst out, "You have no right to speak to me like this! I am a princess, and you, you are a—" She stopped herself.

"I am a king, Melisande," he replied softly, using her name like a prayer for her understanding. "Against my conscience and my wishes, I am a king, the last of my line."

"Do you hold yourself above me now? I know what you are, what you have always been." Her body shook with anger, flushing her cheeks; her beauty flamed.

"A human being! A person, just like you, with dreams and terrors—just like you. I fear, I hope, I hurt, and, yes, I love. Great Goddess, Melisande, listen to me! Please listen, and hear me as you have never heard me before." He took her shoulders and spun her to face him. She tore away but stopped, staring, her fists clenched and shaking.

"Don't touch me. Don't ever touch me."

"There was a time when you were not afraid."

"Long ago, before you left me; before I knew how much you lied to me! My father, my husband, his brother—is there not a man alive who tells the truth?" Her eyes gleamed and, for a moment, he was certain she would weep. "Everything has changed. You don't know me."

"I know that you are not the same, Melisande, I never expected that. I only—"

"Oh, no? What did you expect? Now that you are a king, I should fall into your arms like a common whore?" She swept her arms out as if she would push him away with the angry wind. The birds clamored and screeched, egging her on. "Well I shall not," breathed Melisande, then louder. "Whatever it is that you want, King Rhys, you shall never have it. Sing whatever you wish, I will not hear you."

Kattanan spoke quietly, his voice absolutely clear. "By virtue of rank alone, Your Highness, your rank and mine, I deserve better than how you are treating me."

"So now you seek to instruct me in, what, protocol? Deportment? What is it that you want?" At last, she looked at him, but sidelong, beneath her lashes.

"Respect. If not for me, then for my crown, and for your own, Melisande. No wonder—" He stopped, shaking his head. "Good day, Your Highness." He turned to go.

"What else?" she demanded, not turning after him. "What were you going to say, Your Majesty? What more could you possibly say?"

Breathing slowly, Kattanan turned back to her. "No wonder Wolfram still treated you as a child." He watched her trembling shoulders. "That is all I can possibly say." His throat clenched as he witnessed the shock that broke across her face. She whirled, gathering her skirts, and fled into the trees with her guards in pursuit.

Kattanan's hands were trembling as she vanished beyond the wall. "What happened?" Jordan asked, coming up quietly.

Kattanan shrugged one shoulder, still watching Melisande's wake, where the disturbed flowers lashed their heads in frenzied approval. The cacophonous laughter of the birds grated at his ears. "I went too far, asked too much of her."

"Go back to camp," Jordan said quietly. "You need rest, maybe a song."

"Sing? After that, you think I could sing?" He let Jordan's hand guide him back toward the others. Kattanan took a few steps down the path, but a voice stopped him.

"Your Majesty," said the wizard, still disguised as a hulking guard. "Forgive me. You recall I said there was something I needed to look for in the palace. Now might be a good time; tomorrow, they may not be so careless about checking for wizards at the gate."

Kattanan nodded, but Jordan asked, "Do you need my assistance?"

"If you are still willing, but I don't need you." She tilted her head toward the shaken king, then let her eyes meet Jordan's. "Not that I would turn away your help."

Squaring his shoulders, Kattanan said, "I'll be all right, once I get some peace."

Jordan squeezed Kattanan's shoulder and released him, joining the wizard.

Lyssa glowered. "I'll come, too. A woman is often allowed places neither men nor wizards can go."

"Very well then," the disguised wizard replied faintly. The trio bowed, and Jordan lingered a moment as the other two slipped into the trees.

"She will come round to you, Kat," Jordan said.

"She is a married woman, with a jealous husband. She may not even consent to meet with me again. Certainly not like this." He gestured toward the birdcage.

"Give her time to remember your song."

Kattanan gave a half shrug. "Catch your ladies, Jordan. Go with the Goddess."

"And you, Your Majesty." Jordan caught up with them under the shade of a columned walkway. The wizard had resumed female form—an unremarkable servant. "Just tell me what we're looking for"—Lyssa acknowledged Jordan's arrival with an imperious nod—"and I can seek out Fionvar, or even Orie, and ask—don't look at me like that!" Jordan and the wizard stared, their brows furrowed. "I won't reveal your secrets; I'm not so stupid as that, but they know this place better than any of us."

The wizard glowered fiercely. "We cannot risk revealing our presence, or that of the book to Orie. Goddess knows what he'd do if he knew it was here."

"Fionvar would help, though, if he could," Jordan pointed out, trying to soften the wizard's anger. Instead, he found both women glowering at him. "Lyssa, it is an excellent idea. Alswytha, where is the book likely to be?"

She glanced from one to the other, then grudgingly replied, "When I sought a place to conceal it, I gathered a number of books and sent them to Prince Wolfram, as a well-known scholar. So the books are now in the palace library, or in Wolfram's collection, if it has been kept." The wizard sighed. "Our quest might be a hopeless one."

"It's a book of magic, isn't it?" Lyssa asked, some of her bravado fading.

"It is disguised as Raven duCerulan's *On the Gathering of Herbs and of Their Uses*. A small volume, bound in green and remarkably tedious."

"I will see what I can do. I'd like to speak to Fionvar anyhow."

Lyssa started off, but looked back to Jordan. "What will you do?" she asked pointedly.

Jordan took a breath, noticing the way the color in her cheeks made her face glow with a beauty even more exquisite. "I'd, ah, I'd better stay with the wizard for now. If we're found, they won't suspect who she is if we are together."

"Together," Lyssa echoed, "of course. We can meet back at the funeral grounds at dusk. There should be no one about then—unless someone's dead." She strode off under the arches. She let the spark of anger carry her swiftly between a pair of guards and into the palace proper, where she paused to glance about and set toward the main court.

Fionvar nearly ran into her, shocked to see his sister there, but he made an effort to hear what she needed. He guided her to the library, only to discover Melisande already in residence, there. At the sight of him, she left without a word. He found the little lantern she had set aside and turned the shield to allow a brighter light to spread into the room. Lyssa slipped in around the door, and it was quickly shut again.

She grinned, her face flushed with excitement. "Was that the princess leaving?"

Fionvar nodded, distracted by Melisande's appearance. After Kattanan's entourage had departed, Melisande retired to the kennels—still wearing her fine gown—and refused to admit anyone. The king and Oric had both cornered her there, but she would tell them nothing of the conversation by the birdcage, and they left to take out their frustrations on a cask of wine and whoever happened by. Fionvar had been trying to avoid them when Lyssa ran into him.

On the carrel where the princess had been a stack of books teetered, as if hastily piled. They tumbled as Fionvar approached, and he stared at the cover of the last one, the only one remaining: *A History of the Virgins of the Lady*.

Lyssa's voice interrupted his wondering. "How's this place organized?"

"It would help if you could tell me what you're looking for,"

Fionvar said pointedly. His patience with this day was wearing dangerously thin.

Lyssa flapped her hand in a negligent gesture. "Just some herbal thing."

"Medicinal?"

"General, I think." She frowned. "It was a book of Wolfram's."

Her brother nodded, leading the way toward a section in the back. They started to scan the titles, Fionvar taking the top shelves while Lyssa crawled along the bottom. "Is it in Strelledor?"

Lyssa's red hair tossed as she looked up at him. "I don't think so," she replied, but her voice lacked its usual confidence; Lyssa couldn't read Strelledor.

"Well, let's hope not." He hefted a large volume, but before he'd read the title, she told him, "It would be small."

Back went the giant tome. They inched along in silence for a moment.

"If it's a book of Wolfram's, it may have been destroyed. I don't know what happened to his things after . . ." He let the sentence peter out.

"Let's hope not," she echoed. She straightened up and looked up toward the windows. "I have to go soon, to meet them. Who can we ask about Wolfram's things?"

Fionvar shrugged, his shoulders sagged as he let out a yawn. "Orie and Melisande weren't even here yet. Most of the people who would have been loyal to the prince are gone by now." He pursed his lips.

"You've thought of something," Lyssa prompted.

"Wolfram had a page, Thomas, who used to be a friend of Kattanan's. Trouble is . . ." Fionvar scuffed his foot against the carpet. "He's in the dungeon. Remember during the funeral there was a bell ringing?"

"That was him? So how do we talk to him?"

Fionvar shook his head. "There are guards and gates between us and him. I'll see what I can find out and look for you tomorrow."

"If only there were a way to free Thomas and send him home with Kattanan." Her mail clinked softly as she paced toward the

door. "We'll think of something." She hesitated at the door.
"Fion? Do you think Jordan still has feelings for me?" She
plucked at a sliver of wood.

"Yes, last I knew. Are you considering leaving the Sisterhood?"

"No," she replied quickly, then, "Maybe." She freed the bit of
wood and let it fall from her fingers. "I'd have to, in order to
marry."

"Is that what you want?"

"Jordan would be worth it." Lyssa turned to face her brother,
leaning back against the door, arms folded. "He's handsome, fun;
not a lustful bore like most men."

"That isn't what I asked," Fionvar responded. "Do you want
to marry him?"

"Who wouldn't?"

Fionvar flung up his hands. "Why do I bother? I'm going to
bed," he called over his shoulder. "Do whatever you will." He
left her standing in the corridor.

"Isn't that what I'd do anyhow?" she whispered. She glanced
both ways, then darted across the hall, heading for the funeral
ground, where Jordan would be waiting.

MELISANDE PULLED the silver-handled brush through the
remains of her hair, avoiding her own eyes in the looking glass
before her. She breathed deeply, glad to be free of the confining
gown and the hovering presence of her ladies. For a moment,
she envisioned Kattanan standing at her back, patiently drawing
the brush through the fullness of her hair. She tugged the brush
through a snarl as if the sting could remove the memory of his
touch. Her husband and father had lied to her; her singer, once
so close to her, had lied to her with his every breath; then he had
the effrontery to declare his—his what? She flung the brush
away. What had he declared, really? Now that she sat in her own
chamber, under cover of night, she was no longer certain what
had passed between them. Had her own anger colored her
memory?

Swiftly, she rose and crossed to the tall windows. She cast them open and stepped out into the night. She had chosen her new quarters for this balcony, wide enough for her chair and small table, with a half-domed roof supported by delicately carved stone pillars. It overlooked the dark gardens, and out into the city. On the plain beyond flickered the fires of King Rhys's encampment. King Rhys. As long as he did not stand before her, she could call him that. She could put that name to a distant face, or a ring of fires, as if it belonged to someone long dead. In another world, Lochalyn's youngest prince might well have been among her suitors, a circlet on his golden head, a gift in his hands. But no such gift as his song. *I fear, I hope, I hurt, and, yes, I love,* he had told her, the words echoing back in his unfamiliar voice. He had not said he loved her. Perhaps in her pride and anger, she had added those words of her own accord, from the remarks Orie had made. A simple plea for her forgiveness and understanding, that was all.

At the blackest part of the sky, one star shone brightly, refusing to be separated from her. Was it truly the same that had appeared over Wolfram's fire? An aching crept across the back of her throat, and her eyelids seared, but she would not weep. That was what King Rhys meant when he spoke of wanting, that was all: that she acknowledge the truth of Wolfram's life, and of his death. The little king thought his message would find a receptive audience in her, and he was surprised when it did not. There was no more to it than that. Under the pressure of Orie's words, she had leapt to the wild conclusion that her old singer sought to win her love. Liar he may be, but no fool. She crossed her arms, closing her robe against the rising breeze. She had a husband who loved her, whose baby had begun to grow within her, and she was heir to a kingdom; she had responsibilities—as did he, evidently. Of course it was not love he wanted. She had given him no reason under the stars to care for her, however he might have thought he felt before winning his war. The aching at her throat returned, and the stars dimmed a little. She must control herself, now, and in the future. She must not be so easily swayed.

Melisande considered slipping down the back stairs to the

courtyard to visit her dogs. She thought of their lapping tongues upon her hands, their enthusiasm for the unexpected visit. She wanted to bask in their uncomplicated adoration. No, Orie would hear from the grooms and be hurt that she rejected him for a pack of hounds. Shedding the robe, Melisande crossed to her bed. She turned down the lantern's hood to cast only a subtle golden glow, like the light of a single star, and she snuggled into the embrace of her blankets. At the ball, she would be civility itself. None of them—not Orie, nor her father, nor King Rhys himself—would shake her.

# Chapter 40

THE NIGHT of the ball, Kattanan's squires helped him on with the purple tunic he had worn to recapture his city. His newly polished boots gleamed, as did the hilt of the little dagger he now kept in the left one. When he emerged from the pavilion, Jordan was lounging before it. "My King, you look quite dashing this evening!"

Kattanan grimaced. "I'd love to be dashing—right back into that tent."

Jordan laughed. "Only one more night, then we'll be on our way."

"I can't help but feel that this event is a disaster waiting to happen."

Jordan flung an arm about his shoulders. "How much worse could it get?"

"Not much," Kattanan was forced to admit. Melisande would never accept him, and certainly her father would not; even if Gerrod went through with the apology, it would be with disdain. And they still didn't know what to do about Orie—they found and heard no further evidence of treachery. He thought of Brianna waiting for him on the far side of the mountains, but resolutely pushed the thought aside. Coming down the rise from his pavilion, they encountered Lyssa and Rolf, deeply involved in a discussion of how to hang a sword belt properly while wearing a gown.

"Ye'll not be dancing like that?" Rolf asked dubiously.

"Lyssa, you're a vision!" Jordan swept her up in his arms and twirled her about so that the sword banged hard against his leg when he set her down again. "Ouch! You will make for a dangerous partner."

Kattanan glanced away from them, hearing approaching steps. A beautiful young woman paused by one of the tents, her face, alight as she walked, falling quickly. Until she began to transform, he did not recognize her for the wizard. When she finished her approach, it was in the guise of the burly guardsman, a match for Rolf. Smiling, Kattanan said, "It must be nice not to bother with tailors."

When they reached the castle, the doors of the great hall stood open, and a small consort began to play. Fionvar stood among them, fiddling away. Banners hung from the rafters high above, and sweet-scented herbs were strewn across the floor to make ready for the gathering. At the center of the vast hall, Kattanan stopped short. Above the throne dais, his father's coat of arms hung beside King Gerrod's. It took a moment to recall that his father's arms were now his own, and he wondered who had arranged the banners. Certainly he expected no such civility after his conversations with Melisande.

Kattanan and his followers mounted the broad stairs to the king's feast hall. The gathering awaiting them rose as one—a vast, shimmering shape of velvets, silks, and satins, many in the blue and gold of Bernholt. For a moment, he blanched, realizing that he might be expected to sit next to the king. Then a new fear swept that away, for Gerrod had once more put Melisande between them, with Orie on his far side.

Melisande wore a blue-green gown, woven with gold so that the pleats of the sleeves and skirts twinkled when she rose. It featured neither a low bodice nor the provocative front lacing she had favored at their last meeting. As a result, his eye was drawn more to her face—had she but known the effect this would cause, she'd have abandoned seduction for simplicity two days ago. Her smile was bright, not with the radiance he had known as her singer, but not so cold as he had feared. A golden veil covered her hair, topped with a circlet of elegant golden dogs with sapphire eyes.

King Gerrod and Orie rose last, bowing their heads only, as befit their rank, and Kattanan took the last few steps to the dais with leaden feet. His four guards, including Lyssa and Rolf, moved behind the dais into the shadows, nodding politely to Gerrod's bodyguards. Jordan accepted a seat at the high table with a formal bow and slight smile.

Melisande lifted her goblet as she turned toward Kattanan. "On behalf of Bernholt, I welcome King Rhys of Lochalyn. May Finistrel smile upon his reign!"

The nobles, with Lochalyn's knights among them, cheered for King Rhys. When he'd gotten over his surprise at the courtesy of this greeting, Kattanan lifted his goblet to her. "I thank you for the honor you do me, Your Highness. To the glory of Bernholt and her rulers, may this land prosper and shine beneath the stars forever."

The cheer that rose for Gerrod threatened to overwhelm them, but died down again before too long, and Kattanan and Melisande each took a sip of wine in honor of the other. As the servants offered him the first slice of a spiced venison roast, King Gerrod's arm darted around his daughter to spear the meat for himself, disregarding his royal guest. Kattanan's stomach tightened; his fears seemed about to come true.

Color rose in Melisande's face, while Orie laughed loud and bright, accepting a portion for himself when the others had been served.

"I see you have a royal taster, Your Majesty," Jordan murmured, but Kattanan's warning glance stifled any further jest.

Melisande's face burned. She had resolved to be on her best behavior tonight, only to have her own father take up antagonizing King Rhys, and Orie laughed about it. Bury them both! She straightened her back with an effort, and forced a smile.

"Your cook has outdone himself, Your Highness," Kattanan remarked suddenly.

She blinked. "He travels widely to learn all of the best methods, Your Majesty."

"I should send my own to apprentice with him, Your Highness. I'm afraid our last feast was quite plain."

She felt the corners of her mouth turn up, just a little more. He, too, played at the game of civility. "I am not sure he would pass on the knowledge, Your Majesty. He is somewhat secretive about his ways."

"So many of us are," Orie cut in from his end of the table, loudly, to be sure he was heard. "What sport entertains Your Majesty, when you aren't ruling your kingdom?"

Melisande, clenching her fork, glared down the table to her husband.

Spearing a turnip, Kattanan replied, "I have an interest in music, my lord Prince, and I am reading certain mystic works about the virtues of the Lady."

"She does have many virtues," Orie agreed, winking at Melisande. The flame that had retreated from her cheeks returned now. "As to music, my brother is an excellent fiddler," Orie said. "Do you agree?"

"I believe he played for you at the Great Hall, Your Majesty," the princess cut in. "We shall prevail upon him to play again later."

"I would appreciate that, Your Highness."

King Gerrod belched and laughed at himself. "Have you considered what to do about the Woodmen along our shared border, King Rhys?"

Kattanan faced his questioner. "I do not believe they will be a problem, my lord King."

"Really? During your uncle's reign, they were quite a nuisance."

"I hardly think that 'reign' is the appropriate term, my lord King."

The words had no expression or inflection, neither the strained courtesy of his last remark nor the anger Melisande might have expected. "I am sure my father is simply adjusting to the recent changes, Your Majesty," she said.

"Oh, don't apologize for me, Melisande." Gerrod set down his goblet, again empty. Before she could reply, he cried, "Bring on the ale!"

Ordinarily, this was a cue for the bard to come out as well and regale them with some adventurous story, but the man hesitated, for he had been watching the high table with growing apprehension. Melisande beckoned him on with relief while she desperately searched for a way to rescue the evening. Her father and husband were determined to amuse themselves at the expense of their guest, and she would not have it. Suddenly, a thought sprang to her unbidden: what would Wolfram have done?

Taking advantage of the bard's strident voice as he drew the crowd's attention, Jordan leaned over to whisper, "I don't think anyone is enjoying this party."

"Except Orie, perhaps," Kattanan whispered back, as Orie's laughter again erupted. "I expected no warmer welcome from the king."

To his other side, Melisande had been quiet some time, her eyes on the bard. Her hands gripped each other tightly before her, though, and Kattanan did not think she heard a word of the story. Would this be the last time he sat beside her? If he remained king in Lochdale, and she were queen in Bernholt, there would be other occasions, stiff and formal, as carefully polite as their conversation had been. His heart ached.

As if she suddenly noticed his attention, Melisande turned and smiled. "Is there anything else we may bring you, Your Majesty?"

"No, indeed, Your Highness, but I would thank you on behalf of Thomas."

Kattanan immediately saw that he'd said the wrong thing. Consternation twisted Melisande's face, and she separated her fingers with deliberate care. "I'm afraid, Your Majesty, that now is not the best time to discuss it."

But their words, though quietly spoken, had attracted the notice of her father. "Did you put him up to it then?" Gerrod demanded.

"I've not seen him lately, my lord King, but I am concerned with his welfare."

"Do you always concern yourself with traitors, sir?"

Melisande bowed her head between them.

King Gerrod added, "As well you should be concerned. I think I shall execute the little bastard after all."

At this, Melisande's head shot up. "You cannot be serious, Father."

"You contradict me even now, Melisande?" His eyes narrowed.

"Please, let us talk about it another time. I have no wish to bring this up before the barons." Her voice was soft, soothing, as her spread hand indicated their audience. Many glances flickered back to the bard when she looked their way.

"Well, he's brought it up; he wants to know about his little traitor, and he should know how we deal with traitors." Gerrod snapped his fingers to summon his guards. "Find that boy in the dungeon and kill him."

They blinked at him, and Melisande sprang to her feet so quickly that her chair fell back with a clatter. "Father, this is madness. If you were sober, you'd know it."

"Go," he snapped to the guards, and they reluctantly turned from him.

Hands clasped, Melisande fell to her knees before her father. "I am begging you not to do this. Your Majesty, spare the life of this child. For love of the Lady!" She looked up to him, but his face was stone.

Kattanan turned to Jordan. "Save him," he urged. "Do whatever you have to!"

The Liren-sha leapt to the floor and Kattanan's friends gave pursuit to Gerrod's guards. The bard's strong voice faltered, and Gerrod said, still looking at Melisande, "Perhaps some dancing will lighten the mood. Go on, all of you, and my daughter and I shall join you shortly." He waved a hand to push the courtiers from the room.

The elegant lords and ladies, in strained silence, moved toward the stairs, and Kattanan let his fists relax. Jordan would do what he could, with Lyssa and Rolf to back him up. Just now, he did not want to leave Melisande alone, even if she never knew it.

"Orie," the king prompted, "King Rhys, please go on and amuse yourselves."

Orie grinned, jumping easily down from the dais, but Kattanan did not move. "Come now, Rhys," Orie said, holding the sibilant "s" like a viper, "this matter is none of our concern." His arm outstretched in invitation, or threat—Kattanan could not be sure.

He took a reluctant step back, then turned and made for the stairs, flanked by his two remaining men.

"Don't keep my partner long, Gerrod," Orie called back, following close behind.

When they had gone, Melisande rose, but her father's words struck her numb.

"You are getting so much like your brother."

She sucked in a quick breath and felt a chill in the pit of her stomach. Her father continued to gaze down at her as if he'd never blink. Fury lived in those cold blue eyes.

"Oh, he would always defy me, but I did not expect it from you, Melisande." He reached down a pale hand to touch her temple. "You were always my favorite."

"I did hope you'd not kill all your heirs."

His white brows pinched together. "Are you afraid of me? I do not mean to frighten you," he said, "but I will have order in my palace, do you understand?"

She stared up at him. "What will the barons think of this execution?"

"I am a strong king, that's what they will think. Ever since my recovery, they have doubted my strength. They think I might still be under the wizard's power." Warmth grew in his eyes. "I should have known you were prompted by concern for me."

"Surely, Father, with all that's happened, the barons have no doubts about you."

"If I gave in to your plea, might they not say, 'It's Melisande who rules him, just as that Traitor once ruled.' I am as sorry for the boy as you are, but he is a small sacrifice to make to keep this kingdom together."

Her equilibrium slowly returned. "I can see why you would feel that way," she said, "but I wish—"

"You wish he could be saved? Then I shall save him, quietly, as a gift for you. Come, Princess, walk down with me?" He offered her his hand.

After a moment, she took it, rising to stand before him. She smiled her most radiant. He would save Thomas. "I am sorry, Father."

"Of course you are." With his other arm, he pressed her briefly to his breast, and sighed. "You will be queen one day, and all of this will help to guide you."

"It will," she said into his blue velvet coat; and she knew that it would not guide her quite the way he intended. "Let's go down; I can hear the music."

He laughed, suddenly as warm and merry as she remembered him. "You always were one for the music." Gerrod tucked her hand over his arm and lead her to the hall.

ONCE KATTANAN reached the marble floor of the Great Hall, Orie waved and left him. He was tempted to turn back the way he'd come, but a few guards hovered near the bottom of the stairs, trying to look casual, so he walked slowly beneath the arch into the Hall. It appeared much the way it had the first time he'd seen it, as a member of Baron Eadmund's retinue, but there was something frantic in the dancing, and a tension to every note the consort played. A few ladies curtsied to him, but they did not seek him for a partner—his concerns for Thomas and for Melisande etched every line of his face.

Lacking a better purpose, Kattanan strolled to the throne reserved for him and sat down. After a little while, Melisande and her father appeared at the arch. The king summoned one of his guards over and sent the man scurrying off in the direction his other guards had disappeared. Had she convinced him to try mercy? Hard to tell at this distance, though Gerrod's face glowed with fatherly affection, and Melisande's smile was hopeful despite the darkness of her eyes.

Across the room, the great door opened for a moment, and a figure slipped inside. Kattanan jerked to his feet. For a moment, he was a singer again, watching Orie's stealthy return from the courtyard, and, with a jolt, he realized it was Orie.

The dark man caught his eye and bowed his head briefly, then crossed quickly to where Melisande was standing. Smiling, he led her to the floor.

Kattanan stepped down from the dais and moved through the gathering toward the door. He hesitated before opening it, however, as the memories of that other night flooded through him. Resolutely, he raised the latch and peered into the gloom.

"Your Majesty."

He jumped and whirled, letting the door slam shut behind him. Fionvar held up his hands. "I didn't mean to startle you. Are you well?"

"Just a little worried. Orie just came inside—any idea what he was up to?"

Fionvar frowned. "Someone came to see him, but I didn't recognize the man. It was abundantly clear that he did not want my attention, though."

"I don't like it."

"Nor do I, Your Majesty. I'll be keeping a sharp eye on him, don't doubt it."

"I appreciate that."

"I'm sorry to have missed the feast," Fionvar said, with a slight smile, "I understand it was something to see."

"Quite," Kattanan agreed. "For her sake, I held my tongue, but I should dearly love to give Gerrod the answer he deserves."

"Soon," said Fionvar, and there was an ominous note in his voice.

# Chapter 41

"THIS WAY!" Rolf shouted to the others, pounding suddenly toward the guest chambers. "Back door," he panted. Rolf's face was a mask of determination as he followed the route along which he'd once carried his prince. Down the back stairs, turn along the winding passage—at last they were at the dungeon, a little-used entrance with only one guard behind the gate.

The man looked up, startled. "What—who goes there! Stop!" He drew his sword, but Rolf's enormous hand shot through the bars of the gate to grab his shirt and lift him until they saw eye to eye. The guard's feet kicked the air.

"The keys!" Rolf shouted.

Lyssa quickly cut them from the guard's belt and popped open the lock.

"Where's the boy?"

"Who?" the guard stammered. "I—I don't know wh—"

Rolf slammed the gate open so that the man was held up between it and the rough-hewn wall. "Bury it, man, don't make me kill ye!"

"Outside wall," the man gasped, "first door."

Rolf grinned his thanks to the wheezing guard and let him fall.

They reached the end of the outer corridor in time to see Gerrod's men opening a door at the far end. Their collective roar as they sprang forward echoed down the hall as their pounding boots rattled the hinges.

One of Gerrod's men looked up, his eyes flying open. He got his sword from the scabbard, but found himself tackled by a huge man built like a bull. Rolf, Jordan, and Lyssa stood shoulder to shoulder, swords at the ready, facing the remaining guard through the open door. The guard's worried eyes flicked from one to the other, then he stepped aside. Thomas barreled across the room to grip Rolf's leg, quaking with tears.

"There, now," Rolf mumbled, patting the boy's head. "We'll bring ye away from here. Ye're mother's got a house in town, aye?"

Jordan said, "We had a question for you, Thomas, if we could."

At this, Thomas pulled away a little. "Yes, my lord?" he whispered, tugging at the royal page's tunic he still wore, despite the stains of the dungeon upon it.

"We need to find a book that your prince might have had," Jordan said gently. "Do you know where we should look?"

Thomas returned Jordan's smile, but tremulously. "I took them all away, all I could carry. They're at Mamma's house."

Running footfalls echoed into the hall, and another of Gerrod's guard appeared around the corner. Lyssa's blade flew from the scabbard and she stepped forward, but the man flung up his hands. "Wait! His Majesty has lifted the order to execute."

"He's come to his senses," Rolf muttered.

"Then he won't mind if we escort Thomas to his mother," said Jordan. The little party made their way back to the main corridor, where the guards stood aside, but not without some grumbling. When they reached the courtyard, Rolf stopped, glancing toward the Great Hall.

"Shouldn't've left the king so long," he said, frowning.

Lifting Thomas to his shoulders, Jordan said, "Go back to him, Rolf. We'll return as soon as we can." To Thomas he said, "Did you know Kattanan was a king?"

"I knew he was somebody," the boy replied.

"Maybe the—maybe you should stay, too," Lyssa told the wizard. "You'll be more use to him than I would."

"Maybe so." The wizard eyed the woman. "Just you find that book."

Jordan replied. "What could go wrong, now that we know it's safe?"

"I don't know," the wizard growled, "that's why I worry."

Grinning, Jordan asked the child on his shoulders, "Which way, captain?"

Stretching out his arm past Jordan's ear, Thomas pointed the way, and the three of them set out. Rolf and the wizard watched them go, with a little party of castle guards closing rank behind to be sure of their destination. "That's well done," Rolf said, "though Kat'll be disappointed no' to see the lad."

But as they turned to reenter the hall, a quick movement caught the wizard's attention, and she took a step away, peering into the darkness. "I thought I saw someone I knew." Frowning, the wizard said, "You go on, I want to see for myself."

"Very well." Rolf shrugged and set out to find his king.

Rolf entered the hall just in time to see Kattanan slipping out to one side. He covered the hall in a few long strides, and followed, catching up with him just inside the garden. "Yer Majesty!" he called out. "We got him, Yer Majesty."

Kattanan spun around with a little dagger in his hand, then he relaxed, sliding it back into his boot as Rolf approached, hands up.

"Ye're quick," he observed.

"Jumpy, more like," Kattanan replied. "I should have recognized you sooner."

"No doubt being around these people is makin' ye look over yer shoulder. 'Tis not all a bad thing, especially when yer guards've up and left ye."

Kattanan shook his head. "Was Thomas all right? I wish I could have seen him."

"Aye, Majesty, he's well enough. I think yer princess looked out for him."

"She's not won any credit from her father for that."

Rolf scuffed his boot along the gravel, then said, "I'm surprised to see ye here, not in there where ye'd be close to her."

"Oh, Rolf, she's dancing, with Orie mostly, and he's been

staring at me as if I should burst into flame. What's worse is three or four ladies have been hounding me for a dance."

Suddenly, Rolf laughed aloud, enormous guffaws so that he had to master himself with at effort. "Ye are a king, young, polite—more than I'd say of some—handsome, too, fer the way these ladies watch." He laughed again, and Kattanan flushed.

"I'm not used to such attention," he murmured. "There's a vast difference between entertaining a court and being a part of it."

"Aye, I suppose there'd be." He grinned down at his young friend. "When we go back in, I'll fend off the ladies for ye."

"Thank you, Rolf, but I think I'd like to stay out for a little while. It's suffocating in there." He held his hands behind him, gazing up at the twinkling stars.

Inside the Great Hall, Melisande finished a set with one of the barons and returned to her throne, summoning a page to bring her wine. She searched the crowd as the dancing began again, but did not see her husband there. She did not see King Rhys, either, thank the Lady. Fionvar led the musicians in a complicated tune. The lines of concern on his face relaxed when he was playing; it made him look less like his brother.

Her father sprawled in his great throne a little above hers, with a little cask of ale at his side. Since the illness, he had laughed louder, drunk more, and hunted with a reckless air that made her frightened to think of it. He was determined to prove himself as able as ever he had been, but who was he really fooling?

The dance ended with a flourish, and the dancers bowed to one another before applauding their musicians. Across the hall, she suddenly spotted King Rhys standing to one side, hands behind him, as he'd always done. A few ladies converged upon him, and, to her surprise, one of them led the king to the dance floor. He watched her feet carefully, then began to dance. A long time ago, forever it seemed, she had thought he must be graceful, and, indeed, he was. It must have been something he had learned since he'd left there, for he never had agreed to dance with her.

That strange sensation spread again across the back of her throat until she thought she must choke on it. Gathering up her skirts, Melisande descended the few steps to the floor and fled the room.

STANDING in shadows, gazing down the ill-lit corridor, the wizard caught another glimpse of her quarry. As she ran, she transformed into the maid's guise—swifter, and more silent than the hulking guard. She saw no one else in the halls as she passed, for the nobles would be dancing, the servants watching and tending to their needs, so she was free to speed her steps as she would. How did the other manage to keep ahead of her? She would spy his robe flickering around a corner, or catch sight of him ducking past an archway. Still, she wasn't sure whom she pursued. Surely, with the ban on wizards, he couldn't be there.

Coming to the top of the stair, she paused, listening, then started forward more slowly. A tall, peaked door cut into the wall at the right, and the air around it eddied with some disturbance. A strange odor wafted on that breeze, and Alswytha froze. From the depths of her memory, she recalled the smell—that of flesh decayed, and of the herbs meant to conceal it, that only accentuated the putrid air. She reeled and gagged, the memory flooding through her. She and nine other orphans, raising lambs which they brought to their master's room. She remembered the day the first of her friends went into that room, and did not return.

Some other odor teased at her memory, something added to the scents of childhood, but that did not belong to them. She frowned, trying to push away the memories and concentrate. Her mind would not obey. Her legs refused to move to the stairs. Her fingers, reaching toward the door, seemed sluggish. If she could have, she would have laughed aloud. She was the Wizard of Nine Stars, both revered and feared as the greatest wizard of her time—but memories and herbs had her standing like a statue, too paralyzed already to speak the words that might free her. She might have laughed, or she might have cried.

The door opened, and light silhouetted a stout figure. He reached out a hand and drew her unresisting body toward him. "Oh, my little darling, I've been waiting for you." The Wizard of Broken Shell, clad in his monk's robe, assisted his former ward into Orie's workshop. He shut the door behind her and shot the bolt with a terrible sound of finality.

KATTANAN BREATHED in the scent of oranges and sighed. He must go back in sometime; he would be missed by his guards, if nothing else. They'd not been happy when he insisted on walking out alone. Rolf stood patiently by him, not speaking.

A movement across the orange grove caught his eye, and he squinted to make out the hurrying figure. A lady, evidently coming from the ball, hurried among the trees. Silver glinted upon her head as she emerged onto a pathway, heading for the little chapel. "Melisande," he breathed into the perfumed air. Kattanan turned to Rolf. "I'm going after her."

"Is't wise, Yer Majesty? She'll not be lookin' fer you," he added gently.

"No, but I would still like to apologize . . . for everything."

"As ye wish." Rolf shrugged, starting after him, but Kattanan stopped again.

He looked up at the guard, lips pursed. "Wait here, would you?"

Frowning, Rolf sighed, then repeated, "As ye wish."

Straightening his tunic, Kattanan set out with a purposeful stride. He came quickly to the chapel and found the door standing open, its hinges loose. Inside, a little flame sprang to life, and he saw Melisande on the far side of the altar. She bent to light another candle. The chapel had the same layout as a larger temple, with small niches representing the caves and a hole over the little altar. The difference was the ceiling. As Melisande's candles sparkled into life, the ceiling twinkled with warm light like a roomful of stars. Tiny mirrors caught the candles' flame and sent it dancing about the little room. Kattanan caught his breath, and she spun around, hands to her cheeks. Her eyes gleamed, too, as if with tears.

"Forgive me, Your Highness." He stepped inside. "I didn't mean to frighten you."

"I'm not frightened, Your Majesty, I just—" She set down the candle she was holding, but the trembling of its light had already given her away. "I did not expect to see anyone here."

"I am as surprised to see you, Your Highness, what with the dance going on." He inclined his head toward the candles, taking a step toward the altar, and Melisande. "The Cave of Death, Your Highness."

She studied the stone altar. "I never lit a candle for my brother," she murmured.

Kattanan walked the few paces until only the altar separated them. "I wanted to apologize for what I said to you in the garden. It was cruel and stupid, and I'm sorry."

A brief smile flitted across her face. "It was true, though, Your Majesty. I have always acted as a child, never as the heir to a kingdom."

"Be that as it may, I had no right to say it."

She lifted her head. "I accept your apology, Your Majesty."

Nodding, he watched how the gold of her gown gleamed and receded with her quiet breaths. The warmth of the candles glowed upon her cheeks, and her slightly parted lips. "I wish that things could have been different." Kattanan sighed.

She met his gaze, and did not answer.

Slowly, he reached up and lifted the crown from his head, setting it down upon the altar. He felt a little taller, relieved of that weight. "We have been to each other as master and servant," he said. He reached out and lifted the circlet from her golden veil.

He fingered the chased dogs as he set the circlet down to the other side. Brushing them gently, he went on, "We have been a king, and a princess." He looked back up at her, and his heart quivered within him.

Still, she did not speak, but neither did she move away.

"Until now, we have never faced each other as man and woman."

At this, she nodded once, and a hairpin slipped loose. The golden veil sighed about her face, sliding gracefully down her shoulder to reveal her hair. The thick, auburn locks had been trimmed about her ears, smoothing the ragged edges left by Faedre's knife.

"Oh, your hair," he whispered, reaching out to her.

"Don't touch me," Melisande said suddenly, turning her face from him. Again, he caught the glint of tears in her eyes, and the sound of them in her shaky voice.

One hand stroked the hair from her temple, ever so gently.

She shivered, clutching her elbows as if suddenly chilled.

"I will never be whole," Kattanan said, "but with all that I am, I love you."

The flames danced upon the mirrored walls like a thousand stars. And those stars danced in her eyes as she turned back to face him. His hand still cupped her cheek, feeling the curve of her warm skin as she smiled.

"Which of us is ever whole, Kattanan?" Her tentative fingers touched a lock of his golden hair, following its curl. Melisande leaned over their crowns and kissed him.

Unwillingly, he withdrew from her, mere inches. "But you are married."

"Yes." She kissed him again.

"And I am," he faltered, looking down, but she laughed, just a little.

"Does it matter?" she asked, both her hands now lifting his face toward hers, so that he must meet her eyes.

Tears shone in them, and spilled down, sparkling.

"Does it matter what you are, what you have ever been? Can't you see—" Melisande laughed again, a sad and gentle sound, more for herself than for him. "No," she said, "can you not hear how much I love you?"

Listening to his princess, Kattanan felt the warmth of a tear upon his face, and the warmth of her lips as she kissed it away.

# Chapter 42

STANDING IN the light pouring from the open door, Lyssa fidgeted. Thomas's mother knelt on the doorstep, her arms about her son, her sobs finally quieting. Jordan slipped an arm around Lyssa's waist, smiling down at the reunion, and Lyssa watched her betrothed's face. It suddenly occurred to her that he would want children. A shiver ran through her as she thought of this, and Jordan's hand pulled her a little closer.

At last, the woman drew back from her son and rose. "I can never thank you enough, my lord, my lady. Won't you come in? My house is not grand, but you are welcome to whatever hospitality I can offer. I've got a stew on," she offered.

"Thank you, my lady, but we've not much time. We're with King Rhys of Lochalyn, and he may have need of us."

"Oh, gracious! Of course. Then is there nothing I can do for you?"

"We are looking for a book, my lady, one that belonged to Prince Wolfram."

She made the sign of the Goddess. "Thomas sent some of his things here. I hardly dared accept the cases. Here, I'll show you." She led them through the front room and kitchen past the bubbling stewpot, to a little shed off the back of the house.

"What book?" Thomas piped up, moving to the dim pile of boxes.

"A small herbal book, bound in green."

Thomas tapped a case. "This is the plant books, but they aren't very interesting."

With Lyssa's help, Jordan shifted the indicated box out into the back alley and pried up the lid. They shuffled through the contents for a moment, and Lyssa's hand emerged with the prize. She grinned. "This'll make your friend happy."

"You're sure I can do nothing else for you, my lord?" the mother asked again as she trailed them back to the front door.

"Only take good care of your son." Jordan ruffled the boy's hair, then opened the door, still smiling.

Thomas screamed and ducked behind his mother.

Whirling around, Jordan found himself facing a man on the doorstep, his hand raised as if to knock, a sword in his grip. Jordan nearly shrieked himself.

Squire Montgomery grinned. "They said you were alive, Liren-sha, and I didn't believe it. I'll just have to kill you again."

Recovering himself, Jordan took a quick step forward, forcing the other to retreat from the house. Once in the street, he drew his own sword, left-handed.

Montgomery laughed. "What happened, Wizard's Bane? Lost a sword?"

His crushed hand throbbed suddenly, as if the ruined fingers itched for blood. In the back of his throat, Jordan growled, then he sprang to the attack.

The way stood clear, and Lyssa took it, pulling the door closed behind her, then she gasped as rough hands spun her about. Two men, no, three, grabbed her—snatching the sword from her waist as she struggled. One of her attackers let out a nasty chuckle. "Bury it," Montgomery snapped, easily parrying Jordan's thrust. "Get the book!"

Lyssa suffered the groping hands of his henchmen, wandering somewhat far afield in search of their goal. She stilled, craning her neck to see Jordan. He was fighting for his life, and losing. Vile Montgomery might be, but he was an excellent swordsman. His blade drank blood at Jordan's thigh, then his bad arm, flung up to protect him.

Still, Jordan had lived as the Liren-sha too long not to have learned something from it. He flourished his wild grin, spinning and dodging. Lyssa nearly laughed as she recognized his quick footwork as the steps of a dance. But the duel was no laughing matter.

"Found it!" One of her searchers crowed, holding up the book.

"Disarm the bitch," Montgomery ordered.

"We're not stupid," another called back, her sword in his grip.

Lyssa suddenly let herself flop back into the arms of the man holding her. As he shifted his grip, thinking that she'd fainted, Lyssa slipped sideways. The handle of her hammer slid perfectly into her hand, and its head slammed into her warden's skull.

Laughing, she whirled to the other two. "Come on, men, disarm me!" Lyssa ripped the skirt from her waist to reveal tight leather fighting trousers. She swung the weighted fabric to foul one man's blade and aimed a blow at his companion.

Distracted, Montgomery fell back a moment, and Jordan pressed his advantage. His blade slashed the air, then his opponent's tunic, at last drawing blood.

Lyssa's hammer caught a shoulder with a sickening crunch, and the man yelped. The other man got a leg behind her, casting her to the ground. She rolled, taking him down with her, the hammer aimed for his knee. He cursed, crawling away and staggering to his feet.

"Coward!" she howled. She shook free of the skirt, grasping the hilt of her fallen sword, and brought it up into the starlight. She pushed herself up and tossed back her bloody hair. "Come to me, you son of worms!"

Her hair was wrenched back, and she fell, shouting.

The sound whirled Jordan around. "Lyssa!"

Pain shot up his right arm as it was twisted behind him, and his knees shook.

Montgomery squeezed his hand again, forcing him down. "Drop your sword," he snarled to Lyssa. His grin flared. "The hammer, too, or this man dies a second time."

HIGH ABOVE the dance floor, in the musician's gallery, Fionvar took a break from his playing for a draught of sweet water. Up here, he could watch all that happened below. Just now, he wondered where Orie and Melisande had gone off to. They had not left together, but had probably met outside. It would not be the first time. His heart ached for Kattanan. Fionvar watched his king bow to his partner and move toward the dais. He had not known Kattanan was such a dancer. Perhaps that had been in his lessons since Fionvar had left; surely he had danced at the ball to celebrate his victory.

King Rhys bowed to his partner, then walked deliberately toward King Gerrod.

Fionvar's brows rose. Could he be so bold, after what had happened at dinner? Gerrod was no less surprised, for he moved back in his throne. King Rhys persisted in whatever he was saying, though. Gerrod snapped for a page, who brought up his customary cordial. Both sniffed the drink, then swallowed.

Fionvar's eyes narrowed. Kattanan had no taste for strong liquor. Fionvar shot to his feet and dashed for the stairs, barely managing to keep his footing. "He's an impostor!" He slid the last few stairs, catching his feet and stumbling like a drunk before he regained himself. Dancers scattered out of his way as he ran for the dais. Breathless, he repeated, "He's an impostor, Your Majesty!"

Caught off guard, King Rhys paled, then frowned. "What are you talking about, Fion?"

"You see? He called me 'Fion!'" he gasped.

"That is your name, is it not?" King Gerrod drawled. "What are you on about?"

He looked from one to the other, suddenly aware of how ridiculous he must look. "He is an impostor," he said patiently.

At this, King Rhys smiled a little. "King Gerrod is most certainly not an impostor."

"Not him, Your Majesty, you," Fionvar said. "You are an impostor."

"Well," Gerrod said, "Orie did mention that his brother hadn't gotten much sleep lately. Go on, there's a good man." He patted Fionvar's arm, but Fionvar shook him off.

"You don't understand, Your Majesty." He tried to sound calm and rational.

At this, King Rhys motioned over his two guards. "Would you please escort Fionvar to his quarters and see that he gets some rest?"

"Maybe it's drink," Gerrod slurred.

The guards gestured politely for Fionvar to precede them, but he held his ground. "I am not mad, I am not drunk. Tell them!" He swung around, searching the crowd, and suddenly realized that all of his friends were gone—Lyssa and Jordan had never even come to the ball. Could the wizard have done this? Was she so desperate to revenge herself upon Gerrod? Goddess' Tears, where was Rolf? Even his brother was gone—he spun back to face the kings. "No," he breathed, staring at his king.

"Please," King Rhys repeated, his eyes gone hard.

The guards took Fionvar's arms. "Bury it, Gerrod, you must listen!" They swung him off his feet, still screaming, "He'll kill you, Gerrod! Listen!"

"And give him a sleeping draught, I think," King Rhys added. "I'm sorry."

Four of Gerrod's men joined the struggle, and they carried Fionvar from the hall. He willed himself to stillness, but his mind raced. They took him to his room, where three of them restrained him on his bed, despite the fact that he was no longer struggling. One of the three was a man he knew from Lochdale. "Great Lady! You can't do this! Go after the king, Matthias," he urged, in his most rational tone.

"I'll go once I've seen to you, sir."

The pity in the other man's face made Fionvar madder than ever, but he held his anger in check. "The king is not the king, he's a wizard."

"Just don't listen to him," one of Gerrod's men advised.

Matthias said, "I can't think what's come over him. Look,

Captain, there's a ban on wizards here, you don't suppose one's got past, do you?"

"The wizard was already here," he sobbed in frustration. "He's my brother."

Matthias laughed. "Your brother's a prince, now, what can he possibly have against King Gerrod? Ah—here's the stuff."

Fionvar clamped his lips shut, twisting his head, but they pried his jaws apart. As the bitter liquid passed down his throat, Fionvar sobbed.

MELISANDE LAY watching the stars, especially the one she thought of as Wolfram's. Her head nestled against Kattanan's shoulder, her arm stroking the bare skin of his chest. The hairs there were fine and pale. She knew from her reading that he would never have the forest of hair that Orie had and that her kisses could be placed, with no interference, just over his heart. Her petticoat formed the pallet where they lay, and his velvet tunic pillowed his head. Her discarded corset lay to one side, its laces cut. She shivered, and Kattanan drew her closer.

"We should get dressed," he murmured into her hair. "We have to set an example for the court."

"I can't go back in there," she said, rising to one elbow to gaze down at his face. Her features suddenly clouded. "What if he finds out?"

"I don't know," he said. "I had not thought beyond this moment." Then he laughed, his joy filling up the little chapel. "I had never thought even so far as this moment. I wasn't sure that I could do it."

"What, make love to a woman?" Her smile returned, but fleetingly. "Haven't you read any books on the subject?"

"There are books?"

"Not about that, silly." She poked him gently with her finger. "The history of the Virgins of the Lady. I found a copy in the library. It's very interesting, very detailed."

"Wait a minute," he protested, rising up on his elbow as well.

"You've been studying books? I thought you never wanted to see me again."

"After I met you as King Rhys, my father told me to know my enemy."

"And do you know me?" he asked.

"A little. Every time I see you, I think there is more to learn about you. I could hardly believe when I saw you dancing." She faltered, giving a wry smile. "I thought of how you'd never dance with me."

Kattanan frowned, sitting up. "When was this?"

"When you first came," she explained, rolling her eyes a little. "You sang so beautifully—I wanted to love you then—but you couldn't dance at all."

"No, I know. I still don't."

She sat up, folding her arms. "I saw you, with that lady in the purple dress, cut to here." She pointed emphatically between her breasts. "That's when I finally knew."

Shaking his head, Kattanan reached for his shirt. "It wasn't me; I wasn't there." He pulled the shirt over his head.

"How could it not be you?" Then she gasped. "A wizard?"

"An illusionist," he confirmed, pulling on his hose as fast as he could. His fingers poked through the seam, leaving a naked hole over his knee.

Melisande caught his urgency, jerking on her chemise. "Nine Stars could do it."

"Or her apprentice." He tossed her one of her slippers.

"She has an apprentice?"

Kattanan bowed his head, shoulders slumped. "I don't know how to say it, Melisande, so that you don't think I'm saying it in spite."

"Orie." She stopped still. "You think Orie is posing as you at the ball."

"It's some plot to discredit me, for you, or for Lochalyn, I've no idea, but we must hurry. Bury it, I knew he was up to something!" He shoved his foot into a boot.

"Tell me, Kattanan. Tell me everything."

"There isn't time!"

Melisande placed a hand on his arm. "Then tell it quickly."

"I don't know when he apprenticed, years ago, I guess. He's on his own, now"—he took a deep breath—"he killed Wolfram, and used his blood to heal himself."

"His side? He told me he fell." Her hands clenched together in her lap.

"He called himself the Wizard of the Prince's Blood."

All color drained from Melisande's face. "Oh, Holy Mother," she whispered. "I married him."

He took her face in his hands. "Melisande, you couldn't have known."

"Yes," she whispered, "Yes, I could. That day we had supper, when Wolfram kept treating him as a wizard. I was so angry with him, I couldn't think clearly. I would have married him just to spite Wolfram, just to prove him wrong. When we walked the first circle, I started crying. Brides do, I guess, but I passed the place where Wolfram should have been, and I thought, what if he were right?"

"But you accepted his bracelet," Kattanan whispered, his voice shaky.

The gold bracelet felt cold and hard beneath her fingers. "Because he loved me. I thought that would make everything all right, that my love would grow, in time."

Kattanan jammed his foot into the other boot and stood abruptly. He scanned the floor for his little dagger. Then Melisande's hand came around his shoulders. She pressed herself against his back. "I thought it would grow, but it dwindled. Smaller and smaller, until I clung to him because—" She broke off, and tears seeped into the silk of his shirt. "Because I thought, if I let him go, no one would ever love me again. Wolfram was gone, my father was drunk and angry. Orie and the dogs were all I had."

He placed a gentle kiss on her wrist. "I wish I could have come sooner."

"No," she whispered, "you came just in time."

# Chapter 43

THE INSTANT the guards left his room, Fionvar dragged himself to his feet. He swayed, already feeling the effects. Two beds, two chairs, two tables swam in his vision. He reached his doubled hand out to the two oil lanterns and succeeded in getting hold of one. Crossing unsteadily to the garderobe, he pulled off the wick assembly and tossed back a long swallow of the oil below. His stomach immediately rebelled, and he vomited the oil, the potion, and the excellent dinner. The vile taste brought him back to his senses. He set down the lantern and crept to the windows, grateful for the thick door between himself and the guards.

His eyes refused to focus on the latch, so he felt along the casement until he found it and pushed it free. The window creaked open, and he froze. After a moment, he peered into the torchlit garden. The distance didn't seem too great, so he stuck his feet out, and jumped down, tumbling when he struck ground. His mind reeled, and he lay still.

"What're ye doin'?" a harsh voice demanded. "Gave me a fright, ye did."

"Rolf?" The looming figure was weaving around among the stars. Fionvar pushed himself up to his knees, then rested. "Where's the king?"

"Off walking with Melisande. Here, are ye well?" Rolf laid a hand on Fionvar's shoulder; it felt like a lead weight.

"No, not the slightest bit." He resisted the urge to shake his head. "With Melisande?"

"Aye—I spotted them walking toward the towers."

Fionvar straightened up and tried to stand, but he swayed dangerously, and Rolf caught him by the elbow. "Enough drink for the musicians, eh?"

"Rolf, my brother's disguised as the king, I think he'll kill Gerrod."

Rolf's grip tightened. "What're ye saying?"

"We have to find the king," he said, as clearly as he could.

"Come on, then," Rolf replied gruffly, "though he'll not thank ye for the interruption." He helped Fionvar down the walk. A thin sound of voices drifted down from the near tower. Fionvar pulled away, hauling himself up the stairs along the rusted railing. When he reached the top, with Rolf lending grudging support, the two kings turned to stare.

"You again," Gerrod growled. "I thought you'd been sent to your room."

"I'm sorry, Yer Majesty," Rolf began, shifting awkwardly on the stairs.

"Rolf, thank the Lady!" King Rhys cried. "Fionvar's not well. I'd appreciate it if you can take him back to his room and see that he doesn't get out this time."

"Begging yer pardon, Yer Majesty, but he claims that ye're a fraud." With his great hand on Fionvar's back, he nudged him along the wall until Fionvar stood supported by the stone.

King Rhys laughed, shaking his head. "He said the same thing at the ball, that's why I had him escorted out."

Rolf rested a hand on his sword hilt, eyeing the kings, then Fionvar. "If ye don't mind my asking, where's the princess?"

"Dancing, of course." The smile froze upon Rhys's face as Rolf's eyes narrowed.

Rolf stepped past Fionvar onto the roof. "She accepted yer words, then, did she?"

"What is this man referring to?" King Gerrod demanded. "Isn't he the one who helped the traitor escape?"

"He's a very loyal man," King Rhys said, but he had gone a little pale.

There was a moan behind him, and, from the corner of his

eye, Rolf saw Fionvar slide into a heap at the foot of the wall. In the same moment, Gerrod cried out, arms flailing as King Rhys easily picked him up and swung him over the wall. Gerrod struck the top of the wall and rolled. Rolf leapt forward, his outstretched fingers catching the king's foot. The jerk of the suddenly falling weight flipped him off-balance, and Rolf crashed into the wall, his arm wedged into the crenellation. He cursed the pain, but he did not let go.

"Bury you all!" King Rhys snarled, the borrowed face twisted into a grimace of rage.

"Where's my father?" Melisande screamed from the top of the stairs. Stumbling up beside her, Kattanan caught his breath, staring as if into a mirror.

"It's you," King Rhys hissed, "or is it me?"

"Great Lady," Fionvar mumbled, clutching his head. "Two of everything."

Rolf's legs kicked above the floor. From somewhere over the wall, Gerrod cursed and howled into the wind. King Rhys flung himself upon the burly guard.

"You'll not kill my father!" Melisande flew at him, pulling him away.

"I'll make you queen," he said, "of Bernholt and Lochalyn both, and more." He faced her, eyes flickering over every part of her face.

"That form doesn't suit you," she said, drawing back a little.

"Oh it doesn't?" the false face asked. "I had the impression that you liked it. And I've made at least one improvement, which I think you'll approve." Suddenly his gaze shifted to her uncorseted breasts, her shorn locks freed from their veil. "You whore, you've had him!"

She straightened, chin held high. "And he was better than you ever were."

Orie pushed off, a cry of rage pouring from his lips, his hands reaching for her throat.

Kattanan whirled. "Melisande!"

The fingers closed on air as Orie fell headlong upon the stone, with Fionvar underneath him. Orie scrambled up. Snatching a handful of Melisande's flying skirt, he wrenched her off her feet and flung himself upon her. His face—Kattanan's face—froze in horror, and he groaned.

Melisande gasped as he was pushed aside, with Kattanan's jeweled dagger thrust deep between his shoulder blades.

Kattanan gathered her into his arms, heedless of the blood on his hands. "You're all right," he whispered frantically. "You'll be all right."

"Oh, no," Orie's voice rang out behind them. "You'll never be all right again."

He rose up, features shifting back into his true form. One hand slid over his shoulder and he ripped free the knife. "You can't kill me, eunuch. Not like that."

He flung the blade into the air where it became a hawk and flew away. The gash in his back sealed itself, the blood drawing inward with a sound like weeping.

"Eunuch," he repeated, shaking his head. "You can't kill me."

A broken voice from the darkness whispered, "Run." Fionvar inched his way backward toward Rolf. "Kattanan," he urged, "run."

Melisande grabbed his hand, and they ran—tripping down the stairs, with the wizard's laughter howling after them.

⚬⚬⚬

KNEELING IN the street, Jordan met Lyssa's eyes. The wounded man held a thick knot of her hair wrapped around his hand. Slowly, she let the hammer fall from her grip, then the sword clattered down beside it.

"That's better," Montgomery said. "Bind her. Let's get out of the street." He tucked his own sword into his belt and fumbled out a length of rope.

The first loop tightened about Jordan's imprisoned wrist, and he winced. He heard a window creak open somewhere behind him—they had an audience. Then a whooshing sound. Before he could place it, Montgomery was screaming, and something hot and wet splashed over Jordan's shoulders, stinging.

Lyssa was whooping with laughter, even as she got one

foot under her, and threw herself over backward on top of her captor.

Montgomery still shrieked like a madman, clawing at the angry redness spreading over his face. Lumps of something dripped from his hair and ears—beef, Jordan realized with a start. From the window above, Thomas shouted, "Get him!" as his mother aimed the empty stewpot at the squire's head.

Jordan seized Montgomery's hand and bit him, the fingers spasmodically dropping the sword. Snatching it up, the Liren-sha spun a graceful arc, and shoved the blade home between Montgomery's ribs. The man's cries erupted into a terrible wail, then fell silent as he slumped to the ground.

Her man down, Lyssa called, "Are you hurt?"

"Not much," Jordan replied, gingerly feeling his right hand.

"Orie sent them."

"Must have," Jordan agreed. He retrieved his own sword and turned to Lyssa. "Alswytha's in trouble." Then he frowned. "Where's the book?"

"Oh, bury it!" Lyssa pulled herself up, pointing where the injured man had hobbled away. "I'll go! Get to the palace, Jordan." She thrust her hammer into its loop and set off at a run.

Glancing up to the window, Jordan waved to Thomas and his mother. "Thanks for the hospitality," he called. "The stew was excellent!"

KATTANAN HEARD the impact when Orie's feet struck the ground. The cackling echoed all around them. Their feet pounded the stones as Melisande led the way through the groves. Back to the palace, back to the ball, where surely someone would help them. The path before them burst into flames, and Melisande screamed, stopping short. Orie's voice behind them chanted dark and terrible words. The stones shook beneath their feet.

"Come on!" Kattanan plunged through the narrow band of flames, dragging Melisande along with him.

Wind rose around them, whipping their hair and tossing the

branches. A tree flew through the air, smashing against the wall. Then another aimed for them. Melisande flung them both to the ground. Dirt from the wild roots lashed their faces as they crawled. The stones buckled and rolled beneath their hurrying hands and feet. They fetched up against the wall of the temple. Even as Kattanan exulted in its safety, a massive trunk soared through the air and smashed the spire. The little building shivered. Ducking against the slim shelter of the crumbling wall, he pulled Melisande into his arms.

"I don't want to die," she whispered.

"Oh, Lady of the highest stars," Kattanan sang softly, "Sweet Finistrel set the spheres to singing."

"Though I stand in darkness now," Melisande joined him, her voice shaky, more a breath upon his cheek than a sound at all, "shine your light upon me."

The cackling grew very near, and suddenly light broke in upon them. Orie towered over them, calling lightning from the sky. Again, it cracked the chapel, and Kattanan's scalp tingled.

"Stand up!" Orie's voice thundered.

To his horror, Melisande was rising, resisting his hands. Tears ran from her eyes.

Suddenly, Kattanan remembered her question, *"Where is my father?"* she had asked, and Orie had not yet answered.

She broke free of his embrace, turning toward her husband with terrible slowness.

Orie raised his hand, and her chin tilted upward. He leaned down to kiss her.

Kattanan screamed, "No!"

A dreadful silence fell—the trees dropped from the sky, raining oranges. Orie pulled back, looking wildly around him.

The truth dawned on him, and Kattanan rose. "The Wizard's Bane, Orie, he's returned. You and I are equal."

"No, never," Orie scoffed, but when he reached toward Melisande, she staggered away.

Kattanan sprang forward, not knowing quite what he'd do, but Orie stumbled backward over the downed trees, turned, and ran.

⁂

JORDAN DASHED across the bridge, then hesitated. Something tingled in his blood, and he shut his eyes, turning all his senses inward: he shared the blood of a wizard, and she was calling. Turning, he made for an inside corridor, following its twists and turns, flying up the stairs. The tingle in his blood grew stronger. A corner, an archway, and, at last, a door. Jordan pounded on it with his fist, but there was no sound within. He threw himself against it, wincing with the force of the impact, then again. The third time, the door popped open, and he stumbled in, sprawling onto a dirty floor.

"Nice of you to join us," a man said. "Unexpected, but nice. Go on, get up."

Jordan rose slowly, turning until he could see the speaker, a round man in a monk's robe. He had an arm about Alswytha's shoulders and a knife at her throat. They stood on a landing of the curved stairs that wound up the inside of the chamber.

"Where's the book? Did you get it?"

"Yes, and no," Jordan replied.

"Tell me, Wizard's Bane. I don't have much patience," Broken Shell snapped.

"I can see that," he replied. He searched Alswytha with his eyes. Why was she so still? No magic could hold her, not in his presence. He frowned and blinked. Come to that, he wasn't feeling well himself. Slowly he began turning again.

"Look at me," Broken Shell shrieked.

Jordan sniffed the air and sneezed. The herbs reminded him of something—the night Faedre had gone to his king's tent. He staggered forward, his body beginning to slow, and caught hold of the brazier in both hands. He carried the thing to the door, and threw it out into the hall, slamming the door triumphantly behind. "That's better." Jordan looked up at the two wizards. "What is that stuff?"

"Don't taunt me with questions. Where's the book?"

"Actually, I've no idea. Someplace in the streets of the city, I suppose." He lounged against one of the tables, wrinkling his nose at the foul stench of the place. "This is Orie's workshop? Where's the great man himself, still dancing?"

Her captor dug the tip of the dagger into the woman's neck, just a little.

Jordan stood up, hands out. "Please don't. If you do that, I'd have to kill you, and I'd much rather that she had the pleasure."

Broken Shell laughed, a hearty, boisterous sound. "Without her powers, she is even less than I. And you couldn't reach us in time, so why not tell me?"

"It's rather a long story," Jordan observed, "and this stench is really bothering me. Don't see how you can stand it." He crossed to the curtained arch, ignoring the wizard's protests, and pulled back the curtain. He opened the tall windows to allow in the night breeze. "You see, a friend and I went into town, to the boy's house where he'd sent the prince's books. Oh, see, I've already skipped a part—"

"I don't care!" Broken Shell howled. "Get to the book."

"My friend and I were set upon, once we'd got it." Alswytha's eyelids fluttered at this, and Jordan smiled a little as he continued. "They thought they had us, but we won out, with the help of a cook with impeccable timing. Unfortunately, the man with the book got away." Jordan started pacing around the table with its grisly remains. A few fresh victims lay puddled in their own blood. He grimaced and resolutely turned away. "So my friend went to chase him down, while I came back here. We thought someone might have a plot in store for Nine Stars."

"And you were correct. Will your friend bring the book back?"

"Oh, I imagine so."

Nine Stars twitched her fingers, then they closed into a fist.

"Look"—Jordan spread his arms—"why not come down and have a fair fight?"

"I don't think so."

"Well, I must say, that if you stay up there, the fight will be over too soon."

"To your loss, Wizard's Bane."

"I don't think so," he said softly, for the Wizard of Nine Stars stirred, and spoke.

"Arise," she said, and stretched out her hand to the room.

Letting out an involuntary cry, Broken Shell stabbed his knife deeper, but she bent the knife from his grasp, her blood disappearing as quickly as it had been shed.

"But, the Wizard's Bane!" he said, pointing.

"We have an understanding not to interfere in one another's work."

A soft clattering and scuffling began behind him, and Jordan shuddered. A dark shadow swept upward—an eagle trailing bloody feathers. Something whimpered and dropped from the table, shambling on weak legs up the stairs, one at a time.

"You can do it," Broken Shell breathed. "You can raise the dead."

"No," she said softly. "No one can undo what has been done. What blood remains knows only torment. Torment and revenge."

She ducked as the ragged eagle swooped down, slashing for his head.

Broken Shell shrieked and staggered back. "But I didn't kill them!"

Something small and sharp of tooth clamped onto his leg, and he kicked it free. Another took its place, and another.

"Nine stars shine in my blood," she said. "It is not I alone who call the dead." She turned her back to walk carefully down the stairs.

A snake passed her by, its eyes gone, but its tongue flickered between its fangs. There would be venom enough for one last strike.

# Chapter 44

SKIRTS GATHERED in both hands, Melisande stumbled to a halt when she reached the courtyard. Kattanan came up beside her. "Where?" he panted. The yapping of dogs reached them, and they knew. Melisande sprinted for the door, but Kattanan held back, remembering.

"Hurry!" she called. "The back door!"

Reluctantly, he pushed himself into the yard, wincing as he passed the place where Baron Eadmund had met his death. The barking grew louder.

Melisande shouted as the door popped open. Furry bodies bounded past her, and, from within, Orie's voice yelled, "Kill! Kill!"

Kattanan froze, eyes wide.

The first of the dogs leapt past Melisande, white teeth gleaming as they snapped the air. A dozen and more spilled from the open door, all charging straight for him.

"Stop!" Melisande shouted above the din of claws on stone and the ferocious barking. She dropped her voice to a growl. "Stop right there."

The lead dog faltered and swerved, glancing back to his mistress.

"Down," she ordered, her eyes beating the animals back.

One by one, they sank down onto their bellies, ears lowered, eyes beseeching. The dog nearest Kattanan reached out a delicate tongue and lapped at his boots. He shifted his eyes slowly down toward it, but the dog made no move. Carefully, he lifted one foot, and set it down. Then the other. Hardly daring to breathe, he inched his way among the panting animals. Their dark eyes watched him pass, but they did not rise.

"Good dogs," Melisande was saying, her voice low and soothing. "Good dogs." She held out her hand to him. At last, he took it in his own trembling fingers. She smiled, the way she used to—before the marriage, before Wolfram, before Kattanan had left her. "You are not the only one in control of his voice." She squeezed his hand.

Together, they stepped through the open door. It slammed behind them, and the bar dropped into place. Melisande's hand was wrenched from his, and she shrieked as she was spun away into darkness. Orie's raspy breathing echoed in the chamber. All the windows had been sealed, so that not even a glimmer of starlight reached them.

Somewhere to his right, Melisande whimpered.

"I've got a knife!" Orie called. "Don't move a muscle."

He could find them in the dark, following their sounds, but what then? He had no weapon; he was so rattled he couldn't even tell if Orie was lying. By the time he knew, she might be dead. No good. Kattanan inched toward the far door. Something rustled in the straw, and he froze, but the sound continued, and he heard the soft whining of puppies in the birthing room. Stepping lightly, Kattanan felt his way along the wall, and found the door. "Let her go, Orie," he said to the dark. "I know you don't want to hurt her."

"I might surprise you."

Melisande let out a soft cry, smothered by his hand.

Kattanan fumbled with the latch, calling out, "Great Goddess, Orie, what do you hope to gain? Gerrod knows what you've done." The bolt slid back, and he gently held the latch.

"What you've done," Orie returned. "Gerrod thinks you tried to kill him. All his court—and yours, may I add, saw him leave with you."

"What about your wife?" Kattanan asked, and he threw open the door. Outside, light shone from a hundred windows, casting a feeble glow across the room. Orie clamped one hand over Melisande's mouth. In the other hand he held the edge of a metal plate to her throat.

Kattanan grinned across the darkness, then Orie flung Melisande aside. In one ferocious lunge, Orie bounded across the room. He struck Kattanan full in the chest, knocking the wind out of him. As he struggled for breath, Kattanan skidded across the balcony. His arms flailed, his boots slipped and sought for purchase, then one foot reached back, and found nothing. He found the breath to scream as he struck the stairs.

A sickening crack accompanied the scream, followed by the percussion of his terrible descent. With a thud, the scream ended.

Melisande staggered to the balcony, her face ashen.

Orie turned from the stairs and grinned. "I have always enjoyed silence," he hissed, "haven't you?"

Shaking all over, Melisande steeled herself to look down. She caught a glimpse of his hair, the dark stain of blood spiraling down the golden curls. She wailed.

Orie spun his wife toward him. He caught her face in his cold hands and stopped the sound with a kiss.

ON THE tower, the violent wind had blasted the last of the sleeping draught from Fionvar's head. He heaved himself to the top of the wall and look down the other side. Rolf had a grip on Gerrod's ankle, but the king swung dangerously, and the guard's massive shoulders were wedged firmly into the arrow slit.

"I think we can get him up," he called down to Rolf.

Rolf grunted.

"We'll get you out next, don't worry." He shifted into position, reaching down alongside Rolf's place. "Pull him up a little, would you?"

Rolf hauled up the dangling king until Fionvar could almost get hold of him.

"Bury it," Gerrod gasped, his hair flying in the wind, "I'm not made of wood." Fionvar grabbed the boot, and Rolf shifted his grip to the king's shin, gathering in the other leg.

"Careful!" the king snapped as he bumped against the rough wall.

"You son of a bitch," Fionvar snapped back. To Rolf he said, "My head's still foggy. Why are we saving him?"

"Cursed if I know," Rolf wheezed. "Seemed the thing t' do."

"Pull me up, you cretins! Pull me up, or I'll have your heads!"

Fionvar glared down into the darkness. "You listen to me, Gerrod, because I'm the man with your life in my hands. You can't have my head, you pompous, drunken—"

Far off on the other side of the main bridge, a scream rose into the night, and died away. "Great Lady," Fionvar breathed. He nearly let go of Gerrod, but forced himself to concentrate.

From the same direction, a keening wail shivered him clear through.

It ended just as suddenly.

"Melisande!" Gerrod sobbed. "Where's my daughter?"

"Where's yer son, ye bloody bastard?" Rolf howled back at him.

"Dead by my brother's hands," Fionvar said, "both of them."

"No," the king shouted, his breathing labored. "Ask King Rhys! He threw me here, he brought the traitor's body—"

"Wrong!" Fionvar answered. "Wolfram died to save my life; Finistrel knows why. Orie would've killed me," he whispered, "but Wolfram died instead."

"Orie hired the wizard who sent ye t' yer sickbed, Gerrod," Rolf chimed in.

"Orie learned how to change his appearance; he talked you up here."

"Orie threw ye over, Gerrod."

"Now he's thrown your daughter," said Fionvar. "Just as he murdered your son."

"It's not true," Gerrod sobbed. "She can't be dead, not my Sandy."

Fionvar took a moment to find his breath again, pressing his cheek to the cool stone. The breeze stroked away his tears, and he turned back. "Let's do it." He caught the king's other foot and pulled him up. Rolf glowered at the king's face as he passed him along. Dumping Gerrod onto the floor, Fionvar set to freeing Rolf from the notch. Both men grunted with the effort, but soon they slumped against the wall. Rolf massaged his aching shoulders, wincing at the scraped skin. Sidelong, he watched Fionvar. "I'm thinkin' ye're not so bad."

Fionvar glanced back at him. "Nor are you, Rolf." A half smile brightened the darkness of his features. "I'm glad to know you." He stuck out his hand.

Rolf gripped it. "Any friend of Wolfram's is a friend o' mine."

Gerrod stopped dusting himself off and sighed. "The crown is gone, I guess."

"You can always get another crown," Fionvar said. "Where will you find another prince worthy of the title?"

His head still bowed, Gerrod did not answer. The king's shoulders drooped and trembled as the old man wept for his son.

ORIE PUSHED his wife back against the wall. With one hand, he tore the gown from her shoulders. She shivered in her thin chemise, but promised herself she would not cry. He would get nothing from her. As he cupped her breasts, the stone dug into her back, and she turned her head, gazing at the sky. A cloud drifted across the stars, as if they could not bear to see her. "Oh, Wolfram," she whispered, "I tried."

"Shut up," Orie growled. "I never want to hear that name again, understood!"

"You killed Wolfram," she said, gazing into his eyes.

"Of course I did, you stupid whore." He knotted his hand in her hair. "Give me cause, and I'll kill you, too."

"What, am I not to die?" the words came out nearer a sob.

"Your father's dead, your brother's dead," he spat at her, "your little castrate king is dead—but I'd like to keep you, for my baby's sake, if nothing else." He stroked her belly, pressing his hips into her. "Maybe a few more."

"Kill me, Orie," she pleaded, "or, so help me, I'll find a way."

"Maybe I'll beat the sense out of you." He knocked her head

firmly against the wall so that her teeth slammed together, and she tasted blood. He pressed his lips to hers, forcing his tongue between to taste her blood, and he chuckled. Low in her throat, Melisande whimpered. Her hands held to the wall felt numb. The cold seeped through her body until she felt she'd never be warm again. Melisande shivered, and her husband pressed even closer.

"I'll warm you," he breathed, and a plaintive note had crept into his voice. "Don't you know I love you? Goddess's Tears, Sandy, I never wanted to hurt you." His hands stroked her face, found their way to her breasts and hips, encircled her.

Frozen tears slid down her cheeks. Melisande willed herself dead.

Far below, in the darkness where only the stars could reach, a tiny voice sang, "In the Bernholt Hills you'll find me." It broke off, coughing, then gasped another breath to continue, "Lying with my lady—"

Orie jerked away, frozen just as she was.

"Should be, lying with your lady"—a tiny laugh—"given the circumstances." The voice died away again with a cough.

Orie strode to the wall and looked down. Sprawled at the bottom of the stairs, Kattanan gave a grim half smile. "I didn't think"—he gasped—"I could do it." Blood streamed down his forehead, and his right leg had a bend below the knee. He cradled one arm across his chest and took a shallow breath, and another. "Dancing in the starlight," he sang, "Laughing in the rain."

Melisande crept up, her face lit by the brightest smile Kattanan had ever seen.

"You can't kill me," he told Orie. "Not that way."

The roar grew in Orie's breast again. He grabbed Melisande and thrust her back into the room, where she tumbled in the straw. Then he pounded down the stairs.

Kattanan's smile faltered. He couldn't run—couldn't even crawl away. In his bruised back he felt the vibration of Orie's approach. "You'll always remember she loved me first," he murmured to the darkness. Suddenly Orie was there, quivering with his fury. He reached down and grabbed a handful of Kattanan's shirt to haul him to his feet.

Kattanan yelped with pain. The dizziness grew inside his head, but he fought it down. He must give her time—find help, he urged her—Jordan, Rolf, Fionvar, anyone! Orie shook him back to alertness, sneering when his eyes creaked open again. "I can kill you any number of ways," he snapped, "but I like this one." His hand closed over Kattanan's throat. "Bury me, singer, if you ever sing again."

Lights danced between Kattanan's ears, and he wondered, fleetingly, if that were what the prophecy meant—sing with the stars. His mouth gaped desperately, both hands clawing at Orie's grip, despite the spreading numbness. Even then, on the verge of darkness, a drop of sound reached him. Then another.

His roar running silent at last, Orie half turned from his victim.

Melisande swung, shattering Orie's nose with the first blow.

Orie stared, frowning through the blood. "Sandy, you can't—"

The second blow ruined his handsome features, in a spatter of blood. The third she missed, for his body was already collapsing. The heavy ceramic dog bowl shattered against the rail, the shards cutting her hand. She cast them aside and sank to her knees.

"Please, please, please," she mumbled, as she slipped her arms around Kattanan's shoulders. "Please, please, please."

She cradled him close to her chest, trembling fingers smoothing the hair from his face. "Don't die," she begged him. "Don't leave me now. I've only just found you." Tears dropped onto his forehead, cleaning little pathways through the blood. One drop streaked along his eyelid and came to rest, quivering, upon his lips.

As if he had been waiting for this, his lips parted, and he took a tiny breath. It shuddered through him, but he coughed, and took another. One eye opened, and a little smile trembled into life. "Princess," he whispered.

"I'm here, Kattanan." She clutched him to her breast.

"I thought," he rasped, "I might sing with the stars."

"Not yet," she cried, half in prayer.

Listening to the wild beat of her heart, he murmured, "No, love, not for a very long time."

# Chapter 45

BY SILENT consent, Rolf and Fionvar ignored King Gerrod as they made their way to the courtyard in front of the Great Hall. A richly dressed crowd hovered about the door, unwilling to approach the dogs who crouched about the yard, whimpering. All of the dog's noses were turned toward their door, so the pair began to pick their way across.

"Fion! Where's the king!" Jordan bounded out from the darkness with the wizard at his heels. Seeing Fionvar's expression, the Liren-sha swallowed his greeting and hurried over.

Fionvar tried the door. "Barred." He sighed, rubbing his weary head.

"Stand back," said the wizard. She flung up both hands shouting, "Down and be gone!" in a thundering voice. The door shivered, and fell. Alswytha allowed herself a little smile as all the onlookers stampeded back into the Hall, and the great doors slammed.

Gerrod limped up, calling for his absent guards. "Bury it, where've they gone?" Still smiling, Alswytha turned to face him. "Are you asking me, Your Majesty?"

The king stopped short, shutting his mouth with a snap.

Jordan collected a torch and stepped through the dark doorway. "Kattanan?" From the far side, out in the lower yard, a woman's voice answered, "Here! Come quickly!"

On cue, the dogs leapt to their feet and galloped past the little party, streaming down the stairs with a flurry of yapping and a waving of tails. "Great Lady!" Melisande's voice cried. "Off! Get off, all of you." The torchlight showed a ring of dogs surrounding Melisande at the bottom of the stairs, her chemise and tattered hair spattered with blood. She cradled Kattanan in her lap and did not turn. Jordan skidded the last few steps, falling on his knees beside them.

Melisande let them take him from her, to lay him on the more level floor, and she rose, suddenly feeling the bruises she had earned that evening.

"Melisande?"

She turned to find her father on the last step, his head a little higher than hers, bereft of his crown. The old king took a deep breath. "I am sorry," he said, "for everything. For doubting you." He sighed, his mouth twisting at the unaccustomed awkwardness. "You have always been the most faithful of daughters. And Wolfram was the most faithful of sons." Gerrod took the last step and wrapped his arms around his daughter.

Fionvar followed more slowly. The relief and concern mingled in the wizard's conversation told him his king was safe. What stopped him was the faceless corpse sprawled against the rail, pieces of the shattered bowl sprinkled in his hair. Fionvar's knees felt weak, and he slumped down on the step, head in his hands.

"Hey! Hello! Somebody tell me what's going on," Lyssa demanded from the top of the stairs. "Here's your accursed book!" She started down, finally replacing her hammer as she walked. In the darkness, she nearly tripped over Fionvar, huddled as he was against the wall. She looked from him to the corpse, and back. "Are you all right?"

"Goddess's Tears, Lyssa, leave me alone!" Fionvar shouted.

She opened her mouth, then shut it. Instead, she wrapped her powerful arms around him, refusing to be shaken off. "Fionvar, you did the best you could," she told his matted hair, tucking her head against his. "The best that anyone could have."

"I'm falling apart," he whispered.

Blinking back tears, she nodded. "It's all right. After all those years that you held us together, for this one night, let me hold you."

THEY STAYED at the palace until Kattanan felt ready to take a carriage back over the mountains. His retinue gathered in the main court to make ready their departure. Alswytha for once rode as herself, for she, too, had been a guest of the palace, though King Gerrod forbade her to change her shape and was extremely careful what he said when she was about. The day was bright and clear, but a chill of autumn hung in the air already, and the farthest peaks glistened white in the distance. Kattanan made his way from the Great Hall with the help of a knobbed wooden cane. His right arm was still in a sling across his chest, and his leg was held straight by thin slats of wood. Even after the wizard had healed what she could of his flesh and skin, a scar traced its way from his left cheek to his temple. Atop his head, the crown of his family gleamed. One of the stones had been knocked free in the storm, but it was otherwise unharmed. When it had occurred to Melisande to send someone for their crowns, the servant returned with both. The little temple had utterly collapsed, but the hole in the ceiling had settled gracefully around the altar, leaving their crowns untouched.

Melisande escorted him from the hall, walking at his side at a pace to match his own slow progress. Her father walked on her other side, steadfastly refusing to look at them. By the door of the carriage, Fionvar waited, scuffing his boot. He had quietly taken his brother's body, and discreetly borne it off. If there had been a funeral, Kattanan did not know, and King Gerrod, who might have demanded burial in payment for Orie's treachery, pursued the matter no further.

Melisande brushed by Kattanan, accidentally letting her hand stray on his, atop the cane. She managed to smile. "Lady ride with you, Your Majesty," she told him.

"I will come back when I can," he murmured, "I don't know how long—"

"Hush," she whispered, losing her smile. "I know you will."

Kattanan finally climbed inside. Fionvar got in, shutting the half door firmly behind him and taking a seat opposite his king. As the carriage lurched into motion, Kattanan watched Melisande through the window. She stood shining in the sunlight in a burgundy gown, her hair allowed to fly free in the gentle breeze. Sunlight gleamed on a silver streak that suddenly spilled from her eye, and down her cheek. Then she lifted her hand and made the sign of the Goddess. She raised her hand to her lips, and kissed the fingers as tenderly as if they were his lips. She shut her eyes, seeing only his safe return.

In his memory, Wolfram rode beside him, seeing him off with the same gesture.

Kattanan watched the road ahead as they left the city. In a few short days, he would face the woman who thought she would marry him. In a few short days, he must know what to do. Just now, he did not have the slightest idea.

Alswytha came up to ride beside them. She pushed a scroll of parchment through the window. "I think you should read this, both of you," she said, and her face was grim.

Kattanan took it and read the few lines, and the broad signature at the bottom. He passed it wordlessly to Fionvar, whose frown deepened as he read, then he laughed—a hollow, bitter sound. "He told me he hoped I'd be amused when I found out."

"I didn't know you," Alswytha said. "I didn't know anyone; all I thought of was that it would be nice to have someplace to go home to."

"It would be," Fionvar agreed.

"It should be yours." She thrust the scroll back at him, but he did not take it.

"Oh, no; it's all legal, signed and witnessed. Gamel's Grove was his to bestow as he wished." The flare of anger died away. "Besides, I am not at all sure I want it."

She stared down at the thing in her hand, the price of Orie's apprenticeship. "After what he did with his talent, I am not sure I want to take his title."

Fionvar glanced at her, and a sort of understanding filled his voice when he told her, "It doesn't have to be a legacy of what he was but of what he might have been." He offered a slender smile. "When you take up residence, I'll go with you. I'll introduce you to everyone as some long-lost cousin. I think you would do well there."

"Thank you," Alswytha said, "I would appreciate that." She nodded to the king, and urged her horse a little faster until she passed the carriage.

Something occurred to Kattanan then, a glimmer of an idea. "Fionvar," he said, "when you and Brianna met in Gamel's Grove, what was the song you were playing?"

" 'A Blacksmith to his Lady,' " Fionvar replied, and he looked away.

When they finally reached the plain before Lochdale days later, horses rode out to meet them. Outstripping his men by several paces, Gwythym rode up and reined in by the carriage. "Welcome back, Your Majesty! Am I ever glad to see you!"

Kattanan laughed. "Has the duchess been easy to work with, then?"

"Oh, surely, Majesty! Easy as washing a tiger." He threw back his head to laugh heartily. Then his expression turned sour. "You should know that Lady Faedre's vanished. Seems she seduced one of the guards to let her go."

"Just so long as she stays gone," Kattanan said.

At last, the carriage entered the gates of the city and started up the long slope to the castle. Children waved flags for him, and ladies leaned down from the windows to blow him kisses as the carriage passed. Kattanan blushed. On the steps over the arch, and at the castle gate, ranks of knights awaited them. Carefully, Kattanan rose and took the few steps to the ground. Before him, a rug woven with the leaves of the Rinvien crest led the way to the arch. On the right side, Duchess Elyn and Lady Brianna curtsied, lowering their eyes. They rose as one. Brianna's hair was bound up in braids, accenting her face. Her gown laced up the front—inviting its removal despite the fact that her pregnancy rounded out the sky-blue silk below.

Fionvar dismounted and spent a long time checking his stirrups while his sister ran up to greet the lady with a warm embrace.

Duchess Elyn walked forward and offered her hand to be kissed. Still flustered at the sight of Brianna, Kattanan blinked at her in consternation. His right arm ached, his left hand still gripped the cane. Jordan came up silently beside him, gently slipping free the cane so he could take his grandmother's hand.

When he straightened, he saw the pain that creased her features, mirroring his own. "We are again well met, Grandmother."

"It is good to have you home, Rhys, though it pains me to see you in this condition."

"The sling I may leave off in a week," he replied lightly.

"Excellent," she said, some of the darkness lifting from her eyes. She took the cane from Jordan and returned it to Kattanan. "Just in time for the wedding."

That night, after Evening Prayer, Kattanan sent for Brianna and she came quickly, still wearing her gown and braids as if she had been waiting for him. She curtsied and rose, then smiled at him. "I would like to embrace you, cousin. Would you be hurt?"

He had removed the sling, and flexed his fingers experimentally. "I think I would be fine, if you hug me carefully.

The smile growing, she crossed to him and slipped her arms about him. She felt warm and soft in his arms, and he shut his eyes a moment, and imagined it was Melisande he held. Gently, he moved away. "Before I left, Brianna, you promised me that you would hear me sing. Will you hear me now?"

A hint of trepidation crossed her features, but she nodded. "I promised, if you would hear me speak of our marriage."

He offered her a chair before the fire. "May I take down your hair?"

A frown pinched her brows, but, again, she nodded.

With his left hand, Kattanan slid the pins holding her hair. He untied the ribbons and slowly worked free the strands. He took up a silver brush from the table and stroked it down the flaxen waves. After a moment, he found a fragile rhythm, using his right hand as little as possible. Brianna's eyes were shut, her face caressed by the firelight.

Then, he began to sing. The voice was not his own, it couldn't leap and sparkle in quite the same way, but he had grown used to it and started to find the things it could do.

*"A smith should be a hard man,*
*a man of iron, man of flames.*
*And yet, for thee, I can but weep,*
*Forging my own chains, love*
*I'm forging my own chains."*

Her head rose, shoulders stiffening as her eyes fluttered open, but she had promised, and so she stayed silent.

*"A smith I am, a simple man*
*a man of iron, man of flames,*
*I stand unworthy of your smile*
*Forging my own chains, love*
*I'm forging my own chains."*

Brianna's eyes searched the fire, and she moistened her lips. Her hands came together in her lap. Slowly, one finger traced a line upon her wrist. Her eyes shut as a tear trickled down, then another. To one side, a door opened. Kattanan looked, but did not stop his brushing. Fionvar stood there, mouth open to answer the king's summons. His face burned at the sight.

Holding up a finger to his lips, Kattanan beckoned him forward, to stand by him.

*"Lady, Lady hear my plea*
*A man of iron, man of flames—"*

Kattanan reached for Fionvar's hand, guiding it onto the handle of the brush. He maintained his steady rhythm.

*"You are sun and life to me*
*Forging my own chains, love,*
*I'm forging my own chains."*

Still singing, Kattanan let his hand fall away, so that Fionvar stood lovingly brushing his lady's hair. Bending his head over her, he, too, was weeping silently.

*"Will you yet deny my love?*
*A man of iron—"*

"Rhys," she whispered through the veil of tears. "I can't marry you."

"I know," he said, sitting carefully on the edge of a chair, still out of her sight.

"I love you both," she murmured, "but he—" Her voice cracked, and her head dropped into her hands. She sobbed helplessly.

"I know," he repeated, tenderly.

The brush slipped from Fionvar's numb fingers to fall upon the floor. He knelt behind her, wrapping his arms about her, pressing his face against her neck. Kattanan rose, collected his cane, and left them quietly together.

Fionvar found him the next morning, sound asleep on a bench in his study. When he shut the door, Kattanan's eyes opened, and he pushed himself up.

Fionvar beamed at him. "I don't know how I can ever thank you," he said. Dark circles rimmed his eyes, and stubble showed along his jaw, but the smile was true enough. It slipped away, though, and he hesitated before he added, "I thought, when you asked about the song"—he took a deep breath—"for a moment, I doubted you."

"You should have more faith in your king."

Fionvar laughed. "For all you've done, I certainly should."

Kattanan grinned up at him. "I have thanks enough just hearing you laugh again. I can't tell you what it's been like these past weeks." Then he grew serious. "I don't want to dishonor Brianna by refusing her."

Fionvar drew up a bench and sat down opposite his king. "Go on."

Kattanan shook his head. "Will you trust me, Fionvar?"

"Absolutely."

"I need you to stand as the protector of my crown and kingdom."

"At your wedding," Fionvar said.

"Yes."

"Where you will marry my lady."

"Yes."

Fionvar drew back, letting out a long breath.

"You said you would trust me."

"What are you doing, Your Majesty?"

"I cannot avoid marrying Brianna, both for her sake and the sake of Lochalyn; there must be an heir. I know that what I'm asking you will be absolute torture, and I hope you know that I would not ask it of you lightly or maliciously. You will stand beside me for every moment of the ceremony. You will hold my sword and crown."

After a long pause, Fionvar said, "It would be easier if I knew what happened after that."

"I am sorry, I can't tell you." His eyes held Fionvar's. "Will you trust me?"

The silence stretched. Fionvar studied his hands, then he looked up again. "Yes, Your Majesty, I will."

True to his word, Kattanan planned the full ceremony, from prayer at dawn to presentation at dusk, with a different outfit for virtually every part in between. Duchess Elyn appeared from time to time, to gloat over the preparations, but she otherwise let him alone, giving the court the excuse of his injuries. At his suggestion, Brianna sat in at court for him and relayed the proceedings to him as they shared suppers at his chambers, often joined by Fionvar, Jordan, and Lyssa. Alswytha had made herself scarce lately, but she did come to teach him to play chess, and he asked if it might be possible to learn to control his voice, to return it to the way it used to be. Her eyebrows rose at this, but she nodded noncommittally, and the subject did not come up again.

The day of the wedding started with clouds, causing the duchess to frown, but, by the time the couple had spoken the

Morning Prayer, the sun peeped down onto the altar. Fionvar, awkward in his role, carried the crown on its velvet pillow, and the sword lay beneath it. While Kattanan stood in prayer, Fionvar stood beside him, reminder of the secular power of the groom-to-be. Elyn glowered at this arrangement, but, since the king had no brother to fill the role, she grudgingly admitted that he had made an apt choice. Jordan and Rolf flanked the altar, but neither Lyssa nor the wizard could be found.

Kattanan had shed both the sling and the cane, though he had to set his feet down with great care at every step of the three circuits around the temple. It took forever, and his body ached when they finally stood before the altar.

Brianna faced him and held up a gold marriage bracelet. "The circle unbroken, of our Lady's love," she said, and her eyes flickered to his, then down.

Kattanan held the matching bracelet. "The circle unbroken, of our earthly love."

Hands trembling, he slid the circle over her hand and stood silent as she slid hers onto his wrist. The cold thing rested against his cuff, winking in the candlelight.

The audience cheered—mostly. Fionvar's eyes were cast upward as they finished the ceremony, his hands clutched the pillow like a weapon, but he did not strike.

Kattanan took his wife's hand and led her forth. He brought her down the winding halls and to the steps of the tower from which he would present her to his people. Just as they reached it, the wizard appeared, looking as disheveled as she ever had. Brianna started, then smiled. "I'm so sorry to be late," Alswytha mumbled. "I guess I didn't hear the bell."

"You'll see the most important part," he told her. "Won't you stay?"

"I can't. I'm in the middle of something, really. But I did want to congratulate you." Awkwardly, she flung her arms around him.

A sudden shout behind them made the party turn. A figure hurried up, muffled in a long, hooded riding cloak, breathless. "Blast!" Lyssa's voice called from beneath the hood. "I've missed it, haven't I?"

Kattanan eased the wizard away from him, and again took Brianna's hand. He smiled a little, and Brianna smiled back, then they proceeded up the stairs. On the rooftop, Fionvar brought the crown forward, and Brianna knelt at her husband's feet. Kattanan raised the crown from its pillow. "I proclaim you my queen," he said, "to rule as my equal in all things."

A cheer rose up from those gathered below.

Taking her hand, he helped Brianna rise again to her feet and led her to the low wall, where all could see them.

Lightly, he kissed her hand. Then, glancing back to Fionvar, he smiled, and stepped over the edge.

# Chapter 46

"YOUR MAJESTY!" Fionvar called. He ran to the edge but saw only a few swallows darting in the air. King Rhys had utterly vanished. Brianna swayed, and Fionvar caught her, steadying the crown on her head.

"What's happened to my grandson?" shrilled Elyn. She, too, peered over the edge, to find the astonished crowd below gazing up at her in disbelief. "Where is he?"

Fionvar saw the pallor of her face, and wondered if the duchess herself would faint. He held close the warm weight of Brianna and let the tension drain from his body. Kattanan had done it! Whatever it was he had done, Kattanan had won! Fionvar slowly settled to the ground, supporting the queen in his arms. She would need a strong protector of crown and kingdom, as would their child.

Elyn paced across to Jordan. "What do you know about this?"

"Nothing!" He threw up his hands. "I've hardly seen him." She whirled away to confront Fionvar, but left Jordan suddenly sure. He sprang to the wall and looked not for his king, but for a lady; she was nowhere to be seen, but she could not have gotten far. He turned away, and saw Lyssa coming toward him—so beautiful, so strong. For a moment, he hesitated.

Lyssa laughed, her mouth spread in a wild grin, and she flung back her hood. Her bald scalp gleamed above her red brows. On her skin were traced the intricate paintings of an initiate priestess. "Go, Jordan," she said. "Run!"

And run he did, pounding down the stairs, out into the courtyard, calling, "Alswytha! My lady, wait for me!"

Staring at his sister, Fionvar, too, laughed. Lyssa ran a hand over her scalp and revealed the badge of the Sisters of the Sword emblazoned on her robe.

"Have you all gone mad?" Elyn demanded, fists clenched at her sides. "Where is the king? Why is nobody searching? What has he done?"

"He flew on a dappled steed over the heads of the enemy," Fionvar said.

"He raised the dead," Lyssa added.

Brianna opened her eyes and gazed up at the man who held her. "He brought the Usurper from the castle single-handed, without bloodshed."

"What are you talking about?" Elyn asked, with a hint more of awe than anger.

"What they will say." Fionvar gestured toward the crowd beyond the wall. "He stepped into the stars, and they saw him go."

"He's not a legend," she snapped. "He's the king; he is my grandson."

"He forced Gerrod of Bernholt back on his word and brought a traitor home," Fionvar continued. "He regained your kingdom, Duchess; he put the House of Rinvien back on the throne." He smiled at Brianna, who sat up, touching the crown on her head.

Slowly, Elyn examined each one of them. She nodded, once, firmly—as if it had been as she planned it. "If he ever comes back," she began, but Fionvar shook his head.

"He isn't coming back, Your Excellency. He was your dream,

but this was not his." It was only then that Fionvar noticed Rolf's absence. At least on this road, Kattanan need not travel alone. "Goddess walk with you," he whispered.

And it was true, in Lochdale, that those who had witnessed the disappearance of King Rhys made the sign of the Goddess when they spoke of it. And those who had met him, or served him, suddenly recalled that he had never eaten much, that he was always kind and patient with them, that he had sung the Lady's hours with such feeling. They revered Queen Brianna as his chosen one, the bearer of a child of miracle. With her grandmother close behind her, and her Protector close beside, she wore this new role with grace and beauty. She fondly missed her favorite cousin, and sometimes said at prayer that she was sorry she ever made him mud pies. Her son was born at Finisnez, and he was called Wolfram duRhys. Everyone said that he had his father's eyes.

MELISANDE GAVE birth two months later, surprising her midwife by delivering twins. As was the custom, they waited one cycle of the moon before their Naming Day. A new moon allowed the stars to shine down upon that night and all of the barons came, along with emissaries from foreign courts. King Gerrod swelled with pride, as if the children were a feat of his doing.

The princess greeted each and every guest patiently, searching the crowd for the flash of golden hair, listening, as she always did, for a song. When rumors had reached Bernholt of King Rhys's extraordinary vanishing, the courtiers babbled with excitement about his strange visit among them. Each claimed a miracle for himself, exaggerating Rhys's presence until he sounded no less than holy. Melisande kept her own counsel, hoping beyond hope that his disappearance meant he would soon come to her side. But the snows closed the mountains, and by spring, the mysterious king seemed as distant and untouchable as legend.

As each noble approached, they laid at her feet gifts for her children: tiny fur blankets, delicate necklaces, and silver rattles. When the line was ended, Melisande raised her hand and let the dancing begin. The midwife had said she could dance, but her heart was not in it. Instead, she sat upon her throne, sipping wine, watching her beautiful boy sleeping in Laura's arms. Off to one side, in the richly carved cradle, the girl-child cried for attention, and the midwife gently gathered her into her arms.

The doors opened to admit a party of newcomers, but they took some time to reach the princess, skirting around the dance floor. Melisande sat up straighter, and smiled, her heart racing as she recognized Jordan, with the wizard Alswytha at his side.

"The Countess and Earl of Gamel's Grove," a herald announced, bowing them in.

Jordan swept a low bow, and his lady curtsied, somewhat awkwardly, as Melisande remembered she herself had been a few months ago.

The princess laughed. "Jordan, will your child be the wizard, or the Bane?"

"Don't ask me!" he replied. "I must apologize for our lateness, but I hope you shall forgive me when you have received our gift." His wife stepped aside, and he held out a hand to her. "This gift is a rather special one. It was commissioned of me, and my cohort"—he gestured toward the musician's gallery, where a familiar fiddler swept her a salute with his violin bow—"by King Rhys, before his miraculous disappearance, knowing your love of the dance."

Melisande gasped, and stood, taking the outstretched hand.

"He wanted it to be slow and easy, so that even he might have learned it." Jordan's eyes twinkled. "It's called 'Hearts and Crowns,' and it begins like this."

The dance consisted of a few steps forward, then back, then each partner turning away to the outside, their steps forming half of a heart. When they met again, they exchanged places, reverenced, backed away from each other, then came forward to exchange again. After leading her through it a few times, and demonstrating for the other dancers up on the dais, Jordan determined they were ready. He raised a hand, and Fionvar began his part, a lovely, haunting air for violin and harp.

Smiling as ever, Jordan took Melisande's hand and led her forward, then back. They turned aside to form the heart and, when she reached the point, the hand that reached out for hers was bare and smooth. She looked up and let out a tiny cry.

"Highness," said Kattanan, "I'm sorry I am late." He wore a simple tunic of light wool—a far cry from the king of a few months ago—and his tied-back hair was light brown. The scar that marked his face made him look older, as if he were lately returned from battle. "I had to get married," he told her, "and I had to die."

Melisande blinked fiercely. "I began to think that you would never come."

They exchanged places. "I had to learn to dance," he said. "That was the hardest thing of all." He bowed to her and backed away, his honey-hazel eyes never leaving her face. Her hair, now past her shoulders, was crowned by the circlet of playing hounds.

She approached him, lips trembling and, when they should have exchanged, instead she threw her arms about his neck. "I have missed you so much," she whispered.

"Don't cry," he murmured, pressing her close. "I can't bear to see you cry." But his voice shook, and he broke his own advice. It was a long while before they let each other go, even so far as arm's length so she could lead him to the cradle.

"Your Highness, I'm afraid we must go," said Lady Ethelinda, approaching. She curtsied low despite her girth, and straightened, eyeing the princess's companion. "Do I know you, my lord?"

"I am an old friend of Prince Wolfram's, my lady." He lowered his gaze.

"Hmm. You rather resemble that King Rhys," Ethelinda remarked.

"I have heard it so, my lady, though I don't see it myself."

With a regal bow to Melisande, Ethelinda swept by, giving him no more thought.

Sharing a smile, Kattanan and Melisande knelt side by side at the cradle. Both babies lay quietly, the boy reaching out for his mother.

"Happy Naming Day," Kattanan said. "What are their names?"

Melisande took the boy into her arms and held him out to Kattanan, who accepted him carefully, gazing into the warm hazel eyes. "His name is Alyn." She ruffled the child's baby blond locks, and whispered, "He's yours."

Kattanan lifted his eyes from the child. "You know that's not possible."

"Before you found me in the chapel, there was only one child. I cannot explain it, except to say the Lady willed it so."

A tear shimmered at Kattanan's long lashes, and he blinked it away.

"And her name is Melody." The princess tickled her daughter's chin.

"They're beautiful." Kattanan nestled the boy into his left arm so the child could hear his heartbeat.

Melisande lifted her tiny daughter into her arms, leaning back into Kattanan's embrace. The world danced on around them, as if celebrating life, and Kattanan, ever so softly, sang a lullaby.

Panic at the Disco